RUNNING DEVOTIONALS

Training on God's Word as Coaching for Life's Runs

Habakkuk 2:2 New King James Version (NKJV)

"Then the LORD answered me and said:

*'Write the vision
And make it plain on tablets,
That he may run who reads it.'"*

CH [LTC, RET] ARTHUR. W. COFFEY, JR., D. MIN.

Ordering Information:

For orders and inquiries, please contact:
1-888-375-9818
www.toplinkpublishing.com
bookorder@toplinkpublishing.com

Printed in the United States of America

CONTENTS

PREFACE

This book was born from the crucible of training for marathons, near-death accident and broken family, loss of home and job and dark depression. The pages have ached for a word that speaks on a theme that is timeless.

St. Paul, author of about one-third of the New Testament, summarized his personal journey in his latter writings with words: "⁷ **I have fought the good fight, I have finished the race, I have kept the faith**." 2 Timothy 4:7 New King James Version (NKJV) These words ring in the needed theme. The "walls" and struggles encountered by the runner of a physical marathon also rise up to challenge the runner of mental, emotional, interpersonal, financial and spiritual "marathons."

INTRODUCTION

I invite the reader to join me on the "spiritual pavement" as we train on God's Word. My Bible translation of preference from childhood has been the **King James Version (KJV)**, for its scholarship in translating the Hebrew, Greek, and Aramaic texts. I have also cited, briefly, in this book the **Amplified Bible** for doing the same into modern language, and the **Living Bible,** to assist readers who are not familiar with the Scriptures.

God's Word can speak to and change real-life crises as it did for me—leaving a sense of wonder and comfort about God's Word. Theologically, it would mean encountering Scripture—not just as *logos* (an idea or concept), but as *rhema* (word spoken directly, meant to be personal). How could the Scriptures become more than words on a page?

This devotional book will introduce a body-mind-spirit "transfer of training dynamic." What is that dynamic? Try asking yourself the following questions: 1) What can I learn from a physical run or challenge that will help me with a mental run or challenge and vice versa? 2) What can I learn from a spiritual run or challenge that will help me with both a physical and a mental challenge? And 3) what can I learn from a physical and a mental run or challenge that would become a living parable, a reflection of what I'm learning on the spiritual level of my life?

In this training, I will ask you to consider a hierarchy of God's Word over the human spirit, over the mind, and over the body. If I ask the questions: "Who am I?" and "What is my identity?" God's answer will be, *I am spirit, I have a mind, and I live in a body.* God's Word will address my identity as "spirit," even when I'm knocked out on the operating table. What my spirit—*that part of me that connects with the Word and will live somewhere forever*—hears will then speak to my mind; next, my mind will help direct my body to take steps according to the original Word given. My spirit is that part of my being that can perceive God "talking" to me through his Word about specific conditions in my life. I hear him in the sense that I know that I know. When John the Baptist, still in his mother's womb, sensed the presence of Jesus, who was still in Mary's womb, he "leaped" inside his mother's womb (see Luke 1:41). He had connected with the "Word made flesh"

(John 1:14). "**The spirit of a man is the lamp of the Lord, searching all the inner depths of his heart**" (Prov. 20:27).

My prayer is that the reader will move closer to and relate with God's heart on a deeper level as you move closer to and relate more deeply with His Word (see: John 1:1). "**For physical training is of some value—useful for a little; but godliness (spiritual training) is useful and of value in everything and in every way, for it holds promise for the present life and also for the life which is to come.**" (1 Tim. 4:7–8 The Amplified Bible, or AMP "**Let the words of my mouth, and the meditation of my heart, be acceptable in Thy sight, O Lord, my strength, and my redeemer.**" (Ps. 19:14 KJV). [*Training* is a gerund verb indicating a consistent or daily exercise!]

Ecclesiastes 9:11 (NKJV)
I returned and saw under the sun that—

The race *is* not to the swift, Nor the battle to the strong, Nor bread to the wise, Nor riches to men of understanding, Nor favor to men of skill; But time and chance happen to them all.

Month of Beginnings

COURSE:	REPENTANCE
TRAINEE:	Yesterday, I peered through the eve of a new year. My mind cradled the words: growth, change, newness. I need help with placing first things first.
COACH:	John the Baptist and Jesus began their preaching and teaching ministry with the word "repent." The original Greek word, *metanoia*, used in the writing of the New Testament, has a prefix meaning "*to turn around*" and a suffix translated as "*mind*." Hence, repentance literally means to turn your mind around.
TRAINEE:	Wrong thinking leads me to wrong speaking and wrong acting. But repentance, for me, amounts to no more than New Year's Resolutions, "made only to be broken."
COACH:	The Apostle Paul had the same struggles. Stop now and read about it in Romans 7:13-24; next, read James 1:13-15
TRAINEE:	I agree with everything he outlined in the struggle. So, what can be done to make changes in my life?
COACH:	You see your need for God's help; that's the first step.
WORD:	**"Blessed *are* the poor in spirit, for theirs is the kingdom of heaven."** **Matthew 5:3**
TRAINEE:	So, "poor in spirit" means seeing how much I need God?
COACH:	We train more on this tomorrow.
TRAINEE:	O.K., I'm ready.

-continued-

JANUARY 2

COURSE: TRANSFORMATION OR MAKING CHANGES

WORD: **"The fear of the LORD is the beginning of wisdom: and the knowledge of the holy is understanding." Proverbs 9:10**

COACH: We begin with three levels in "the fear of the Lord." The first is fear of consequences for going against God's will in any area of your life.

TRAINEE: I need to fear the One who could cast both body and soul into an eternity of hell fire. This level, however, does not hold any lasting power for me to make changes in my life. Being sorry just for the pickle I get myself in, when the dust settles, finds me right back in my old ways.

COACH: Level two is fear of missing out on God's best.

TRAINEE: This level of sorrow holds a bit more muscle for change but, over time, loses its grip as I fall back into my old pattern and choose to "settle for less" (*one of the Greek New Testament meanings for sin*).

COACH: Level three is fear (sorrow) of wounding God's heart anymore with your sins. This is what the Apostle Paul called "Godly sorrow."

WORD: **"For godly sorrow produces repentance leading to salvation, not to be regretted; but the sorrow of the world produces death." 2 Cor. 7:10 NKJV**

TRAINEE: How does this level happen for me?

COACH: Be ready for tomorrow's training.

JANUARY 3

COURSE: MOTIVATION FOR CHANGE

COACH: Suppose you had a friend who took your place when you were found guilty of a crime? What would that do to your misbehavior?

TRAINEE: It would put a damper on it.

COACH: That's what Jesus did for you; He stepped up for you. He had you in mind while He was on the Cross. Again:

WORD:	**"For godly sorrow produces repentance *leading* to salvation, not to be regretted; but the sorrow of the world produces death."** 2 Corinthians 7:10 (NKJV)
TRAINEE:	What is "Godly Sorrow?"
COACH:	Think about Jesus waging war against the forces of evil throughout the universe and for all of our earthly time. Look deeper into the selfless price he paid in the battle against sin, death, and disease.
TRAINEE:	From where does the power for change come?
COACH:	Read the Apostle Paul's message to the early church, saying that the cross is the very heart of God's power for salvation (1 Cor. 1:18).
TRAINEE:	What does this mean? Would the cross somehow hold the DNA necessary for me to get on the road to repentance, that is, to creatively give me a new mind and heart with which to make real-life changes?
COACH:	Read what Matthew [26-27], Mark [14-15], Luke [22-23] and John [18-19] wrote about the arrest, trail, and crucifixion of Jesus. Tell me later what you learned.

JANUARY 4

COURSE:	THE WORD AND CHANGE
TRAINEE:	I learned enough to see why medical science now says that crucifixion is the most agonizing and cruel form of death ever invented by man. How can I let this speak to my mind and heart?
COACH:	You need to become more fanatical in training on the "spiritual pavement" than you are on the "physical pavement."
TRAINEE:	I don't understand.
COACH:	Ask God to help you become hungry for His Word, to read, meditate, memorize, pray it. Like King David, this "hides His Word in your heart." Psalm 119:11
WORD:	**"Thy word have I hid in mine heart, that I might not sin against thee"** *Ps.* 119:11 KJV

COACH: Can you glance at your temptation and then look firmly at the cross, glance again at the temptation and turn again to see the cross, and recall that you were on His mind then and there. That "cross look," you will find, is the power to overcome.

TRAINEE: I need a daily exercise on which to train for this.

COACH: We step up the pace over the next three days.

WORD: **"For physical training is of some value—useful for a little; but godliness (spiritual training) is useful and of value in everything and in every way, for it holds promise for the present life and also for the life which is to come."** 1 Tim. 4:7–8 the Amplified Bible

JANUARY 5

COURSE: CONFESSIONAL HONESTY WITH GOD

TRAINEE: What's the first exercise; do I need to do some warm-ups?

COACH: You need to become confessional and honest with the Father!

WORD: **"If we say that we have no sin, we deceive ourselves, and the truth is not in us. If we confess our sins, He is faithful and just to forgive us our sins and to cleanse us from all unrighteousness."** 1 John 1:9 NKJV

TRAINEE: To what is He being faithful?

COACH: He is being "faithful" and "just" to what His Son carried out and paid for on the Cross when He said: "It is finished!"

TRAINEE: So, what's my next training step?

COACH: Take a step of faith; make a decision to trust God at His Word in seeking forgiveness. Be settled that being confessional and honest and His forgiveness is something very personal—as it was for King David [see Psalm 51], helping David's heart move closer to God's heart].

TRAINEE: Dear Father, in the Name of Jesus, I ask You to help me to take the same faith journey as King David—moving from adultery, murder, deceit—to what he wrote in Psalm 51 where he found that "Godly sorrow [2 Cor. 7:10]" that 'produces a repentance that leads to salvation" and, later, found You to say: **"David has a heart after my Own heart."** Amen.

WORD: **"...the LORD hath sought him a man after his own heart, and the LORD hath commanded him to be captain over his people,..."** 1 Samuel 13:14 KJV

JANUARY 6

COURSE: RUNNING ON THE ROAD TO REPENTANCE

COACH: That's your next step on this course?

TRAINEE: What, exactly, is repentance; and, how does it happen?

COACH: Again, when you are sorry in your own heart for what you have done against God's heart with your sin, St. Paul says that this kind of sorrow will produce a repentance that leads to salvation and never brings regret." 2 Corinthians 7:10

WORD: Psalm 34:18 **"The Lord is near to those who have a broken heart, And saves such as have a contrite spirit."** NKJV

Psalm 51:17 **"The sacrifices of God are a broken spirit, A broken and a contrite, O heart— These God, You will not despise."** NKJV

TRAINEE: I need help in growing closer to God.

COACH: Your journey into letting Jesus become YOUR "closest person" begins when you read those accounts of the Passion of Christ in Matthew [26-27], Mark [14-15], Luke [22-23] and John [18-19]. Reading, meditating and praying through it will help you see that if you were the only person on earth and were standing there watching what was happening to Him, He would still go through with it for you. It would be personal and for you. In a real sense, those Words take you there!

TRAINEE: So, the more I hold God's Word in my mind and heart, the more I am actually holding Jesus there.

WORD: **"In the beginning was the Word, and the Word was with God, and the Word was God . . . And the Word was made flesh, and dwelt among us, . . ."** [see: John 1:1-14]

-continued-

JANUARY 7

TRAINEE:	What Scriptures will be good for me to "hide in my heart" on this "road to repentance?
WORD:	2 Cor. 7:10, Ps. 119:11, 1 John 1:9, Psalm 51:17, Romans 12:2, Romans 1:16, 1 Corinthians 1:18, Philippians 2:13; 4:8
COACH:	Again, the "cross look," you will find, is the power to overcome; it is the way to "cast down imaginations of the heart" (2 Cor. 10:5), "mortify [*put to death*] the deeds of the body" (Rom. 8:13) and "crucify (the) self" (Gal. 2:20)
TRAINEE:	What gets my mind, gets me? I need a picture of this "casting down" exercise.
COACH:	A farmer working his garden turns the dirt for planting. His hand mistakenly picks up a clump of fresh cow manure; instantly, he throws it down—not to hold another second.
TRAINEE:	"Deadening deeds of my body?"
COACH:	See someone on a life-support system in a hospital; the decision is made to remove the supports and let the person die.
TRAINEE:	When I stop entertaining plans to sin, I'm "deadening the deeds of the flesh." And, "Crucify the self;" that sounds harsh.
COACH:	Most crucifixion deaths were caused by suffocation. Just like water replaces the air in the lungs when someone drowns, you need to replace the junk in your mind with what the four gospel writers had to say about the passion of Christ.
WORD:	"… **that I may know Him and the power of His resurrection, and the *fellowship of His sufferings*, being *conformed to His death*, if, by any means, I may attain to the resurrection from the dead**" Phil. 3:10–11.

JANUARY 8

COURSE:	HELP WITH REPENTANCE
TRAINEE:	I need help to carry out these exercises.
COACH:	Let me coach you to pray two Scriptures with the confidence that praying His Word is the same as asking Him something He wants and, therefore, He will hear it [1 Jn. 5:14-15]. Pray Philippians 2:13 and the "Godly sorrow" words of 2 Cor. 7:10 from training days 2 & 3 by putting your name in those verses and praying them.
WORD:	**"For it is God which worketh in you both to will and to do of is good pleasure."** Philippians 2:13King James Version (KJV)
TRAINEE:	Is this part of what it means for me to be "found in Christ," to be a "new creation," to "have the mind of Christ" (see 2 Cor. 5:17; Phil. 3:9; 1 Peter 4:1) or to connect me in yesterday's exercise to "the fellowship of his sufferings" and being "conformed to his death?"
WORD:	**"For the preaching of the cross is to them that perish foolishness; but unto us which are saved it is the power of God."** 1 Corinthians 1:18 King James Version (KJV)
TRAINEE:	After I have prayed for this help, what then? On what will I train?
COACH:	Meditate on this Word for tomorrow's exercise:
WORD:	**"And do not be conformed to this world, but be transformed by the renewing of your mind, that you may prove what is that good and acceptable and perfect will of God."** Romans 12:2 (New King James Version)

JANUARY 9

-continued-

COACH:	King David said:
WORD:	**"Your word I have hidden in my heart, That I might not sin against You."** Psalm 119:11 NKJV

TRAINEE: The more I hold God's Word in my mind and heart, the more I am actually holding Jesus there [see: John 1:1-14].

COACH: I coach you, if you have not already done so, to make your search for Jesus and then your decision for Him: i.e., to accept Him as your Lord and Savior based on what He accomplished for you on the Cross when He said: 'It is finished!" The Word can make you into a new person.

WORD: **"And he that sat upon the throne said, behold, I make all things new."** Revelation 21:5 KJV

"Brethren, I do not count myself to have apprehended; but one thing *I do,* forgetting those things which are behind and reaching forward to those things which are ahead, I press toward the goal for the prize of the upward call of God in Christ Jesus. Therefore let us, as many as are mature, have this mind; and if in anything you think otherwise, God will reveal even this to you." Philippians 3:13-15 NKJV

TRAINEE: I certainly am looking forward to this new person and closeness to my Creator and Savior!

COACH: We begin with tomorrow's course on obedience. You will come to know as much about God—and only as much as you come to obey.

TRAINEE: I guess it's like the words of the hymn: "Trust and obey for there is no other way to be happy in Jesus . . ."

JANUARY 10

COURSE: THE WISDOM OF OBEDIENCE

WORD: **"And do not be conformed to this world, but be transformed by the renewing of your mind, that you may prove what is that good and acceptable and perfect will of God."** Romans 12:2 (New King James Version)

TRAINEE: "Renewing of your mind;" what is this like? I guess "transformed" means to be changed?

COACH: Yes; and, "Renewing" is a gerund verb meaning an on-going exercise. The next five days, I want you to train on five forms of obedience.

TRAINEE:	I trust the Holy Spirit to teach, comfort, help, convict and counsel me through the Word!
COACH:	Your Heavenly Father is not so concerned about your *obedience of wisdom* as about the *wisdom of obedience.*
TRAINEE:	What does this do for me?
COACH:	It protects you from the bad consequences of going against His will. "Casting down the imaginations of [your] heart" accomplishes this.
TRAINEE:	Why?
COACH:	Because what gets your mind gets you!
WORD:	**"Casting down imaginations, and every high thing that exalts itself against the knowledge of God, and bringing into captivity every thought to the obedience of Christ; and having in a readiness to revenge all disobedience, when your obedience is fulfilled**. 2 Cor. 10:5-6 KJV"

JANUARY 11

COURSE:	THE <u>FAITH</u> OF OBEDIENCE
COACH:	He is not as concerned about the *obedience of faith* as about the *faith of obedience.*
TRAINEE:	And, what does this form of faith do for me?
COACH:	It protects you from missing out on God's best.
TRAINEE:	What do I exercise when I do this?
COACH:	You make a faith-decision over against sinful feelings that come out of your heart and circumstances that are pulling on your desires. To "*deaden deeds of* [your] *flesh* <u>Rom. 8:13</u>" will enable this decision.
WORD:	**"For if ye live after the flesh, ye shall die: but if ye through the Spirit do mortify the deeds of the body, ye shall live."** Romans 8:13 KJV
COACH:	This exercise in faith can be rewarded.

WORD:	**"But without faith, it is impossible to please him: for he that cometh to God must believe that he is, and that he is a rewarder of them that diligently seek him."** Hebrews 11:6 KJV
	*"**Be it done unto you according to your faith**. MT. 9:29 KJV"*
TRAINEE:	I think I can do these two forms of obedience.
COACH:	Tomorrow's course will hold more of a challenge. Jesus said if you love Him you should obey Him. St. Paul said that faith without works is dead. Get a good night's rest.

JANUARY 12

COURSE:	THE <u>SACRIFICE</u> OF OBEDIENCE
COACH:	He is not so much interested in your *obedience of sacrifice* as He is in your *sacrifice of obedience*.
TRAINEE:	This sounds a bit more strenuous. What will I be doing?
COACH:	In giving up your sin desire you "crucify [your] flesh Gal. 2:20; 2 Cor. 5:15." This may seem painful to your heart.
TRAINEE:	When I make this "sacrifice," what will it produce?
COACH:	This exercise will protect you from *wounding God's heart* anymore with your sin. He told the people of Israel that he wanted their obedience more than their sacrifices.
TRAINEE:	Does this mean He wants my obedience more than my worship?
COACH:	He delights in the true worship that comes from your heart; and He desires to see that worship take the form of obedience.
WORD:	**"And Samuel said, Hath the LORD as great delight in burnt offerings and sacrifices, as in obeying the voice of the LORD? Behold, to obey is better than sacrifice, and to hearken than the fat of rams."** 1 Sam. 15:22 KJV.
TRAINEE:	So, more than hands lifted up in praise, He wants my hands to refrain from wrong deeds and turn them to the right ones.
COACH:	Carry on! We look deeper into praise in tomorrow's training regimen.

JANUARY 13

COURSE:	THE <u>PRAISE</u> OF OBEDIENCE
COACH:	He is not centered so much on your *obedience of praise* as he is your *praise of obedience*. True worshipers will worship the Father with honest respect and love; for the Father is looking for such to worship Him.
WORD:	"**. . . .the true worshippers shall worship the Father in spirit and in truth:**" John 4:23 (KJV)
COACH:	"*. . . in spirit and in truth.* Are you being true or caring for someone when your actions do not back up your words?
TRAINEE:	So my faith and praise need to become active in love.
COACH:	Well said. Do you not find yourself more motivated or willing to do for someone when they have poured out themselves so deeply and sacrificially for you?
TRAINEE:	Yes! I can see I need to get in touch with what has been done for me. But just how do I make this connection with what God has done for me?
COACH:	Your journey into letting Jesus become your "closest person" will begin with tomorrow's training.
TRAINEE:	I look forward to it.
COACH:	That's good and proper. Read and study again:
WORD:	[Samuel replied, "**Has the Lord as much pleasure in your burnt offerings and sacrifices as in your obedience? Obedience is far better than sacrifice. He is much more interested in your listening to him than in your offering the fat of rams to him.**" 1 Sam. 15:22 (TLB)

JANUARY 14

COURSE:	THE <u>LOVE</u> OF OBEDIENCE
COACH:	God wants you to show him the *love of obedience*.
WORD:	"*If a man love me, he will keep my words*… Jn. 14:23 KJV."
TRAINEE:	Help me with how I go about "*keeping*" His Word.

COACH: Start reading what Matthew [26-27], Mark [14-15], Luke [22-23] and John [18-19] wrote about the arrest, trail, and crucifixion of Jesus.

TRAINEE: What can I expect in this study?

COACH: Again, reading it will help you see that if you were the only person on earth and were standing there watching what was happening to Him, He would still go through with it for you. It would be personal and for you. In a real sense, those Words can take you there!

TRAINEE: How can words on a page do that?

COACH: Truly, the more you hold God's Word in your mind and heart, the more you are holding Jesus there [see: John 1:1-14].

TRAINEE: For me, then, to read God's Word is the same as reading Jesus?

COACH: Your question leads us to train the next couple days on the question: "Who is Jesus?"

TRAINEE: I need that exercise!

COACH: Again, when Jesus said, "Blessed are the **poor in spirit**," the original text means, "Happy is the man who knows how much he needs God." So, when you see how much you need Him, that's not a step backward but a step forward?

-continued-

JANUARY 15

WORD: **"He is the image of the invisible God, the firstborn over all creation. For by Him all things were created that are in heaven and that are on earth, visible and invisible, whether thrones or dominions or principalities or powers. All things were created through Him and for Him. And He is before all things, and in Him all things consist. And He is the head of the body, the church, who is the beginning, the firstborn from the dead, that in all things He may have the preeminence."** Colossians 1:16-18 NKJV

TRAINEE: Then, Jesus is the Creator; He is God.

COACH: Before the "*Word became flesh and dwelt among us*" [see: John 1:1-14] Jesus was the Word that God the Father "sent out" to speak creation into existence as He spoke: "Let there be . . ."

TRAINEE: Does this mean that God is two persons?

WORD: **"For there are three that bear witness in heaven: the Father, the Word, and the Holy Spirit; and these three are one."** 1 John 5:7 NKJV

COACH: You will not find the name Trinity in the Bible; but, you see God introduce Himself as: 1. A loving, creative Father. 2. A saving, redeeming Son. 3. An ever-present, powerful Holy Spirit.

When Jesus was here, He said: "**He who has seen me has seen the Father** [John 14:9]." He, also, said; "**The Father and I are one** [John 10:30]." St. Paul writes to you: "**God was in Christ reconciling the world to Himself**" [2 Corinthians 5:19.]

JANUARY 16

-continued-

TRAINEE: Help me understand how "God was <u>in</u> Christ."

COACH: Jesus is called **Emmanuel**; it means: "*God with us.*" Christianity is the practice of a growing relationship between us and God. A Christian, therefore, is a follower and believer in Christ who trains regularly on the Word.

TRAINEE: Does this mean that it was God being crucified?

COACH: "Pilate had placed a board on the cross saying, "Jesus of Nazareth, the king of the Jews." The Hebrew consonants formed the word YHWH. The Jewish authorities, then, asked Pilate to take the sign down. Because Pilate answered, "What I have written, I have written," the sign reflected God the Father's handwriting. When Moses asked God who he should say sent him to Egypt to free his people, God said to tell them that YHWH, "I Am," had sent him. Jesus and these words hanging on the cross were saying—as he had already said when asked about his identity and origin—"Before Abraham was, **I Am**." The soldiers who had come to arrest him fell down when Jesus answered their question, "Are you the Christ?" by saying, "I Am."

YHWH, from which you take the English word Jehovah, is written from right to left in Hebrew. The letter Y, Hebrew Yod, means "hand"; the next letter, Hei, means "grace"; the next letter, Waw [pronounced Vav], means "nail" or "peg; and then, again, Hei is "grace." The name means, "I am who I" am." Jesus on the Cross, hands outstretched with nails in them, was saying, "I am God!" (See John 19:19–22.) The Father was saying: "Here I am, in Christ, reconciling the world to myself."

JANUARY 17

COURSE: **-STEPS ON THE ROAD TO REPENTANCE-:**

TRAINEE: Can You make a summary of what we have talked about so far?

COACH: The following, from the Billy Graham Evangelical Association, will help:

1. "<u>Recognize your Condition</u> and admit you are lost in sin. Romans 3:23 says, "**For all have sinned and come short of the glory of God.**" Sin has a penalty: "**For the wages of sin is death; but the gift of God is eternal life through Jesus Christ our Lord.**" Romans 6:23

2. <u>Religion and Good Works are not the Answer.</u> "**There is a way that seemeth right unto a man, but the end thereof are the ways of death.**" Proverbs 14:12 In other words, our thoughts and ways are not what matters. God's Word, the Bible, provides true answers of grace and forgiveness. Ephesians 2:8-9 says: "**For by grace are ye saved through faith; and that not of yourselves: it is a gift of God: Not of works, lest any man should boast.**" If I could work my way to heaven, then why did Jesus have to die?

3. <u>The Good News---Jesus Christ Provides the Way!</u> "**For God so loved the world that He gave His only begotten Son, that whosoever believeth in Him should not perish, but have everlasting life.**" John 3:16 He became the payment for our sin. In Romans 5:8, the Bible says, "**But God commendeth His love toward us, in that, while we were yet sinners, Christ died for us.**" Christ died for us so that we can go and be with Him in Heaven! *–continued-*

JANUARY 18

-continued-

4. <u>Believe and Receive Christ</u>. "**For whosoever shall call Upon the name of the Lord shall be saved**." Romans 10:13 That promise, directly from God, tells us that if we pray to Him and ask Him to forgive our sin and turn to Him alone to be our Savior, He will save and give us the free gift of eternal life. You can make that decision today by sincerely praying something like this:

"Dear God, I know that I am separated from you because of sin. I confess that in my sin, I cannot save myself. Right now, I turn to You alone to be my Savior. I ask You to save me from the penalty of my sin and I trust You to provide eternal life to me. Amen."

COACH: I look forward to seeing your response announcing your Decision for Christ as your Lord and Savior—that it has become settled in your heart and mind, never to regret!

TRAINEE: Where will this training lead me; what will I find myself doing; what changes will I see?

WORD: "**For if we would judge ourselves, we should not be judged. But when we are judged, we are chastened of the Lord, that we should not be condemned with the world.**" 1 Corinthians 11:27-32 (KJV)

TRAINEE: That's the ultimate goal and change; what about the meantime; how will that "shape up"?

COACH: Your daily walk with God will center on what it means to "wait on Him." We begin this course with tomorrow's training.

TRAINEE: Looking forward to it. *–continued-*

JANUARY 19

TRAINEE: How does waiting on God make me transformed?

WORD: "**But they that wait upon the Lord shall renew their strength; they shall mount up with wings as eagles; they shall run, and not be weary; and they shall walk, and not faint.**" Isaiah 40:31 (KJV)

TRAINEE: How can "wait" address my being "transformed?

COACH: The forms of obedience exercised last week will amount to "waiting on the Lord."

TRAINEE: I'm not seeing how this change in me will take place.

COACH: "*Transformed,*" in the Greek translation of the Scriptures, gives you the word "metamorphosis;" cocoon, caterpillar, butterfly.

TRAINEE: So, what will be my identity?

COACH: In addition to being "found in Christ," your identity will not be so much in 'who' you are but in '<u>Whose</u>' you are! Again, recall the words of the Apostle Paul in experiencing his transformation:

WORD: …"**but one thing *I do,* forgetting those things which are behind and reaching forward to those things which are ahead, I press toward the goal for the prize of the upward call of God in Christ Jesus.**" Philippians 3:13-14 (NKJV)

TRAINEE: Sounds wide open and too big to grasp. What would be a good title or heading to go over this entire course about repentance?

COACH: "*SHEMA*"

TRAINEE: No idea what that means.

COACH: Be ready for tomorrow's training; it means to "hear."

-continued-

JANUARY 20

WORD: **"Jesus said unto him, Thou shalt love the Lord thy God with all thy heart, and with all thy soul, and with all thy mind. This is the first and great commandment. And the second is like unto it, Thou shalt love thy neighbour as thyself. On these two commandments hang all the law and the prophets."** Matthew 22:37-41 (KJV)

TRAINEE: Does this mean that I will be moved, motivated, to obey Him?

COACH: What did Jesus say?

TRAINEE: If I love Him, I will keep His Word. What happened to St. Paul; how did he change from the old person to the new person?

COACH: Paul was transformed (grew and changed) from the confession of being "*chief of sinners, 1 Tim. 1:15*" having "*nothing good in (him), Romans 7:18*" deserving "*only condemnation and death,*" being a "*wretched being, Romans 7:24*" to stating he was "*more than a conqueror through (Christ, Jesus) who loved (him), Romans 8:37*" that he could "*do all things through Christ who strengthens (him) Philippians 4:13,*" that "*God's strength is made perfect in (his) weakness, 2 Corinthians 12:9,*" and finally to say, "*It is no longer I (self-centered ego) Paul who live, but Christ within me, Galatians 2:20.*"

TRAINEE: What Word from the Word will help me the most to know these kind of changes in me?

COACH: Again, it is the Word about the Cross; this Word speaks most powerfully. Read, again and again, those accounts of the Passion of Christ in Matthew [26-27], Mark [14-15], Luke [22-23] and John [18-19]. These Words will take you there and speak to your heart and mind. You will "hear." -continued-

JANUARY 21

WORD: **For I am not ashamed of the gospel of Christ: for it is the power of God unto salvation to every one that believeth; to the Jew first, and also to the Greek.** Romans 1:16 KJV

TRAINEE: Help me understand this "power" that is in Jesus.

COACH: During this coming week, we look at the names given to Jesus in the Bible.

TRAINEE: Do these names hold the "power of God?"

COACH: The first of the seven titles is: "Jesus, Name above all names." The word "name" in the Scriptures means power. Another way to understand this first title is to read: "Jesus, power above all powers."

TRAINEE: I'm ready for the Word.

WORD: **Wherefore God also hath highly exalted him, and given him a name which is above every name:** Philippians 2:9 KJV

Far above all principality, and power, and might, and dominion, and every name that is named, not only in this world, but also in that which is to come: Ephesians 1:21 KJV

TRAINEE: Can I consider that any kind of evil or sin is a name [power] and that Jesus is a name [power] over it; that problems, stress, sufferings, and death are names [powers], and that Jesus is a name [power] above them? I could go on with the list, but with each should I automatically consider the Name of Jesus greater and more powerful?

COACH: I like the way you put your question. Let it be your catalyst to move deeper into your study of Jesus, as the Word introduces you to Him. -continued-

JANUARY 22

WORD: **"And my spirit hath rejoiced in God my Saviour."** Luke 1:47 KJV

COACH: The second Name for Jesus Christ is Savior (Hebrew: *Yeshua [Jesus]* "God's salvation" *HaMashiach [Christ]* "the anointed, sent one,") becomes a title describing who Jesus is: i.e., the saving One and the anointed One Who is sent.

TRAINEE: So what's in a name?

COACH: Read again the accounts of the Passion of Christ in Matthew [26-27], Mark [14-15], Luke [22-23] and John [18-19]. These chapters will show you how Jesus lived up to His Name's sake.

WORD: **"For by grace are ye saved through faith; and that not of yourselves: it is the gift of God: Not of works, lest any man should boast."** Ephesians 2:8-9 KJV

"For God sent not his Son into the world to condemn the world; but that the world through him might be saved." John 3:17 (KJV) [see, also, verse 16]

"And it shall come to pass, that whosoever shall call on the name of the Lord shall be saved." Acts 2:21 KJV

"Neither is there salvation in any other: for there is none other name under heaven given among men, whereby we must be saved" Acts 4:12 KJV

"That if thou shalt confess with thy mouth the Lord Jesus, and shalt believe in thine heart that God hath raised him from the dead, thou shalt be saved." Romans 10:9 (KJV)

"For whosoever shall call upon the name of the Lord shall be saved." Romans 10:13 KJV

-continued-

JANUARY 23

WORD: **"In that day shall the branch of the LORD be beautiful and glorious,"** Isaiah 4:2a KJV

"But there the glorious LORD will be unto us a place of broad rivers and streams;" Isaiah 33:21a KJV

TRAINEE: Give me a good definition of "glorious."

COACH: Dictionaries say: "Exhibiting attributes, qualities or acts worthy to receive glory; noble; excellent; splendid; illustrious; inspiring admiration . . ." Part of this "glory" is the title "glorious Lord." Lordship is rule, reign and governing authority.

TRAINEE: "Beautiful savior, glorious Lord;" he knows how to save and deliver as Savior and how to train me into the faith of obedience as my Lord.

COACH: Carry on.

WORD: **"And because of what Christ did, all you others too who heard the Good News about how to be saved, and trusted Christ, were marked as belonging to Christ by the Holy Spirit, who long ago had been promised to all of us Christians. His presence within us is God's guarantee that he really will give us all that he promised; and the Spirit's seal upon us means that God has already purchased us and that he guarantees to bring us to himself. This is just one more reason for us to praise our glorious God."** (Eph. 1:13–14 TLB)

JANUARY 24

COURSE: IMMANUEL

COACH: Again, Jesus is called Immanuel; it means: *"God with us."*

TRAINEE: How is He "with me?"

COACH: To you, He says: **"Let your conversation be without covetousness; and be content with such things as ye have: for he hath said, I will never leave thee, nor forsake thee."** Hebrews 13:5 KJV

"And ye shall seek me, and find me, when ye shall search for me with all your heart. And I will be found of you, saith the LORD" Jeremiah 29:13-14 KJV

TRAINEE: What steps do I take to "seek Him" so that I can be "found" by Him?

COACH: You need to let Jesus become your closest person. To seek the kingdom first (Matt. 6:33) is to "seek Him." This closeness means getting into the Word and the Word into you. Jesus *is* the Word [see: John 1:1-14].

WORD: **"Yes, everything else is worthless when compared with the priceless gain of knowing Christ Jesus my Lord. I have put aside all else, counting it worth less than nothing, in order that I can have Christ, and become one with him, no longer counting on being saved by being good enough or by obeying God's laws, but by trusting Christ to save me; for God's way of making us right with himself depends on faith— counting on Christ alone."** (Phil. 3:8–9 TLB)

JANUARY 25

COURSE: BLESSED REDEEMER

TRAINEE: How am I to understand "redemption?"

WORD:	**"For the grace of God that bringeth salvation hath appeared to all men, Teaching us that, denying ungodliness and worldly lusts, we should live soberly, righteously, and godly, in this present world; Looking for that blessed hope, and the glorious appearing of the great God and our Saviour Jesus Christ; Who gave himself for us, that He might redeem us from all iniquity, and purify unto himself a peculiar people, zealous of good works."** Titus 2:11-14 (KJV)
TRAINEE:	I need a picture of "redemption."
COACH:	A man owned a precious, valuable ring. Somehow, the diamond suffered a deep scratch. The owner took the diamond to one dealer after another, but no one could remove the flaw. Finally, he came across an old master in the gem trade who took the ring back into his study for a good while, where he proceeded to paint a rose at the top of the scratch. The scratch became the stem of the rose, forming a most beautiful design in the diamond. In a similar manner, God can show you how he can take the scratches in your life and redeem them into the stem of the rose.
TRAINEE:	And this is made possible by what Jesus accomplished on the Cross?
WORD:	**"For it is God which worketh in you both to will and to do of his good pleasure."** Philippians 2:13 (KJV)
TRAINEE:	I needed that understanding.
COACH:	Carry on.

JANUARY 26

COURSE:	LIVING WORD
WORD:	**"For the word of God is quick, and powerful, and sharper than any two-edged sword, piercing even to the dividing asunder of soul and spirit, and of the joints and marrow, and is a discerner of the thoughts and intents of the heart."** Hebrews 4:12 KJV
TRAINEE:	I'm to understand that Jesus is the Word and you are telling me how He—as the Word—can know me?

COACH: When we pray, that's us talking to God; when we read His Word, the Holy Spirit is talking to us through the Word as we meditate on it. Just as good conversation serves as a platform to bring you closer with people, the same goes between you and your Creator.

TRAINEE: Can I train on how He can divide my soul and spirit and know my thoughts and motivations in my heart?

COACH: God is person. Talk to Him in your prayer life, telling Him what you feel, fear and need, even though He already knows. Talk it out to Him and know that He knows you better than you know your own self and is closer to you than you are to your own self. He wants to be in communication with you because you are made "*in His image and likeness.*"

TRAINEE: I need to talk with Him every day.

COACH: It has been said: "One week without prayer can make one weak."

TRAINEE: I'm ready to continue this tomorrow; it helps me to see that I am known by my Creator!

JANUARY 27

-continued-

COACH: Pray as if speaking with someone who knows all about you and still loves you more than you could ever imagine. Believe that you have presented your needs to the One Who receives your requests, no matter how poorly you may have presented them. Know that God hears not only your words, but even more, He hears and understands your heart.

WORD: **"But the Lord said unto Samuel, Look not on his countenance, or on the height of his stature; because I have refused him: for the Lord seeth not as man seeth; for man looketh on the outward appearance, but the Lord looketh on the heart."** 1 Samuel 16:7 KJV

TRAINEE: Could I say that when I'm reading God's Word, He, the Word, is actually reading me?

WORD: **"Thou knowest my downsitting and mine uprising, thou understandest my thought afar off."** Psalm 139:2 KJV

"Call unto me, and I will answer thee, and show thee great and mighty things, which thou knowest not." Jeremiah 33:3 (KJV)

TRAINEE: Dear Father, I ask in the Name of Jesus that you help me to journey in heart closer to Your heart and find a deeper talking and listening relationship with You. Help me see prayer as speaking to you and to see reading your word as listening to You. Amen.

COACH: It has been said, "A Bible stored in the mind is worth a dozen stored on the shelf." Have You ever seen a Bible worn and torn owned by someone who was *worn and torn*?

TRAINEE: No, Sir.

JANUARY 28

COURSE: PRACTICING THE PRESENCE

TRAINEE: How and on what?

COACH: Recall that "Godliness [spiritual training]" is profitable for both this life and the life to come. [See: 1 Tim. 4:7–8]

TRAINEE: I do this training when I read, meditate, memorize His Word, and at times, I pray It.

COACH: Reading, meditating and memorizing God's Word leads you to a renewed mind, which transforms. For example, doing a study exercise on the Matthew, Mark, Luke and John accounts of the arrest, trial, scourging and crucifixion of Jesus, placing you where you can see that He suffered all that for you, personally—as though you were the only person on this planet! What Jesus accomplished on the Cross delivers you from: 1. the guilt and penalty of your sin; 2. the habit and dominion of your sin; 3. one day from the very presence of sin. Hold this truth in mind and heart; it "practices the presence."

TRAINEE: How does God describe His Own Word?

COACH: God's Word can become, as he describes it, "sent out" (Is. 55:10–11); "active and alive" (Heb. 4:12); "watched over and performed" (Jer. 1:12).

TRAINEE: How could the Scriptures become more than words on a page?

COACH:	Let your faith be expectant about the training for tomorrow.
WORD:	"**. . . for he who comes to God must believe that He is, and that He is a rewarder of those who diligently seek Him.**" Hebrews 11:6b KJV
TRAINEE:	I can do that.

JANUARY 29

-continued-

TRAINEE:	I want to think more deeply about what God said, that the only way I can please him is through faith. Why is that?
COACH:	Because God has everything except one thing; He doesn't have your faith, a trusting relationship with you, unless you give it to him.
TRAINEE:	If I don't have something to give Him, how can I give it?
COACH:	I'm encouraged that you are looking to God to provide. When Jesus was here on the earth, sometimes people would come up to Him asking for help; sometimes He would turn to them and say things like: "be it done unto you <u>according</u> to your faith;" "your faith has made you whole;" "your faith has made you well." This shows you that God is watching you to see if you really trust Him to answer your prayers. My question to you is, do you see yourself having this **trusting relationship** with Him? Before we journey further into your needs, can you wrestle with this question and get back to me. There are ways to find your trust level become stronger.
TRAINEE:	But, what if sometimes, my faith doesn't feel anything?
COACH:	Faith is not a feeling; it is a decision.
TRAINEE:	That decision is not in me; my faith is too weak.
COACH:	Faith is not a human attribute; it is a God-given (1 Cor. 12:9) ability to choose to trust him at his word, often against feelings, against circumstances. There's nothing weak about it; it's your use of it that's weak.
TRAINEE:	Yes, Sir, I stand at attention and sharply salute!
COACH:	Prepare to train deeper on this tomorrow.

JANUARY 30

-continued-

WORD: **"Now faith is the substance of things hoped for, the evidence of things not seen."** Hebrews 11:1 KJV "**. . . according as God hath dealt to every man the measure of faith**." Romans 12:3b KJV

COACH: Substance is your assurance; evidence is your conviction. Notice that He has not given one level (measure) of faith to some and another level to others; to every . . . the measure . . .

TRAINEE: So I have as much faith to use as anyone else?

COACH: Rely on the Word to strengthen your use of your faith gift, (Romans 10:17). Remember, also, that the righteousness of Christ has been 'imputed' (Romans 4:22-24) to you. The Word and Jesus are one, (John 1:1-14).

TRAINEE: So, when God says that "the prayers of a righteous man availeth much" (James 5:16), when I pray something that God wants and use my faith gift, a lot can happen?

WORD: **So then faith cometh by hearing, and hearing by the word of God.** Romans 10:17 KJV"

TRAINEE: I need to daily strengthen my faith gift by reading and meditating on His Word.

COACH: Again, Scripture says: "**So then faith comes by hearing, and hearing by the word of God.**" Romans 10:17 Therefore, I coach you to search out Jesus by reading and meditating on the Word. God's Word will bring Conviction and understanding to your heart and mind.

TRAINEE: Dear Father, in the Name of Jesus, lead me deeper and closer to Your heart in a trusting relationship.

JANUARY 31

-continued-

TRAINEE: Dear Father, in the Name of Jesus, strengthen my grip on the gift of faith so that it becomes that trusting relationship, to trust You in Your Word. Amen.

COACH: Practice giving God thanks *"in"* and *"for"* all things; this exercise will lift up your faith. There is a relationship between your trust level and God's activity in your life.

TRAINEE: What Word do you have for me on giving thanks?

COACH: I coach you to wrestle with the following "praise prescription" and see how you are led:

WORD: **In everything give thanks: for this is the will of God in Christ Jesus concerning you.** 1Thessalonians 5:18 KJV

Giving thanks always for all things unto God and the Father in the name of our Lord Jesus Christ; . . . Ephesians 5:20 KJV

By him therefore let us offer the sacrifice of praise to God continually, that is, the fruit of our lips giving thanks to his name. Hebrews 13:15 KJV

Be careful for nothing; but in every thing by prayer and supplication with thanksgiving let your requests be made known unto God.

And the peace of God, which passeth all understanding, shall keep your hearts and minds through Christ Jesus. Philippians 4:6-7 KJV

TRAINEE: What about the times this "thanks" will be tough, hard to do?

COACH: You will see that day when *"gritted-teeth thanks"* and *"tearful thanks"* becomes *"joyful thanks!"* Look to October's training.

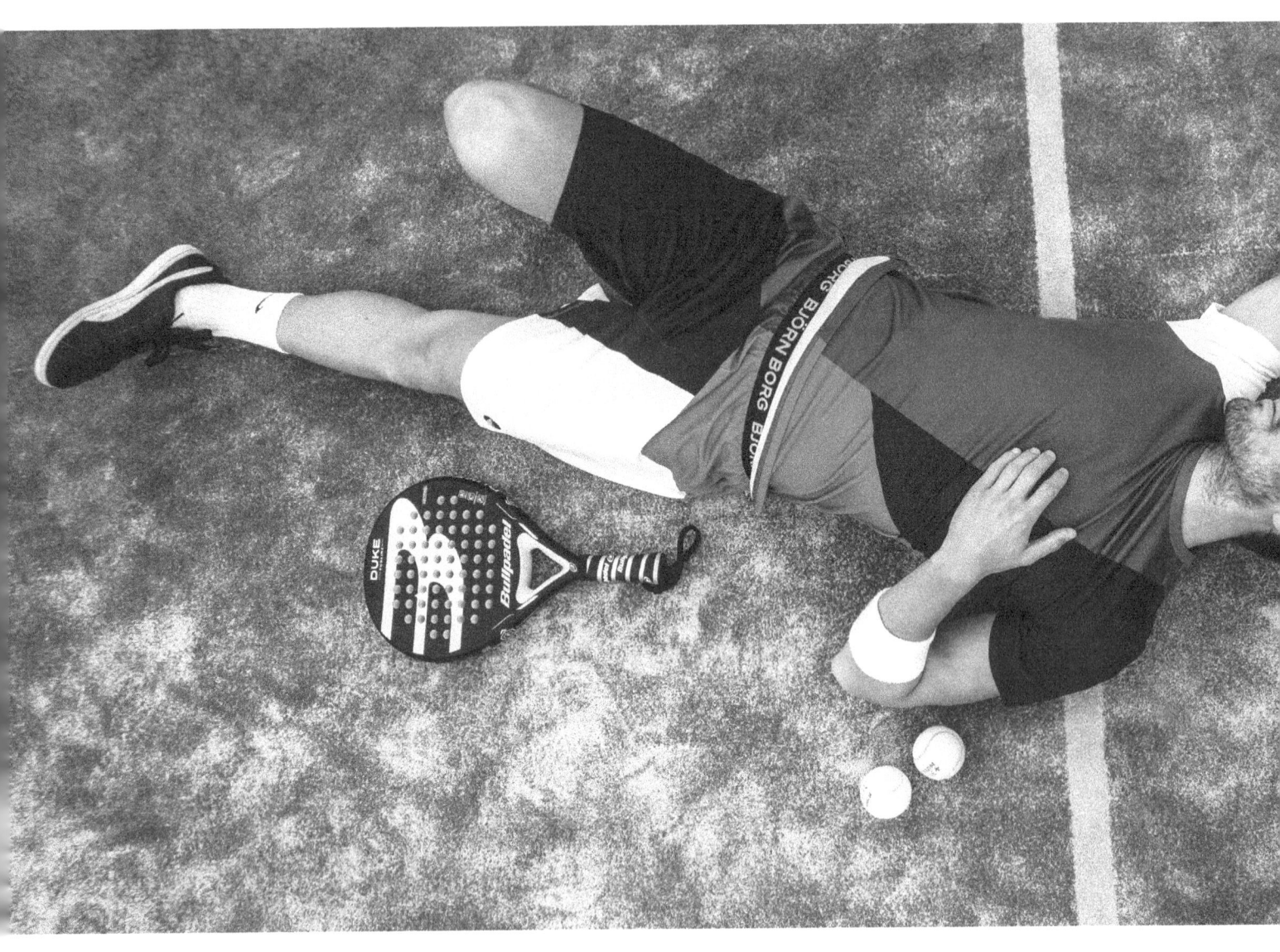

FEBRUARY 1

Month of Discontent

COURSE: DISCOURSE IN DISCONTENT

TRAINEE: The world we live in—everywhere I look—the one word to describe it: "*Discontent!*"

COACH: God promises to go with you through your trials; He doesn't promise to always take them away. It calls for a major "never-the-less" of faith posture on your part. Sometimes the level of stress or hardship is a compliment to the faith potential that God sees in you. E.g., see Job—God had confidence in Job.

WORD: **"My brethren, count it all joy when you fall into various trials, knowing that the testing of your faith produces patience. But let patience have *its* perfect work, that you may be perfect and complete, lacking nothing."** James 1:2-4 NKJV

COACH: The commentary on that verse reads: "If a believer endures a trial, he or she will be perfect, meaning 'having reached the end,' and complete, meaning "whole." [Nelson NKJV Study Bible]

TRAINEE: How did people in the "Bible days" make it through stress and strain?

COACH: Read what the Apostle Paul said in the midst of shipwreck, snake bite, plots against his life, defections, imprisonment, beatings so severe he was left for dead, and being the mutual target between two warring factions [*Orthodox Jews and newly formed followers of Jesus*]…:

WORD: **"For I reckon that the sufferings of this present time are not worthy to be compared with the glory which shall be revealed in us."** Romans 8:18 (KJV)

FEBRUARY 2

-continued-

TRAINEE:	My "weights" are not getting any lighter; in fact, with each step in life's runs they're getting heavier.
COACH:	Run in faith!
TRAINEE:	I don't feel like it.
COACH:	Again, faith is not a feeling, it is a decision.
TRAINEE:	That decision is not in me.
COACH:	Recall that faith is not a human attribute; it is a God-given (1 Cor. 12:9) ability to <u>choose</u> to trust him at his word, often against feelings, against circumstances. Recall the Word on how to resolve the "tug-of war" between faith and feelings:
WORD:	**"But they that wait upon the Lord shall renew their strength; they shall mount up with wings as eagles; they shall run, and not be weary; and they shall walk, and not faint."** Isaiah 40:31 (KJV)
COACH:	**"God's strength is made perfect *in* (focus on the word *in*) (your) weakness"** (1 Cor. 12:9). When Jesus said, **"Blessed are the poor in spirit;"** the original text reads, *"Happy is the man who knows how much he needs God."*
TRAINEE:	So, again, when I see my weakness and how much I need him, that's not a step backward but a step forward?
COACH:	Carry on.
TRAINEE:	Too much suffering with what I'm carrying in the run.
WORD:	Again, ***Change it to a moment (1 Cor. 15:52), and count it all joy when you fall into various trials*** . . . (James 1:2–4).
TRAINEE:	This is going to take a lot of training!

FEBRUARY 3

-continued-

COACH: Again, in the midst of his own surrounding troubles, read some of the coaching St. Paul gave to the people of the Early Church:

WORD: **"We are pressed on every side by troubles, but not crushed and broken. We are perplexed because we don't know why things happen as they do, but we don't give up and quit. We are hunted down, but God never abandons us. We get knocked down, but we get up again and keep going. These bodies of ours are constantly facing death just as Jesus did; so it is clear to all that it is only the living Christ within who keeps us safe.**

That is why we never give up. Though our bodies are dying, our inner strength in the Lord is growing every day. These troubles and sufferings of ours are, after all, quite small and won't last very long. Yet this short time of distress will result in God's richest blessing upon us forever and ever! So we do not look at what we can see right now, the troubles all around us, but we look forward to the joys in heaven which we have not yet seen. The troubles will soon be over, but the joys to come will last forever." 2 Corinthians 4:8-10; 16-18 Living Bible (TLB)

TRAINEE: That reads as a good *"pep-talk,"* but I still need a plan on how to get there.

COACH: Read and give some good meditation time to the following Word from your Creator; the Prophet Isaiah says to God:

WORD: **"Thou wilt keep him in perfect peace, whose mind is stayed on thee: because he trusteth in thee."** Isaiah 26:3 KJV

COACH: To have your mind stayed on His Word is the same as having it stayed on Him. Read Ps. 139:1-12 to see how He knows you.

TRAINEE: Why is He the same as the Word?

FEBRUARY 4

-continued-

COACH: Jesus <u>is</u> the Word and the Word <u>is</u> Jesus. Let it sink-in how St. John explains this reality in John 1:1-14.

WORD: **"And they that know Thy name will put their trust in Thee: for thou, Lord, hast not forsaken them that seek thee."** Psalm 9:10 (KJV)

TRAINEE: I see my heart like a balloon strapped to a persistently dripping water faucet, each drop tearfully reminding me of all the "weights" of the world—surrounding and within me. I can't even use the faith given me to bear up under them. This certainly has become the "winter of my discontent;" it is the "dark night of my soul."

WORD: **"Be still and know that I am God"** (Ps. 46:10 New International Version).

COACH: This "stillness" is the setting in which you can "hear" His Holy Spirit counsel and comfort you through the Word.

WORD: **"Come to Me, all you who labor and are heavy-laden and overburdened, and I will cause you to rest—I will ease and relieve and refresh your souls. Take My yoke upon you, and learn of Me; for I am gentle (meek) and humble (lowly) in heart, and you will find rest—relief, ease and refreshment and recreation and blessed quiet—for your souls. For My yoke is wholesome (useful, good)—not harsh, hard, sharp or pressing, but comfortable, gracious and pleasant; and My burden is light and easy to be borne"** (Matt. 11:28–30 AMP).

TRAINEE: O.K. I'm ready to go deeper into honestly looking at what is inside me—to let the One Who knows me best speak.

FEBRUARY 5

-continued-

WORD:	**"For if we would judge ourselves, we would not be judged. But when we are judged, we are chastened by the Lord, that we may not be condemned with the world."** (1 Cor. 11:31–32 KJV).
COACH:	A great leader in the faith of the Early Church, St. Augustine, said something that has stood the test of time: *"Every man's heart is restless 'til he finds his rest in God."*
TRAINEE:	How can I find this rest, to *'be still and know that God is God?'* My mind is like a computer programmed by what I put into it.
WORD:	**"For as he thinketh in his heart, so is he"** (Prov. 23:7 KJV).
TRAINEE:	What captures my mind captures me.
COACH:	The Word was clear concerning the standard to which Your mind is to be trained:
WORD:	**"Therefore, prepare your minds for action; be self-controlled; set your hope fully on the grace to be given you when Jesus Christ is revealed. As obedient children, do not conform to the evil desires you had when you lived in ignorance. But just as he who called you is holy, so be holy in all you do; for it is written: 'Be holy, because I am holy.'"** (1 Peter 1:13–16 NIV)
TRAINEE:	My mind can be dragged away from God's will. In computer language, this is expressed as "garbage in, garbage out."
COACH:	Your "judging of yourself" helps open your heart to what God can replace in it.
TRAINEE:	You have my attention; I'm ready for step one.

FEBRUARY 6

COURSE: MEDITATE ON THESE THINGS:

WORD: **"Finally, brethren, whatever things are true, whatever things are noble, whatever things are just, whatever things are pure, whatever things are lovely, whatever things are of good report, if there is any virtue and if there is anything praiseworthy—meditate on these things."** (Philippians 4:8 NKJV)

COACH: It is your nature to sin against God because mankind is in a fallen condition due to the disobedience Adam and Eve committed in the Garden of Eden—the beginning of Creation. Satan, your number one enemy, is called the "Prince of this World;" in this role, he works hard at tempting you to sin. This is one reason for the Cross of Christ.

TRAINEE: Can I truly glance at my temptation and then look firmly at the cross, glance again at the temptation and turn again to see the cross, and recall that I was on His mind then and there?

COACH: That "cross look," you recall, is the power to overcome; it is the way to "cast down imaginations of the heart" (2 Cor. 10:5), "crucify (my) self" (Gal. 2:20), and "put to death the deeds of the body" (Rom. 8:13). Just like Moses repeatedly said, *Behold the mighty hand of God* in delivering the children of Israel out of Egyptian bondage and through the Red Sea, there at Golgotha God was saying to you, *Behold the mighty outstretched arms of my Son in delivering you out of bondage to sin, your Red Sea.*

TRAINEE: Can you help me take a deeper look at the Cross?

COACH: We address that "look" the next several days.

FEBRUARY 7

-continued-

COACH: Think about His bodily wounds; they form the outline of a door. You are to enter heaven by the "narrow door" (Matt. 7:13–14).

TRAINEE:	I thought about Golgotha ("place of the skull"), Calvary ("cranium"), and the crown of thorns, and I thought about how my head is the first place to sweat during a run. Then it makes sense that I can be transformed (changed) by the renewing or training of my mind on what happened to Jesus then and there. From his head to my head, is there a meeting of the minds—the "mind of Christ"?
COACH:	Medical science tells you that it is humanly possible to be under so much stress that one could sweat drops of blood (the Greek words *hematidrosis* and *agonia* are used only once in the Scriptures to describe such stress and agony).
TRAINEE:	At this point in my thinking, my coach has me ponder the fact that Jesus, being also fully human as well as fully God, did exactly that—sweated drops of blood—in the garden of Gethsemane. I begin to see how *deadly* serious Jesus is about wanting to help me grow and change through the Father's grace.
COACH:	Yes, agape love, like faith, is a decision, not a feeling. We train still deeper into the Passion of your Lord tomorrow—the Cross as the "power of God." Again:
WORD:	**"For the preaching of the cross is to them that perish foolishness; but unto us which are saved it is the power of God."** 1 Corinthians 1:18King James Version KJV)

-continued-

FEBRUARY 8

COACH:	A shortage of wood called for prisoners to carry a crossbeam that would be fastened to a tree. Bulky nails went into His hands; executioners twisted His body to the side as they nailed through the sides of his ankles to the tree. Twisted and, thereby, having less capacity for air, he would suffocate faster.
TRAINEE:	What impact did all this have on the bystanders?
WORD:	**"As many were astonished at thee; his visage was so marred more than any man, and his form more than the sons of men."** (Is. 52:14 KJV)

COACH: Jesus was about eye level with his mother, John, the soldiers, and other bystanders as he hung suspended on the tree, slightly above ground level. So, again, his mother could see into his eyes as he asked her to look at John and then said, "*Behold your son*" and, to John, "*Behold your mother.*"

TRAINEE: So it would have been easy to thrust a spear into his side.

COACH: With his lungs screaming for air, the only way to breathe was to sit back on a plank nailed to the tree. But as soon as he did, his body weight caused pain to shoot like bullets from the nails in his hands and run throughout his body. So after a split second, he would have to push back up with his feet, where there was no air. So it went throughout the whole crucifixion process, for six hours. In the midst of that agony, the spitting, the insults, and so on, the bystanders could hear him say:

WORD: **"Father, forgive them, for they know not what they do."**

TRAINEE: I thought crucifixion sometimes lasted for a day or more.

FEBRUARY 9

-continued-

COACH: He died in the ninth hour (three o'clock), the time normally set for killing the lamb during Jewish Passover.

TRAINEE: I find that significant!

COACH: It was customary to break the legs of those hanging on the cross in order to speed up the suffocation process, but Scripture says that God's lamb (Jesus) would not have his bones broken (see Ex. 12:46; John 19:36). They did not break Jesus' bones because he died before the others.

TRAINEE: Why?

COACH: He had been scourged during his trial. This means the Roman soldiers whipped him with a long leather-type strap with metal hooks or pieces of bone placed at intervals. He was beaten on his back and front; each time, those hooks tore out chunks of flesh. He almost bled to death before he got to Golgotha—beaten beyond human recognition (see Ps. 22:6 and Is. 53).

TRAINEE:	This explains why he fell with that heavy crossbeam on the way to Golgotha.
COACH:	Psalm 22 states much that occurred on the cross; Jesus had spoken many of those words about himself: see Psalm 22:6. The word *worm* used there is from the Hebrew word *Tolah*, which is the name of a worm that is round in shape like a beetle. When it is pregnant and ready to give birth, it will climb to the top of a tree. When there, its heart will explode and it gives birth.
TRAINEE:	Christ's heart may well have exploded while hanging at the top of his tree.

FEBRUARY 10

-continued-

COACH:	Can you let what happened to his heart give birth to change your heart?
TRAINEE:	As I stood there at Golgotha in the midst of the above understanding, God had me picture myself standing in front of the cross as though I were the only one there. He then said to my heart, *You need to see that all of this is done for you as though you were the only person on this earth!* God, the Father, above all things, being a *just* God, demands that my sin be punished.
WORD:	"That is, God was in Christ reconciling the world to Himself, not imputing their trespasses to them, and has committed to us the word of reconciliation" (2 Cor. 5:19a, see and meditate on vs.21 NKJV)
COACH:	Can you see him stripped, bound, and scourged, with a crown of thorns forced into his skull, long square nails pounded into his palms and feet, and a spear thrust into his side, hoisted onto the cross, where his nerve centers flashed the most excruciating pain a human can experience—and, all for you, personally?"
TRAINEE:	My Coach helped me look deeper into Matthew's, Mark's, Luke's, and John's accounts of this event.

COACH: Those words hold the power to place you there. At the point of unfathomable agony and despair, a cry came from the cross: *"Eli, Eli, lama sabachthani?"* Jesus uttered this in Hebrew, which means, "My God, my God, why have you forsaken (original meaning: "forgotten") me?" (Matt. 27:46).

TRAINEE: Was this a lack of faith on his part?

FEBRUARY 11

-continued-

COACH: No! Being fully human as well as fully God, He suffered every dimension of pain and agony that you would have on that cross. Plus, he was not only receiving into himself everything that the enemy had been allowed to do through the Roman soldiers and bystanders, he was also taking all the punishment and wrath from God the Father for all the sins of humanity, past, present, and future!

WORD: **"For he hath made him to be sin for us, who knew no sin; that we might be made the righteousness of God in him."** (2 Cor. 5:21 KJV)

TRAINEE: And Jesus surely had seen the Father look away from him because God will not look upon sin.

COACH: This "looking away" by the heavenly Father gave Jesus a severe taste of hell in the truest definition of that word: "separation from God." Furthermore, he had said earlier, "The Father and I are one" and "He who has seen me has seen the Father."

TRAINEE: Does this mean that Jesus actually felt his identity or spirit being torn in two? I began to see that his love reaches that far for me. Jesus endured the cross for me personally in total empathy, not sympathy. It would be tantamount to blasphemy for me to give in to the suggestions of the enemy and thereby believe that God can't forgive someone so wretched as me. This understanding is what started to move or motivate me, more than any other force, to want his will to be done in my life.

COACH: Herein lies the power of God from the cross.

WORD: **"For the preaching of the cross is to them that perish foolishness; but unto us which are saved it is the power of God."** 1 Corinthians 1:18 King James Version KJV)

FEBRUARY 12

COURSE: DISCONTENT

WORD: **"Not that I speak in respect of want: for I have learned, in whatsoever state I am, therewith to be content."** Philippians 4:11 (KJV)

COACH: You have seen the discontent the world provides.

TRAINEE: I need something to lift me from the discontent that lives within me. How did St. Paul "learn" to be content?

COACH: Do you recall the Word about "Godly sorrow?"

TRAINEE: Yes, I identify with the following Word:

WORD: **"For I admit my shameful deed—it haunts me day and night. It is against you and you alone I sinned, and did this terrible thing. You saw it all, and your sentence against me is just."** (Ps. 51:3–4 TLB)

COACH: When Jesus said from the cross, *"It is finished,"* that was not a cry of defeat but a statement of victory. The Hebrew words used were what someone would write on a bill when it was paid in full. The original Greek word for that text reads, *"It is accomplished."* In Bible days, if you heard someone running through the streets shouting *"Tetelestai! Tetelestai!"* it meant their marketplace bill had been paid in full. My sin and God's forgiveness—mission impossible, accomplished!

TRAINEE: All that He suffered was done and accomplished for me?

COACH: In April, we train more deeply on what was accomplished through His seven last Words from the Cross.

FEBRUARY 13

COURSE: SELF-WORTH

TRAINEE: I've tried all the self-esteem exercises and nothing lasts.

COACH: Scripture tells you that Jesus was a "man of sorrows" and acquainted with grief [Isaiah 53:3 NKJV]." It is not feelings or self-worth that saves you; it is your decision to accept what Jesus accomplished on the cross.

TRAINEE: I made that decision, but I still don't feel worthy.

WORD: **"Blessed be God, even the Father of our Lord Jesus Christ, the Father of mercies, and the God of all comfort; Who comforteth us in all our tribulation, that we may be able to comfort them which are in any trouble, by the comfort wherewith we ourselves are comforted of God."** 2 Corinthians 1:3-4 KJV

COACH: The love poured out on the Cross for you is the basis for your being able to love yourself. Can you make a faith-decision to let that love encircle your worth, based on how much you are loved by our Creator and Savior!

TRAINEE: Dear Father, in the Name of Jesus, I ask that Your Holy Spirit would coach me through the Scriptures as my teacher, counselor, comforter, helper and One Who convicts me of what is true. Amen.

COACH: Good prayer.

WORD: **…to know the love of Christ which passes knowledge; that you may be filled with all the fullness of God. Ephesians 3:19**

COACH: See, also, 1 John 4:9; Romans 8:39

FEBRUARY 14

COURSE: SUFFERING

TRAINEE: Too much suffering, everywhere I turn. Suffering…suffering…suffering!

COACH: Center your thinking on those who suffered in the days the Bible was being formed. Read again some of their expressions about it:

WORD: **"We are pressed on every side by troubles, but not crushed and broken. We are perplexed because we don't know why things happen as they do, but we don't give up and quit. We are hunted down, but God never abandons us. We get knocked down, but we get up again and keep going. These bodies of ours are constantly facing death just as Jesus did; so it is clear to all that it is only the living Christ within who keeps us safe.**

That is why we never give up. Though our bodies are dying, our inner strength in the Lord is growing every day. These troubles and sufferings of ours are, after all, quite small and won't last very long. Yet this short time of distress will result in God's richest blessing upon us forever and ever! So we do not look at what we can see right now, the troubles all around us, but we look forward to the joys in heaven which we have not yet seen. The troubles will soon be over, but the joys to come will last forever." 2 Corinthians 4:8-10; 16-18 Living Bible (TLB)

". . . that I may know Him and the power of His resurrection, and the fellowship of His sufferings, being conformed to His death, if, by any means, I may attain to the resurrection from the dead." Philippians 3:10-11 (NKJV)

TRAINEE: Helps me place some of my suffering in perspective.

FEBRUARY 15

-continued-

COACH: The Apostle Paul summed up our journey with death and suffering by saying:

WORD: **"For to me, to live is Christ, and to die is gain**." Philippians 1:21 NKV [*And, again:*]

             "For I consider that the sufferings of this present time are not worthy to be compared with the glory which shall be revealed in us." Romans 8:18 NKJV

TRAINEE: To what was St. Paul comparing?

COACH: When you lose a loved one who is a believer, you can simply give thanks for their graduation? For, here is a description of their new existence:

WORD: **"But as it is written: "Eye has not seen, nor ear heard, nor have entered into the heart of man the things which God has prepared for those who love Him."** 1 Corinthians 2:9 NKJV

TRAINEE: So, God has been at work for my future here and in His Kingdom?

COACH: Read how broad and in depth He is doing it:

WORD: **"Now unto him that is able to do exceeding abundantly above all that we ask or think, according to the power that worketh in us,** " Ephesian 3:20 KJV

COACH: How much can you ask; how much can you think or imagine? Trust God to be in your past, now; in your present, now; and in your future, now. He has no space or time limits as you do. Therefore, He can perform the Scriptures the way he describes in the above Ephesians 3:20 Word.

FEBRUARY 16

COURSE: SIN

COACH: The problem:

WORD: **"No, you yourselves do wrong and cheat, and you do these things to your brethren! Do you not know that the unrighteous will not inherit the kingdom of God? Do not be deceived. Neither fornicators, nor idolaters, nor adulterers, nor homosexuals, nor sodomites, nor thieves, nor covetous, nor drunkards, nor revilers, nor extortioners will inherit the kingdom of God."** 1 Corinthians 6:8-10 New King James Version (NKJV)

TRAINEE: I need the answer!

WORD: **"And do not be conformed to this world, but be transformed by the renewing of your mind, that you may prove what is that good and acceptable and perfect will of God."** Romans 12:2 (New King James Version)

COACH: Again, "renewing" is a gerund verb, meaning and pointing you to a consistent and daily exercise on His Word. What did King David say about his sin condition? **"Thy word have I hid in mine heart, that I might not sin against thee"** Ps. 119:11 KJV

TRAINEE: I need help with this "exercise!"

WORD: **". . . for it is God who works in you both to will and to do for His good pleasure.** Philippians 2:13 (New King James Version)

TRAINEE:	Can you give me a picture of how God is going to give me this help?
COACH:	We train more deeply tomorrow.

FEBRUARY 17

-continued-

COACH:	God will never "bulldoze" His will over anyone, but you will see Him do the Scriptures in your life.
WORD:	**"Blessed is the man who endures temptation; for when he has been approved, he will receive the crown of life which the Lord has promised to those who love Him."** James 1:12 (New King James Version) [see, also vs. 13-15]
TRAINEE:	That's well and good for the next life, but where is the real help I need while still here on this earth? I sure will need that medicine—especially in treating those very trying or impossible temptations.
WORD:	**"For no temptation (no trial regarded as enticing to sin), [no matter how it comes or where it leads] has overtaken you and laid hold on you that is not common to man [that is, no temptation or trial has come to you that is beyond human resistance and that is not [a]adjusted and [b]adapted and belonging to human experience, and such as man can bear]. But God is faithful [to His Word and to His compassionate nature], and He [can be trusted] not to let you be tempted and tried and assayed beyond your ability and strength of resistance and power to endure, but with the temptation He will [always] also provide the way out (the means of escape to [c]a landing place), that you may be capable and strong and powerful to bear up under it patiently."** 1 Corinthians 10:13 (Amplified Bible)
COACH:	When you say, "*I can't*;" God, who knows you better than you know your own self, says, He will give you a "way of escape"—making you "able to bear it." Tomorrow, we begin with a picture of that "power of God" that beams from the Cross. Prepare yourself for a stark and sober look!

FEBRUARY 18

-continued-

COACH: Again, read those accounts of the Passion of Christ in Matthew [26-27], Mark [14-15], Luke [22-23] and John [18-19]. Those Words take you there for needs of forgiveness and overcoming!

TRAINEE: I'm ready for that picture that reflects the Cross.

COACH: Think for a moment. What if you were to go down town and rob the bank, arrested, tried, convicted, and, just as the judge is getting ready to bring down the gavel and pronounce sentence, your friend [Ralph] in the back of the court raises his hand and says: *"Judge, let me take his punishment for him."* The judge turns to your friend, brings down the gavel and pronounces sentence on Ralph. If that should happen, what would that do to your intentions to not rob any more banks? [*see again: Corinthians 1:18 NKJV*]

TRAINEE: The world we live in would say: *"well, if Ralph is going to do that, I'll just go out and rob some more banks, 'cause Ralph is going to take care of it."*

COACH: That, in effect, is what people said to St. Paul as he explained how God's Grace always "abounds to cover the sin." Paul answered with: "Certainly not! God forbid!" So, what if you have a heart; what would Jesus's payment for your sin do to move you into obedience and service of Him?

WORD: **"And now, little children, abide in Him, that when He appears, we may have confidence and not be ashamed before Him at His coming."** 1 John 2:28 NKJV

COACH: Honest confession, followed by true repentance (*God's Word hidden in your heart making for changes in thoughts, words, decisions, actions*) will set the stage for standing before Him unashamed.

FEBRUARY 19

-continued-

WORD: **"Not everyone who says to Me, 'Lord, Lord,' shall enter the kingdom of heaven, but he who does the will of My Father in heaven. Many will say to Me in that day, 'Lord, Lord, have we not prophesied in Your name, cast out demons in Your name, and done many wonders in Your name?' And then I will declare to them, 'I never knew you; depart from Me, you who practice lawlessness!'** Matthew 7:21-23 NKJV

COACH: Will He see those places His Word has made a "mark" on your heart, causing changes, repentance, to be formed in your life? It is not enough for you to know God, God must know you.

TRAINEE: You have coached me to understand that when I hold God's Word in my mind and heart, I am holding Him there.

COACH: All sin must be repented of, forsaken and prayer made for God's Spirit to dwell in you and assist you to grow into His perfect image. The problem with sin is when you begin to identify with it and believe that is who you are. That is a deception of Satan. Because of Christ's death, you have become the righteousness that God desires. Christ redeems you from all your fallen-ness. See again,

WORD: **"For God sent not his Son into the world to condemn the world; but that the world through him might be saved."** John 3:17 (KJV)

"But if a wicked man turns from all his sins which he has committed, keeps all My statutes, and does what is lawful and right, he shall surely live; he shall not die. None of the transgressions which he has committed shall be remembered against him; because of the righteousness which he has done, he shall live. Ezekiel 18:21-22 NKJV

FEBRUARY 20

COACH: A. W. Tozer wrote a good summary of this course on sin:

"Earth is a shadow of heaven—sin excepted, of course. Heaven shines downward and throws its shadows; and those shadows we call the earth and the things therein.

Wherever sin is found, however, it is a shadow of hell and never can be of heaven. Sin is a disease, a deformity, a plague, a blight, a treason, a rebellion, an error, a sacrilege, and a perversion. It is all of those things and so it can be no part of heaven, for there is nothing of heaven in it and nothing in heaven like it. Sin is a sinister presence in the universe, which God has permitted to be here for a little while. Its days are limited and numbered by the determinate counsel and foreknowledge of God.

When His good pleasure comes, He is going to destroy sin from the universe and beat it and chase it out of His universe until there is no sin left. So earth is the shadow of heaven."

TRAINEE: I've heard it said, "*We are to be in the world but not off the world.*"

WORD: **"Ye are of God, little children, and have overcome them: because greater is he that is in you, than he that is in the world."** 1 John 4:4 KJV

COACH: See John, chapter 17 for the High Priestly prayer Jesus prayed for you. Verses 20-21 reads: **"I do not pray for these alone, but also for those who will believe in Me through their word; that they all may be one, as You, Father, are in Me, and I in You; that they also may be one in Us, that the world may believe that You sent Me."** NKJV

FEBRUARY 21

COURSE: TRIALS

WORD: **"In this you greatly rejoice, though now for a little while, if need be, you have been grieved by various trials, that the genuineness of your faith, *being* much more precious than gold that perishes, though it is tested by fire, may be found to praise, honor, and glory at the revelation of Jesus Christ, ..."**1 Peter 1:6-7_(NKJV)

COACH: Study the following from His Word about trials: Psalm 119:50, 67, 71, 92, 107.

TRAINEE: I see that His Word is my strength and my comfort.

WORD: **"But He knows the way that I take [He has concern for it, appreciates, and pays attention to it]. When He has tried me, I shall come forth as refined gold [pure and luminous]."** Job 23:10 (Amplified Bible)

TRAINEE: What about death and broken heartedness?

COACH: Heartbreak triggers immediate thoughts of loss—maybe the death of a loved one or a relationship. But soul-crushing grief isn't necessarily limited to the absence of someone dear.

TRAINEE: But, I'm not alone?

COACH: **"…the Lord your God goes with you. He will never leave you nor forsake you"** (Deuteronomy 31:6). He knows the number of tears you've cried, and His heart breaks, too, because He loves you. Talk openly to God as you would a friend; He's listening and eager to hear from you. [See, also, Isaiah 43:1-2]

WORD: **"He is near to the brokenhearted; He saves the crushed in spirit"** Psalm 34:18.

TRAINEE: This is a comfort to me! Some more Words tomorrow, please.

FEBRUARY 22

-continued-

WORD: **"For my father and my mother have forsaken me, but the Lord will take me in"** Psalm 27:10.

COACH: God promises to restore and give you a "new heart and a new spirit [Ez. 36:26]" God has created a longing in you to find your heart moving closer to His. Recall St. Augustine's words: *"Every man's heart is restless 'til he finds His rest in God."*

WORD: **"You number my wanderings; Put my tears into Your bottle; *Are they not in Your book?*"** Psalm 56:8 NKJV

TRAINEE: I need some more Words about death.

WORD:	**"So we are always confident, knowing that while we are at home in the body we are absent from the Lord."** 2 Corinthians 5:6
	"We are confident, yes, well pleased rather to be absent from the body and to be present with the Lord." 2 Corinthians 5:8
COACH:	Look at what King David said when he lost his son: 2 Samuel 12:15-23. Verse 23 reads:
WORD:	**"And he said, "While the child was alive, I fasted and wept; for I said, 'Who can tell whether the Lord will be gracious to me, that the child may live?' 23 But now he is dead; why should I fast? Can I bring him back again? I shall go to him, but he shall not return to me."**
COACH:	Recall, again, the Words of the Apostle Paul.
WORD:	**"For to me, to live is Christ, and to die is gain."** Philippians:21 NKV
TRAINEE:	So, for believers, we are not a loser either way.

FEBRUARY 23

COURSE:	RESISTING SATAN
COACH:	Satan cannot stand God's Word. It has been his target since the beginning of time, especially when the "Word became flesh and dwelt among us [Jesus}."
	Therefore, I coach you to open your Bible and read some of it out loud next time these attacks come. He can't read your mind, but hears you speak. The Word, at this point, will become a weapon.
WORD:	**"The Lord is my rock and my fortress and my deliverer; My God, my strength, in whom I will trust; My shield and the horn of my salvation, my stronghold."** Psalm 18:2 NKJV
	"No weapon that is formed against thee shall prosper; and every tongue that shall rise against thee in judgment thou shalt condemn. This is the heritage of the servants of the Lord, and their righteousness is of me, saith the Lord." Isaiah 54:17 KJV Again:
	"Ye are of God, little children, and have overcome them: because greater is he that is in you, than he that is in the world." 1 John 4:4

COACH: Remember that the Word is Jesus and Jesus is the Word [John 1:1-14]. Jesus is Satan's greatest foe and that's the reason for Satan's attacks through history: e.g., 1. Satan motivating Cain to slay Abel in the days of Adam and Eve; 2. Satan stirring the heart of Pharaoh to kill the Hebrew male children in the days of Moses; 3. The planned destruction of the Jews by Haman as told in the book of Esther; 4. Satan coaching King Saul to kill David, from whose line Jesus would be born. And, he especially tempts and tries to trip those who place their faith in Jesus.

FEBRUARY 24

COURSE: THE DEMONIC

COACH: Satan's goal is to have his way in human lives--to control or at least win a hearing and become a persuasive force. He can do this in three ways in the life of a Christian: by temptation to sin, by oppression, or by using deception and lies to gain a stronghold of sinful thoughts and actions.

TRAINEE: I've already stated that what gets my mind gets me.

COACH: Speaking to Christians, the Apostle Paul says:

WORD: **"And do not give the devil an opportunity [to lead you into sin by holding a grudge, or nurturing anger, or harboring resentment, or cultivating bitterness].**" Ephesians 4:27 (AMP)

COACH: Christians must actively resist the devil.

WORD: **"Submit yourselves therefore to God. Resist the devil, and he will flee from you.** James 4:7 KJV

COACH: Paul also explains how believers can take their stand against the devil. These verses point to the fact that our strongest defense against evil is to stand firm in our faith in Jesus Christ and in a lifestyle of obedience to God's Word.

WORD: **"Finally, my brethren, be strong in the Lord, and in the power of his might. [11]Put on the whole armour of God, that ye may be able to stand against the wiles of the devil."** Ephesians 6:10-11 KJV

COACH: Read and reflect on Ephesians 6:10-20 to see what pieces of armor to put on and what they provide in warfare with the enemy. This armor will protect from his camouflage tactics.

FEBRUARY 25

COURSE: SIN [THE PROBLEM]

COACH: Again, the problem; read and heed:

WORD: **"No, you yourselves do wrong and cheat, and *you do* these things *to your* brethren! Do you not know that the unrighteous will not inherit the kingdom of God? Do not be deceived. Neither fornicators, nor idolaters, nor adulterers, nor homosexuals, nor sodomites, nor thieves, nor covetous, nor drunkards, nor revilers, nor extortioners will inherit the kingdom of God."** 1 Corinthians 6:8-10 (NKJV)

". . . knowing this: that the law is not made for a righteous person, but for *the* lawless and insubordinate, for *the* ungodly and for sinners, for *the* unholy and profane, for murderers of fathers and murderers of mothers, for manslayers, ¹⁰for fornicators, for sodomites, for kidnappers, for liars, for perjurers, and if there is any other thing that is contrary to sound doctrine, ¹¹according to the glorious gospel of the blessed God which was committed to my trust." 1 Timothy 1:9-11 (NKJV)

"And He said, "What comes out of a man, that defiles a man. For from within, out of the heart of men, proceed evil thoughts, adulteries, fornications, murders, thefts, covetousness, wickedness, deceit, lewdness, an evil eye, blasphemy, pride, foolishness. All these evil things come from within and defile a man." And He said, "What comes out of a man, that defiles a man. For from within, out of the heart of men, proceed evil thoughts, adulteries, fornications, murders, ²²thefts, covetousness, wickedness, deceit, lewdness, an evil eye, blasphemy, pride, foolishness. All these evil things come from within and defile a man." Mark 7:20-23 (NKJV)

FEBRUARY 26

COURSE: Sin [continued]

WORD: **"Now the works of the flesh are evident, which are: adultery, fornication, uncleanness, lewdness, idolatry, sorcery, hatred, contentions, jealousies, outbursts of wrath, selfish ambitions, dissensions, heresies, envy, murders,**[b] **drunkenness, revelries, and the like; of which I tell you beforehand, just as I also told** *you* **in time past, that those who practice such things will not inherit the kingdom of God.** Galatians 5:19-21 (NKJV)

               "For if we sin willfully after we have received the knowledge of the truth, there no longer remains a sacrifice for sins, but a certain fearful expectation of judgment, and fiery indignation which will devour the adversaries. Anyone who has rejected Moses' law dies without mercy on *the testimony of* **two or three witnesses. Of how much worse punishment, do you suppose, will he be thought worthy who has trampled the Son of God underfoot, counted the blood of the covenant by which he was sanctified a common thing, and insulted the Spirit of grace? For we know Him who said, "Vengeance is Mine, I will repay," says the Lord.** [b] **And again, "The Lord will judge His people."** Heb. 10:26-30 NKJV

               "F*it is* **impossible for those who were once enlightened, and have tasted the heavenly gift, and have become partakers of the Holy Spirit, and have tasted the good word of God and the powers of the age to come, if they fall away, to renew them again to repentance, since they crucify again for themselves the Son of God, and put** *Him* **to an open shame."** Heb. 6:4-6 (NKJV)

TRAINEE: This Word is heavy. You have graphically shown me the problem; I now desperately need the answer!

FEBRUARY 27

COURSE: SIN [THE ANSWER]

COACH: The Answer; read and head:

WORD: "For godly sorrow produces repentance *leading* to salvation, not to be regretted; but the sorrow of the world produces death." 2 Corinthians 7:10 (NKJV)

"And do not be conformed to this world, but be transformed by the renewing of your do mind, that you may prove what *is* that good and acceptable and perfect will of God." Romans 12:2 (NKJV)

"But what does it say? *"The word is near you, in your mouth and in your heart"* (that is, the word of faith which we preach): that if you confess with your mouth the Lord Jesus and believe in your heart that God has raised Him from the dead, you will be saved. For with the heart one believes unto righteousness, and with the mouth confession is made unto salvation." Romans 10:8-10 (NKJV)

"Blessed *is* the man who endures temptation; for when he has been approved, he will receive the crown of life which the Lord has promised to those who love Him." James 1:12 (NKJV)

"No temptation has overtaken you except such as is common to man; but God *is* faithful, who will not allow you to be tempted beyond what you are able, but with the temptation will also make the way of escape, that you may be able to bear it." 1 Corinthians 10:13 (NKJV)

-continued-

FEBRUARY 28

"If we say we have no sin [refusing to admit that we are sinners], we delude and lead ourselves astray, and the Truth [which the Gospel presents] is not in us [does not dwell in our hearts]. If we [freely] admit that we have sinned and confess our sins, He is faithful and just (true to His own nature and promises) and will forgive our sins [dismiss our lawlessness] and [continuously] cleanse us from all unrighteousness [everything not in conformity to His will in purpose, thought, and action]. 1 John 1:8-9 (Amplified Bible)

"THEREFORE, [there is] now no condemnation (no adjudging guilty of wrong) for those who are in Christ Jesus, who live [and] walk not after the dictates of the flesh, but after the dictates of the Spirit.

For the law of the Spirit of life [which is] in Christ Jesus [the law of our new being] has freed me from the law of sin and of death.

For God has done what the Law could not do, [its power] being weakened by the flesh [the entire nature of man without the Holy Spirit]. Sending His own Son in the guise of sinful flesh and as an offering for sin, [God] condemned sin in the flesh [subdued, overcame, deprived it of its power over all who accept that sacrifice]," Romans 8:1-3 (Amplified Bible)

"For God so greatly loved and dearly prized the world that He [even] gave up His only begotten (unique) Son, so that whoever believes in (trusts in, clings to, relies on) Him shall not perish (come to destruction, be lost) but have eternal (everlasting) life." John 3:16 (Amplified Bible)

AMAN

FEBRUARY 29

COURSE: SELF-ESTEEM

TRAINEE: How can I love me, care for me?

COACH: We will exercise you off the *"seesaw effect"* of putting others down in order to feel better about yourself. It does not work. The *"altruistic ego effect"* of helping others as a means of feeling good about yourself is better, but not the Father's best.

TRAINEE: I'm listening.

COACH: Your deepest need is the answer to this question: "does anyone really know me?" Let the following Word from the Father sink deep into your soul.

WORD: **"Then the word of the L**ORD **came to me, saying: "Before I formed you in the womb I knew you; Before you were born I sanctified you;"** Jeremiah 1:4-5a NKJV

COACH: Again, one of your great spiritual leaders, St. Augustine, in the fourth century, stated: *"Every man's heart is restless 'til he finds his rest in Thee."* Your identity and ability to love and forgive yourself comes not so much from knowing *who* you are as in knowing *whose* you are. Complete today's course by exercising, meditating, on Psalm 119—all of it. The psalmist knows where you are. The Word is "active and alive."

WORD: **"My soul melts from heaviness; Strengthen me according to Your word."** Psalm 119:28 NKJV

"My flesh and my heart fail; *But* **God** *is* **the strength of my heart and my portion forever."** Psalm 73:26 NKJV

TRAINEE: I need to let God be "my all in all."

COACH: Amen.

Month of Wind

COURSE:	LEARNING/GROWING BY THE WORD
TRAINEE:	You've given me a good taste; I need rich servings every day.
COACH:	It's good for you to be hungry for His Word.
WORD:	**"Blessed *are* those who hunger and thirst for righteousness, for they shall be filled." Matthew 5:6** NKJV
COACH:	I would coach you to ask God's **Holy Spirit to guide** you in seeking the Scriptures for answers. When Jesus got ready to ascend back to Heaven, He told the disciples that the comforter, counselor would come and He would teach them and bring to their remembrance all things Jesus had said. The Holy Spirit fully knows the mind of the Father and fully knows your needs; therefore, He is the best one to bring the two together as you seek for answers. Like the wind, Jesus said, He works in you; you don't see the wind but you sense its effects.
TRAINEE:	I'm listening.
COACH:	The Holy Spirit comes to your aid to: 1. Counsel, 2. Teach, 3. Help, 4. Comfort, and 5. Convict. Those five functions are the actual names the Bible gives to the Holy Spirit. He does these for you by pointing and unfolding to you the Scriptures.
WORD:	**"But the Helper, the Holy Spirit, whom the Father will send in My name, He will teach you all things, and bring to your remembrance all things that I said to you."** John 14:26 NKJ
TRAINEE:	Dear Father, in the Name of Jesus, I ask that Your Holy Spirit give me discernment by coaching me through Your Word. Amen.

MARCH 2

-continued-

COACH: Scripture for inviting the Holy Spirit to join you:

WORD: **"The Sovereign Lord has given me his words of wisdom, so that I know how to comfort the weary. Morning by morning he wakens me and opens my understanding to his will"** Isaiah 50:4 NKJV

"But when the Father sends the Advocate as my representative —that is, the Holy Spirit—he will teach you everything and will remind you of everything I have told you."   John 14:26 NLT.

"And the Holy Spirit helps us in our weakness. For example, we don't know what God wants us to pray for. But the Holy Spirit prays for us with groaning's that cannot be expressed in words" Romans 8:26. NKJV

"But you will receive power when the Holy Spirit comes upon you. And you will be my witnesses, telling people about me everywhere in Jerusalem, throughout Judea, in Samaria, and to the ends of the earth" Acts 1:8 NKJV.

". . . for it is not you speaking, but the Spirit of your Father speaking through you." Matthew 10:20. AMP

"May He grant you out of the riches of His glory, to be strengthened *and* spiritually energized with power through His Spirit in your inner self, [indwelling your innermost being and personality]," Ephesians 3:16. AMP

"I advise you to obey only the Holy Spirit's instructions. He will tell you where to go and what to do, and then you won't always be doing the wrong things your evil nature wants you to." Galatians 5:16 (TLB)

TRAINEE: I feel more full and encouraged!

MARCH 3

-continued-

COACH: Dr. Billy Graham summed it up well with the following:

"To walk in the Spirit is a challenging and inspiring exercise, for it combines activity with relaxation. To walk means to place one foot in front of the other. If you stop doing this, you are no longer walking-you are standing still. Walking always implies movement, progress, and direction. Sin shall no longer rule or dominate you when you are allowing the Holy Spirit to live Christ's life through you. It is living by faith, living by trust, living in dependence upon God." https://billygraham. org/devotion/depend-on-him/

TRAINEE: But how does this take place? What has to change for me to do this?

COACH: You don't want to rely on your own strength; recall Peter trying to walk on the water when he saw Jesus. You need the Holy Spirit living in you to coach you through each day. God, the Father, freely gives the Holy Spirit to all who sincerely ask.

WORD: **"If you then, being evil, know how to give good gifts to your children, how much more will *your* heavenly Father give the Holy Spirit to those who ask Him!" Luke 11:13**

TRAINEE: Lord, so often I have walked on my own instead of walking by the help of Your Spirit. Guide my footsteps this day, I pray in Jesus' name. Amen.

COACH: Honest and confessional; good prayer. You're holding some hope.

WORD: **"Now hope does not disappoint, because the love of God has been poured out in our hearts by the Holy Spirit who was given to us." Romans 5:5**

TRAINEE: Yes, Sir!

MARCH 4

COURSE: THE DAY-BY-DAY JOURNEY

TRAINEE: I'm impressed, but how do I go about putting this all together?

COACH: Have you ever watched a child with building blocks, trying to stack one upon another? Just the slightest shift in stacking those blocks can make the whole structure off balance, causing them to all tumble down. So it is with the building blocks of God's Word. For example, the first block handed you by the Holy Spirit was centered on His work to "convict of Truth":

WORD: **"O Lord, You have searched me (thoroughly) and have known me.... Search me (thoroughly), O God, and know my heart! Try me, and know my thoughts!"** Ps. 139:1, 23 (AMP)

"I, the Lord, search the mind, I try the heart, even to give every man according to his ways, according to the fruit of his doings." Jer. 17:10 (AMP)

COACH: The second block:

WORD: **"If we say that we have no sin, we are only fooling ourselves, and refusing to accept the truth. But if we confess our sins to him, he can be depended on to forgive us and to cleanse us from every wrong. (And it is perfectly proper for God to do this for us because Christ died to wash away our sins)."** 1 John 1:8–9 (TLB)

COACH: Other blocks: see Paul's journey of being transformed; he grew and changed from confession of being: *"chief of sinners* [T Tim. 1:15]," *"nothing good in (him)* [Rom. 7:18]," deserving *"only condemnation and death* [Rom. 5:12, 16, 18; 7:5, 10, 13]," *"a wretched being* [Rom. 7:24]" to stating he was: [cont.]

-continued-

MARCH 5

WORD: "*. . . more than a conqueror through (Christ, Jesus) who loved (him)* [Rom. 8:37]," that he could "*do all things through Christ who strengthens (him)* [Phil. 4:13]," that "*God's strength is made perfect in (his) weakness* [2 Cor. 12; 9]," and finally, to say, "*It is no longer I (self-centered ego) Paul who live, but Christ within me* [Gal. 3:18]."

COACH:	One block builds upon the other. The Holy Spirit knows which building blocks from the Word to hand you at the right time. You need only remember which block (Word) is the cornerstone of the house of God's grace. It is none other than the Word from the cross—all this so you can be: *"transformed by the renewing of your mind* [Rom. 12:2]."
COACH:	This means you can practice saying every day: "Today, I can stop *'having a form of godliness and denying the power thereof.'"*
WORD:	**"For the message of the cross is foolishness to those who are perishing, but to us who are being saved it is the power of God."** 1 Cor. 1:18 (NIV)
COACH:	Meditate and memorize (God's M & M's). Again, ask God to help you become increasingly hungry for His Word, letting it sink-in deep.
WORD:	**"And Jesus said to them, "I am the bread of life. He who comes to Me shall never hunger, and he who believes in Me shall never thirst." John 6:35** NKJV
TRAINEE:	So, the Word is my "bread."

MARCH 6

COURSE:	GOD'S PERSONAL WORD
COACH:	God's Word can speak to and change real-life crises—leaving a sense of wonder and comfort about His Word. Theologically, it would mean encountering Scripture—not just as *"Logos,"* but as *"Rhema."* These two words were in the original Greek New Testament texts for the word *"word"*: *Logos,* meaning "idea," "thought," "concept," or "creative energy that generated the universe," according to Strong's 3056; and *Rhema* (see Rom. 10:17), meaning that the hearer is changed, motivated and personally and directly addressed by that Word (Jesus).

When you still yourself to read the Bible, you are reading *logos* and cannot turn it into *Rhema,* but the Holy Spirit can. Using the Scriptures, He lives up to his description as "teacher, helper, counselor, comforter and one who convicts of truth" (John 14:26; John 16:7–15; Rom. 8:26). When a verse of Scripture strikes you as *rhema,* you know that it is time to sit up, salute and say, "Yes, sir;" and become expectant—*you know that you know that you know.*

The Thomas Nelson King James Study Bible will help you search for key words in the concordance; e.g., *faith, hope, love, forgiveness* . . . and then pore over the Scriptures surrounding those key words in search of words that the Holy Spirit would choose to "speak" to you in that "R*hema* fashion." If the Word of God says it, it is true; it is done! When the Holy Spirit guides the *logos* Word from the Bible into your heart and mind as *rhema*, then you have assurance and conviction. Jesus also said, "***It has been written, Man shall not live and be upheld and sustained by bread alone, but by every word that comes forth from the mouth of God***" Matt. 4:4 AMP.

MARCH 7

COURSE:	WOUNDED-HEALERS
COACH:	God loves to use Your wounds to build "wounded healers."
TRAINEE:	I can't put the two together.
COACH:	A wounded healer is someone who has been there, who has gone through the pain, problem, crisis, sin condition, weakness, habit, addiction, and so on. So, like an Army scout, he is the best person to come back and take the rest of the troops through the same territory.
TRAINEE:	I have some pains, wounds to memory and body.
COACH:	This places you in good company.
TRAINEE:	Why?
COACH:	Because Jesus was the greatest wounded healer of all times.
WORD:	"**By his wounds, his stripes, we are healed**" (Is. 53:5; 1 Pet. 2:24).
COACH:	What kind of wounds might you be carrying as we train? Feel free to adopt from these months what you sense to be helpful.
TRAINEE:	I need some examples.
COACH:	From the months of January, February, and March:
WORD:	"**They that wait upon the Lord shall renew their strength**" Is. 40:31
	For I consider that the sufferings of this present time are not worthy to be compared with the glory which shall be revealed in us Rom. 8:18
	. . . endure unto the end, same shall be saved Mk 13:13 [KJV]

MARCH 8

COURSE: HEALING

COACH: Ask God to "send out [Is, 55:10-11]" His healing Word for you. His Word where He says:

"I am the Lord Thy God, Who healeth thee . . ." Ex. 15:26

"For I will restore health unto thee and heal thee of thy wounds" Jer. 30:17

"Ye are healed by the stripes of Jesus." Is. 53:4-5/1Pet. 2:24

"Thy body is the temple of the Holy Spirit . . ." 1 Cor. 6:19

"Ye are fearfully and wonderfully made and God knows all the inner parts . . ." Ps. 139:13-16

"The curse of the Law [sin, death, disease] has been broken [by what Jesus accomplished on the Cross . . ."] Gal. 3:13-14

"God desires above all things that ye prosper and be in health-even as thy soul prospers" 3 Jn. 2

"They that wait upon the Lord shall renew their strength . . ." Is. 40:31

"We have none of these diseases . . ." Ps. 103:3

"We are the healed of the Lord . . ." Ps. 107:20/James. 5:16

"God's Word is health [medicine] to all thy flesh" Pr. 4:22

[Promise about prayer in His will; His Word is His will]: 1 Jn. 5:14-15

TRAINEE: To pray His Word, I pray His will to be done in His way/time.

MARCH 9

COURSE: WIND AND THE WORD

TRAINEE: How are they related?

COACH: Jesus said the Holy Spirit works "like the wind." You see the effect of it but not the wind itself. Recall His Names: Counselor, Comforter, Helper, Teacher, One Who Convicts of Truth; they, again, are the way He uses and applies the Word to and in your life. Look at how Dr. Billy Graham put it in one of his devotional writings:

"If we look to our own resources, our own strength, or our own ability, as Peter did when he walked on the water, we will fail. You cannot live the Christian life by yourself. The Holy Spirit must live in you and express Himself through you. Living for Christ is a day-by-day experience. It is a continuous dependence upon the Spirit of God. It is believing in His faithfulness.

Prayer for the day

Lord, so often I have walked on my own instead of walking in Your Spirit. Guide my footsteps this day, I pray in Jesus' name." https://billygraham.org/devotion/depend-on-him/

WORD: **"But when the Father sends the Advocate as my representative —that is, the Holy Spirit—he will teach you everything and will remind you of everything I have told you"** John 14:26.

"And the Holy Spirit helps us in our weakness. For example, we don't know what God wants us to pray for. But the Holy Spirit prays for us with groaning's that cannot be expressed in words" Romans 8:26.

TRAINEE: Yes, like the wind!

MARCH 10

-continued-

TRAINEE: I need coaching from the Holy Spirit to direct the Word to me about my sin condition. Have I committed the "sin unto death?" What is it?

COACH: Read carefully Hebrews 4:4-6; 10:26-30.

TRAINEE: I can't dodge the fact that my sin was "willful and deliberate."

COACH: So was King David's. The *"sin unto death"* is a lifestyle of deliberate sin against God with no desire to repent of it.

TRAINEE: I have sorrow over my sin against God and have not decided to go my own way or to reject Jesus, and my heart feels the thump effect of that triangle as it is rolled over—the edges of my conscience not worn off; however, I'm deeply afraid of offending God by my hypocrisy and deceitful heart.

COACH: Beautiful! You recall that *"working out your salvation with fear and trembling"* is amplified to read:

WORD: **"(Self-distrust, that is, with serious caution, tenderness of conscience, watchfulness against temptation; timidly shrinking from whatever might offend God and discredit the name of Christ)."** Phil. 2:12 (AMP)

King David wrote:

"You aren't interested in offerings burned before you on the altar. It is a broken spirit you want—remorse and penitence. A broken and a contrite heart (*the Amplified Bible says* **"broken down with sorrow for sin and humbly and thoroughly penitent"**)**, O God, you will not ignore.** Ps. 51:16–17 (TLB)"

TRAINEE: That helps!

MARCH 11

COURSE: MY UNTRUSTWORTHY HEART AND FEELINGS

WORD: **"The heart is deceitful above all things, and it is exceedingly perverse and corrupt and severely, mortally sick! Who can know it (perceive, understand, be acquainted with his own heart and mind)?"** Jer. 17:9 (AMP)

COACH: The real crime here is unbelief. Your sin is not only idolatry, but not believing his Word too is. He saw your struggle with it; therefore, he was patient with you in it. You can still come boldly to him (see Eph. 3:12, Heb. 4:16) despite the long history of your struggle.

WORD: **"It is of the Lord's mercies that we are not consumed because his compassions fail not."** Lam. 3:22 (KJV)

COACH: *Heart* is the Old Testament's word for the seat of your emotional system sitting in the right brain. God made that portion of the brain for a reason. Feelings are his creation and, therefore, are good. Speaking of Jesus, the writer of Hebrews says that he was *"anointed with gladness beyond his comrades"* (Heb. 1:9). Yet he also was described by Isaiah as *"a man of sorrows, and acquainted with grief"* (Is. 53:3).

However, Jesus was never enslaved to his own emotional reactions. How he felt was never the issue; personal insult never provoked him, unless it affected the Father. He *saw* things from the Father's perspective.

WORD: **"For even Christ did not please himself but, as it is written: 'The insults of those who insult you have fallen on me'"** Rom. 15:3 NIV.

MARCH 12

COURSE: FEELINGS VS. FAITH

COACH: If you don't choose to adopt God's feelings, you settle for your own.

TRAINEE: On one hand, I am not to "*let the sun go down on (my) anger;*" on the other hand, I am to "*be angry but sin not*" (see Eph. 4:26). It's like the saying, "Going to pieces is sometimes what keeps you from falling apart."

COACH: The balance comes in choosing to see or perceive people, circumstances, and so on from God's view.

TRAINEE: How is this done?

COACH: Part of what it means for you to "*deny yourself and take up your cross*" falls under the prayer that says, "Dear Father, I give my emotions to you and ask that you give me yours." Is this not what the apostle Paul learned?

WORD: **"Put them all away: anger, wrath, malice, slander, and foul talk.... Put on compassion, kindness, lowliness, meekness, and patience, forbearing one another ... and forgiving one another."** Col. 3:8, 12, 13

COACH: You are not a robot, programmed by feelings into action. Notice the word *put* in the above text. It is a decision.

WORD: **"Reckon ... yourselves to be dead ... unto sin."** Rom. 6:11 (KJV)

TRAINEE: Yet again, what enables this choice?

COACH: It takes an act of faith to make such decisions about feelings. That faith moves into action when you lock it into the Word.

MARCH 13

COURSE: BENEFITS OF FAITH CHOICES

COACH: The benefits of such a transformation through the renewal of the mind (see Rom. 12:2) are as follows:

While you may see differently than most of the world—for example, Jeremiah was called "*the weeping prophet*"—you will have an extraordinary objectivity in your outlook. When you look at the news and see the insane actions of a hardened criminal and ask, "How do you feel about this, Father?" you will find yourself moving away from the vindictive, reactionary, self-righteous response to a desire to see this criminal in the position of the penitent thief hanging on the cross next to Jesus, causing you to pray for salvation in the midst of punishment.

You'll be free to enter God's emotions rather than remain bound to your own. The reason Jesus could voice a cry of victory—"It is finished"—from the cross is because he saw what the Father saw. Great or small, whatever the concern, it pays to see it from God's perspective.

Listen to the Word that coaches you to see that the one Beatitude—**"Blessed are the poor in spirit, for theirs is the kingdom of heaven"**—again, with the Greek text reading, **"How blest are those who know their need of God; the kingdom of Heaven is theirs"**—is completely true. Matthew 5:3 (NEB) states that you are to choose to be happy when you come to know how much you need God.

TRAINEE: This is new thinking for me.

MARCH 14

COURSE: BLESSINGS IN DISGUISE:

He prayed for strength that he might achieve;
He was made weak that he might obey.
He prayed for health that he might do great things;
He was given infirmity that he might do better things.

He prayed for riches that he might be happy;
He was given poverty that he might be wise.
He prayed for power that he might have the praises of men;
He was given weakness that he might feel the need of God.

He prayed for all things that he might enjoy life;
He was given life that he might enjoy all things.
He had received nothing that he asked for – all that he hoped for;
His prayer was answered – he was most blessed.

-Author unknown-

COACH: You are only one, but still, you are one.

TRAINEE: I cannot do everything. And because I cannot do everything, I will not refuse to do the something that I CAN do! With God's help!

MARCH 15

COURSE: CLOSER TO CHRIST

COACH: Conduct your personal Bible study on the following, open to the coaching of the Holy Spirit:

TRAINEE: Will the Word bring me closer to Him?

COACH: God says: **"Thou wilt keep him in perfect peace, whose mind is stayed on thee: because he trusteth in thee."** Isaiah 26:3 KJV Again, to have your mind stayed on His Word is the same as having it stayed on Him. Why? Because He is the Word and the Word is Him.

WORD: Read John 1:1-14. Verse 14 says: **"And the Word became flesh and dwelt with us."** NKJV

I.   Honest Confession: [1 John 1:8-9, Psalm 34:18, Psalm 51:17]

II.   Redemption/Forgiveness/Grace: [Hebrews 12:16]

III.   Obedience: [Philippians 2:13, 2 Corinthians 7:10, 2 Corinthians 10:5, Galatians 2:20, 1 Corinthians 1:18, 2 Corinthians 12:9]

IV.   Service: [Philippians 4:13, Romans 8:37]

V.   Praise: [1 Thessalonians 5:16-18, Ephesians 5:20, Hebrews 13:15, Philippians 4:6-7]

TRAINEE: His Word tastes good!

WORD: **"For the ear tests words as the palate tastes food."** Job 34:3 NKJV

MARCH 16

COURSE: SIN-CONDITIONS: A Summary and Review

THE PROBLEM:

WORD: No, you yourselves do wrong and cheat, and *you do* these things *to your* brethren! [9]Do you not know that the unrighteous will not inherit the kingdom of God? Do not be deceived. Neither fornicators, nor idolaters, nor adulterers, nor homosexuals,[a] nor sodomites, [10] nor thieves, nor covetous, nor drunkards, nor revilers, nor extortioners will inherit the kingdom of God. 1 Corinthians 6:8-10 New King James Version (NKJV)

For if we sin willfully after we have received the knowledge of the truth, there no longer remains a sacrifice for sins, [27]but a certain fearful expectation of judgment, and fiery indignation which will devour the adversaries. [28]Anyone who has rejected Moses' law dies without mercy on *the testimony of* two or three witnesses. [29]Of how much worse punishment, do you suppose, will he be thought worthy who has trampled the Son of God underfoot, counted the blood of the covenant by which he was sanctified a common thing, and insulted the Spirit of grace? [30]For we know Him who said, "Vengeance is Mine, I will repay,"[a] says the Lord. [b] And again, "The LORD will judge His people." Heb. 10:26-30 NKJV

. . . knowing this: that the law is not made for a righteous person, but for *the* lawless and insubordinate, for *the* ungodly and for sinners, for *the* unholy and profane, for murderers of fathers and murderers of mothers, for manslayers, [10]for fornicators, for sodomites, for kidnappers, for liars, for perjurers, and if there is any other thing that is contrary to sound doctrine, [11]according to the glorious gospel of the blessed God which was committed to my trust. 1 Timothy 1:9-11 New King James Version (NKJV)

MARCH 17

-continued-

And He said, "What comes out of a man, that defiles a man. For from within, out of the heart of men, proceed evil thoughts, adulteries, fornications, murders, [22]thefts, covetousness, wickedness, deceit, lewdness, an evil eye, blasphemy, pride, foolishness. [23] All these evil things come from within and defile a man." Mark 7:20-23 New King James Version (NKJV)

Now the works of the flesh are evident, which are: adultery,[a] fornication, uncleanness, lewdness, ²⁰ idolatry, sorcery, hatred, contentions, jealousies, outbursts of wrath, selfish ambitions, dissensions, heresies, ²¹ envy, murders,[b] drunkenness, revelries, and the like; of which I tell you beforehand, just as I also told *you* in time past, that those who practice such things will not inherit the kingdom of God. Galatians 5:19-21 New King James Version (NKJV)

COACH: *During the season of **Lent** in the Church Year, you have a focused opportunity to discern and examine your journey to overcome your sin-conditions, varied as they may be. Tomorrow's Words speak directly to God's answer to your struggle. Prepare your mind and heart for them to speak and make their mark on your heart.*

TRAINEE: Looking for and expecting the "Answer" to this most grievous "Problem!"

MARCH 18

COURSE: THE ANSWER: A Summary and a Review

"For godly sorrow produces repentance *leading* to salvation, not to be regretted; but the sorrow of the world produces death." 2 Corinthians 7:10 (New King James Version)

"And do not be conformed to this world, but be transformed by the renewing of your mind, that you may prove what *is* that good and acceptable and perfect will of God." Romans 12:2 (New King James Version)

"But what does it say? *"The word is near you, in your mouth and in your heart"*[a] (that is, the word of faith which we preach): ⁹ that if you confess with your mouth the Lord Jesus and believe in your heart that God has raised Him from the dead, you will be saved. ¹⁰ For with the heart one believes unto righteousness, and with the mouth confession is made unto salvation." Romans 10:8-10 (New King James Version)

. . . "for it is God who works in you both to will and to do for *His* good pleasure." Philippians 2:13 (New King James Version)

. . . "Blessed *is* the man who endures temptation; for when he has been approved, he will receive the crown of life which the Lord has promised to those who love Him." James 1:12 (New King James Version

"No temptation has overtaken you except such as is common to man; but God *is* faithful, who will not allow you to be tempted beyond what you are able, but with the temptation will also make the way of escape, that you may be able to bear *it*." 1 Corinthians 10:13 (New King James Version)

MARCH 19

-continued-

"If we say that we have no sin, we deceive ourselves, and the truth is not in us. If we confess our sins, He is faithful and just to forgive us *our* sins and to cleanse us from all unrighteousness." 1 John 1:8-9 (New King James Version)

Free from Indwelling Sin

"T*here is* therefore now no condemnation to those who are in Christ Jesus,[a] who do not walk according to the flesh, but according to the Spirit. 2 For the law of the Spirit of life in Christ Jesus has made me free from the law of sin and death. 3 For what the law could not do in that it was weak through the flesh, God *did* by sending His own Son in the likeness of sinful flesh, on account of sin: He condemned sin in the flesh, . . ." Romans 8:1-3 (New King James Version)

"For God so loved the world that He gave His only begotten Son, that whoever believes in Him should not perish but have everlasting life." John 3:16 (**New King James Version**)

AMEN

MARCH 20

COURSE:

THE ANSWER: A SUMMARY
THE REAL VALUE IN
READING GOD'S WORD
IS NOT JUST THE KNOWLEDGE INSELF,
BUT
THE HEART UNDERSTANDING IT SETS
TO
THE BOUNDARIES OF GOD'S
THOUGHT
THINKING GOD'S THOUGHTS AFTER
HIM
FRAMES HIS PURPOSE AND COUNSEL
IN A
BELIEVER'S HEART.
AND,
IT SETS THE BOUNDARIES FOR
FERVENT & EFFECTUAL PRAYERS.

TRAINEE: Dear Father, again, help me be more hungry for Your Word!

MARCH 21

COURSE: THE **WORD**

COACH: God says you are "blessed" when hungry for His Word [Matthew 5:6]; and that His Word "endures forever [Isaiah 40:8]."

TRAINEE: When I read His Word, what am I taking in?

COACH: In the 55th chapter of Isaiah, God talks in "living-room" conversation style about His Word. He says that it is like the rain and snow that comes down and waters the earth, causing the seeds to germinate and bear forth fruit/grow. Then He says that It "always accomplishes that which It is sent out to do, never returns to Him void or empty." The Apostle Paul speaks about the Word as "**active and alive, sharper than a two-edge sword, able to divide between bone and marrow, soul** [personality] **and spirit** [that part which is eternal] **and to discern and know the deepest thoughts and motivations of the heart** [Hebrews 4:12]." And God says that He "**watches over His Word to perform It** [Jeremiah 1:12]." The wisdom writer tells us that God's Word is "**medicine to all (our) flesh** [Proverbs 4:22]. St. John wrote that the "**Word became flesh and dwelt among us** [John 1:14]."

TRAINEE: That's quite a summary; how do I open up for all that to happen?

COACH: To meditate and memorize His Word [God's M & M's] is to receive into the hierarchy of your being [spirit-mind-body] the same force sent out at the beginning of creation when God spoke His Word and said: "**Let there be . . . and there was.**" Genesis 1:3.

MARCH 22

COURSE: PRAYER AND THE WORD

COACH: Right prayers bring right results! Like wartime, infra-red, computerized weapons, the most on-target form of praying is to pray God's Own Word right back to Him. He says that prayers prayed in His will are "**heard and answered** [1 John 5:14-15]." His Word is His will! Increasingly engage spiritual "readiness training" by exercising daily on His Word. Paul wrote to Timothy: "**For bodily exercise profiteth little; but godliness is profitable unto all things, having promise of the life that now is, and of that which is to come** [1 Timothy 4:8]."

TRAINEE: Can you give me some good examples of praying the Word?

COACH: If your circumstances are chaotic, pray Romans 8:28; if your life is disobedient, pray Philippians 2:13; if you have broken relationships, pray Ephesians 1:16–19, 3:14–19 by placing your name or the name of another in these Scriptures as you pray—*making it personal.*

TRAINEE: As I pray these Words with my name in them, what happens?

COACH: The Holy Spirit is the power source now ready for the complete flow of the Word; see yourself stepping out, not quitting, but with the nevertheless-of-faith connection. Would this not be the reason Jesus said, *"And whatsoever ye shall ask in my name, that will I do, that the Father may be glorified in the Son"* (John 14:13 KJV)? Scripture tells us that prayers made in the name of Jesus that are in the Father's will are heard, and are, therefore, in God's eyes already answered (1 John 5:13–14).

TRAINEE: A lot to think about!

MARCH 23

COURSE: WORD ABOUT THE WORD

TRAINEE: How does God talk about His Word to us?

WORD: **"For the Word that God speaks is alive and full of power—making it active, operative, energizing and effective; it is sharper than any two-edged sword, penetrating to the dividing line of the breath of life (soul) and (the immortal) spirit, and of joints and marrow (that is, of the deepest parts of our nature) exposing and sifting and analyzing and judging the very thoughts and purposes of the heart."** Heb. 4:12 (AMP)

THE WORD

1 Thessalonians 2:13 (New King James Version) **"For this reason we also thank God without ceasing, because when you received the word of God which you heard from us, you welcomed *it* not *as* the word of men, but as it is in truth, the word of God, which also effectively works in you who believe."**

<u>Hebrews 1:1-3</u> (New King James Version) **"God, who at various times and in various ways spoke in time past to the fathers by the prophets, [2] has in these last days spoken to us by** *His* **Son, whom He has appointed heir of all things, through whom also He made the worlds; [3] who being the brightness of** *His* **glory and the express image of His person, and upholding all things by the word of His power, when He had by Himself purged our sins, sat down at the right hand of the Majesty on high, . . ."**

<u>Hebrews 11:3</u> (New King James Version) **"By faith we understand that the worlds were framed by the word of God, so that the things which are seen were not made of things which are visible."**

-continued-

MARCH 24

<u>1 Peter 1:23</u> (New King James Version) **". . . having been born again, not of corruptible seed but incorruptible, through the word of God which lives and abides forever, because** *" All flesh is as grass, And all the glory of man as the flower of the grass. The grass withers, And its flower falls away, But the word of the LORD endures forever."*

<u>1 Peter 2</u> *". . . as newborn babes, desire the pure milk of the word, that you may grow thereby, . . ."*

<u>2 Peter 3:5-7</u> (New King James Version) **"For this they willfully forget: that by the word of God the heavens were of old, and the earth standing out of water and in the water, [6] by which the world** *that* **then existed perished, being flooded with water. [7] But the heavens and the earth** *which* **are now preserved by the same word, are reserved for fire until the day of judgment and perdition of ungodly men."**

<u>1 John 1:1</u> (New King James Version) **"What Was Heard, Seen, and touched that which was from the beginning, which we have heard, which we have seen with our eyes, which we have looked upon, and our hands have handled, concerning the Word of life—"**

<u>1 John 5:7</u> (New King James Version) **"For there are three that bear witness in heaven: the Father, the Word, and the Holy Spirit; and these three are one.**"

<u>Revelation 19:11-13</u> (New King James Version) **"Now I saw heaven opened, and behold, a white horse. And He who sat on him** *was* **called Faithful and True, and in righteousness He judges and makes war.** [12] **His eyes** *were* **like a flame of fire, and on His head** *were* **many crowns. He had**[a] **a name written that no one knew except Himself.** [13] **He** *was* **clothed with a robe dipped in blood, and His name is called The Word of God."**

Philippians 4:7 The peace of God that passes all understanding, keep your hearts and minds through Christ Jesus]

MARCH 25

COURSE: RIGHT PRAYERS THAT BRING RIGHT RESULTS

COACH: Again, to pray His Word is to pray His will.

WORD: 1 John 5:14-15 New King James Version (NKJV) **" Now this is the confidence that we have in Him, that if we ask anything according to His will, He hears us. And if we know that He hears us, whatever we ask, we know that we have the petitions that we have asked of Him."**

TRAINEE: What about broken relationships? That's a huge problem in this world!

COACH: Where you see a word underlined in the following two prayers the Apostle Paul prayed for the Early Church, place the name of anyone, with whom your relations are estranged or broken. Pray it for them until your heart wants for them what this prayer asks.

WORD: "I have never stopped thanking God for You. I pray for you constantly, asking God, the glorious Father of our Lord Jesus Christ, to give you wisdom to see clearly and really understand who Christ is and all that he has done for you. I pray that your hearts will be flooded with light so that you can see something of the future he has called you to share. I want you to realize that God has been made rich because we who are Christ's have been given to Him! I pray that you will begin to understand how incredibly great His power is to help those who believe Him. EPHESIANS 1:16-19 TLB

-continued-

MARCH 26

"When I think of the wisdom and scope of his plan I fall down on my knees and pray to the Father of all the great family of God—some of them already in heaven and some down here on earth—that out of his glorious, unlimited resources he will give you the mighty inner strengthening of his Holy Spirit. And I pray that Christ will be more and more at home in your hearts, living within you as you trust in him. May your roots go down deep into the soil of God's marvelous love; and may you be able to feel and understand, as all God's children should, how long, how wide, how deep, and how high his love really is; and to experience this love for yourselves, though it is so great that you will never see the end of it or fully know or understand it. And so at last you will be filled up with God himself." EPHESIANS 3:14-19

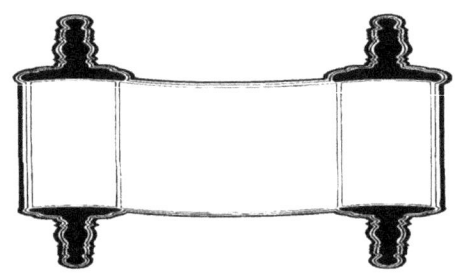

MARCH 27

TRAINEE: God tells me that I am to show Him the love of obedience as I "*forget not all thy benefits* <u>Psalm 103:2</u>" and hear him say, "*If you love me, you will obey me* <u>John 14:15</u>."

COACH: Read the following verses from Psalm 91. Where you see "*set his love upon Me,*" understand it to include: "*set his obedience upon Me.*"

WORD: Psalm 91:14-16 New King James Version (NKJV)

> **"Because he has set his love upon Me,**
> **therefore I will deliver him;**
> **I will set him on high,**
> **because he has known My name.**
> **He shall call upon Me,**
> **and I will answer him;**
> **I** *will be* **with him in trouble;**
> **I will deliver him and honor him.**
> **With long life I will satisfy him,**
> **And show him My salvation."**

TRAINEE: Circling the letters [*d, i, e*] in the word *obedience* reminds me that I need to "die" to self as a way of setting my love on him."

COACH: *Carry on.*

MARCH 28

COURSE: LIFE'S WEIGHTS, HILLS

TRAINEE: Weights and hills come in different "packages," different sizes.

COACH: The Old Testament Hebrew word for *spirit* (phonetically, *ru*-wach) means "breath, wind."

TRAINEE: In school, we learned that at the time of earth's formation, the wind was strong over it. "Was that God?"

WORD: **"In the beginning of creation, when God made heaven and earth, the earth was without form and void, with darkness over the face of the abyss, and a mighty wind that swept over the surface of the waters"** Gen. 1:1–2 NEB. **"The Spirit of God was moving (hovering, brooding) over the face of the waters"** Gen. 1:2b AMP.

TRAINEE: "Are you going to be the 'wind beneath my wings'?"

WORD: **"The wind blows wherever it pleases. You hear its sound, but you cannot tell where it comes from or where it goes to. So it is with everyone born of the Spirit"** John 3:8 NIV.

COACH: The Holy Spirit is the breath of life to all of your hills and weights. Your training courses will coach you to see parallels between the physical hills and the "hills of temptation."

WORD: **"Since we live by the Spirit, let us keep in step with the Spirit"** Gal. 5:25 (NIV).

COACH: In the original Greek text, the words "keep in step" have a depth of meaning far greater than just "being moved along;" they are a command that military logistics describe as "to get in line with, to make decisions, to take steps and initiate actions in accord with, continually." We continue your training tomorrow.

MARCH 29

-continued-

TRAINEE: I can use the "nevertheless-of-faith" principle to offer words of praise and trust as I begin to run the "hills of life" when I'm almost completely out of breath.

COACH: Again, faith is not a human attribute or a feeling; it is a gift (1 Cor. 12:9) from God that enables you to make the decision to trust him to act.

TRAINEE: I don't know if that "decision" is in me.

COACH: There is nothing weak about faith; it's just your use of it that's weak. I'm coaching you to dive back into the Word when your use of this faith gift becomes weak; then the Word addressing your impossibilities will strengthen your grip (Rom. 10:17). You just need to remember its origin. God does not give you, his child, something that is frail or unstable. It is His strength given to you that enables you to stand on his Word simply by making a decision to do so—sometimes against feelings and circumstances.

WORD: **"And without faith it is impossible to please God"** (Heb. 11:6a NIV).

TRAINEE: The Word flatly tells me that the only way I can be pleasing to Him is to exercise that faith gift. Why is that?

COACH: God has everything except one thing. He doesn't have your faith, a trusting relationship with you, unless you give it to him.

WORD: **"For whatsoever is born of God overcometh the world: and this is the victory that overcometh the world, even our faith"** (1 John 5:4 KJV).

-continued-

MARCH 30

TRAINEE: A question coaches me further. What can I learn from Jesus when it comes to facing the weights and hills with faith?

COACH: *Do you see what Jesus did when facing* his *hill?* "**Because the Lord God helps me, I will not be dismayed; therefore, I have set my face like flint to do his will, and I know that I will triumph**" Is. 50:7 TLB.

TRAINEE: I ask for more coaching. "Can I '*set my face like flint*' against the hills of temptation because Jesus runs with me? When he said from the cross, '*It is finished*,' did he have the finish line in sight? Can I, too, run by faith to the goal, knowing there will come a point at which I see that *cross*over line?"

WORD: "**He that shall endure unto the end, the same shall be saved**" Mark 13:13 (KJV).

TRAINEE: I'm continually and more deeply seeing the Holy Spirit as my coach. I said to him, "*You are making the Word become the wind beneath my wings.*"

WORD: "**And so, dear brothers, I plead with you to give your bodies to God. Let them be a living sacrifice, holy—the kind he can accept. When you think of what he has done for you, is this too much to ask? Don't copy the behavior and customs of this world, but be a new and different person with a fresh newness in all you do and think.** *Then* (emphasis mine) **you will learn from your own experience how his ways will really satisfy you.**" Rom. 12:1–2 TLB [Verse 2 in the King James Version reads, "be ye transformed by the renewing of your mind."]

TRAINEE: Good coaching!

MARCH 31

COURSE: SOME PRELIMINARY QUESTIONS

TRAINEE: For example, when I confess my sins to God as I pray to Him, does He sees me, by faith, accept His Word about forgiveness? (1 John 1:9)

COACH: Have you noted how a baby, laying soiled in the crib, is taken up, cleaned up and securely held in the arms of its parents before feeding again? We train next month on how your Heavenly Father does that cleansing for you as you become soiled from your sin condition.

TRAINEE: Yes, I need that, daily.

COACH: Your faith in His Word about this will make the way clear and open for it to happen.

TRAINEE: I need to remember it is the Word Itself that will strengthen my use of this faith gift.

COACH: Abraham's faith was counted as being the same as righteousness.

WORD: **And being fully persuaded that, what he had promised, he was able also to perform. And therefore it was imputed to him for righteousness. Now it was not written for his sake alone, that it was imputed to him; But for us also, to whom it shall be imputed, if we believe on him that raised up Jesus our Lord from the dead**; Romans 4:21-24 (see, also, vs. 1-8; Lu. 19:9; Ps. 32:1-2

TRAINEE: Can I see the "righteousness of Christ" <u>imputed</u> to me?

COACH: Be ready tomorrow for the month of water to answer your question.

Month of Water

COURSE: FORGIVENESS

TRAINEE: I need a good picture or understanding of forgiveness.

COACH: Again, have you ever watched when a baby has soiled itself and the mother simply picks it up, washes, redresses, feeds and rocks it 'til contentment settles in for that little one?

TRAINEE: Yes, I've seen such; but how does that apply to me?

COACH: When you confess your sins and God forgives you, He does four things: 1. He chooses to forget your sin. He told Israel: "I remember your sins no more." 2. He erases your sin; He doesn't see it anymore. 3. He heals your life from what sin has done to it. 4. He covers your sin so that you are freed from the bondage to sin.

    The original Greek words for those four things He does are the ones that give you the words: "forget [pronounced na-*me*-sius, gives us the word *amnesia*], erase [pronounced *eph*-e-say, gives us *to erase*], heal [pronounced *ther*-o-*pu*-o, leads to *therapy*], and cover [pronounced *tow*-lah, gives us *to cover*]." He also says He will remove your sin as far as the East is from the West. How far is that? Finally, He says those sins that are like scarlet, He will make white as snow.

WORD: "**. . . having wiped out the handwriting of requirements that was against us, which was contrary to us. And He has taken it out of the way, having nailed it to the cross. Having disarmed principalities and powers, He made a public spectacle of them, triumphing over them in it.**" Colossians 2:14-15 (NKJV)

APRIL 2

-continued-

TRAINEE: The past few days have given good training, but I'm hungry for more.

COACH: Excellent! God likes that hunger.

WORD: **"Blessed *are* those who hunger and thirst for righteousness, For they shall be filled**." Matthew 5:6 NKJV

COACH: During the next several days, you can dive deeper into some of the different dimensions of forgiveness.

TRAINEE: I'm ready.

WORD: **"The LORD hath taken away thy judgments, he hath cast out thine enemy: the king of Israel, even the LORD, is in the midst of thee: thou shalt not see evil any more.**

   In that day it shall be said to Jerusalem, Fear thou not: and to Zion, Let not thine hands be slack.

   The LORD thy God in the midst of thee is mighty; he will save, he will rejoice over thee with joy; he will rest in his love, he will joy over thee with singing." Zephaniah 3:15-17 (KJV)

TRAINEE: Will He always forgive this much, and how many times?

COACH: When the disciples asked Jesus if they should forgive as many as 7-times, He answered 70 times 7. This is quite significant because the number "7" in Hebrew stands for perfection and on-going, un-ending time-infinity.

WORD: **". . . and forgive us our sins, just as we have forgiven those who have sinned against us.**" Matthew 6:12 (TLB)

TRAINEE: So, He is asking us to forgive the way He forgives and as much as He does?

APRIL 3

-continued-

COACH:	Now, if God is going to do all that for you because of what His Son accomplished for you on the Cross, can you accept it the whole nine yards by taking the step of forgiving yourself?
WORD:	**"If we confess our sins, He is faithful and just to forgive us our sins and to cleanse us from all unrighteousness."** 1 John 1:9 NKJV
COACH:	He is being "faithful" and "just" to what His Son carried out on the Cross when He said: "It is finished!" Read the background to the Passion of Christ in Isaiah 53 and Psalm. 22.
TRAINEE:	I read the brutal things done to Him, but I still feel guilty and accused.
COACH:	Satan is also called the "accuser."
WORD:	**"And I heard a loud voice saying in heaven, Now is come salvation, and strength, and the kingdom of our God, and the power of his Christ: for the accuser of our brethren is cast down, which accused them before our God day and night."** Revelation 12:10
COACH:	But following your confession and repentance, Jesus is your High Priest Who defends you when the accuser is bringing charges against you. Again, Jesus is your High Priest, interceding for you to the Father when you turn to God the Father and confess your sins.
TRAINEE:	Can you give me some words about this?
WORD:	**"Wherefore in all things it behoved him to be made like unto his brethren, that he might be a merciful and faithful high priest in things pertaining to God, to make reconciliation for the sins of the people."** Hebrews 2:17

APRIL 4

-continued-

"Seeing then that we have a great high priest, that is passed into the heavens, Jesus the Son of God, let us hold fast our profession." Hebrews 4:14 KJV

"For we have not an high priest which cannot be touched with the feeling of our infirmities; but was in all points tempted like as we are, yet without sin". Hebrews 4:15 KJV

COACH: Keep in mind also that it was not too late for the thief on the cross next to Jesus to be forgiven and saved. That thief had what St. Paul described as "Godly sorrow." [see, again, 2 Cor. 7:10] He confessed his sin to Jesus [Luke 23:40-43].

TRAINEE: As horrible as the crucifixion was, I am to see it in a good light?

COACH: When Jesus said *"It is finished,"* that was not a cry of defeat; the original Greek word for "finished" means *accomplished*. So, He was actually announcing a victory: "It is *accomplished*." Mission impossible <u>accomplished</u>!

TRAINEE: I need to make my search for and decision for Jesus as my personal Lord and Savior!

COACH: Place your request in the form of a prayer.

TRAINEE: Dear Father, in the Name of Jesus, I ask that You help me to take a step of faith, make a decision, to trust You at Your Word in seeking forgiveness. Help me to see and be settled that being confessional and honest and your forgiveness is something very personal—*as it was for King David* [see Psalm 51], *helping his heart move closer to Your heart*. Dear Holy Spirit, help me to search and make my decision for Jesus as Lord and Savior. Amen.

-continued-

APRIL 5

COACH: After you have confessed your sins and asked for mercy, forgiveness, and deliverance over all your sin, then take the posture of thanks and praise for His help on the road to repentance.

TRAINEE: What will that posture of praise and thanks do for me?

COACH: As you turn to God for his comforting forgiveness, He can use his redeeming will much like the man who, in a story, owned a beautiful diamond ring. This man's ring would have brought a lot on the market. Somehow, the diamond suffered a deep scratch. The owner took the diamond to one dealer after another, but no one could remove the flaw. Finally, he came across an old master in the gem trade who took the ring back into his study for a good while, where he proceeded to paint a rose at the top of the scratch. The scratch became the stem of the rose, forming a most beautiful design in the diamond. In a similar manner, God can begin showing you how he can take the scratches in your life and redeem them into the *stem of the rose*.

TRAINEE: Yes, I really need to come to that point of just trusting him to act on my behalf.

COACH: Rely on the Word to strengthen your use of your faith gift.

WORD: **"So then faith cometh by hearing, and hearing by the word of God."** Romans 10:17 KJV

COACH: Remember also that the righteousness of Christ has been 'imputed' to you.

WORD: **"But for us also, to whom it shall be imputed, if we believe on him that raised up Jesus our Lord from the dead; ..."** Romans 4:22-24 King James Version (KJV)

APRIL 6

COURSE: FORGIVING OTHERS

WORD: **And the Word was made flesh, and dwelt among us, (and we beheld his glory, the glory as of the only begotten of the Father,) full of grace and truth.** John 1:14 (KJV)

COACH: God's great love for you is what brings all the above to your mind and heart and life!

TRAINEE: Forgiving others; sometimes it is hard to carry out, especially when the wounds go deep.

COACH: I share with you the story of Corrie Ten Boom as an example of how forgiveness can be given in harsh or extremely difficult circumstances. As you may know, Corrie Ten Boom was a prisoner of war in a Nazi concentration camp because she had aided Jewish personnel in their efforts to escape and hide. While there, she watched a German SS guard take her sister and others, whom she had grown to love, to the gas chamber. Had the war not ended at the precise point that it did, Corrie would have been next.

After the war, Corrie wrote about her experiences in books and toured Germany on speaking engagements. Following one particular tour, after speaking superbly on the subject of forgiveness (*some of her books on the subject were best-sellers*), she was greeting people and signing copies of her books when, suddenly, her eyes drifted up the aisle and locked onto the gaze of the German SS guard. He was marching down the aisle with his hand extended, saying, "Good evening, Fraulein. It's so good to see you again." Immediately, she dropped her head down and whispered, "Dear Father, I cannot forgive this man."

-continued-

APRIL 7

And she had just gotten through delivering a speech on forgiveness that moved many people. While her head was still down, she turned her thoughts into this prayer: "Dear Jesus, you're going to have to give me your forgiveness to give to this man." As soon as this prayer was formed, she was able to lift her eyes to those of the SS guard, stretch out her hand to take his, and speak the words of forgiveness. In time, her emotions caught up with what her spirituality had done in making a decision, taking that step of faith, to forgive this man. A new book on forgiveness, even better than the others she had written on it, emerged from this experience."

TRAINEE: I can pray like that also when it is hard.

COACH: The Word truthfully states that the *"sins of the fathers"* are passed on from generation to generation (Num. 14:18). Scientific research in deoxyribonucleic acid (DNA) has discovered that the footprint of the father remains in the genetic code until the third and sometimes the fourth generation. And the law of *"being judged"* as a result of *"judging"* is as accountable and predictable as the law of gravity [see: Matthew 7:1-5].

Modern-day psychological inquiry has established the fact that, as the Bible outlines, only forgiveness can break that generational curse. Of interest is the development of a new therapy that addresses this pattern; it is called "reconciliation therapy" and could be seen as a secular way of talking about forgiveness. You do not want your children to experience this "being judged" (Num. 14:18 AMP).

TRAINEE: My perennial prayer is that they take my request to heart and find a way to forgive, for both the good of others and for theirs!

COACH: Good prayer.

APRIL 8

-continued-

TRAINEE: Again, God sees me, by faith, accepting His forgiveness?

COACH: To review: He takes those sins and not only "forgets, erases, heals, covers (*meaning of the four original Greek words for forgiveness*), removes them as far as the East is from the West, makes the scarlet ones white as snow, but also imputes to you the righteousness of Christ!

TRAINEE: Will this action carry me to and through the Final Judgment?

WORD: **"It is of the Lord's mercies that we are not consumed, because his compassions fail not. They are new every morning: great is thy faithfulness. The LORD is my portion, saith my soul; therefore will I hope in him."** Lamentations 3:22-24 (KJV)

COACH: The only way you can avoid hearing Jesus, as your judge, say to you, **"Depart from me; I never knew you"** (Matt. 7:21–23), is to, by <u>faith</u>, have the Word [Jesus] living (Heb. 4:12) and abiding (John 15:7) in your heart. That gives him a picture of your heart being moved by Him. Because He himself is the Word, if He sees that the Word has made a mark on your heart—producing changes—then He can say, *"I know you."* For you to refuse to "hide God's Word in your heart" is tantamount to telling Jesus *"there is no room in the inn."*

TRAINEE: Like the apostle Paul, I need to *"press on to the mark"* (Phil. 3:14). Assurance of salvation, from where does it come?

WORD: **"Because he hath appointed a day, in the which he will judge the world in righteousness by that man whom he hath ordained; whereof he hath given assurance unto all men, in that he hath raised him from the dead.** Acts 17:31 KJV

APRIL 9

COURSE: THE ROAD TO THE CROSS

TRAINEE: What will I find on this road?

COACH: You will find it to be the "Road to Repentance."

TRAINEE: I need to understand this "cross" connection to repentance.

COACH: Read slowly David's penitential Psalm 51, letting each Word sink in deeply! See God's response: James 4:5-10 to you.

TRAINEE: O. K., I've done that twice. You've said several times that the Word holds power to "take me there;" I'm ready for that journey.

COACH: Let's look for a moment at the example of a wine press, slowly and deliberately turning to squeeze and then without loosening its grip, tightening up again and again. Crucifixion, like a wine press, would often crush the prisoner's bones. Gethsemane, which means "place of the oil press," is where Jesus agonized over his decision; he knew what was coming! Again, medical science tells us that it is humanly possible to be under so much stress that one could sweat drops of blood, as Jesus did there while making a death-defying decision for you.

TRAINEE: At this point in my thinking, your coaching has me ponder the fact that Jesus, being also fully human as well as fully God, did exactly that—sweated drops of blood—in the garden of Gethsemane. I'm beginning to see how *deadly* serious Jesus is about wanting to help me grow and change through the Father's grace.

WORD: **"In the beginning was the Word, and the Word was with God, and the Word was God . . . The same was in the beginning with God."** John1:1-2 KJV

APRIL 10

-continued-

COACH: Pilate had placed a board on the cross saying, "Jesus of Nazareth, the king of the Jews." The Hebrew consonants formed the word *Yahweh*.

TRAINEE: You have drawn me several times to that Word.

COACH: Again, when Moses asked God who he should say sent him to Egypt to free his people, God said to tell them that Yhwh, "I Am," had sent him. Jesus and these words hanging on the cross were saying—as he had already said when asked about his identity and origin—"Before Abraham was, *I Am*." The soldiers who had come to arrest him fell down when Jesus answered their question, "Are you the Christ?" by saying, "I Am." Read and meditate on Colossians 1:15–23 to address the identity of Jesus as being the great "*I Am*."

WORD: **"Who is the image of the invisible God, the firstborn of every creature: For by him were all things created, that are in heaven, and that are in earth, visible and invisible, whether they be thrones, or dominions, or principalities, or powers: all things were created by him, and for him: And he is before all things, and by him all things consist." . . . And he is the head of the body, the church: who is the beginning, the firstborn from the dead; that in all things he might have the preeminence. For it pleased the Father that in him should all fullness dwell; and, having made peace through the blood of his cross, by him to reconcile all things unto himself; . . . And you, that were sometime alienated and enemies in your mind by wicked works, yet now hath he reconciled in the body of his flesh through death, to present you holy and unblameable and unreproveable in his sight:** Colossians 1:15-22 (KJV)

APRIL 11

-continued-

TRAINEE: I need to stop here and get something straight.

COACH: Go ahead.

TRAINEE: It sounds like I can't do anything to save myself or do anything to open my way to Heaven.

COACH: You are exactly correct.

WORD: "Many will say to me in that day, Lord, Lord, have we not prophesied in thy name? and in thy name have cast out devils? and in thy name done many wonderful works?

And then will I profess unto them, I never knew you: depart from me, ye that work iniquity." Matthew 7:22-23 (KJV)

"But to him that worketh not, but believeth on him that justifieth the ungodly, his faith is counted for righteousness.

Even as David also describeth the blessedness of the man, unto whom God imputeth righteousness without works, . . ." Romans 4:5-7 (KJV)

"And if by grace, then is it no more of works: otherwise grace is no more grace. But if it be of works, then it is no more grace: otherwise work is no more work." Romans 11:6 KJV

"Knowing that a man is not justified by the works of the law, but by the faith of Jesus Christ, even we have believed in Jesus Christ, that we might be justified by the faith of Christ, and not by the works of the law: for by the works of the law shall no flesh be justified." Galatians 2:16 KJV

"For by grace are ye saved through faith; and that not of yourselves: it is the gift of God: Not of works, lest any man should boast." Ephesians 2:8-9 (KJV)

APRIL 12

-continued-

"Who hath saved us, and called us with an holy calling, not according to our works, but according to his own purpose and grace, which was given us in Christ Jesus before the world began, . . ."2 Timothy 1:9 KJV

"Not by works of righteousness which we have done, but according to his mercy he saved us, by the washing of regeneration, and renewing of the Holy Ghost; . . ." Titus 3:5 KJV

TRAINEE: O. K., That's enough to convince me of no works!

COACH: You need to understand "works" as not applying to payment for your salvation; that payment was made in full by Jesus. God the Father's resurrection of His Son, Jesus, is the ultimate stamp of approval for that payment!

TRAINEE: How, then, do works fit in the picture?

COACH: Works become part of your grateful response to the Grace that has saved you.

WORD: **"Thou believest that there is one God; thou doest well: the devils also believe, and tremble. But wilt thou know, O vain man, that faith without works is dead? Was not Abraham our father justified by works, when he had offered Isaac his son upon the altar? Seest thou how faith wrought with his works, and by works was faith made perfect?"** James 2:19-22 (KJV)

"For as the body without the spirit is dead, so faith without works is dead also." James 2:26 KJV

COACH: See also Revelation 17:8 [register of saved;] 20:12-13 [register of unsaved].

APRIL 13

COURSE: CONTINUING ON THE ROAD TO THE CROSS.

TRAINEE: I see more clearly the need for this journey.

COACH: Like Israel's Passover Lamb in Egypt, Jesus became your Passover Lamb (see: 1 Corinthians 5:7; 1 Peter 1:19)! Herein lays the power of God from the cross. The first Adam ushered sin into the world by a tree; the second Adam, Jesus, carried sin away on a tree.

"So, since Christ suffered in the flesh (for us, for you), arm yourselves with the same thought and purpose (patiently to suffer rather than fail to please God). For whoever has suffered in the flesh (having the mind of Christ) has done with (intentional) sin—has stopped pleasing himself and the world, and pleases God, so that he can no longer spend the rest of his natural life living by (his) human appetites and desires, but (he lives) for what God wills. For the time that is past already suffices for doing what the Gentiles like to do, living (as you have done) in shameless, insolent wantonness, in lustful desires...." 1 Peter 4:1–3a (AMP)

TRAINEE: How then can I have "the mind of Christ"?

COACH: When you have God's Word hidden and settled in your mind and heart, you have the "mind of Christ." **Wherefore lay apart all filthiness and superfluity of naughtiness, and receive with meekness the engrafted word, which is able to save your souls.** James 1:21 KJV (see 2 Cor. 5:17; Phil. 3:9; 1 Pet. 4:1-3a). The cross stands sentinel to your past, present, and future at once; the "cross look" is life and death available for all people; for it is the power to overcome our sinful condition!

APRIL 14

COURSE: GOOD FRIDAY & THE SEVEN LAST WORDS

COACH: As you approach Good Friday, we take a deep look into the seven "lasting" Words Jesus spoke from the Cross. As you look at the crucifixion, recall it is the most agonizing and cruel form of death ever invented by man.

TRAINEE: Golgotha ("place of the skull"), I could see how the rock structure does look like a skull.

COACH: Listen again to a description of this event: A shortage of wood called for prisoners to carry a crossbeam that would be fastened to a tree. Bulky nails went into His hands; executioners twisted His body to the side as they nailed through the sides of His ankles to the tree. Twisted and, thereby, having less capacity for air, He would suffocate faster. People in those days were shorter than modern people are; therefore, Jesus was about eye level with his mother, John, the soldiers, and other bystanders as He hung suspended on the tree, slightly above ground level. So His mother could see into His eyes as he asked her to look at John and then said, "Behold your son" and to John, "Behold your mother." It would have been easy to thrust a spear into His side. With His lungs screaming for air, the only way to open the cavity was to sit back on a plank nailed to the tree. But His body weight would cause pain to shoot like bullets from the nails in His hands and run throughout His body. So after a split second, He would have to push back up with his feet, where there was no air. So it went throughout the whole crucifixion process, for six hours. In the midst of that agony, the spitting, the insults, and so on, the bystanders could hear Him say, "Father, forgive them, for they know not what they do."

-continued-

APRIL 15

TRAINEE: Did Words from the Cross cause the Roman Centurion there to say: "*Truly, this man was the Son of God* (Mark 15:39);"

COACH"   Not only was Jesus receiving into himself everything that the enemy had been allowed to do through the Roman soldiers and bystanders, he was also taking all the punishment and wrath from God the Father for all the sins of humanity, past, present, and future. And Jesus surely had seen the Father look away from him because God will not look upon sin. This "looking away" by the heavenly Father gave Jesus a severe taste of hell in the truest definition of that word: "separation from God." Furthermore, he had said earlier, "*The Father and I are one*" and "*He who has seen me has seen the Father.*" Does this mean that Jesus actually felt his identity or spirit being torn in two?

Word:	**"And at the ninth hour Jesus cried out with a loud voice, saying, "Eloi, Eloi, lama sabachthani?" which is translated, "My God, My God, why have You forsaken Me?"** Mark 15:34 **"For he hath made him to be sin for us, who knew no sin; that we might be made the righteousness of God in him."** 2 Cor. 5:21 (KJV)
COACH"	Scripture tells that he died in the ninth hour (three o'clock), the time normally set for killing the lamb during Jewish Passover. Again, do you find that significant! It was customary to break the legs of those hanging on the cross in order to speed up the suffocation process, but Scripture says that God's lamb (Jesus) would not have his bones broken (see Ex. 12:46; John 19:36). They did not break Jesus' bones because he died before the others. Why?

-continued-

APRIL 16

TRAINEE:	He had been scourged. That's why he fell with that heavy crossbeam on the way to Golgotha; he almost bled to death!
COACH:	Jesus died after only six hours as opposed to the usual day and a half or two. Psalm 22 states much that occurred on the cross; Jesus had spoken many of those words about himself. He spoke verse six when he said, "I am as a worm." Again, the word *worm* used there is from the Hebrew word, *Tolah*, which is the name of a worm that is round in shape like a beetle. When it is pregnant and ready to give birth, it will climb to the top of a tree. When there, its heart will explode and it gives birth. Medical science now raises the possibility that, given all that came down on Jesus in body, mind, and spirit, his heart may well have exploded while hanging at the top of his tree.
TRAINEE:	Could I let what happened to his heart give birth to change my heart? As I stood there at Golgotha in the midst of the above understanding, God had me picture myself standing in front of the cross as though I were the only one there. He then said to my heart, *You need to see that all of this is done for you as though you were the only person on this earth!*

COACH   God, the Father, above all things, being a *just* God, demands that your sin be punished.

WORD: **"To the praise of the glory of his grace, wherein he hath made us accepted in the beloved"** (Eph. 1:6 KJV; see also Ps. 66:18, John 9:31).

TRAINEE: Can I glance at my temptation, then look firmly at the cross, glance again at the temptation and turn again to see the cross, and recall that I was on his mind then and there.

APRIL 17

COURSE: SEVEN LAST WORDS

COACH: Another way to express this course: *"the Seven Lasting Words.*

TRAINEE: Can you give them to me as He said them?

SEVEN LASTING WORDS FROM THE CROSS

WORD: 1. *"Father, forgive them, for they do not know what they do."* Luke 23:34 NKJV

COACH: Can you look at the Cross with everything happening there to Jesus, and then hear Him say these words and still find it hard to forgive others?

WORD: 2. *"And Jesus said to him, "Assuredly, I say to you, today you will be with Me in Paradise."*

COACH: Can you take assurance of your salvation as you hear Jesus say this to a hardened criminal who asked to be saved as he, too, was dying? Jonathan Edwards remarked: *"The only thing I can contribute toward my salvation is the sin which made it necessary."* (*Midnight Call Magazine*, Int'l, June 2014, page 24)]

WORD: 3. *"When Jesus therefore saw His mother, and the disciple whom He loved standing by, He said to His mother, "Woman, behold your son!" Then He said to the disciple, "Behold your mother!"* John 19:26-27 NKJV

COACH: In the midst of agony, He was thinking ahead for those He loved. Does He do the same for you?

WORD: **4. "And about the ninth hour Jesus cried out with a loud voice, saying, "Eli, Eli, lama sabachthani?" that is, "My God, My God, why have You forsaken Me?"** Matthew 27:46 NKJV

APRIL 18

-continued-

COACH: Again, did He sense His identity being torn in two, separated from the Father Who will not look upon sin?

WORD: **5. "After this, Jesus, knowing that all things were now accomplished, that the Scripture might be fulfilled, said, "I thirst!"** John 19:28 NKJV

COACH: Martin Luther used to say: "*The Holy Scriptures are the 'crib' in which the baby Jesus lies . . . (Midnight Call Magazine, Int'l April 2013, p. 7)*" For Jewish people, as well as non-Jewish, to read Isaiah 53, Psalm 22, Jeremiah 31, Micah 5:2-5, Daniel 9:24-27, Isaiah 7:14, Zechariah 12:10, Matthew's gospel (*focused on Jewish values*) and a host of other passages, is to see the direct connection with Messianic prophecy and the life of Jesus on this earth, especially what He experienced on the Cross.

WORD: **6. "So when Jesus had received the sour wine, He said, "It is finished!" And bowing His head, He gave up His spirit.** John 19:30 NKJV

COACH: Notice, He "gave up" His spirit; no one took His life from Him. His Cross was His gift to you!

WORD: **7. And when Jesus had cried out with a loud voice, He said, "Father, 'into Your hands I commit My spirit.'" Having said this, He breathed His last.** Luke 23:46 NKJV

COACH: He reached the point where all had been paid; now He could be, again, one with the Father.

TRAINEE: What is my part, now?

COACH: Prayerfully, look at the crucifixion with eyes that see He was going through all this, personally, for you.

-continued-

APRIL 19

TRAINEE: The hymn "Were You There?" takes on new meaning with such an image. As I look upon that scene and ask myself how people could do such a thing to Jesus, my coach points out a horrible picture—a picture of me, standing there with a hammer in my hand. Could I stand there and continue on with an unrepentant mind, entertaining the lusts of the heart? It is then that I understand that Jesus, being fully God, cast his eyes into the past, present, and future while on the cross. He saw me and my sin two thousand years ahead of time, and I was on his mind as he hung there.

Again, I am beginning to see the power of the "Cross-look!"

TRAINEE: I will look, knowing that He saw me two-thousand years ago and my need for His Grace to pour over and through my life.

COACH: That "look" is the kind that moves your heart closer to His heart!

APRIL 20

COURSE: THE RESURRECTION

COACH: The Resurrection of Jesus is not a fact 'til it is a fact in the heart of the believer!

TRAINEE: How did it happen?

WORD: **"And when they had fulfilled all that was written of him, they took him down from the tree, and laid him in a sepulchre. But God raised him from the dead: And he was seen many days of them which came up with him from Galilee to Jerusalem, who are his witnesses unto the people."** Acts 13:29-31 (KJV)

"That if thou shalt confess with thy mouth the Lord Jesus, and shalt believe in thine heart that God hath raised him from the dead, thou shalt be saved." Romans 10:9 KJV

"Who by him do believe in God, that raised him up from the dead, and gave him glory; that your faith and hope might be in God." 1 Peter 1:21 KJV

COACH: You recall how Mary Magdalene had run to the tomb, found it empty and told the disciples who could not believe it?

WORD: "The first day of the week cometh Mary Magdalene early, when it was yet dark, unto the sepulchre, and seeth the stone taken away from the sepulchre.

Then she runneth, and cometh to Simon Peter, and to the other disciple, whom Jesus loved, and saith unto them, They have taken away the LORD out of the sepulchre, and we know not where they have laid him.

Peter therefore went forth, and that other disciple, and came to the sepulchre.

APRIL 21

-continued-

So they ran both together: and the other disciple did outrun Peter, and came first to the sepulchre.

And he stooping down, and looking in, saw the linen clothes lying; yet went he not in.

Then cometh Simon Peter following him, and went into the sepulchre, and seeth the linen clothes lie,

And the napkin, that was about his head, not lying with the linen clothes, but wrapped together in a place by itself." John 20:1-7 (KJV)

TRAINEE: A very live account; I can see it happening.

COACH: Let it sink in deeper by reading what Matthew, Mark, Luke, John, Paul, Peter, and others wrote about it.

TRAINEE: I plan on it.

COACH: Look again in the above text at John's account; note the last verse. The "napkin" [*head piece*] was separate from the other clothes of His crucifixion attire. Note that it was folded and left separate.

TRAINEE: Why is that significant?

COACH: The Jewish leaders feared that someone would try and steal the body of Jesus to make it look like a resurrection; so, they asked for Roman guards at the tomb. Also, grave robbers would not take the time to fold that napkin and set it separately aside. It is Jewish custom during the course of a meal to neatly fold one's napkin and lay it in the chair if their plan was to leave the table and come back later to finish the meal.

TRAINEE: How does this apply to the resurrection?

COACH: This was one, among many, signs that say: *HE'S COMING BACK!*

APRIL 22

COURSE: PRAYER AND REPENTANCE

COACH: One regimen of fitness to help produce a repentant mind centers in a profound manner on the prayer Jesus taught his disciples to pray as a model prayer. For example, ask yourself, "Can I pray—

Our—while I am self-centered;
Father—and not show that I daily look to him that way;
Who art in heaven—if I pursue only earthly things;
Hallowed be thy name—if I am not "set apart" for him;
Thy kingdom come—and not trade my control for his control;
Thy will be done—and continue to give in to my will, not his;
On earth as it is in heaven—and not be a willing instrument of his peace here and now;
Give us this day our daily bread—and not feed others in need;
Forgive us our trespasses as we forgive those who trespass against us—and continue to nurture bitterness and resentment;
Lead us not into temptation—if I seek out settings as open targets for temptation;
Deliver us from evil—while not using the sword of the Word;
Thine is the kingdom—and not continually be his servant;

Thine is the power—and fear people and circumstances more;
Thine is the glory—if I act primarily for self-recognition;
Forever and ever—and worry about the footsteps ahead;
Amen—and not really mean it."

APRIL 23

-continued-

TRAINEE: I've tried this and that to change my thinking [*be repentant*], but it simply doesn't work. I identify with St. Paul in the struggle to stop doing what I do not want to do (see Rom. 7).

COACH: Yet, God's Word is persistent and encouraging:

WORD: **"Therefore then, since we are surrounded by so great a cloud of witnesses (who have borne testimony of the Truth), let us strip off and throw aside every encumbrance—unnecessary weight—and that sin which so readily (deftly and cleverly) clings to and entangles us, and let us run with patient endurance and steady and active persistence the appointed course of the race that is set before us....**

Looking away (from all that will distract) to Jesus, Who is the Leader and the Source of our faith (giving the first incentive for our belief) and is also its Finisher, (bringing it to maturity and perfection). He, for the joy (of obtaining the prize) that was set before Him, endured the cross, despising and ignoring the shame, and is now seated at the right hand of the throne of God.

Just think of Him Who endured from sinners such grievous opposition and bitter hostility against Himself—reckon up and consider it all in comparison with your trials—so that you may not grow weary or exhausted, losing heart and relaxing and fainting in your minds. You have not yet struggled and fought agonizingly against sin, nor have you yet resisted and withstood to the point of pouring out your (own) blood." Heb. 12:1–4 (AMP)

APRIL 24

-continued-

TRAINEE: I need more rigid training.

COACH: Keep in mind the following Word from April 13.

WORD: **"So, since Christ suffered in the flesh (for us, for you), arm yourselves with the same thought and purpose (patiently to suffer rather than fail to please God). For whoever has suffered in the flesh (having the mind of Christ) has done with (intentional) sin—has stopped pleasing himself and the world, and pleases God, so that he can no longer spend the rest of his natural life living by (his) human appetites and desires, but (he lives) for what God wills. For the time that is past already suffices for doing what the Gentiles like to do, living (as you have done) in shameless, insolent wantonness, in lustful desires...."** 1 Peter 4:1–3a (AMP)

TRAINEE: Again, I need help with having *"the mind of Christ"*?

COACH: Again, when you have God's Word hidden and settled in your mind and heart, you have the "mind of Christ."

TRAINEE: What's a good prayer for me to begin this 'hiding" and "settling" of the Word?

COACH: Ask to become hungry for His Word /Jesus.

WORD: **"Blessed are they which do hunger and thirst after righteousness: for they shall be filled."** Matthew 5:6 KJV

         "And the Word was made flesh, and dwelt among us, (and we beheld his glory, the glory as of the only begotten of the Father,) full of grace and truth." John 1:14 (KJV)

APRIL 25

COURSE: WASHING IN GOD'S WORD

COACH: Are you thirsty?

TRAINEE: Thirsty for what?

COACH: Jesus had a conversation with a woman about water; not physical water but spiritual water.

WORD: **"But whosoever drinketh of the water that I shall give him shall never thirst; but the water that I shall give him shall be in him a well of water springing up into everlasting life."** John 4:14 (KJV)

COACH: Are you thirsty for something in life that you haven't found? You may be a Church goer, baptized, confirmed, a good person… but deep in your heart, there is an emptiness.

TRAINEE: What should I do?

COACH: Go to the Cross for that "living water." The hell that you deserve because of all your sins was placed on Jesus. As the woman at the well talked with Jesus, a thousand searchlights were turned on as she could tell He knew all her secret sins. She asked Him for that 'living water.'

TRAINEE: I'm asking, too, but what is my first step to drink from it?

COACH: The Rev. Billy Graham used to lead people in the following prayer: *"Lord Jesus, I have sinned. I am sorry for my sin. I am willing to change my way of life and come to you by faith. I don't understand it all, but by faith, I receive You as my Savior and my Lord and Master."*

TRAINEE: I feel washed and clean.

APRIL 26

COURSE: THE BANK OF HEAVEN

COACH: All mankind owes a debt.

WORD: **"For all have sinned, and come short of the glory of God;"** Romans 3:23 (KJV)

"For the wages of sin is death; but the gift of God is eternal life through Jesus Christ our Lord." Romans 6:23 (KJV)

TRAINEE: I can never pay my way out!

COACH: Jesus paid it in full by shedding His blood for our redemption!

WORD: **"But God commendeth his love toward us, in that, while we were yet sinners, Christ died for us."** Romans 5:8 (KJV)

"There is therefore now no condemnation to them which are in Christ Jesus, who walk not after the flesh, but after the Spirit." Romans 8:1 KJV

" But as many as received him, to them gave he power to become the sons of God, even to them that believe on his name:" John 1:12 (KJV)

COACH: Read these Words with the understanding: *"Pay to the Order of: 'Who-so-ever Believes' the sum of Eternal Life."*

WORD: **"For God so loved the world, that he gave his only begotten Son, that whosoever believeth in him should not perish, but have everlasting life."** John 3:16 (KJV)

COACH: This payment was endorsed by the thief on the Cross and all sinners saved by Grace. You can 'cash in" by honest confession and acceptance of what Jesus accomplished for you on the Cross. [see: 1 Jn. 1:8, 10; 1 Pet. 3:18; 2:24; Rom. 10; 13]

APRIL 27

COURSE: PROTECTION PRAYING

TRAINEE: As I look at my family, what is a good "whole-person" prayer?

COACH: "Dear Father, I now place the Name Jesus over _____ with the understanding that His Name now also hovers over <u>all</u> those in the household and that:

1. Their bodies are the temple of the Holy Spirit; they are fearfully and wonderfully made; and nothing from the outside or from the inside of their bodies will hurt them;

2. Their minds are the mind of Christ; their minds are "stayed on thee;" therefore, they are kept in perfect peace;

3. Their spirit is connected to Your Spirit as You bring all things good through Your Word." Amen.

Pray these petitions with the understanding that God can answer them in light of the Ephesians 3:20 Word--" . . . **exceedingly, abundantly, above all we can ask or think** . . ." See the Name, Jesus, hovering over each and every member of the household like a huge umbrella covering **all** their needs. Further understand that He knows every cell of their bodies, every impulse of their minds and every dimension of their human spirit whom He foreknew before they were conceived in their mother's womb (see Jeremiah 1:5; Psalm 139).

TRAINEE: The **S**ON empowers all for their bodies and minds as the **S**UN energizes the solar system.

-continued-

APRIL 28

-continued-

WORD: **"You made all the delicate, inner parts of my body, and knit them together in my mother's womb. Thank you for making me so wonderfully complex! It is amazing to think about. Your workmanship is marvelous--and how well I know it. You were there while I was being formed in utter seclusion! You saw me before I was born and scheduled each day of my life before I began to breathe. Every day was recorded in your Book!"** Psalms 139:13-16 TLB

COACH: Thank Him for doing Philippians 2:13 in working to **help** their minds "to will and do His good pleasure" in their lives. Pray that His Holy Spirit shape and mold the spirit of each in your household so that minds and bodies will conform to serve Him. In the Words of Joshua:

WORD: **"But as for me and my household, we will serve the Lord** (Joshua 24:15b)."

COACH: All this based on God's knowledge of you and of your household. In His foreknowledge, He knows who will, like King David, want to be developing a "heart after His own heart [1 Sam. 13:14."]

TRAINEE: How can one claim the above statements for someone else?"

COACH: Don't talk overly much about God to your children, but rather, talk to God about them, so He can speak to them directly, in His time. God has so closely formed the bond of marriage and family that you can pray and claim His Word for family members. Read tomorrow, some bold texts, focused on the question of salvation, to address this authority to claim God's Word and will for families.

-continued-

APRIL 29

WORD: **"They replied, 'Believe in the Lord Jesus, and you will be saved--you and your household.'"** Acts 16:31 NIV

"He will give and explain to you a message by means of which you and all your household [as well] will be saved [from eternal death]." Acts 11:14 AMP. B.

"For the promise (of the Holy Spirit) is to and for you and your children, . . ." Acts 2:39 AMP. B.

". . . but I have not lost confidence, because I know who it is that I have put my trust in, and I have no doubt at all that he is able to take care of all that I have entrusted to him until that Day." 2 Timothy 1:12 JB

"And I am convinced and sure of this very thing, that He Who began a good work in you will continue until the day of Jesus Christ--right up to the time of His return--developing [that good work] and perfecting and bringing it to full completion in you." Philippians 1:6 AMP. B.

TRAINEE: Can I say our children's bodies are the "temple of the Holy Spirit" because they are baptized?

COACH: Belief and baptism are the conception factors giving birth to the Spirit of Jesus living in them. To claim they have "the mind of Christ" can only be done as God's Word is taught and provided to them. Jesus **is** the Word (see John 1). As the Word abides in them, so does the "mind of Christ."

TRAINEE: I'm beginning to get a picture of how this can happen.

APRIL 30

COURSE: HEADSHIP AND SUBMISSION

TRAINEE: Some of church history has viewed the husband's headship as to say: "*Jump;*" to which the wife is to submit by saying: "*How high?*"

COACH: God has a different view. Read the following Word both from your viewpoint and from your wife's viewpoint.

WORD: **"Wives, submit to your own husbands, as to the Lord. For the husband is head of the wife, as also Christ is head of the church; and He is the Savior of the body. Therefore, just as the church is subject to Christ, so *let* the wives *be* to their own husbands in everything."** Ephesians 5:22-24 NKJV

TRAINEE: Help me understand how the husband "is the Savior of the body" for the wife.

WORD: **"Husbands, love your wives, just as Christ also loved the church and gave Himself for her, . . ."** Ephesians 5:25 (NKJV)

COACH: That's the "headship" to which the wife "submits."

TRAINEE: I've usually thought of it as the man being physically stronger and more at ease in tackling the hard or harsh issues of life.

COACH: That can be natural and a "given;" however, I challenge you to pray for God to help you see her the way He wants you to see her. You relate to people the way you see them. This exercise is anticipating the training for "The Month of Vision."

TRAINEE: I can do that. All I need to do is just trust my Heavenly Father to know best and to do best. The closer I move toward Him, the better I can see my wife.

Month of Vision

COURSE:	"BECOMERS"
COACH:	God sees his children as "becomers." He knew you in your future; he knew that your spirit, your heart, would respond to his Word. Being in the past, present, and future all at the same time, he could, then, work those times together toward good! Do you see the depth of what I've just said?
WORD:	**"No one can come to me unless the Father who sent Me draws him; and I will raise him up at the last day."** John 6:44 (KJV)
COACH:	The Holy Spirit coaches us to understand: *So the Father chose you before creation, drew you, gave you faith to believe, promises to keep you, keeps you, and now works in you.*
TRAINEE:	Then my salvation depends on my response to His call because he chose me before I was born, knowing ahead of time that I would respond to him. And when I have the conviction of sin, this is his Holy Spirit, working with me, and a sign that the Father is working with me. If he saved me while I was still evil, he would not 'unsave' me because I continue to sin.
COACH:	You have a good understanding.
TRAINEE:	How, then, do I move into that third level in the "fear of the Lord.
COACH:	We train in this Month of Vision [May] for a deeper understanding and heart-felt knowledge of Who Jesus is and the price paid.
TRAINEE:	I'm ready.

MAY 2

COURSE:	CLIMBING TO A HIGHER LEVEL: (How to draw close to God)
TRAINEE:	Just how do we move into that third dimension of "the fear of the Lord?"

COACH: The Word tells you how:

WORD: **"Seek first his kingdom and his righteousness, and all these things will be given to you as well."** Matt. 6:33 (NIV)

           "Delight yourself in the Lord and he will give you the desires of your heart." Ps. 37:4 (NIV)

TRAINEE: How do I delight in and seek him first?

COACH: By loving him for just *Who* he is. He is your heavenly Father. Think for a moment: do parents want their children to love them just because of what they can give them, or do they want their children to love them simply because of *who* they are? So it is with God.

TRAINEE: How does that happen?

COACH: It happens as you take in his Word. Recall the first chapter of John's gospel. He states that the Word, Jesus (see Rev. 19:13), was, in the beginning, sent out (see Gen. 1 and Is. 55:10–11). Then he says that the Word *was* God. You could stop right there and know that to delight in God's Word is to receive him into your heart and mind. But John continues, saying, "and the Word was *with* God."

TRAINEE: What does that mean?

COACH: This requires vision.

MAY 3

-continued-

COACH: The creation narrative tells that God said, "Let there be … and there was." He also said, "Let us make man in our own image."

TRAINEE: To whom was he talking?

COACH: The answer to this comes in John, chapter one, where he states that "the Word became flesh and dwelt among us." You know this to be Jesus, born in Bethlehem, dying on a cross, and rising from the dead.

WORD: "He is the image of the invisible God, the firstborn over all creation. For by Him all things were created that are in heaven and that are on earth, visible and invisible, whether thrones or dominions or principalities or powers. All things were created through Him and for Him. And He is before all things, and in Him all things consist." Col. 1:15–17 (NKJV)

"But in these last days he has spoken to us by his Son, whom he appointed heir of all things, and through whom he made the universe. The Son is the radiance of God's glory and the exact representation of his being, sustaining all things by his powerful word." Heb. 1:2–3a (NIV)

"By the word of the Lord the heavens were made, and all the host of them by the breath of his mouth." Ps. 33:6 (KJV)

TRAINEE: Putting all the above together, what do we have?

-continued-

MAY 4

COACH: You have a consistent and persistent message that God's Word *is* God and that Jesus was pre-existent at the very point of creation as the Word. To take it into your mind and heart, to read and meditate God's Word is to receive him (Jesus).

WORD: "You are already clean because of the word I have spoken to you. Remain in me, and I will remain in you." John 15:3–4a (NIV)

COACH: God wants you to desire and delight in his Word because to do so is to desire and to delight in Him! His own words say this:

WORD: "My son, keep my words and store up my commands within you. Keep my commands and you will live; guard my teachings as the apple of your eye." Prov. 7:1–2 (NIV)

"O taste and see that the Lord is good: blessed is the man that trusteth in him." Ps. 34:8 (KJV)

"When your words came, I ate them; they were my joy and my heart's delight." Jer. 15:16a (NIV)

"How sweet are your words to my taste, sweeter than honey to my mouth!" Ps. 119:113 (NIV)

COACH: When you eat something good, it benefits your whole system.

WORD: **"But his delight and desire are in the law of the Lord, and on His law—the precepts, the instructions, the teachings of God—he habitually meditates (ponders and studies) by day and by night."** Ps. 1:2 (AMP)

-continued-

MAY 5

TRAINEE: Is this the reason God was so pleased with Solomon's choice of wisdom for God's gift to him—out of all the things he could have selected—so pleased that he gave him everything else?

COACH: To choose wisdom is to choose God's Word, and to choose his Word is to choose Jesus.

WORD: **"He was clothed with garments dipped in blood, and his title was 'The Word of God.'"** Rev. 19:13 (TLB)

"So we have these three witnesses: the voice of the Holy Spirit in our hearts, the voice from heaven at Christ's baptism, and the voice before he died. And they all say the same thing: that Jesus Christ is the Son of God." 1 John 5:7–8 (TLB)

TRAINEE: God promises to be close to me with his Word?

WORD: **When thou goest, it shall lead thee; when thou sleepest, it shall keep thee; and when thou awakest, it shall talk with thee.** Prov.6:22 KJV

COACH: No wonder Paul told the early Church:

WORD: **"I can do all things through Christ which strengtheneth me."** (Phil. 4:13 KJV) **"God's strength is made perfect in my weakness."** (2 Cor. 12:9 KJV) **"We are more than conquerors through him that loved us."** (Rom. 8:37 KJV

"It is no longer I who live but Jesus within me." (Gal. 2:20 NIV)

COACH: The Father knows the Word you need; the Son is the strength and life of that Word in you; and the Spirit delivers that Word to you in a most timely way.

MAY 6

COURSE: PRAYER AND REPENTANCE

TRAINEE: I see that by the predominance of our discussion, prayer becomes a most important exercise in staying spiritually fit.

COACH: You need to let the following Word be your training guide, especially the words italicized here: "… **that I may know Him and the power of His resurrection, and the** *fellowship of His sufferings*, **being** *conformed to His death*, **if, by any means, I may attain to the resurrection from the dead**" (Phil. 3:10–11).

TRAINEE: Again, is this part of what it means for me to be "*found in Christ*," to be a "*new creation*," or to "*have the mind of Christ*" (see 2 Cor. 5:17; Phil. 3:9; 1 Peter 4:1)?

COACH: I believe that you, at this point, would say, "*Yes, I'm progressing in my training on the Word, but I sense that there remains a still-deeper root system for the ground of my being as I run on the road to repentance. How will the "cast down, deaden, crucify" exercise connect me to "the fellowship of his sufferings" and being "conformed to his death?"*

What you "see" is what you get. If you continue to see yourself locked into the same sinful mode of operation, you would remain in bondage to what you see. You have heard the expression "Seeing is believing." Let's rearrange it to say "Believing is seeing."

TRAINEE: I will keep on keeping on.

-continued-

MAY 7

COURSE: PERSISTANT REPENTANCE

WORD: **"You have not yet struggled and fought agonizingly against sin, nor have you yet resisted and withstood to the point of pouring out your (own) blood."** (Heb. 12:1–4 AMP)

"So, since Christ suffered in the flesh (for us, for you), arm yourselves with the same thought and purpose (patiently to suffer rather than fail to please God). For whoever has suffered in the flesh (having the mind of Christ) has done with (intentional) sin—has stopped pleasing himself and the world, and pleases God, so that he can no longer spend the rest of his natural life living by (his) human appetites and desires, but (he lives) for what God wills. For the time that is past already suffices for doing what the Gentiles like to do, living (as you have done) in shameless, insolent wantonness, in lustful desires...." (1 Peter 4:1–3a AMP)

TRAINEE: How, then, can I have "the mind of Christ"?

COACH: When you have God's Word hidden and settled in your mind and heart, you have the "mind of Christ."

Feelings are actually thought choices, and you are seeing that God backs that up. But understanding is not enough. This calls for an intense conditioning and training program for the mind.

TRAINEE: The "spiritual pavement" beckons.

WORD: **Those who live according to the sinful nature have their minds set on what that nature desires; but those who live in accordance with the Spirit have their minds set on what the Spirit desires.**

-continued-

MAY 8

The mind of sinful man is death, but the mind controlled by the Spirit is life and peace. (Rom. 8:5–6 NIV)

COACH:	Again, what captures your mind captures you. Your thoughts, as Martin Luther wrote in his treatise, *On Bondage of the Will*, can place you in a state of bondage to sin, or you can place them in bondage to Jesus by **"bringing into captivity every thought to the obedience of Christ"** (2 Cor. 10:5 KJV).
TRAINEE:	My freedom lies in the exchange of one bondage for the other. Without this exchange, I remain in bondage to sin and death and cannot free myself. But, given the exchange, I am in bondage to Jesus and His holy ways.
WORD:	**"And being found in fashion as a man, he humbled himself, and became obedient unto death, even the death of the cross"** (Phil. 2:8 KJV).
COACH:	You will come to see that temptation itself is not sin. However, temptation that is allowed to dwell in and be entertained in the mind (see "Sermon on the Mount," Matt. 5:17–48) and that proceeds out of your mind, marching into wrong words and wrong actions, is sin.
WORD:	**Let no one say when he is tempted, "I am tempted by God;" for God cannot be tempted by evil, nor does He Himself tempt anyone. But each one is tempted when he is drawn away by his own desires and enticed. Then, when desire has conceived, it gives birth to sin; and sin, when it is full-grown, brings forth death.** James 1:13-15 (NKJV)

MAY 9

COURSE:	VISION [Part One]
WORD:	**And it shall come to pass in the last days, says God, that I will pour out my spirit on all flesh; your sons and your daughters shall prophesy, your young men shall see visions, your old men shall dream dreams.** (Acts 2:17 KJV)
TRAINEE:	"Will I perish without vision?"
COACH:	What vision do you now have?
TRAINEE:	To see moving from one level of performance to another.
COACH:	That is your body vision. What about your heart vision?

TRAINEE: "I'm not sure what you mean."

WORD: **That is what the Scriptures mean when they say that God made Abraham the father of many nations. God will accept all people in every nation who trust God as Abraham did. And this promise is from God himself, who makes the dead live again and speaks of future events with as much certainty as though they were already past.… But Abraham never doubted. He believed God, for his faith and trust grew ever stronger, and he praised God for this blessing even before it happened.** (Rom. 4:17, 20–22 TLB)

COACH: Do you see the hills of temptation being run and overcome?

TRAINEE: Something Robert Kennedy once said has stuck with me through the years: "*Some see things that are and ask why. I see things that are not and ask why not.*"

COACH: I like that.

MAY 10

COURSE: VISION [[Part Two]

WORD: **Where there is no vision, the people perish: but he that keepeth the law, happy is he.** Proverbs 29:18 KJV

COACH: Let God's Word become like a pair of eye glasses, perfectly adjusting your vision of God's will and plan for you in this life. His Word will build trust in you to believe God can do His Word in the very setting of life.

WORD: **"Now to Him who is able to do exceedingly abundantly above all that we ask or think, according to the power that works in us,"** Ephesians 3:20 (NKJV)

"And we know that all things work together for good to those who love God, to those who are the called according to *His* purpose." Romans 8:28 NKJV

. . . for it is God who works in you both to will and to do for *His* good pleasure. Philippians 2:13 NKJV

"For godly sorrow produces repentance *leading* to salvation, not to be regretted; but the sorrow of the world produces death." 2 Cor. 7:10 NKJV

"For I know the thoughts that I think toward you, says the LORD**, thoughts of peace and not of evil, to give you a future and a hope."** Jeremiah 29:11 NKJV

TRAINEE: How can God do Romans 8:28?

COACH: We train the next several days as answer to your question. Be in prayer for the Holy Spirit to be your counselor, comforter, helper, teacher and the One Who can convince you of what is true. He will use the Word to be that for you.

MAY 11

COURSE: GOD'S HELP

TRAINEE: How does God work his Word in Romans 8:28?

COACH: A translation of the Greek text reads:

WORD: **"For God is in all things working toward good for those who love Him and are called according to His purpose."**

COACH: The KJV best reflects this original text:

WORD: **"And we know that all things work together for good to them that love God, to them who are the called according to his purpose."** Rom. 8:28 (KJV)

TRAINEE: "How does God actually *do* this?"

COACH: How would you react if a famous cook asked you to sample some lard, baking soda, oil, raw eggs, or flour, each one by itself? The thought of sampling an ingredient has little, if any, appeal. But what happens when that cook begins to mix a number of these and other ingredients *together* into delicious, flaky, somewhat moist-looking biscuits or a cake? The totally unique factor of God's "working all things together toward good" is that he can even take the ingredients supplied by Satan (the evil planted in your lives by Satan and by your deceptive hearts) and *work* them toward good. God has done this through the redeeming will performed by his Son. Yet there is an important Word of caution here. Let tomorrow's Scriptural correlation bear on your mind.

TRAINEE: I will wait with expectation.

-continued-

MAY 12

WORD: **Jesus answered, If a person (really) loves Me, he will keep My word—obey My teaching" (John 14:23a AMP). And "For it is not merely hearing the Law (read) that makes one righteous before God, but it is the doers of the Law who will be held guiltless and acquitted and justified.** (Rom. 2:13 AMP)

TRAINEE: So, for me, a wise and right prayer says, "Dear Father, help me obey the great commandment—the Shema—more and more." God wants me to show him that I love him by obeying him. And does "casting down imaginations of the heart," "deadening the deeds of the flesh" and "crucifying the self" constitute the love of obedience?

COACH: Yes! And the conclusion to that verse [*Rom. 8:28*] says, "to them who are the called according to his purpose" (Rom. 8:28b KJV). God has a purpose in showering his grace down on you and for exercising his redeeming will through your life. He looks at your heart to see what impact the cross of his Son has made, leading you into obedience.

TRAINEE: My prayer is that he would help me line up more and more with his perfect will; therefore, again, I pray Philippians 2:13 so as to have healthier material with which he can work and less garbage from me. I want to be used and called "according to His purpose(s)" as a most willing participant, wanting what he wants! -continued-

MAY 13

WORD: **"For the eyes of the Lord search back and forth across the whole earth, looking for people whose hearts are perfect toward him, so that he can show his great power in helping them."** 2 Chron. 16:9a (TLB)

COACH: God knows you better than you know yourself; He is closer to you than you are to your own self.

TRAINEE: He knows me that well and close to me that much, yet He still loves Me?

COACH:	The opposite of love is not anger, not even hate; the opposite of love is indifference. Therefore:
WORD:	**"He that is slow to anger is better than the mighty; and he that ruleth his spirit than he that taketh a city."** Proverbs 16:32 (KJV)
TRAINEE:	I want to be pleasing to God. Yes, I recall our training on faith.
	But, I need to exercise it to grow stronger.
COACH:	Good. There is another kind of faith that pleases God—when you see or feel nothing. God used Abraham as an example of this kind of faith. God had good things to say about his faith.
WORD:	**"These all died in faith, not having received the promises, but having seen them afar off were assured of them,**[a] **embraced** *them* **and confessed that they were strangers and pilgrims on the earth."** Hebrews 11:13 NKJV
COACH:	No rapid results; but one immediate result: God was pleased.
TRAINEE:	So, He may wait to answer for a long time so that I find a blessing in trusting and waiting on Him in a personal way during that time.

MAY 14

COURSE:	CLIMBING TO A HIGHER LEVEL
TRAINEE:	Let me ask again about moving into that third dimension of "the fear of the Lord?"
COACH:	Again, the Word tells you how:
WORD:	**"Seek first his kingdom and his righteousness, and all these things will be given to you as well."** Matt. 6:33 (NIV)
	"Delight yourself in the Lord and he will give you the desires of your heart." Ps. 37:4 (NIV)
TRAINEE:	So, the "delight" in Him and to "seek" Him first is to be pleasing to Him.
COACH:	Carry on.

WORD: **I will stand my watch and set myself on the rampart, and watch to see what he will say to me, and what I will answer when I am corrected. Then the Lord answered me and said: "Write the vision and make it plain on tablets, that he may run who reads it. For the vision is yet for an appointed time; but at the end it will speak, and it will not lie. Though it tarries, wait for it; because it will surely come, it will not tarry.** (Hab. 2:1–3 KJV)

For I will work a work in your days which you would not believe, though it were told you. (Hab. 1:5 KJV)

COACH: The more you live in this posture of centering your mind and heart on Him, the more you will find yourself wanting to serve Him and to offer Him the praise of obedience

TRAINEE: I like that summary!

MAY 15

COURSE: THE VIOLINIST

COACH: The story is told about a ragged boy with a violin under his arm that roamed the streets of a great city in Italy. Homeless, he wandered from place to place for food and shelter, literally living off the streets. Somehow he had gained possession of a violin and used an exceptional gift he had for music to learn the instrument. He became good enough to stand on the street corners and play for the passing crowds who would gather to listen, entranced by what they heard. After he finished playing, they tossed coins at his feet.

In this same city lived a world-renowned violin player. One day, he happened to pass by the place where the ragged boy was playing. His attention was arrested by the unusual quality of the music. He lingered until the crowd had passed on and then said to the little violin player, "Son, to whom do you belong?" "I don't belong to anybody," the boy answered. "Well, where do you live?" was the next question. "I don't have any place to live. I just sleep on the streets or wherever I can."

The man thought for a moment and then asked, "How would you like to come home with me? I'll give you some food and clothes and take care of you. The young lad's eyes lit up like light sockets as he said, "Mister, I'd love it!"

So the great musician took him to his own home. He had the boy cleaned and dressed up; and, as the days grew into weeks, months, years, the man became like a father to him. For several years he poured into the eager young mind and heart all he knew about playing the violin. Imagine a large porous sponge dropped into a bucket of water. That's how naturally the boy absorbed all that the great music master had to offer.

MAY 16

-continued-

Finally, the boy was ready for his first public recital, and the word went out that a great new musical prodigy was about to appear on the concert stage. On the night of the performance, the house was filled to capacity; even the balcony was packed like sardines. At last the boy came out, put the violin beneath his chin, and began to let the bow ride the strings from that instrument as the crowd had never heard before. He made this violin "talk" to them. At every pause, there was a deafening applause.

For some reason, however, the boy did not seem to pay any attention to the ovations. He kept his eyes turned upward and continued to play on and on. The audience was mystified by his strange manner. Finally, one of the persons present said, "I don't understand why he is so insensible to all this thunderous applause. He keeps looking up all the time. I'm going to find out what is attracting his attention!" Moving about in the concert hall, the observer found the answer. There, in the topmost balcony was the old music master, peering over the banister toward his young pupil. He was nodding his head and smiling, as if to say, "You are doing well, my boy; play on!" And the boy did play on, not seeming to care about the applause from the audience. He kept his gaze upward. He was playing to please the master only. He had eyes for the master only.

TRAINEE: That's the picture needed "*for me and my household!*"

COACH: Amen.

MAY 17

COURSE: VISION ENVISIONED

TRAINEE"   How much can God do; how big can He answer my prayers?

COACH: How much can you imagine or conceive?

WORD: **"Now to Him who is able to do exceedingly abundantly above all that we ask or think, according to the power that works in us, . . ."** Ephesians 3:20 (NKJV)

"For My thoughts *are* not your thoughts,
Nor *are* your ways My ways," says the LORD**.**
"For *as* the heavens are higher than the earth,
So are My ways higher than your ways,
And My thoughts than your thoughts.

"For as the rain comes down, and the snow from heaven,
And do not return there,
But water the earth,
And make it bring forth and bud,
That it may give seed to the sower
And bread to the eater,
So shall My word be that goes forth from My mouth;
It shall not return to Me void,
But it shall accomplish what I please,
And it shall prosper *in the thing* for which I sent it. Isaiah 55:8-11[NKJV]

TRAINEE: So, I need to trust God at His Word over against the odds.

WORD: **"But without faith it is impossible to please him: for he that cometh to God must believe that he is, and that he is a rewarder of them that diligently seek him."** Hebrews 11:6 KJV

MAY 18

COURSE:	CONFIDENCE COURSE
TRAINEE:	I do have more vision for the search in light of the goal.
COACH:	There is one single platform upon which all the Words rest.
WORD:	**"And because of what Christ did, all you others too who heard the Good News about how to be saved, and trusted Christ, were marked as belonging to Christ by the Holy Spirit, who long ago had been promised to all of us Christians. His presence within us is God's guarantee that he really will give us all that he promised; and the Spirit's seal upon us means that God has already purchased us and that he guarantees to bring us to himself. This is just one more reason for us to praise our glorious God."** Eph. 1:13–14 (TLB)
	"These things have I written unto you that believe on the name of the Son of God; that ye may know that ye have eternal life, and that ye may believe on the name of the Son of God." 1 John 5:13 (KJV)
TRAINEE:	That says it all. Thank you!
COACH:	The next two days, we begin to deepen your heart, drawing from the former months of training, especially the month of water.
TRAINEE:	Will this month be like taking a longer bath in the Word.
COACH:	Good way to put it!

MAY 19

COURSE:	BEING BORN AGAIN
WORD:	**"Jesus replied, "With all the earnestness I possess I tell you this: Unless you are born again, you can never get into the Kingdom of God.... Men can only reproduce human life, but the Holy Spirit gives new life from heaven; so don't be surprised at my statement that you must be born again! Just as you can hear the wind but can't tell where it comes from or where it will go next, so it is with the Spirit. We do not know on whom he will next bestow this life from heaven."** John 3:3, 6–8 (TLB)

TRAINEE: What enables me to be "born again?"

WORD: **The Spirit gives life; the flesh counts for nothing. The words I have spoken to you are spirit and they are life.… He went on to say, "This is why I told you that no one can come to me unless the Father has enabled him."** John 6:63, 65 (NIV)

"For you have been born again, not of perishable seed, but of imperishable, through the living and enduring word of God." 1 Peter 1:23 (NIV)

TRAINEE: God works a lot with the wind.

COACH: He works a lot <u>like</u> the wind.

WORD: **"He bowed the heavens also, and came down: and darkness was under his feet. And he rode upon a cherub, and did fly: yea, he did fly upon the wings of the wind. He made darkness his secret place; his pavilion round about him were dark waters and thick clouds of the skies.** Psalm 18:9-11 KJV"

continued-

MAY 20

TRAINEE: Can you summarize the Cross and the Word?

COACH: The Word about the cross becomes the platform for what it means to be "born again"—that is, to have God's Word conceived in your heart, giving you a personal, trusting relationship with Jesus Christ as your Lord and Savior. Note how the Word clearly tells that it is the Spirit who "baptizes" you with the Word and Who, in turn, becomes born in you.

TRAINEE: That's a giant step up from the "churchianity" or "religiosity" of today's world!

COACH: God is *always* as good as his Word, and He watches over His Word to see what it will perform in your heart.

TRAINEE: When I pray, therefore, is God watching to see if I will exercise the faith of obedience so as to answer my prayer "according to my faith"?

WORD: **"God looks down from heaven upon the children of men, To see if there are *any* who understand, who seek God."** Psalm 53:2 NKJV

"From the place of his habitation he looketh upon all the inhabitants of the earth. Psalm 33:14 KJV**"**

"... for the LORD seeth not as man seeth; for man looketh on the outward appearance, but the Lord looketh on the heart. 1 Samuel 16:7 KJV**"**

MAY 21

COURSE: A REVIEW

COACH: Recall, training on His Word prospers...: **having promise of the life that now is, and of that which is to come** [1 Timothy 4:8]."

TRAINEE: Why do I need to review; I understand pretty well, so far.

COACH: Refresh your mind and heart on the training exercise for January 10, 11, 12, 13, 14.

TRAINEE: O. K., that was a good reminder and summary.

COACH: Yes, it can serve as a platform for helping your heart search for God— moving closer in your heart to His heart.

TRAINEE: Can you show me some of His Words to help me with this?

WORD: **"And thou, Solomon my son, know thou the God of thy father, and serve him with a perfect heart and with a willing mind: for the LORD searcheth all hearts, and understandeth all the imaginations of the thoughts: if thou seek him, he will be found of thee; but if thou forsake him, he will cast thee off for ever."** 1 Chronicles 28:9 KJV

"And they that know thy name will put their trust in thee: for thou, LORD, hast not forsaken them that seek thee." Psalm 9:10 (KJV)

"Seek ye the LORD while he may be found, call ye upon him while he is near:" Isaiah 55:6 (KJV)

"Search me, O God, and know my heart: try me, and know my thoughts:" Psalm 139:23 KJV

-continued-

MAY 22

"O lord, thou hast searched me, and known me. Thou knowest my downsitting and mine uprising, thou understandest my thought afar off. Thou compassest my path and my lying down, and art acquainted with all my ways . . ." Psalm 139:1

"And ye shall seek me, and find me, when ye shall search for me with all your heart." Jeremiah 29:13 KJV

"Search the scriptures; for in them ye think ye have eternal life: and they are they which testify of me." John 5:39 KJV

TRAINEE:	These Words from the Old Covenant and from John's Gospel in the New Covenant hold promise and motivate me.
COACH:	Good!
TRAINEE:	Is there a Word about this searching exercise from Jesus Himself?
WORD:	"But seek ye first the kingdom of God, and his righteousness; and all these things shall be added unto you." Matthew 6:33 LKV
	"Again, the kingdom of heaven is like unto treasure hid in a field; the which when a man hath found, he hideth, and for joy thereof goeth and selleth all that he hath, and buyeth that field." Matthew 13:44 KJV
	"And said, Verily I say unto you, Except ye be converted, and become as little children, ye shall not enter into the kingdom of heaven." Matthew 18:3 KJV
TRAINEE:	These Words give me vision, also.

-continued-

MAY 23

COACH:	Again, "Imputed" means <u>placed</u> in your account.
TRAINEE:	As though someone "imputed," placed $10,000 into my bank account, thereby making it truly mine?
COACH:	Use today's training on the Word as preparation for the coming month.

WORD: "And therefore it was imputed to him for righteousness. Now it was not written for his sake alone, that it was imputed to him; But for us also, to whom it shall be imputed, if we believe on him that raised up Jesus our Lord from the dead; . . ." Romans 4:22-24 (KJV)

"Therefore, just as through one man sin entered the world, and death through sin, and thus death spread to all men, because all sinned— (For until the law sin was in the world, but sin is not imputed when there is no law. Nevertheless death reigned from Adam to Moses, even over those who had not sinned according to the likeness of the transgression of Adam, who is a type of Him who was to come." Romans 5:12-14 (NKJV)

"And the scripture was fulfilled which saith, Abraham believed God, and it was imputed unto him for righteousness: and he was called the Friend of God." James 2:23 KJV

"Having therefore these promises, dearly beloved, let us cleanse ourselves from all filthiness of the flesh and spirit, perfecting holiness in the fear of God." 2 Corinthians 7:1 KJV

TRAINEE: I'm looking forward to next month's training.

COACH: Good. God looks for open hearts!

MAY 24

COURSE: GOD'S PLAN OF SALVATION--ENVISIONED

WORD: "To Him all the prophets witness that, through His name, whoever believes in Him will receive remission of sins." Acts 10:43 (NKJV)

Therefore, if anyone *is* in Christ, *he is* a new creation; old things have passed away; behold, all things have become new. 2 Corinthians 5:17 (NKJV)

COACH: Salvation is free; yet, it is not cheap!

TRAINEE: Yes, there was great need and huge cost. Good medicine checks first for vital signs; what are the spiritual vital signs of salvation?

COACH: <u>First</u>, see that you are to be judged: <u>2 Corinthians 5:9–10</u>. <u>Second</u>, see that you are viewed and evaluated by the judge through the cover of Jesus' blood: <u>Romans 4:3–8</u>. <u>Third</u>, see that you receive this coverage through a step of faith, choosing to believe it is real and true: <u>Romans 3:27–31</u>. <u>Fourth</u>, see that you are not to cleverly "cheapen" that coverage by some manipulative use of that faith: <u>Romans 3:5–8; 6:1–2</u>. <u>Fifth</u>, see that you are to exercise faith also as an act of obedience, belief that acts on that belief: <u>Romans 1:5</u>. <u>Sixth</u>, see that you are to practice daily placing your faith in what has been worked out for you; this is your part: <u>Philippians 2:12</u>. <u>Seventh</u>, see that when you backslide or "break training," your Coach has a re-entry plan to bring you back into training: <u>Philippians 2:13</u>.

TRAINEE: It is good that there is a re-entry into the faith.

COACH: We march deeper into the plan in tomorrow's training.

TRAINEE: Good.

-continued-

MAY 25

WORD: **"'Return, faithless people; I will cure you of backsliding.' 'Yes, we will come to you, for you are the Lord our God.'"** Jer. 3:22 (NIV)

    "He hath shewed thee, O man, what is good; and what doth the Lord require of thee, but to do justly, and to love mercy, and to walk humbly with thy God?" Micah 6:8 (KJV)

TRAINEE: If I think I've "got it made," that's when I break training (not running in his grace).

COACH: Read and heed Paul's words on this:

WORD: **"I don't mean to say I'm perfect. I haven't learned all I should even yet, but I keep working toward that day when I will finally be all that Christ saved me for and wants me to be.**

No, dear brothers, I am still not all I should be but I am bringing all my energies to bear on this one thing: Forgetting the past and looking forward to what lies ahead, I strain to reach the end of the race and receive the prize for which God is calling us up to heaven because of what Christ Jesus did for us.

I hope all of you who are mature Christians will see eye to eye with me on these things, and if you disagree on some point, I believe that God will make it plain to you—if you fully obey the truth you have." Phil. 3:12–16 (TLB)

COACH: Again, the Word provides a "way of escape" (1 Cor. 10:13) from your backsliding:

-continued-

MAY 26

WORD: "**His divine power has given us everything we need for life and godliness through our knowledge of him who called us by his own glory and goodness. Through these he has given us his very great and precious promises, so that through them you may participate in the divine nature and escape the corruption in the world caused by evil desires.**" 2 Peter 1:3–4 (NIV)

"**So also the Lord can rescue you and me from the temptations that surround us.**" 2 Peter 2:9 (TLB)

TRAINEE: Many times I hear on television and radio the message that says that all you have to do is accept Christ as your personal Savior or just believe in order to be saved. These are some favorite Scriptures often quoted:

"**For God so loved the world, that He gave His only begotten Son, that whosoever believeth in Him shall not perish, but have everlasting life**" John 3:16 (KJV).

133

"**But what does it say? 'The word is near you; it is in your mouth and in your heart,' that is, the word of faith we are proclaiming: That if you confess with your mouth, 'Jesus is Lord,' and believe in your heart that God raised him from the dead, you will be saved**" Rom. 10:8–9 (NIV).

COACH: But let's look at another Scripture. Speaking about the last judgment, Jesus had the following to say:

WORD: "**Not every one that saith unto me, Lord, Lord, shall enter into the kingdom of heaven; but he that doeth the will of my Father which is in heaven. Many will say to me in that day, Lord, Lord, have we not prophesied in thy name? and in thy name have cast out devils? and in thy name done many wonderful works? And then will I profess unto them, I never knew you: depart from me, ye that work iniquity.**" Matt. 7:21–23 (KJV)

-continued-

MAY 27

COACH: Did they believe? Yes, they called Him "Lord." But were they saved? No. Why? Because, they, like you, have a sin problem. Jesus put it plainly when speaking to his own people in Galilee: "**But unless you repent, you too will all perish**" Luke 13:3 (NIV).

TRAINEE: I'm listening.

COACH: In the parable of the sheep and the goats, the goats believed, but were they saved? No. Why? Because their faith was not active in love. They had not "done it unto the least of these" and, therefore, had "not done it unto (Jesus)." When the people of the early church asked Peter what they should do to be saved, he answered: "**Repent—change your views, and purpose to accept the will of God in your inner selves instead of rejecting it**" (Acts 2:38 AMP). Have a fellowship with Christ's sufferings as you reach out to those in need (see Matt. 25:31–46). If Jesus, the Word, lives in your heart, you will not have to hear Him say, "**Depart from me, for I never knew you.**" Peter told the church to "**repent . . . and turn to God, so that your**

-continued-

MAY 28

sins may be wiped out, that times of refreshing may come from the Lord" (Acts 3:19 NIV; see also Acts 17:30, Mark 2:17).

TRAINEE: From where does the power come?

COACH: When God says, "The fear of the Lord is the beginning of wisdom," this does not just mean a fear of the consequences or the "pickle" you get in when stepping out of his will or even the fear of missing out on his best. It is the fear of wounding his heart anymore because of your sin. It is the posture of King David, writing Psalm 51 while reflecting on his adultery with Bathsheba, the murder of her husband, and the avalanche of harm it did. David became sorry for what he had done against God's heart, will, and Word. So David writes, "**For I know my transgressions, and my sin is always before me. Against you, you only, have I sinned and done what is evil in your sight**" (Ps. 51:3–4 NIV). The apostle Paul nailed it down with these words:

WORD: "**For godly sorrow worketh repentance to salvation not to be repented of: but the sorrow of the world worketh death**" 2 Cor. 7:10 (KJV). Other translations read that godly sorrow "produces" a repentance.

TRAINEE: What does godly sorrow look like?

COACH: Can you stand before the cross of Jesus and see him taking into his body and mind all that Satan could do through the Roman soldiers and bystanders and even hear him cry out in pain in his spirit as he felt the wrath of the Father; "Father, why have you forsaken me?"

MAY 29

-continued-

God, the Father, will not look upon sin. "**God made him who had no sin to be sin for us, so that in him we might become the righteousness of God**" (2 Cor. 5:21 NIV). In that agony of body, mind, and spirit on the cross, can you look there and see that you were on his mind as he hung there? Would you then step back and not be moved to repent? See the power in these words: "**For the message of the cross is foolishness to those who are perishing, but to us who are being saved it is the power of God**" (1 Cor. 1:18 NIV). All Israel will be saved when they see the one they have pierced (see Zech. 12:10; Jn. 19:37; Rev. 1:7). The New Covenant will be written on their hearts. The same is true for you as you see the piercing your sins (past, present, and future) have done. Godly sorrow over these sins will, therefore, transform you by the renewing of your mind, giving you the "mind of Christ."

TRAINEE: So when Jesus says that "many are called but few chosen" and that we should enter by the "narrow door," what does this mean?

COACH: If you somehow try to show the Father that you deserve the kingdom because you have performed greatly or by pointing to your awards for service, then you are too big to fit through the "narrow door." Notice the outline of markings on Christ as he hung on the cross. His wounds form the shape of a door. No one comes to the Father except through Jesus and the "power of the cross" (see John 14:6). Mt. Sinai found its completion in Mt. Calvary!

MAY 30

COURSE: A SUMMARY

TRAINEE: I'm impressed, but how do I go about putting this all together?

COACH: Go back to that example of a child with building blocks, trying to stack one upon another? Just the slightest shift in stacking those blocks can make the whole structure off balance, causing them to all tumble down. So it is with the building blocks of God's Word. Recall that the first block handed you was centered on the Holy Spirit's work to "convict of Truth":

WORD: **"O Lord, You have searched me (thoroughly) and have known me.... Search me (thoroughly), O God, and know my heart! Try me, and know my thoughts!** Ps. 139:1,23 (AMP)

COACH: The second block:

WORD: **"If we say that we have no sin, we are only fooling ourselves, and refusing to accept the truth. But if we confess our sins to him, he can be depended on to forgive us and to cleanse us from every wrong. (And it is perfectly proper for God to do this for us because Christ died to wash away our sins).**" 1 John 1:8–9 (TLB)

COACH: Other blocks came through the journey of the apostle Paul, who was transformed (grew and changed) from the confession of being "chief of sinners," having "nothing good in (him)," deserving "only condemnation and death" to stating he was "more than a conqueror through (Christ, Jesus) who loved (him)," that he could "do all things through Christ who strengthens (him)," that "God's strength is made perfect in (his) weakness" and finally to say, "It is no longer I (self-centered ego)

-continued-

MAY 31

Paul who live, but Christ within me." One block builds upon the other. Again, the Holy Spirit knows which building blocks from the Word to hand you at the right time. You need only remember which block (Word) is the cornerstone of the house of God's grace. It is none other than the Word from the cross—all this so you can be transformed by the renewing of your mind as you cast down the imaginations of the heart, deaden the deeds of the flesh and crucify the self. This means you can practice saying every day, "Today, I can stop having a form of godliness and denying the power thereof."

WORD: **"For the message of the cross is foolishness to those who are perishing, but to us who are being saved it is the power of God."** 1 Cor. 1:18 (NIV)

TRAINEE: Dear Father, in the Name of Jesus, I ask that You help me see You as my "closest Person"; guide me to have—*like what You said about King David*—"a heart after Your Own heart."

COACH: Yes, and this was after David's sins of adultery, murder, and efforts at deceit.

TRAINEE: I'm encouraged.

COACH: Next month's training will address the fire needed to burn away anything against the will of Your Heavenly Father.

TRAINEE: I will look with expectation.

COACH: That's a good posture for growth and change.

Month of Fire

COURSE: UNTRUSTWORTHY HEART RENEWED

WORD: **"And He said, "What comes out of a man, that defiles a man. For from within, out of the heart of men, proceed evil thoughts, adulteries, fornications, murders, thefts, covetousness, wickedness, deceit, lewdness, an evil eye, blasphemy, pride, foolishness. All these evil things come from within and defile a man."** Mark 7:20-23 (NKJV)

COACH: Again, the power for repentance (turning around and being obedient) is found in the cross and what Jesus accomplished there for us. St. Paul used the term "Godly sorrow." When I am sorry in my own heart for what I have done against God with my sin, the Apostle Paul says that this kind of sorrow will **"produce a repentance that leads to salvation and never brings regret."** 2 Corinthians 7:10 Read Psalm 51 to see how this kind or sorrow turned King David's heart from adultery, murder, and deceit to becoming someone whom God could call: **"A man after God's Own heart** [Acts 13:22]."

TRAINEE: How can I start seeing people and conditions through those kind of glasses? I'm so wrapped up into what I feel that I hardly ever think about what God would feel.

COACH: The more you take in His Word to your heart and mind, the more you are wearing those glasses.

TRAINEE: Why?

WORD: **"In the beginning was the Word, and the Word was with God, and the Word was God."** John 1:1-14 (NKJV)

JUNE 2

COURSE: JESUS'S FEELINGS/EMOTIONS

COACH: Recall the scene on Palm Sunday, where almost two million people prepared for the Passover celebration. As the Pharisees tried to stop the people from singing praises to Jesus, Jesus told the Pharisees that if the people kept quiet, "the very stones would cry out (see Luke 19:28–44)." That, by the way, makes perfect sense. Jesus, being the "Word made flesh" who created the rocks, would certainly have gotten a response from the rocks if the people did not give it. They would have demonstrated for a fact that they, too, have life or exist because of Him. These were the Father's feelings as He watched His Son enter Jerusalem. Yet, a little while later, Jesus' mood shifted dramatically. He approached Jerusalem and wept over it (see Luke 19:41–44). These verses show that He was feeling what the Father felt as He saw their future, the destruction of Jerusalem in AD 70.

Later, His mood changed again. Angered by the activity at the temple, He began driving out the merchants and overturning their tables. Archaeologists have discovered that those tables were very heavy; it took a lot of adrenaline to turn them over. Psalm 69:9 and John 2:17 tell us that zeal for His Father's house consumed Jesus. As stated, the opposite of love is not anger or even hatred, it is indifference. Jesus strongly felt what the Father felt then and there.

TRAINEE: This was the Word and God's feelings working together?

COACH: Read again John 1:1-14 to see the Word is God, is Jesus.

-continued-

JUNE 3

WORD: **"For even Christ did not please himself but, as it is written: 'The insults of those who insult you have fallen on me'"** Rom. 15:3 (NIV).

COACH: If you don't choose to adopt God's feelings, you settle for your own.

TRAINEE: But from where did the feelings of Jesus come? What was His source?

COACH: When He saw people and their needs, when He encountered conditions of their sinfulness, He felt the heart of His Father Who had sent Him here; He saw and felt as did the Father.

TRAINEE: As I do the exercise of recalling what God feels in connection with His Word, how will I know it is affecting my view of things?

COACH: You will become aware that people and their circumstances all have a history which has given shape and form to their own perceptions, behaviors, and feelings.

WORD: **"For we do not have a High Priest who cannot sympathize with our weaknesses, but was in all *points* tempted as *we are, yet* without sin."** Hebrews 4:15 (NKJV)

COACH: You will also begin to sympathize instead of judge; to want to help instead of ignoring and resenting.

TRAINEE: I can feel you getting ready to remind me that this shift in feelings is also a decision on my part, not just a feeling to do so.

COACH: That understanding prepares your heart for tomorrow's training.

-continued-

JUNE 4

COACH: When you take God's Word to heart, this enables you to make such decisions about feelings. That faith moves into action when you lock it into the Word. God's Word gives you what His feelings are concerning anything you face or see or experience. When you stand on His feelings through a faith-decision, He is pleased. (See Heb. 11:6.)

We review from the March 13th training the benefits of such a transformation through the renewal of the mind (see Rom. 12:2) as follows:

While you may see differently than most of the world—for example, Jeremiah was called "the weeping prophet"—you will have an extraordinary objectivity in your outlook. When you look at the news and see the insane actions of a hardened criminal and ask, "How do you feel about this, Father?" you will find yourself moving away from the vindictive, reactionary, self-righteous response to a desire to see this criminal in the position of the penitent thief hanging on the cross next to Jesus, causing you to pray for salvation in the midst of punishment.

You'll be free to enter God's emotions rather than remain bound to your own. The reason Jesus could voice a cry of victory—"It is finished"—from the cross is because he saw what the Father saw. Great or small, whatever the concern, it pays to see it from God's perspective.

TRAINEE: Thank you, this helps.

COACH: We look a step deeper tomorrow.

-continued-

JUNE 5

TRAINEE: I'm ready for more.

COACH: The Beatitudes (Matt. 5:1–12), for example, tell you that you are "blessed" (happy) when poor in spirit, mournful, persecuted, and so on. These verses, when added to the following—"This is the day that the Lord hath made; we *will* rejoice and be glad in it" (Ps. 118:24 KJV), "for the joy of the Lord is your strength" (Neh. 8:10b KJV)—establish a biblical platform for feelings to also become faith-decisions.

TRAINEE: Based on the Beatitudes, am I to somehow develop the attitude of gratitude? One might say it is a "to-be attitude."

COACH: Develop, instead, a hunger for His Word; this will help you see through the Father's eyes, giving shape to your feelings, words, and decisions. The rest will be good history.

-continued-

WORD:	**"All Scripture is given by inspiration of God, and is profitable for doctrine, for reproof, for correction, for instruction in righteousness, that the man of God may be complete, thoroughly equipped for every good work."** 2 Tim. 3:16-17 (NKJV)
TRAINEE:	In that light, can we do a review of what's been said from the months before concerning obedience?
COACH	I'm glad to see that hunger in you. Our summary will center on His Word, which, as you now know, is the person of Jesus, Himself.
TRAINEE:	Yes, Sir.

-continued-

JUNE 6

COURSE:	OBEDIENCE REVIEWED BY THE WORD
WORD:	**"See, I have set before thee this day life and good, and death and evil; In that I command thee this day to love the LORD thy God, to walk in his ways, and to keep his commandments and his statutes and his judgments, that thou mayest live and multiply: and the LORD thy God shall bless thee in the land whither thou goest to possess it."** Deuteronomy 30:15-16 KJV

"Then it shall come to pass, because you listen to these judgments, and keep and do them, that the LORD your God will keep with you the covenant and the mercy which He swore to your fathers." Deuteronomy 7:12 NKJV [Blessings of Obedience: Samuel Adams wrote on 17 August 1780 to his daughter: "If you carefully fulfill the various duties of Life, from a Principle of Obedience to your Heavenly Father, you shall enjoy that peace which the world cannot give nor take away." (*Biography of Samuel Adams*)]

"Therefore keep the words of this covenant, and do them, that you may prosper in all that you do." Deuteronomy 29:9 New King James Version NKJV

"**Oh, that they had such a heart in them that they would fear Me and always keep all My commandments, that it might be well with them and with their children forever!**" Deuteronomy 5:29 NKJV

"**The things which you learned and received and heard and saw in me, these do, and the God of peace will be with you.**" Philippians 4:9 NKJV

"**Then it shall come to pass, because you listen to these judgments, and keep and do them, that the LORD your God will keep with you the covenant and the mercy which He swore to your fathers.**"

-continued-

JUNE 7

Deuteronomy 7:12 NKJV [Blessings of Obedience: I repeat, Samuel Adams wrote on 17 August 1780 to his daughter: "If you carefully fulfill the various duties of Life, from a Principle of Obedience to your Heavenly Father, you shall enjoy that peace which the world cannot give nor take away." (*Biography of Samuel Adams*)] READ AGAIN

"**Therefore keep the words of this covenant, and do them, that you may prosper in all that you do.**" Deuteronomy 29:9 New King James Version NKJV

"**Oh, that they had such a heart in them that they would fear Me and always keep all My commandments, that it might be well with them and with their children forever!**" Deuteronomy 5:29 NKJV

"**The things which you learned and received and heard and saw in me, these do, and the God of peace will be with you.**" Philippians 4:9 NKJV

"**Whoever therefore breaks one of the least of these commandments, and teaches men so, shall be called least in the kingdom of heaven; but whoever does and teaches *them*, he shall be called great in the kingdom of heaven.**" Matthew 5:19 NKJV

"Therefore whoever hears these sayings of Mine, and does them, I will liken him to a wise man who built his house on the rock: and the rain descended, the floods came, and the winds blew and beat on that house; and it did not fall, for it was founded on the rock." Matthew 7:24-25 NKJV

-continued-

JUNE 8

"Jesus answered and said to him, "If anyone loves Me, he will keep My word; and My Father will love him, and We will come to him and make Our home with him." John 14:23 NKJV [see in context verses 21-24]

"If you know these things, blessed are you if you do them." John 13:17 NKJV

"If you keep My commandments, you will abide in My love, just as I have kept My Father's commandments and abide in His love." John 15:10 NKJV

"But he who looks into the perfect law of liberty and continues *in it*, and is not a forgetful hearer but a doer of the work, this one will be blessed in what he does." James 1:25 NKJV

" . . .(for not the hearers of the law *are* just in the sight of God, but the doers of the law will be justified;" Romans 2:13 NKJV [Paul's statements of our no longer being "under the law" do not mean the law is no longer our standard; it means we, through Jesus, are no longer under the guilt, dominion and penalty of the law. (see Rom. 6:14-15; Gal.3:23; 5:18]

"**Most assuredly, I say to you, he who hears My word and believes in Him who sent Me has everlasting life, and shall not come into judgment, but has passed from death into life.**" John 5:24 NKJV [Life and Judgment are through the Son. The word: "*hears*" is like our military expression: "*attention to orders;*" it means with intention to follow through/obey. Sometimes my Daddy would give me a corrective word and then tilt his head to the side and look at me sharply saying: "Do you hear me?" He was asking me if I was hearing him with the mind to obey. "*Hear*" is what Jesus said about the faith that obeys: "**I tell you that he will avenge them speedily. Nevertheless when the Son of man cometh, shall he find faith on**

-continued-

JUNE 9

the earth?" Luke 18:8 KJV We, like Joshua, need to say in these deceitful and divergent times: "**but as for me and my house, we will serve the LORD.**"]

"**For whoever does the will of My Father in heaven is My brother and sister and mother.**" Matthew 12:50 NKJV

"**And the world is passing away, and the lust of it; but he who does the will of God abides forever.**" 1 John 2:17 NKJV

"**And hereby we do know that we know him, if we keep his commandments. He that saith, I know him, and keepeth not his commandments, is a liar, and the truth is not in him. But whoso keepeth his word, in him verily is the love of God perfected: hereby know we that we are in him.**"1 John 2:3-5 KJV

"**Not everyone who says to Me, 'Lord, Lord,' shall enter the kingdom of heaven, but he who does the will of My Father in heaven.**" Matthew 7:21 NKJV

"**And whatever we ask we receive from Him, because we keep His commandments and do those things that are pleasing in His sight.**" 1 John 3:22 NKJV

"So Samuel said: "Has the LORD *as great* delight in burnt offerings and sacrifices, As in obeying the voice of the LORD? Behold, to obey is better than sacrifice, *And* to heed than the fat of rams." 1 Samuel 15:22 NKJV

[see, also: Philippians 2:13, 2 Corinthians 7:10-11, 2 Corinthians 10:5, Galatians 2:20, 1 Corinthians 1:18, 2 Corinthians 12:9]

JUNE 10

COURSE:	BURNING OUT SELF
COACH:	Let the following Word address your self-centeredness
WORD:	"But the cowardly, unbelieving, abominable, murderers, sexually immoral, sorcerers, idolaters, and all liars shall have their part in the lake which burns with fire and brimstone, which is the second death." Revelation 21:8 (NKJV)
	"But brother goes to law against brother, and that before unbelievers!
	Now therefore, it is already an utter failure for you that you go to law against one another. Why do you not rather accept wrong? Why do you not rather *let yourselves* be cheated? No, you yourselves do wrong and cheat, and *you do* these things *to your* brethren! Do you not know that the unrighteous will not inherit the kingdom of God? Do not be deceived. Neither fornicators, nor idolaters, nor adulterers, nor homosexuals, nor sodomites, nor thieves, nor covetous, nor drunkards, nor revilers, nor extortioners will inherit the kingdom of God." 1 Corinthians 6:6-10 (NKJV)
TRAINEE:	Will this burning away really hurt; what will I lose or no longer have as a part of me?
COACH:	To release sin that has become like a familiar friend may hurt, but this action on your part will open the door wide for God's blessing, protection, and provision.
TRAINEE:	I need that. What is the first step in this exercise of cutting away?
COACH:	Tomorrow we begin with "surgical" inspection of your heart.

JUNE 11

COURSE: YOUR UNTRUSTWORTHY HEART!

COACH: God says He "looks upon the heart." Do you have a heart relationship with Him, centered on the Cross? Ask the Holy Spirit to guide you through His Word—becoming hungry for the Word—so as to make your decision for Jesus as Lord and Savior, truly finding your heart moving closer to the Father's heart!

WORD: **"I will bless the LORD who has given me counsel; My heart also instructs me in the night seasons."** Psalm 16:7 (NKJV)

COACH: After you have confessed your sins, like King David, ask in the Name of Jesus for the Father's mercy, His forgiveness and His deliverance over all your sins. Then take the posture of thanks and praise for His help on the road to repentance, as you take a long and good look at the Cross!.

King David confessed his sins of adultery, murder, and deceit; God forgave him. Read again David's confession in Psalm 51. Recall that later in David's life, God said: "David has a heart after My Own heart."

TRAINEE: I need to be more mindful of God's feelings than of my feelings and desires.

COACH: If you don't choose to adopt God's feelings, you settle for your own.

TRAINEE: I need help seeing or knowing what our Heavenly Father is feeling about this and that.

COACH: Good, you are, again, blessed in seeing that need. We begin tomorrow taking a deeper look into His feelings.

TRAINEE: Looking forward to it.

JUNE 12

COURSE: EXCHANGE OF FEELINGS

COACH: By review, the benefits of such a transformation through the "renewal of the mind (see Rom. 12:2)" are as follows:

A. While you may see differently than most of the world, you will have an extraordinary objectivity in your outlook. When you look at the news and see the insane actions of a hardened criminal and ask, "How do you feel about this, Father?" you will find yourself moving away from the vindictive, reactionary, self-righteous response to a desire to see this criminal in the position of the penitent thief hanging on the cross next to Jesus, causing you to pray for salvation in the midst of punishment.

B. Again, you'll be free to enter God's emotions rather than remain bound to your own. The reason Jesus could voice a cry of victory—"It is finished"—from the cross is because he saw what the Father saw. Great or small, whatever the concern, it pays to see it from God's perspective.

TRAINEE: Remind me of how I start seeing how He feels about things.

COACH: It's His Word; you will begin sensing and seeing what He feels by the feelings found in the Word. Read again:

WORD: **"All Scripture is given by inspiration of God, and is profitable for doctrine, for reproof, for correction, for instruction in righteousness, that the man of God may be complete, thoroughly equipped for every good work.**" 2 Tim. 3:16-17 (NKJV)

TRAINEE: My heart moves closer to His heart as I "hide His Word" there.

JUNE 13

COURSE: GOD'S PERFECT WILL AND HIS REDEEMING WILL

TRAINEE: What is the difference between these two "wills"?

COACH: God's *perfect will* was for Adam and Eve to have never sinned in the Garden of Eden. In spite of His will, they used their free will to go against His. God found another route to bring them back into his peace and presence. This new way is his *redeeming will*, involving his Son and the cross.

Although God's *perfect will* was for the people of Israel to march out of Egypt and into the Promised Land, free will choices led the Israelites away from God's timely best. Their choices cost them a forty-year journey through the wilderness for a trip that should have taken about three weeks by camel. Nevertheless, God's *redeeming will* led them into the Promised Land. God can do the same with marriage and family.

TRAINEE: Does this mean that his *redeeming will*, when worked through marriage and family, is somehow to be considered a second-class will?

COACH: No! If it were, then what God did through his Son and the cross would have to be similarly rated. There is no church body in all of Christendom prepared to do so. God can take the broken pieces of your marriages and families and find a way to redeem them, too. His will is his will, period!

WORD: **"In him we have redemption through his blood, the forgiveness of sins, in accordance with the riches of God's grace that he lavished on us with all wisdom and understanding."** Eph. 1:7–8 (NIV)

JUNE 14

COURSE: THE DAY BY DAY JOURNEY

TRAINEE: I'm impressed, but how do I go about putting this all together?

COACH: I draw your attention a third time to that child with building blocks, trying to stack one upon another. Just the slightest shift in stacking those blocks can make the whole structure off balance, causing them to all tumble down. So it is with the building blocks of God's Word. Again, the first block handed you was centered on the Holy Spirit's work to "convict of Truth":

WORD: **"O Lord, You have searched me (thoroughly) and have known me.... Search me (thoroughly), O God, and know my heart! Try me, and know my thoughts!"** Ps. 139:1,23 (AMP)

"I, the Lord, search the mind, I try the heart, even to give every man according to his ways, according to the fruit of his doings." Jer. 17:10 (AMP)

COACH: The second block:

WORD:
"If we say that we have no sin, we are only fooling ourselves, and refusing to accept the truth. But if we confess our sins to him, he can be depended on to forgive us and to cleanse us from every wrong. (And it is perfectly proper for God to do this for us because Christ died to wash away our sins)." 1 John 1:8–9 (TLB)

"If we say that we have no sin, we deceive ourselves, and the truth is not in us. If we confess our sins, he is faithful and just to forgive us our sins, and to cleanse us from all unrighteousness." 1 John 1:9 (KJV)

-continued-

JUNE 15

COACH:
Recall, other blocks came through the journey of the apostle Paul, who was transformed (grew and changed) from the confession of being *"chief of sinners,"* having *"nothing good in (him),"* deserving *"only condemnation and death"* to stating he was *"more than a conqueror through (Christ, Jesus) who loved (him),"* that he could *"do all things through Christ who strengthens (him),"* that *"God's strength is made perfect in (his) weakness"* and finally to say, *"It is no longer I (self-centered ego) Paul who live, but Christ within me."* One block builds upon the other. The Holy Spirit knows which building blocks from the Word to hand you at the right time. You need only remember which block (Word) is the cornerstone of the house of God's grace. It is none other than the Word from the cross—all this so you can be transformed by the renewing of your mind, again, as you *"cast down the imaginations of the heart,"* *"deaden the deeds of the flesh"* and *"crucify the self."* This means you can practice saying every day, "Today, I can stop *having a form of godliness and denying the power thereof."*

WORD:
"For the message of the cross is foolishness to those who are perishing, but to us who are being saved it is the power of God." 1 Cor. 1:18 (NIV)

COACH:
Do you sense the Holy Spirit working as your; Counselor, Comforter, Helper, Teacher and to Convict you of Truth?

WORD: **And when He has come, He will convict the world of sin, and of righteousness, and of judgment.** John 16:8 NKJV

TRAINEE: I thank Him for using the Word to work with me that way.

JUNE 16

COURSE: THE SIN UNTO DEATH

TRAINEE: What is it?

COACH: The "wall" Scriptures [Heb. 6:4-6; 10:26-30] that fell on you in the February 26 training.

TRAINEE: I broke through that wall, but I can't dodge the fact that my sin was as those Hebrew's Scriptures describe: *"willful and deliberate."*

COACH: So was King David's.

TRAINEE: The apostle Paul wrote that his sin was in ignorance.

COACH: So there are degrees of sin? Does the Word say that?

TRAINEE: I have not decided to go my own way or to reject Jesus, and my heart feels the thumping effect of that triangle as it is rolled over—the edges of my conscience not worn off; however, I'm deeply afraid of offending God by my hypocrisy and deceitful heart.

COACH: Beautiful! You recall that "working out your salvation with fear and trembling" is amplified to read:

WORD: **"(Self-distrust, that is, with serious caution, tenderness of conscience, watchfulness against temptation; timidly shrinking from whatever might offend God and discredit the name of Christ)."** Phil. 2:12 (AMP)

TRAINEE: Can I in truth believe that, like King David, I am "a man after God's own heart"?

COACH: From now own, watch carefully for the clever deceptions of the enemy. He can even quote Scripture in his effort to torment and deceive. We look further into his nature and tactics tomorrow.

-continued-

JUNE 17

COACH: The word *devil* comes from your word *traduce*, meaning "to expose, shame or blame by means of falsehood and misrepresentation" (*Merriam Webster's Collegiate Dictionary*, Tenth Edition). Ezekiel 13:22a is a good description of his tactics. The Holy Spirit, however, will never torment you with the Word. He convicts of sin and of the Father's forgiveness (John 16:8–11). He is the Comforter.

WORD: **And He will establish you to the end—keep you steadfast, give you strength, and guarantee your vindication, that is, be your warrant against all accusation or indictment—[so that you will be] guiltless and irreproachable in the day of our Lord Jesus Christ, the Messiah.** 1 Corinthians 1:8 (AMP) [see, also: 11 Corinthians 5:21; Hebrews 10:14]

TRAINEE: His conviction of sin and the comfort of His grace would certainly rescue us, as a nation, from the "soap-opera mentality."

COACH: Israel, as a nation, fared better as David developed "Godly sorrow." God will not bless people who try to serve him while they, at the same time, hold onto a bosom lust. The real crime here is unbelief. Your sin is not only idolatry; it is failing to believe his Word. He saw your struggle with it; therefore, he was patient with you in it. You can still come boldly to him (see Eph. 3:12, Heb. 4:16) despite the long history of your struggle.

WORD: **"It is of the Lord's mercies that we are not consumed, because his compassions fail not."** Lam. 3:22 (KJV)

JUNE 18

COURSE: The Power of His Word to Overcome [*A Summary*]

POWER

OF

HIS

WORD

COACH:

I   Honest Confession:

If we confess our sins, he is faithful and just to forgive us our sins, and to cleanse us from all unrighteousness. 2 Cor. 7:10

1 John 1:19

Godly sorrow brings repentance that leads to salvation and leaves no regret, but worldly sorrow brings death.

That if you confess with your mouth the Lord Jesus and believe in your heart that God has raised him from the dead, you will be saved. Rom. 10:9

-continued-

JUNE 19

II. THOUGHTS CAPTIVE TO JESUS

<u>2 Corinthians 10:5</u>
We demolish arguments and every pretension that sets itself up against the knowledge of God and we take captive every thought to make it obedient to Christ.

<u>Galatians 2:20</u>
I have been crucified with Christ and I no longer live, but Christ lives in me. The life I live in the body, I live by faith in the Son of God, who loved me and gave himself for me.

<u>1 Corinthians 1:18</u>
For the message of the cross is foolishness to those who are but to us who are being saved it is the power of God.

<u>Romans 8:13</u>
For if you live according to the sinful nature, you will perish, die; but if by the Spirit you put to death the misdeeds of body, you will live.

<u>2 Corinthians 12:9</u>
But he said to me, "My grace is sufficient for you, for my power is made perfect in weak-weakness, so that Christ's power may rest on me. Therefore I will boast all the more gladly about my weaknesses."

-continued-

JUNE 20

III. PLACE THE NAME OF JESUS OVER THE MIND

<u>Philippians 2:9</u>
Therefore God exalted Him to highest place and gave Him the Name that is above every name.

<u>Philippians 4:13</u>
I can do everything God asks me to with the help of Christ who gives me strength and power.

<u>Romans 8:37</u>
In all these things we are more than conquerors through Him Who love us.

<u>Romans 12:2 (KJV)</u>
Be ye transformed by the renewing of your mind

<u>James 1:13 (KJV)</u>
Let no man say when he is tempted, I am tempted of God: for God cannot be tempted with evil, neither tempteth he any man:

JUNE 21

COURSE: **GOD:**   **A SUMMARY**

COACH: On the one hand He:

Is a just God demanding punishment of evil. [Deut. 32:4; Is. 45:21; Acts 3:14]

An angry God when viewing sin. [Ex. 32:22; Num. 32:13-14; Deut. 7:4]

One Who will not be mocked. [Gal. 6:7]

Chastens [trains, teaches, compels], disciplines.

Speaks fearfully in Heb. 6:4-6 & 10:26-30 about sin.

Grants no remission without repentance. [Mt. 3:7-9; Lu. 3:3, 8; 24:47; Acts 2:38; 26:18-20; 2 Cor. 7:9-10; Heb. 6:1, 6]

Will not hear prayer when iniquity is regarded in the heart [Ps. 66:18]

Says if I love Him I will obey Him. [Jn. 14:15, 21 23]

TRAINEE: I can seem close to Him and appear to know Him and still be a "Judas."

-continued-

JUNE 22

COACH: On the other hand He:

Has paid for it all. [1 Cor. 6:20; 7:23]

Makes His strength perfect in my weakness. [2 Cor. 12:9]

Helps me see that faith is a decision, not a feeling. [Lu. 22:42]

Is a rewarder of my faith. [Col. 3:24; Heb. 11:6; 2 Jn. 1:8; Rev. 22:12]

Says that if I judge myself I will not be judged [1 Cor. 11:31-32]

Helps me do what He wants [Phil. 2:13; 4:13], [1 Cor. 1:18], [Rom. 12:2]

Says sorrow for what I have done against Him leads me to repentance [2 Cor. 7:10]

TRAINEE: Coaches me to:
Make the *sacrifice-of-obedience*
Exercise the *faith-of-obedience*
Have the **wisdom-of-obedience**.
Offer Him the *praise-of-obedience*.
Show Him the *love-of-obedience*.

JUNE 23

COURSE: REPEATED SIN AND GOD'S GRACE

COACH: You are not to frustrate the work of the Holy Spirit with repeated sin in your life.

WORD: **"And do not grieve the Holy Spirit of God [but seek to please Him], by whom you were sealed *and* marked [branded as God's own] for the day of redemption [the final deliverance from the consequences of sin]."**
Ephesians 4:30Amplified Bible (AMP)

COACH Remember God's promise and faithfulness to forgive even repeated sin.

WORD:	**"If we say that we have no sin, we deceive ourselves, and the truth is not in us. If we confess our sins, he is faithful and just to forgive us our sins, and to cleanse us from all unrighteousness."** 1 John 1:8-9 (KJV)
COACH:	Recall, when the disciples asked Jesus how many times we should forgive, saying as many as 7-times, Jesus answered 70 times 7. This is powerful because the number "7" in Hebrew stands for perfection and on-going time or infinity. God says He has "sealed" our salvation because of our faith relationship to Him through His Son, Jesus. He is being "faithful and just" to what His Son carried out on the Cross when He said: "It is finished!"
TRAINEE:	Now, if God is going to do all that for me because of what His Son accomplished for me on the Cross, can I accept it the whole nine yards by taking the step of forgiving myself?
COACH:	**"But if you do not forgive men their trespasses, neither will your Father forgive your trespasses."** Matthew 6:15 (NKJV

JUNE 24

COURSE:	REPEATED SIN AND GOD'S DISCIPLINE
COACH:	God knows what you need for true change or repentance. Sometimes He sharply disciplines; other times He will allow a time of stressful waiting.
TRAINEE:	Tell me about the stressful waiting.
WORD:	**"I will bear the indignation of the Lᴏʀᴅ, because I have sinned against him, until he plead my cause, and execute judgment for me: he will bring me forth to the light, and I shall behold his righteousness."** Micah 7:9 (KJV)
TRAINEE:	I need to understand *"indignation," "plead my cause"* and *"execute judgment."*

COACH: His "*indignation*" is the distress He allows you to feel or experience because of your sin. Can you see Jesus as the One Who stands before the Father to "*plead* [defend] (your) *cause*" [personal and/or legal]? To "*execute judgment*" means that you are declared guilty before God because you have sinned against Him. To "*bring (you) forth to the light*" addresses God's forgiveness and those who are against you.

TRAINEE: I need to, somehow, get back into a right relationship with Him.

COACH: I addition to yesterday's Word about His forgiveness when you confess your sins, the following Word underscores:

WORD: **"And they shall teach no more every man his neighbour, and every man his brother, saying, Know the LORD: for they shall all know me, from the least of them unto the greatest of them, saith the LORD: for I will forgive their iniquity, and I will remember their sin no more."** Jeremiah 31:34 (KJV)

-continued-

JUNE 25

"For I will be merciful to their unrighteousness, and their sins and their iniquities will I remember no more." Hebrews 8:12 (KJV)

"And their sins and iniquities will I remember no more." Hebrews 10:17 (KJV)

COACH" "As God had delivered Israel in the past because of His righteousness, so He would deliver a repentant Israel in the future." [Thomas Nelson New King James Study Bible, p 1511]

TRAINEE: But, what is the deeper part of my being confessional and repentant to Him?

WORD: **"Lament and mourn and weep! Let your laughter be turned to mourning and *your* joy to gloom. Humble yourselves in the sight of the Lord, and He will lift you up."** James 4:9-10 (NKJV)

TRAINEE: I need the Holy Spirit to talk with me some more on this Word, as well.

COACH: Again the commentary from the King James Study Bible will give good guidance. It reads: "When a believer who has fallen into sin responds to God's call for repentance, he or she should place laughter and joy aside to reflect on the sin with genuine sorrow [2 Cor. 7:9,10]. In this verse, laughter seems to refer to the loud revelry of pleasure-loving people. They immerse themselves in a celebration of their sins in an effort to forget God's judgment. A Christian should never laugh at sin. However, Christian sorrow leads to repentance, repentance leads to forgiveness, and forgiveness leads to true joy over one's reconciliation with God. [see: Ps. 32:1; 126:2; Prov. 15:13]

-continued-

JUNE 26

WORD: **"For He says: "In an acceptable time I have heard you, And in the day of salvation I have helped you."** 2 Corinthians 6:2 (NKJV)

COACH: St. Paul quoted Isaiah 49:8 as a reminder that God is ready to listen, help and deliver if only we would turn to Him in faith and humility.

TRAINEE: What does it mean for me when God "lifts me up" and there is a restored right relationship with Him?

COACH: I'm glad you asked that! It means God's Everlasting Love.

WORD: **"What then shall we say to these things? If God *is* for us, who *can be* against us?"** Romans 8:31 (NKJV)

**"The LORD *is* near to those who have a broken heart,
And saves such as have a contrite spirit."** Psalm 34:18 (NKJV)

**"Because he has set his love upon Me, therefore I will deliver him; I will set him on high, because he has known My name. He shall call upon Me, and I will answer him;
I *will be* with him in trouble;
I will deliver him and honor him.
With long life I will satisfy him,
And show him My salvation."** Psalm 91:16-18 NKJV

**"The horse *is* prepared for the day of battle,
But deliverance *is* of the L**ORD**."** Proverbs. 21:31 NKJV

TRAINEE: I'm with you; can we still go deeper?

COACH: Tomorrow's training will take us there.

TRAINEE: Looking forward to it!

-continued-

JUNE 27

COURSE: GOD'S COMPLETE FORGIVENESS, CLEANSING, AND RENEWAL—
THE JOY OF FORGIVENESS

WORD: **"Blessed *is he whose* transgression *is* forgiven, *Whose* sin *is* covered. Blessed *is* the man to whom the L**ORD** does not impute iniquity, And in whose spirit *there is* no deceit."** Psalm 32:1-2 (NKJV)

"Thanks be to God [for my deliverance] through Jesus Christ our Lord! So then, on the one hand I myself with my mind serve the law of God, but on the other, with my flesh [my human nature, my worldliness, my sinful capacity—I serve] the law of sin." Romans 7:25Amplified Bible (AMP)

"In Him we have redemption [that is, our deliverance and salvation] through His blood, [which paid the penalty for our sin and resulted in] the forgiveness *and* complete pardon of our sin, in accordance with the riches of His grace." Ephesians 1:7Amplified Bible (AMP)

COACH: "Redemption" includes ransom in full and deliverance. Therefore, you can approach God boldly about your needs.

WORD: **" Let us therefore come boldly unto the throne of grace, that we may obtain mercy, and find grace to help in time of need."** Hebrews 4:16(KJV)

"For godly sorrow produces repentance *leading* to salvation, not to be regretted; but the sorrow of the world produces death." 2 Corinthians 7:10 (NKJV)

COACH: Salvation, in this verse, includes rescue and safety. Tomorrow we train on what should be your response to such outpouring of His Grace to you.

JUNE 28

COURSE: YOUR RESPONSE TO HIS GRACE

COACH: The tremendous response God makes to you in His Grace calls for a response on your part.

TRAINEE: Most of your coaching has come from the Word; is there a Word about my response?

COACH: Heed and read.

WORD: **"Rest in the Lord, and wait patiently for Him;**
Do not fret because of him who prospers in his way,
Because of the man who brings wicked schemes to pass. Cease from anger, and forsake wrath;
Do not fret—*it* only *causes* harm. For evildoers shall be cut off; But those who wait on the Lord,
They shall inherit the earth.
For yet a little while and the wicked *shall be* no *more*;
Indeed, you will look carefully for his place,
But it *shall be* no *more*. " Psalm 37:7-10 (NKJV)

"Be anxious for nothing, but in everything by prayer and supplication, with thanksgiving, let your requests be made known to God; *7* and the peace of God, which surpasses all understanding, will guard your hearts and minds through Christ Jesus." Philippians 4:6-7 (NKJV)

COACH: Note that this last Word wants you to give God thanks as part of your prayers.

TRAINEE: Does this mean I am to give Him thanks when I pray and see no answer?

COACH: In the next two days, we will review prayer made in His will.

JUNE 29

COURSE:	THE WORD AND PRAYER
TRAINEE:	So, how can I *know* whether or not my prayer (talking/listening relationship with God) on a given concern is in God's will?
COACH:	First, if inner conviction is there, it is "**the assurance of things hoped for, the conviction of things not seen**" (Heb. 11:1). (The KJV reads, "substance of things hoped for, the evidence of things not seen." Something substantial gives assurance, like a title deed in hand. Evidence goes with conviction.
TRAINEE:	I need something to back up my conviction, to know God is really talking to me when I pray.
COACH:	Second, does God's Word confirm and address your conviction? Does the Word echo your prayer? If so, you have the strongest confirmation possible—when you pray God's own Word.
COACH:	Third, do you have godly, wise counsel of others who are steeped in the faith? "**For by wise counsel you can wage your war, and in an abundance of counselors there is victory and safety**" Prov. 24:6 (AMP).
COACH:	Fourth, do you have an inner peace, much like that eye of the hurricane—calm, balanced, and stable while everything around you is chaotic? Can you turn over and go to sleep? If so, that's another confirmation.

Fifth, is there circumstantial evidence? This may occur following some prayers; with others, it may not exist. Should it not, rest firmly on the confirmation of God's Word. That Word will lift up faith. God's Words are events!

-continued-

JUNE 30

Sixth, is there unconfessed sin? This blocks God's hearing (1 John 5:13–15; Is. 59:1–3, 12–15) of your prayers. Confession and God's forgiveness clear the way. "**He that covereth his sins shall not prosper: but whoso confesseth and forsaketh them shall have mercy.**" Prov. 28:13 (KJV)

Seventh, look for the final/actual provision, which is the ultimate confirmation of God's will in the matter. In the military, you do not go anywhere until you have orders in hand. Your number one Commander-in-Chief does deliver those orders from his Word as a final provision.

Pray continually, "without ceasing." Seven days without prayer will make "one weak." Be like the woman who knocked on the door for a loaf of bread until, said Jesus, the householder, opened up to her. Do not regard God as hard of hearing but be persistent. To "pray-through" means nothing short of not giving up, to go the distance.

WORD: **"For whoever would come near to God must (necessarily) believe that God exists and that He is the Rewarder of those who earnestly and diligently seek Him (out)."** Heb. 11:6b (AMP)

"You will seek me and find me when you seek me with all your heart. I will be found by you, declares the Lord." Jer. 29:13–14a NIV; (see Deut. 4:29; Prov. 8:17)

COACH: Following the above steps, be persistent in giving God thanks for his answer, even before your eyes see it. "See it" with the "eyes of faith."

Make it a practice to remind yourself how well the Father can answer your prayer (Eph. 3:20).

Month of Endurance

COURSE:	"THE BUCK STOPS HERE"
COACH:	So read the little motto on President Harry Truman's desk. This applies to the training you've had on repentance. Some Words to summarize:
WORD:	**"Truly, these times of ignorance God overlooked, but now commands all men everywhere to repent, because He has appointed a day on which He will judge the world in righteousness by the Man whom He has ordained. He has given assurance of this to all by raising Him from the dead."** Acts 17:30-31 (NKJV)
	"I tell you, no; but unless you repent you will all likewise perish." Luke 13:3 (NKJV)
	"Now I rejoice, not that you were made sorry, but that your sorrow led to repentance. For you were made sorry in a godly manner, that you might suffer loss from us in nothing. For godly sorrow produces repentance *leading* to salvation, not to be regretted; but the sorrow of the world produces death." 2 Corinthians 7:9-10 (NKJV)
	"Likewise, I say to you, there is joy in the presence of the angels of God over one sinner who repents." Luke 15:10 (NKJV)
COACH:	Dr. Billy Graham put it this way: "When we receive Jesus Christ, the result is a transformed life and new joy and new peace, with the assurance that we are going to heaven. You can know that today." [Decision March 1993]
TRAINEE:	Thank You for that summary from the Word!

JULY 2

COURSE: STRENGTH TO ENDURE

WORD: "... **be clothed with humility** ... 1 Peter 5:5"

COACH: When the "I" reigns, the "spiritual eye" sees the world and people in distortion. Putting God first is your first step in enduring what and who is in the world.

WORD: **"Whom have I in Heaven *but You*? And *there is* none upon earth *that* I desire besides You. My flesh and my heart fail; *But* God *is* the strength of my heart and my portion forever."** Psalm 73:25-26 (NKJV)

"Seek the Lord and His strength; Seek His face evermore!" Psalm 105:4 (NKJV)

"But the word of the LORD endures forever." 1 Peter 1:25a (NKJV)

"Finally, my brethren, be strong in the Lord and in the power of His might. Put on the whole armor of God, that you may be able to stand against the wiles of the devil." Ephesians 6:10-11 NKJV

"I can do all things through Christ who strengthens me." Philippians 4:13 NKJV

"Blessed *is* the man who endures temptation; for when he has been approved, he will receive the crown of life which the Lord has promised to those who love Him." James 1:12 NKJV

"You therefore must endure hardship as a good soldier of Jesus Christ." 2 Timothy 2:3 NKJV

TRAINEE: Again, thank You for the Word!

JULY 3

COURSE: PERSEVERANCE IN SERVING G0D

COACH: The Greek New Testament word for serving [leitougia] is applied to God's call for you to serve Him [Rom. 12:7]. Read Matthew 25:31-40 to see that when you serve people, at the same time, you are serving God. And, when troubles arise in this race, those very troubles can produce perseverance.

WORD: **"And not only *that,* but we also glory in tribulations, knowing that tribulation produces perseverance;"**

"For you have need of endurance, so that after you have done the will of God, you may receive the promise:" Hebrews 10:36 NKJV

". . . knowing that the testing of your faith produces patience." James 1:3 NKJV

COACH: When your life seems to be going nowhere, Jesus is still working in you to complete His plan for you. Set your face like flint to serve and persevere; this is a grand way to follow His example.

TRAINEE: Can I treat it like a marathon? When I get to mile 19 or 20, the "wall" hits. It's the point of decision as to whether to go on or quit. The weight is formidable, causing the mind to go limp in its ability to order the body to continue.

COACH: Yes, as you have seen, the Holy Spirit is the One Who enables those steps to continue as He brings the hierarchy of Word over spirit, over mind, and over body, to keep the feet moving

WORD: **"The steps of a *good* man are ordered by the LORD,
And He delights in his way.."** Psalm 37:23 NKJV

JULY 4

COURSE: TRIALS

COACH: Let the Word speak to you about endurance here, too.

WORD: **In this you greatly rejoice, though now for a little while, if need be, you have been grieved by various trials, that the genuineness of your faith, *being* much more precious than gold that perishes, though it is tested by fire, may be found to praise, honor, and glory at the revelation of Jesus Christ,** 1 Peter 1:6-7 NKJV

For I consider that the sufferings of this present time are not worthy *to be compared* with the glory which shall be revealed in us. Romans 8:18 NKJV

This *is* my comfort in my affliction, for Your word has given me life. Psalm 119:50 NKJV

CH [LTC, RET] Arthur. W. Coffey, Jr., D. Min.

But He knows the way that I take [He has concern for it, appreciates, and pays attention to it]. When He has tried me, I shall come forth as refined gold [pure and luminous]. Job 23:10 (Amplified Bible)

COACH: Practice the joy of the Lord Who is closer to you than you to yourself.

TRAINEE: I understand; I can offer up to Him what's eating me.

COACH: His response of peace to you midst stress fills November.

WORD: "**. . . Do not sorrow, for the joy of the LORD is your strength.**" Nehemiah 8:10b NKJV

"But let all those rejoice who put their trust in You;
Let them ever shout for joy, because You defend them;
Let those also who love Your name
Be joyful in You." Psalm 5:11 NKJV

JULY 5

COURSE: RUNNING THE RAGE, RESENTMENT, REJECTION

TRAINEE: The dark night of the soul.

COACH: Your honest expression of anger is healthy.

TRAINEE: I feel some of February's discontent.

WORD: "**Be angry, and do not sin**": do not let the sun go down on your wrath, nor give place to the devil.**" Ephesians 4:26-27 NKJV

"So then, my beloved brethren, let every man be swift to hear, slow to speak, slow to wrath; for the wrath of man does not produce the righteousness of God." James 1:19-20 NKJV

TRAINEE: What about despair, desperation, depression?

COACH: Read St. Pauls' experience of these: Philippians 3:7-14; Romans 8:18-25. You can see problems turned into stepping stones. Your disappointment can be the Father's appointment; your impossibility can be His possibility. Recall that His 'strength can be made perfect in your weakness.'

WORD: "**But Jesus looked at *them* and said to them, "With men this is impossible, but with God all things are possible.**" Matthew 19:26 NKJV

COACH:	Spend some quality time with Peter's expression of a way of escape: 2 Peter 1:3-11
TRAINEE:	That's deep and good, but what about the escape from my sense of shame and failure?
COACH:	We exercise that tomorrow.

JULY 6

COURSE	ENDURING GOD'S RESPONSE TO OUR SIN
WORD:	**"And do not grieve the Holy Spirit of God, by whom you were sealed for the day of redemption."** Ephesians 4:30 AMP. B.
TRAINEE:	So, I cause God to grieve because of my sin.
COACH:	Yes, and His grief also contains anger and a justice that demands punishment.
TRAINEE:	Can I find a way to endure His reaction to my sin?
WORD:	**"I will bear the indignation *and* wrath of the Lord** **Because I have sinned against Him,** **Until He pleads my case and executes judgment for me.** **He will bring me out to the light,** **And I will behold His [amazing] righteousness *and* His remarkable deliverance."** Micah 7:9 AMP. B.
COACH:	To repeat, for you to "bear the indignation and wrath of the Lord" can include the distress you experience due to your sin. A commentary explains that for God to "plead your case" means He will defend you both personally and legally.
TRAINEE:	Why would He turn from wrath to defense?
COACH:	Have you confessed your sins and asked for His forgiveness?
WORD:	**"If we confess our sins, He is faithful and just to forgive us our sins and to cleanse us from all unrighteous**ness." 1 John 1:9 NKJV
TRAINEE:	Yes, I have confessed my sins, but to what is He being "faithful and just" in the forgiveness of my sins?

JULY 7

-continued-

COACH: He is being "faithful" and "just" to what His Son carried out on the Cross when He said: "It is finished!" Look at what He does about your sin.

WORD: . . . **"For I will forgive their iniquity, and their sin I will remember no more."** Jeremiah 31:34b NKJV

"For I will be merciful to their unrighteousness, and their sins and their lawless deeds I will remember no more." Hebrews 8:12 NKJV

The writer of Hebrews repeats;... **then He adds, "Their sins and their lawless deeds I will remember no more."** Hebrews 10:17 NKJV

COACH: Does that help you begin to grasp why He would defend you?

TRAINEE: Sounds like He had been looking at me in my future to shine light on the darkness of my sinful present.

WORD: **"For He says: "In an acceptable time I have heard you, And in the day of salvation I have helped you." Behold, now *is* the accepted time; behold, now *is* the day of salvation."** 2 Corinthians 6:2 NKJV

COACH: The NKJV Bible commentary on this Scripture explains that St. Paul quoted Isaiah 49:8 to encourage the Corinthians that He was "ready to listen to them and to help them. He would deliver them, if only they turned to Him in faith."

TRAINEE: Is this the reason He invites us to call on Him in times of need?

WORD: **"Let us therefore come boldly to the throne of grace, that we may obtain mercy and find grace to help in time of need."** Hebrews 4:16 NKJV

COACH: The following training summarizes your response to Him.

JULY 8

-continued-

WORD:	**"I thank God—through Jesus Christ our Lord! So then, with the mind I myself serve the law of God, but with the flesh the law of sin."** Romans 7:25
	"In Him we have redemption through His blood, the forgiveness of sins, according to the riches of His grace." Ephesians 1:7 NKJV
COACH:	"Redemption" in this Ephesians Word means you are ransomed and delivered completely.
TRAINEE:	I'm ready to hear your coaching about my response.
COACH:	God calls you to regret your sin.
WORD:	**"Lament and mourn and weep! Let your laughter be turned to mourning and *your* joy to gloom. Humble yourselves in the sight of the Lord, and He will lift you up."** James 4:9-10 NKJV
COACH:	You are reconciled with God; He will lift you up. This means He will take away and cover your sins. Read again:
WORD:	**Blessed *is he whose* transgression *is* forgiven,** **Whose sin *is* covered. Blessed *is* the man to whom the Lord does not impute iniquity,** **And in whose spirit *there is* no deceit.** Psalm 32:1-2 NKJV
	"For godly sorrow produces repentance *leading* to salvation, not to be regretted; but the sorrow of the world produces death." 2 Corinthians 7:10 NKJV
COACH:	In addition to regret over your sin, He calls you to rest in His Grace.
TRAINEE:	Help me with "rest in His Grace."
COACH:	Tomorrow.

-continued-

JULY 9

COACH: When you consent to be loved by God, this also constitutes the repentance He is looking for.

TRAINEE: That seems pretty radical.

COACH: When Jesus forgave the woman caught is adultery, He seemed more concerned that she not feel condemned.

WORD: **Rest in the Lord, and wait patiently for Him . . .** Psalm 37:7 (NKJV)

            "The Lord is near to those who have a broken heart,
            And saves such as have a contrite spirit." Psalm 34:18(NKJV)

            "What then shall we say to these things? If God is for us, who can be against us?" Romans 8:31 (NKJV)

            Do not be anxious or worried about anything, but in everything [every circumstance and situation] by prayer and petition with thanksgiving, continue to make your [specific] requests known to God. And the peace of God [that peace which reassures the heart, that peace] which transcends all understanding, [that peace which] stands guard over your hearts and your minds in Christ Jesus [is yours]. Philippians 4:6-7 (AMP)

TRAINEE: I need to let the amazing outpouring of His Grace sink deeply into my heart and settle there.

WORD: **For the message of the cross is foolishness to those who are perishing, but to us who are being saved it is the power of God.** 1 Cor. 1:18 NKJV

JULY 10

COURSE: ENDURING THE DISCIPLINE OF THE LORD

TRAINEE: How can His discipline of my sinning be a part of His Grace?

COACH: **"For whom the Lord loves He corrects, just as a father the son in whom he delights."** Proverbs 3:12 NKJV

TRAINEE: But sometimes it hurts.

WORD:	**"Do not labor for the food which perishes, but for the food that endures to everlasting life, which the Son of Man will give you, because God the Father has set His seal on Him."** John 6:27 NKJV
TRAINEE:	Help me understand what is being said here.
COACH:	Hide God's Word deep within your heart. Seek it first above all else.
TRAINEE:	How will His Word protect me from doing the bad things in life that have brought me only trouble?
COACH:	Recall King David's sins of adultery and murder; read his response to God concerning them:
WORD:	**"Thy Word have I hid in mine heart, that I might not sin against thee."** Psalm 119:11 KJV
TRAINEE:	Help me make the connection between His Word and my motivation to stop sinning so much.
COACH:	The Word is Jesus; Jesus is the Word. [see John 1:1-14]
WORD:	**"For the message of the cross is foolishness to those who are perishing, but to us who are being saved it is the power of God."** 1 Corinthians 1:18 NKJV

JULY 11

COURSE:	KNOWING GOD AND MY OBEDIENCE
COACH:	You will come to know as much about God—and only as much—as you come to obey.
TRAINEE:	I see that as I come to know more about my wife—become closer to her—the more I love her.
COACH:	And vice versa. See what Jesus, speaking for Himself and on behalf of your Heavenly Father, says about that love:
WORD:	**"If ye love me, keep my commandments."** John 14:15 KJV
TRAINEE:	So, knowing and loving God's Word—*hiding it in my heart*—holds the power to move my heart into obedience, because I'm actually knowing and loving Him. Is that a fair statement?

WORD: **"And be not conformed to this world: but be ye transformed by the renewing of your mind, that ye may prove what is that good, and acceptable, and perfect will of God."** Romans 12:2 KJV

TRAINEE: Upon what do I renew my mind so that this "transformation" can take place?

COACH: Go back and renew your training from February 16-20.

TRAINEE: I will look forward to what changes the Word will make in me.

WORD: **"Therefore, if anyone is in Christ, he is a new creation; old things have passed away; behold, all things have become new.** 2 Corinthians 5:17 NKJV

COACH: Recall the training centered on faith and love being rooted in a decision, not just a feeling.

TRAINEE: I remember.

JULY 12

COURSE: THE AVALANCHE OF STRESS AND CONCERNS

COACH: Can you name them?

TRAINEE: The list seems to grow every day; it's too long to express.

WORD: **"For as he thinketh in his heart, so is he: . . ."** Provers 23:7 KJV

COACH: As you think, so are you; carrying a heavy stress list can weigh you down.

TRAINEE: I can say 'Amen' to that!

COACH: Consider the following Word:

WORD: **Casting all your care upon him; for he careth for you.** 1 Peter 5:7 KJV

COACH: How big is the word "all" in that verse; can you think of something it does not cover?

TRAINEE: No.

COACH: Meditate upon the following Word:

WORD: **"Now to Him who is able to do exceedingly abundantly above all that we ask or think, according to the power that works in us. . ."** Ephesians 3:20 NKJV

TRAINEE: So, I need not limit God to the level of my own thinking.

WORD: **"The fear of the LORD *is* the beginning of wisdom, And the knowledge of the Holy One *is* understanding."** Proverbs 9:10 NKJV Amp. B. reads: ". . . is the beginning *and* the preeminent part of wisdom [its starting point and its essence],"

COACH: To "fear" Him is to stand in awe and great respect of Him!

JULY 13

COURSE: ENDURANCE AND RECEIVING GOD'S BLESSINGS

COACH: His blessings include redemption, deliverance, and provision. They come most readily as you practice obedience [endure] in the face of trials and temptations. Some of these blessings are:

WORD: **Therefore being justified by faith, we have peace with God through our Lord Jesus Christ:** Romans 5:1 KJV

And such were some of you [before you believed]. But you were washed [by the atoning sacrifice of Christ], you were sanctified [set apart for God, and made holy], you were justified [declared free of guilt] in the name of the Lord Jesus Christ and in the [Holy] Spirit of our God [the source of the believer's new life and changed behavior]. 1 Corinthians 6:11 AMP. B.

Christ hath redeemed us from the curse of the law, being made a curse for us: for it is written, Cursed is every one that hangeth on a tree: Galatians 3:13 (KJV)

Who hath delivered us from the power of darkness, and hath translated us into the kingdom of his dear Son: Colossians 1:13 (KJV)

For he shall give his angels charge over thee, to keep thee in all thy ways. Psalm 91:11 (KJV)

But my God shall supply all your need according to his riches in glory by Christ Jesus. Philippians 4:19 (KJV)

Blessed be the God and Father of our Lord Jesus Christ, who hath blessed us with all spiritual blessings in heavenly places in Christ: Ephesians 1:3 (KJV)

JULY 14

COURSE: THE SECURITY OF HIS BLESSINGS

TRAINEE: How are these blessings "nailed down" for me to count on and hold close?

COACH: You are a "son of God, heir of God, an inheritor."

WORD: **For as many as are led by the Spirit of God, they are the sons of God.** Romans 8:14 (KJV)

And if [we are His] children, [then we are His] heirs also: heirs of God and fellow heirs with Christ [sharing His spiritual blessing and inheritance], if indeed we share in His suffering so that we may also share in His glory. Romans 8:17 (AMP)

Christ hath redeemed us from the curse of the law, being made a curse for us: for it is written, Cursed is every one that hangeth on a tree:

That the blessing of Abraham might come on the Gentiles through Jesus Christ; that we might receive the promise of the Spirit through faith. Galatians 3:13-14 (KJV)

And the testimony is this: God has given us eternal life [we already possess it], and this life is in His Son [resulting in our spiritual completeness, and eternal companionship with Him]. He who has the Son [by accepting Him as Lord and Savior] has the life [that is eternal]; he who does not have the Son of God [by personal faith] does not have the life. 1 John 5:11-12 (AMP)

COACH: You are most comprehensively blessed!

WORD: **Blessed *shall* you *be* when you come in, and blessed *shall* you *be* when you go out.** Deuteronomy 28:6 (NKJV)

JULY 15

COURSE: AUTHORITY OVER THE ENEMY

TRAINEE: I'm no match for Satan's attacks to my life. He surely studies my weaknesses.

WORD: **Listen carefully: I have given you authority [that you now possess] to tread on serpents and scorpions, and [the ability to exercise authority] over all the power of the enemy (Satan); and nothing will [in any way] harm you.** Luke 10:19 (AMP)

Let the redeemed of the LORD say so, whom he hath redeemed from the hand of the enemy; Psalm 107:2 (KJV)

Little children (believers, dear ones), you are of God *and* you belong to Him and have [already] overcome them [the agents of the antichrist]; because He who is in you is greater than he (Satan) who is in the world [of sinful mankind]. 1 John 4:4 (AMP)

And the LORD will make you the head and not the tail; you shall be above only, and not be beneath, if you heed the commandments of the LORD your God, which I command you today, and are careful to observe *them*. Deuteronomy 28:13 (NKJV)

And they overcame him by the blood of the Lamb, and by the word of their testimony; and they loved not their lives unto the death. Revelation 12:11 (KJV)

COACH: Let the Word of God encourage your mind and heart to see the true identity He has given you through what Jesus, His Son, accomplished for you on the Cross when He said: "It is finished."

JULY 16

COURSE: THE NEW PERSON/ THE NEW UNDERSTANDING

COACH: When you look at the pictures the enemy paints for your world, you do not have to be moved by what you see.

WORD: **While we look not at the things which are seen, but at the things which are not seen: for the things which are seen are temporal; but the things which are not seen are eternal.** 2 Corinthians 4:18 (KJV)

TRAINEE: I can hear you tell me to "walk by faith and not by sight."

WORD: **. . . for we walk by faith, not by sight [living our lives in a manner consistent with our confident belief in God's promises]** 2 Corinthians 5:7 (AMP)

COACH: Your faith relationship to God enables you to labor together with Him.

WORD: **For we are God's fellow workers; you are God's field,** *you are* **God's building.** 1 Corinthians 3:9 (NKJV)

TRAINEE: Help me understand what this means in a more concrete way.

COACH: **And I will give unto thee the keys of the kingdom of heaven: and whatsoever thou shalt bind on earth shall be bound in heaven: and whatsoever thou shalt loose on earth shall be loosed in heaven.** Matthew 16:19 (KJV)

WORD: **Be ye therefore followers of God, as dear children;** Ephesians 5:1 (KJV)

            You are the light of [Christ to] the world. A city set on a hill cannot be hidden; Matthew 5:14 (AMP)

COACH: Let His Word fill your mind with a different world-picture.

JULY 17

COURSE: ENDURING "UNANSWERED" PRAYER

TRAINEE: Why do my prayers seem delayed or blocked at times?

COACH: They need, first, to be God's will—something He wants. Second, what seem like delays could be for the purpose of strengthening your faith, helping you truly wait on and trust Him. Check the following as possible blockages to that faith:

WORD: Being prideful [James 4:6]

            He knows something that we don't [John 11:5-6]

            Grumbling, complaining [Deut. 1:26-35; Ephesians 5:20]

            Un-forgiveness, grudges, resentments [Matthew 6:14-15; 18:21-35]

            Asking something against His will [James 4:2-3]

            Unconfessed sin [Isaiah 59:1-2; Acts 5:1-10]

TRAINEE: So, God always answers prayer when we stand in right relationship with Him and His will. That's hard for me.

COACH: Passage after passage, in both testaments, attests to the fact that the Heavenly Father always sees you as His child. He says for you to ask and have faith in Him like a child. Have you ever run across a situation where the child had to become perfect before the parents would answer them and provide? The above can block or delay answers; however, He does always answer prayer. Sometimes the parent will say to the child: "no," "not yet," "yes," . . . Each of those is an answer.

-continued-

JULY 18

TRAINEE: What will help remove those "blockages" to my prayers?

COACH: Monks from the first century learned from Jesus's teachings on prayer to begin daily prayer with an honest confession of their weaknesses and need for Him. This is a step toward removing pride. It helps release trust and praise that He will answer with His best; this also opens your spirit to His Spirit, Who helps you pray in the Father's will.

WORD: **Blessed [spiritually prosperous, happy, to be admired] are the poor in spirit [those devoid of spiritual arrogance, those who regard themselves as insignificant], for theirs is the kingdom of heaven [both now and forever].** Matthew 5:3 Amplified Bible (AMP)

TRAINEE: If God knows everything anyway—all my thoughts, feelings, motives, needs, etc.— then, why is it so important to pray with this confessional honesty?

COACH: It helps you pray more in His will and to truly look to Him to answer your prayers the way He says He can answer them.

WORD: **"Now unto him that is able to do exceeding abundantly above all that we ask or think, according to the power that worketh in us,"** Ephesians 3:20 (KJV)

COACH: How omnipotent [all-powerful]; omniscient [all-knowing]; omnipresent [all present] can you allow God to be with your faith? You ask, from where does that kind of trust come? It is a decision on your part to:

WORD: **"Trust in the L**ORD **with all your heart, And lean not on your own understanding; In all your ways acknowledge Him, And He shall direct your paths."** Proverbs 3:5-6 NKJV

JULY 19

COURSE: THE WEIGHTS

TRAINEE: The road looks long and lonely. How do I meet the pavement?

COACH: One mile, one step, one day at a time. Do not run with the weight of the years behind and the days ahead.

TRAINEE: I know we're built to handle stress only in 24-hour packages. But what's the reliable formula to avoid weighing the miles, the months, the mountains before I meet them?

COACH: <u>Decide</u> to trust God during those 'alone' times. Pray, read His Word; train yourself to believe that you are His Child. Welcome the training; center yourself upon the day, the step at hand. Like breathing and heart beats, move in the "now:" the present is more than a chain link between the past and future.

WORD: **Trust in the L**ORD **with all thine heart; and lean not unto thine own understanding. In all thy ways acknowledge him, and he shall direct thy paths.** Proverbs 3:4-6 (KJV)

So do not worry *or* be anxious about tomorrow, for tomorrow will have worries *and* anxieties of its own. Sufficient for each day is its own trouble. Matthew 6:34 (AMPC)

TRAINEE: Too many thoughts!

WORD: **Casting down imaginations, and every high thing that exalteth itself against the knowledge of God, and bringing into captivity every thought to the obedience of Christ;** 2 Corinthians 10:5 KJV

For as he thinketh in his heart, so is he: Proverbs 23:7 KJV

TRAINEE: I know; faith is a decision.

JULY 20

COURSE:	FAILURE REDEEMED
COACH:	Your needs, weaknesses, will become part of the training ground enabling you to help others with the same needs.
TRAINEE:	Can I be trained by pain?
COACH:	Yes, into that *wounded-healer.*
WORD:	**And He said to me, "My grace is sufficient for you, for My strength is made perfect in weakness." Therefore most gladly I will rather boast in my infirmities, that the power of Christ may rest upon me. Therefore I take pleasure in infirmities, in reproaches, in needs, in persecutions, in distresses, for Christ's sake. For when I am weak, then I am strong.** 2 Corinthians 12:9-10 (NKJV)
	But He *was* wounded for our transgressions, *He was* **bruised for our iniquities; The chastisement for our peace *was* upon Him, And by His stripes we are healed.** Isaiah 53:5 (NKJV)
	Who his own self bare our sins in his own body on the tree, that we, being dead to sins, should live unto righteousness: by whose stripes ye were healed. 1 Peter 2:24 (KJV)
COACH:	Look deeper into the blessing and hope that names you "Children of God." So, as Jesus called the Heavenly Father "ABBA," so can you. What Jesus accomplished on the Cross and your faith in Him allows you to be family and say "ABBA, Father."

JULY 21

COURSE:	COPING WITH THOUGHTS, ACTIONS, FEELINGS
COACH:	All these concerns need to be consciously, deliberately and individually placed under God's authority.
TRAINEE:	And, how do I do that? These mammoth explosions are, collectively, too much for the human dilemma.
COACH:	Read and heed the Word.

WORD:	**Casting down imaginations, and every high thing that exalteth itself against the knowledge of God, and bringing into captivity every thought to the obedience of Christ;** 2 Corinthians 10:5 (KJV)
TRAINEE:	I can't do that; I don't have that kind of power.
COACH:	Place the Name of Jesus over each and every thought as they arise: e. g, pain is a name; Jesus is above it. Depression is a name; Jesus is above it. Anger is a name; Jesus is above it. Brokenness is a name; the Name of Jesus is above it . . .
TRAINEE:	But teach me what to do when all these names come cascading, surrounding me all at once.
COACH:	Look to God as the all-knowing, creative, loving, perfect father; trust Jesus, God's Son, to address your needs and concerns with healing, redemption, reconciliation. Look to the Holy Spirit, as God's presence and power with you, to deliver the Father's ruling Word through His Son to each and every thought. The Father, Son, and Holy Spirit are One.
WORD:	**"And in that day you will ask Me nothing. Most assuredly, I say to you, whatever you ask the Father in My name He will give you. Until now you have asked nothing in My name. Ask, and you will receive, that your joy may be full.** John 16:23-24 (NKJV) [see: Proverbs. 18:10; Philippians. 2:9-11]

JULY 22

COURSE:	THE "WORK" OF SHEDDING WORK-A-HOLIC SKIN
TRAINEE:	What Word do you have for a recovering workaholic?
COACH:	"Wait." This word has two-fold meaning. Sometimes it means for you to "be still and know that God is God"; other times it means to move and serve, like a waiter.
TRAINEE:	How am I to know which is meant?
COACH:	Through the Father's perspective, one may accomplish as much by changing a baby's diaper as the one who evangelizes the world.
WORD:	**For since the world began no one has seen or heard of such a God as ours, who works for those who wait for him!** Isaiah 64:4 (TLB)

There are many ways in which God works in our lives, but it is the same God who does the work in and through all of us who are his. 1 Corinthians 12:6 Living Bible (TLB)

TRAINEE: Help me understand that better.

COACH: When tired, learn to do as Jesus did when upon this earth; stop all work and rest apart from your work. These times of rest and prayer to the Father will replenish your spirit, mind, and body—finding you accomplishing more by doing less. His Word will keep you in perfect peace.

TRAINEE: I'm listening.

COACH: Busyness is not part of the Father's plan. When St. Paul wrote that he "can do all things through Christ who strengthens [him]," he did not mean that he was to perform all things but that the strength for each task comes from God.

WORD: **He lets me rest in the meadow grass and leads me beside the quiet streams. He gives me new strength. He helps me do what honors him the most.** Psalm 23:2-3 (TLB) [see, also: Exodus 35:2; 2 Thessalonians 3:10-12; Ecclesiasticus 3:17; Psalm 90:17]

Roll your works upon the Lord [commit and trust them wholly to Him; He will cause your thoughts to become agreeable to His will, and] so shall your plans be established *and* succeed. Proverbs 16:3 (AMPC)

JULY 23

-continued-

TRAINEE: Do these two types of waiting ever merge?

WORD: **What *does it* profit, my brethren, if someone says he has faith but does not have works? Can faith save him? If a brother or sister is naked and destitute of daily food, and one of you says to them, "Depart in peace, be warmed and filled," but you do not give them the things which are needed for the body, what *does it* profit? Thus also faith by itself, if it does not have works, is dead.** James 2:14-17 (NKJV)

Then said they unto him, What shall we do, that we might work the works of God? Jesus answered and said unto them, This is the work of God, that ye believe on him whom he hath sent. John 6:28-29 King James Version (KJV)

COACH: God's strength moves through you best when you are at rest.

TRAINEE: I'm to trust Him to give me rest as I work my best.

COACH: God wants you to work your best; He says: "*if you do not work, you do not eat.*" 2 Thess. 3:10. Pray as though everything depends on God.

TRAINEE: Thank you. I can be a confessing and recovering workaholic.

JULY 24

COURSE: FREEDOM VERSUS BONDAGE OF THE WILL

TRAINEE: "Born Free, as Free as the Wind Blows;" I like that song.

COACH: So do I; that is the way the Father has made you through your spiritual rebirth.

TRAINEE: If He created nothing bad, then why are we full of potential to sin and go wrong with our lives?

COACH: He formed you in His Own image, with freedom of choice. God wants people to love Him because they simply choose to, because of Who He is and His desire to have a relationship with us. If He wanted robots, that is what He could have made. Jesus says: "If you love Me, you will keep [*obey*] My Word." Can you hear Him say to you: "I want you to freely surrender your will the way I did in the Garden of Gethsemane."

TRAINEE: But I don't, and I can't always want what the Father wants.

COACH: Are you <u>willing</u> to let Him help you want what He wants?

TRAINEE: Yes.

WORD: **For God is at work within you, helping you want to obey him, and then helping you do what he wants.** Philippians 2:13 (TLB)

COACH: One of the Church reformers, Dr. Martin Luther, explained the petition of the Lord's Prayer that says: 'Thy will be done on earth as it is in Heaven' to mean you 'request that His will may be done <u>also</u> in and by you. His will is done with or without your prayer.' Praying in His will means agreeing with God.

JULY 25

-continued-

WORD: **So the Word that goes from my mouth does not return to me empty, without carrying out my will and succeeding in what it was sent to do.** Isaiah 55:11 JB

COACH: Only when you freely allow your will to be bound to the Father's will are you free at last.

TRAINEE: And what about Satan's will and my will; how are those wills bound/stopped? When I look at my hypocrisy and weakness, I agree wholeheartedly with how the Apostle Paul explained it.

WORD: **For I know that in me (that is, in my flesh,) dwelleth no good thing: for to will is present with me; but how to perform that which is good I find not.**

For the good that I would I do not: but the evil which I would not, that I do. Now if I do that I would not, it is no more I that do it, but sin that dwelleth in me.

I find then a law, that, when I would do good, evil is present with me. For I delight in the law of God after the inward man: But I see another law in my members, warring against the law of my mind, and bringing me into captivity to the law of sin which is in my members.

O wretched man that I am! who shall deliver me from the body of this death? Romans 7:18-24 King James Version (KJV)

COACH: The Father will never lead you where His Grace cannot redeem your sinful will. Your training will lead to the Month of Victory; by that time, you will have come to know something of the Father's power through the Name He has given His Son.

TRAINEE:	I could use some more training days about such changes.
COACH:	All you need do is ask. Rest well; the next courses are tough.

JULY 26

COURSE:	RUNNING IN GOD'S PERFECT WILL OR IN HIS REDEEMING WILL
TRAINEE:	What's the difference between the two?
COACH:	Reviewing the June 13 training exercise, the Father's perfect will was for Adam and Eve to live in the Garden of Eden, a condition of perfect peace. Because they exercised their free will regarding the "Tree of Knowledge," they had to vacate the Father's best. However, He responded with His redeeming will by another plan to, again, offer His best; this plan involved His Son and a cross.
	The Father's perfect will was for Israel to exodus Egypt and go straight into the Promised Land. Because they, also, exercised their free will regarding "other gods," they delayed the Father's best by 40 years. However, God, again, responded with His redeeming will by letting His justice become His mercy, re-calling His "lost sheep," restoring and renewing the covenant with His chosen people.
TRAINEE:	So, Father knows best.
COACH:	Yes, a wise child pursues the Father's perfect will. Ask Him to help you to want and do what He wants [Philippians 2:13]."
WORD:	**For my thoughts are not your thoughts, neither are your ways my ways, saith the LORD.**
	For as the heavens are higher than the earth, so are my ways higher than your ways, and my thoughts than your thoughts. Isaiah 55:8-9 (KJV)
	Jesus said to them, "My food is to do the will of Him who sent Me, and to finish His work. John 4:34New (NKJV)

JULY 27

COURSE: DISTINGUISHING THE FATHER'S '*WILL*' WORD FROM HIS '*WILL BE*' WORD

COACH: Again, the Father's Word for the word 'Word,' when first written down in the Greek text, translates as: <u>Logos</u> [word as thought, idea, communication]; Rhema [word as speech, prophecy, instruction].

TRAINEE: Why two words for "word?"

COACH: Logos, in written form, expresses the Father's will about a given subject. Rhema is that Word which, when sent out from the Father, creates a change, heals, restores, shapes what <u>will be</u>. For example, a mother calls for the children to come wash for supper. No response. She calls out to the front yard again - nothing. Then the father sticks his head out the window and firmly says: 'get yourselves in here and wash up right now or else.' As fast as lightening, the children are at the table with clean hands ready to eat. Now, that's Rhema

TRAINEE: Let's go back over the past two days of training. If I pray about anything involving other people—for example, healing of relationships—what if their will is not in it? The Father's will about it is in bold Logos print, but what can His Rhema-Word perform if free human will blocks the path?

COACH: A trainee proposes, but God disposes. Yet, as I said, the Father will never 'bulldoze' His will over any of His children; however, what did the Word say on January 24-26? Let each Word settle in your mind. Meditate again on Philippians 2:13.

TRAINEE: I need some examples of how the Father causes His Word to become active and alive when free will is standing in the way.

JULY 28

-continued-

COACH: What do the names Moses, Naaman, Saul of Tarsus mean to you?

TRAINEE: I don't know; they turned out to be pretty good leaders. What should they mean to me?

COACH:	Each had a will. Moses did not want to go down into Egypt to lead the people out of bondage as the Father willed him to do. So, He used a burning bush, conversations with brother, Aaron, etc. to give Moses every chance to freely change his will. He did.
	Naaman, foreign ruler outside Israel, did not want to have his leprosy treated by following the prophet Elisha's instructions to bathe in the Jordan. It's dirty water and Elisha's manner of contact were too much for Naaman's ego. But the Father worked through Naaman's soldiers, reasoning repeatedly, 'til Naaman freely changed his mind [will], bathed in the Jordan and was healed.
	Saul of Tarsus is a little more of a challenge, going 180 degrees against the Father's will. He arrested and persecuted followers of Jesus. Therefore, as Saul traveled to Damascus to do more of the same, the Father used blinding light and the voice of His Son to give Saul every chance to freely surrender his will. He did; Saul became St. Paul of the early Church.
TRAINEE:	Thank You, that helps. I need to pray Philippians 2:13, not only for me but for others as well.
COACH:	Yes. Such prayer places your faith on the line where He wants it.

JULY 29

COURSE:	KEEP THE STRIDE; KEEP THE PACE; KEEP THE FAITH
COACH:	Don't expect to win when you say: *'I'll slack off on these miles and make up the difference in some of the miles down the road.'*
TRAINEE:	But I can always look at my watch to see if I've got time to spare—to take it easier for a while, can't I?
COACH:	Train without cheating. The world says: *'keep the pace with us'*; God says: *'Keep pace, stride, faith with Him.'* You can suit your pace to His, trusting His strong stride as you weigh the odds, but then stretching out with the 'nevertheless' of faith.
WORD:	**Search me, O God, and know my heart: try me, and know my thoughts: And see if there be any wicked way in me, and lead me in the way everlasting.** Psalm 139:23-24 (KJV)

For whatever God says to us is full of living power: it is sharper than the sharpest dagger, cutting swift and deep into our innermost thoughts and desires with all their parts, exposing us for what we really are. He knows about everyone, everywhere. Everything about us is bare and wide open to the all-seeing eyes of our living God; nothing can be hidden from him to whom we must explain all that we have done.

But Jesus the Son of God is our great High Priest who has gone to heaven itself to help us; therefore let us never stop trusting him. This High Priest of ours understands our weaknesses since he had the same temptations we do, though he never once gave way to them and sinned. So let us come boldly to the very throne of God and stay there to receive his mercy and to find grace to help us in our times of need.
Hebrews 4:12-16 (TLB)

JULY 30

COURSE:	DISCIPLINE OF BODY, MIND, SPIRIT.
TRAINEE:	I'm learning body discipline, but what about mind and spirit?
COACH:	You recall that the time comes during the course of long distance running when your body taps your mind on the 'shoulder' saying: 'I wanna quit.' But you overrule the body as your mind tells it to go on. But, later down the road, your mind shakes hands with your body and they both tap you on the shoulder, saying: '*we wanna quit.*' That's when and where your spirit must speak the faith-Word over them both, saying: '*nevertheless, we continue.*' This month of 'endurance' finds you training at the heart of this challenge. Just as mathematics discipline the mind to think, so does prayer disciplines the spirit to trust.
TRAINEE:	I need help in understanding this better.
COACH:	Grow to know Him by persistently flinging your frets at His feet. Then, daily discipline your mind to leave them there, chiseling your innermost feelings [heart] into a masterpiece mosaic of peace and trust. The training months of August and November will find you running this course, daily. For now, review the training Word from January 4, plus this one.

WORD: **Trust in him at all times; ye people, pour out your heart before him: God is a refuge for us. Selah.** Psalm 62:8 (KJV)

                        Cause me to hear Your loving-kindness in the morning, for on You do I lean *and* in You do I trust. Cause me to know the way wherein I should walk, for I lift up my inner self to You. Psalm 143:8 (AMPC)

COACH: Pray the above psalms; answers to them will set the stage for training your whole being—body, mind, spirit.

-continued-

JULY 31

COACH: As you discipline your spirit with the Word and in prayer fellowship with the Father, the craving of your heart will not be after externals or even such internals as happiness or freedom from stress. The true longing of your heart will be for a deepening, personal, trusting-relationship at the heart level. This is the Olympics of the Spirit—to become one with God Who created you. No greater race run; no gold more cherished. Love for the Father will automatically increase your capacity to love family, friends, and even enemies. I request that you end today's training in prayer.

TRAINEE: Dear Father, help my body be obedient to my mind; help my mind be obedient to my spirit; help my spirit be obedient to Your Word—coached by Your Spirit in *'Chariots of Fire.'*

WORD: ***And this, so* that I may know Him [experientially, becoming more thoroughly acquainted with Him, understanding the remarkable wonders of His Person more completely] and [in that same way experience] the power of His resurrection [which overflows and is active in believers], and [that I may share] the fellowship of His sufferings, by being *continually* conformed [inwardly into His likeness even] to His death . . .**

Not that I have already obtained it [this goal of being Christlike] or have already been made perfect, but I actively press on so that I may take hold of that [perfection] for which Christ Jesus took hold of me *and* **made me His own. Brothers and sisters, I do not consider that I have made it my own yet; but one thing** *I do*: **forgetting what** *lies* **behind and reaching forward to what** *lies* **ahead, I press on toward the goal to win the [heavenly] prize of the upward call of God in Christ Jesus.** Philippians 3:10-14 (AMP)

Month of Hope

COURSE:	FAITH IS FLAWLESS
COACH:	It is a gift from the Father. Training in the spiritual realm is much like that of the physical realm. At one stage you work on endurance, at stamina, at another breath; so the trials and challenges of each day teach you the same qualities.
WORD:	**For we walk by faith [we regulate our lives and conduct ourselves by our conviction or belief respecting man's relationship to God and divine things, with trust and holy fervor; thus we walk] not by sight** *or* **appearance.** 2 Corinthians 5:7 (AMPC)
	Don't waste time arguing over foolish ideas and silly myths and legends. Spend your time and energy in the exercise of keeping spiritually fit. Bodily exercise is all right, but spiritual exercise is much more important and is a tonic for all you do. So exercise yourself spiritually, and practice being a better Christian because that will help you not only now in this life, but in the next life too. 1 Timothy 4:7-8 (TLB)
COACH:	The Holy Spirit cannot fail you; you gaze into the unknown; He knows all. You could not bear to know all; He, therefore, chooses to reveal as you are able to absorb. Trust the will of your Father Who knows and does best. The months ahead will find you training on a road less traveled but powerful in the exercise of your faith.
WORD:	**Thy word is a lamp unto my feet, and a light unto my path.** Psalm 119:105 (KJV)
	Let us not lose sight of Jesus, who leads us in our faith and brings it to perfection. Hebrews 12:2 JB

AUGUST 2

COURSE: TALKING WITH MY HEAVENLY FATHER IN THE MOST DIRECT—
ON TARGET—WAY POSSIBLE.

TRAINEE: My mind is so numb; I know I need to be talking with the Father about a lot of things but where to begin?

COACH: The Holy Spirit will speak with the Father <u>for</u> you during times like these.

TRAINEE: How can He do that for me?

COACH: He knows the Father's mind completely, and He knows yours. He knows the content, motives, and intentions of your mind. The Father is God; the Son is God; the Holy Spirit is God; the three are One. The Holy Spirit is the presence of the Father and the Son with you, now.

TRAINEE: Dear Father, You know best; dear Jesus, You have bought the best for me; dear Holy Spirit, You deliver the Father's best.

WORD: **Then what am I to do? I will pray with my spirit [by the Holy Spirit that is within me] , . . . 1 Corinthians 14:15 AMP.B.**

And in the same way—by our faith—the Holy Spirit helps us with our daily problems and in our praying. For we don't even know what we should pray for nor how to pray as we should, but the Holy Spirit prays for us with such feeling that it cannot be expressed in words. And the Father who knows all hearts knows, of course, what the Spirit is saying as he pleads for us in harmony with God's own will. Romans 8:26-27 (TLB)

AUGUST 3

COURSE: PRAYING/RUNNING WITHOUT CEASING

TRAINEE: Folks think I'm crazy for praying and running so much; they see no evidence of any good.

COACH: Pray anyway; run anyway.

TRAINEE: How much and why?

WORD: Now Jesus was telling the disciples a parable to make the point that at all times they ought to pray and not give up *and* lose heart, saying, "In a certain city there was a judge who did not fear God and had no respect for man. There was a [desperate] widow in that city and she kept coming to him and saying, 'Give me justice *and* legal protection from my adversary.' For a time he would not; but later he said to himself, 'Even though I do not fear God nor respect man, yet because this widow *continues* to bother me, I will give her justice *and* legal protection; otherwise by continually coming she [will be an intolerable annoyance and she] will wear me out.'" Then the Lord said, "Listen to what the unjust judge says! And will not [our just] God defend *and* avenge His elect [His chosen ones] who cry out to Him day and night? Will He delay [in providing justice] on their behalf? I tell you that He will defend *and* avenge them quickly. However, when the Son of Man comes, will He find [this kind of persistent] faith on the earth?" Luke 18:1-8 Amplified Bible (AMP)

Be happy [in your faith] *and* rejoice *and* be glad-hearted continually (always); Be unceasing in prayer [praying perseveringly]; Thank [God] in everything [no matter what the circumstances may be, be thankful and give thanks], for this is the will of God for you [who are] in Christ Jesus [the Revealer and Mediator of that will]. 1 Thessalonians 5:16-18 (AMPC)

AUGUST 4

-continued-

For God is in all things working toward good for those who love Him and are called according to His purpose. Romans 8:28 [*Original Hebrew Text*]

TRAINEE: Well, if God is in all things causing them to work for my good, why should I pray?

COACH: Prayer prepares the soil of your soul for the seed of the Word, sown into your mind and cultivated by the Holy Spirit. Praying helps place you in God's will. This merging of wills creates a oneness that results in the flow of the Holy Spirit's power and presence through you as you pray for people and concerns. Therefore, pray in all things continually.

TRAINEE: I have to keep starting over in prayer; and, I need a model to go by.

COACH: <u>Always</u> start your conversation with the Father by being confessional—honest. This will, then, lead you into *"moments-of-truth"* as you see *"eye-to-eye."* Use the prayer Jesus taught His disciples to pray as your model on what and how to pray; let each petition of that prayer become a meditative mantra for your mind. That will open you to your listening role in prayer, conversation, with the Father.

WORD: **He would not have listened if I had not confessed my sins.** Psalm 66:18 Living Bible (TLB)

And when you pray, you shall not be like the hypocrites. For they love to pray standing in the synagogues and on the corners of the streets, that they may be seen by men . . . But you, when you pray, . . . pray to your Father who *is* in the secret *place;* and your Father who sees in secret will reward you openly . . . For your Father knows the things you have need of before you ask Him. In this manner, therefore, pray: [*The Lord's Prayer follows*]. Matthew 6:5-13 NKJV

AUGUST 5

COURSE: REGAINING CONFIDENCE AND SELF-RESPECT.

TRAINEE: When I allow myself to feel the weight of the wreck I've made in this life, it's too much to lift or carry.

COACH: Your training for the months of <u>Discontent</u> and <u>Water</u> spoke most profoundly to your 'weight' problem. For now, this month of <u>hope</u>, allow yourself to identify with another who felt exactly like you.

WORD: **For I do not understand my own actions [I am baffled and bewildered by them]. I do not practice what I want *to do*, but I am doing the very thing I hate [and yielding to my human nature, my worldliness—my sinful capacity]. Now if I *habitually* do what I do not want to do, [that means] I agree with the Law, *confessing* that it is good (morally excellent). So now [if that is the case, then] it is no longer I who do it [the disobedient thing which I despise], but the sin [nature] which lives in me . . . For the good that I want to do, I do not do, but I practice the very evil that I do not want . . .**

So I find *it to be* the law [of my inner self], that evil is present in me, the one who wants to do good. For I joyfully delight in the law of God in my inner self [with my new nature], but I see a different law *and* rule of action in the members of my body [in its appetites and desires], waging war against the law of my mind *and* subduing me and making me a prisoner of the law of sin which is within my members. Wretched *and* miserable man that I am! Who will [rescue me and] set me free from this body of death [this corrupt, mortal existence]? Thanks be to God [for my deliverance] through Jesus Christ our Lord! So then, on the one hand I myself with my mind serve the law of God, but on the other, with my flesh [my human nature, my worldliness, my sinful capacity—I serve] the law of sin. Romans 7:15-25 Amplified Bible (AMP)

AUGUST 6

-continued-

COACH: Could you have made the '*weight*' sound any heavier?

TRAINEE: No, I guess not.

COACH: When your arch enemy, the Accuser, tries to freshen your memory concerning failures and sins, use the name of Jesus on him. This will restore your mind to a mountain top perspective of the '*wreck*.' You need that view so you can rise from the valley of "discontent." Climb and give Jesus the cumbersome weights from your pack.

WORD: **Cast your burden on the LORD [release it] and He will sustain *and* uphold you; He will never allow the righteous to be shaken (slip, fall, fail).** Psalm 55:22 (AMP)

Come to Me, all *you* who labor and are heavy laden, and I will give you rest. Take My yoke upon you and learn from Me, for I am gentle and lowly in heart, and you will find rest for your souls. For My yoke *is* easy and My burden is light." Matthew 11:28-30 (NKJV)

TRAINEE: What steps do I take in shifting this weight to Jesus?

COACH: Any physical, mental, emotional, spiritual, relational, circumstantial burden God allows you to keep is for a reason—much like a physician who effects a cure, allowing only the necessary pain. Shift the remaining weight to Jesus by quietly trusting Him—letting your trust grow in God 'til you know a quiet confidence and a new self-respect centered on how much God loves you.

WORD: **For the Lord GOD, the Holy One of Israel has said this,**

"In returning [to Me] and rest you shall be saved,
In quietness and confident trust is your strength."
But you were not willing . . . Isaiah 30:15 (AMP)

AUGUST 7

COURSE: LEARNING BIG THINGS THROUGH THE PRACTICE OF LITTLE THINGS.

TRAINEE: I want to do great things for people and be a '*hero of the faith.*'

COACH: You are now a '*babe in the faith*' and growing up in the faith will require daily bread [The Word].

TRAINEE: Take me a step deeper into the growth-Word connection.

COACH: The Holy Spirit knows your mind and personality [soul] completely; trust Him in this. You will discover that what you do in the small, daily tasks are what most often either antagonize or attract others. Perform—as a SFC [*Servant First Class*]—the simple duties; drop your anxious watch for answers to your prayers for big things. Learn of God's will in the small, simple things; this will fit you for the larger desires of your heart. To learn of Him is to move from baby food to the richer protein of His Word.

WORD: **Delight yourself in the LORD, And He will give you the desires *and* petitions of your heart.** Psalm 37:4 (AMP)

His lord said unto him, Well done, thou good and faithful servant: thou hast been faithful over a few things, I will make thee ruler over many things: enter thou into the joy of thy lord. Matthew 25:21 King James Version (KJV)

TRAINEE: I need to let His Word be settled in my mind and heart before anything worthwhile comes from my hands.

COACH: Yes. And when the Word begins to stir your heart to serve others in love, let Psalm 25:14-22 be a guide for applying yourself to that service. Remember Who it is that sent you; you are actually serving Him!

AUGUST 8

COURSE: DISCOVERING GOD'S PLANS FOR ME

WORD: **For I know the plans *and* thoughts that I have for you,' says the LORD, 'plans for peace *and* well-being and not for disaster, to give you a future and a hope. Then you will call on Me and you will come and pray to Me, and I will hear [your voice] *and* I will listen to you. Then [with a deep longing] you will seek Me *and* require Me [as a vital necessity] and [you will] find Me when you search for Me with all your heart.** Jeremiah 29:11-13 (AMP)

TRAINEE: I want to be all I can be. God seems to know me well enough to help make this happen?

WORD: **Before I formed you in the womb I knew you [and approved of you as My chosen instrument], And before you were born I consecrated you to Myself as My own]; I have appointed you as a prophet to the nations."** Jeremiah 1:5 (AMP)

For from the very beginning God decided that those who came to him—and all along he knew who would—should become like his Son, so that his Son would be the First, with many brothers. And having chosen us, he called us to come to him; and when we came, he declared us "not guilty," filled us with Christ's goodness, gave us right standing with himself, and promised us his glory. Romans 8:29-30 (TLB)

COACH: The Father's knowledge and love of you is complete; **practice** remembering this. He has a plan for your life. You frustrate that plan if you neglect the exercise [s] of today while worrying about the course for tomorrow.

WORD: **This plan of mine is not what you would work out, neither are my thoughts the same as yours! For just as the heavens are higher than the earth, so are my ways higher than yours, and my thoughts than yours.** Isaiah 55:8-9 (TLB)

AUGUST 9

COURSE: LUST ADDICTION/SEX AS SUBSTANCE ABUSE

TRAINEE: I'm a 'womanizer.'

COACH: Yes, you are. So was King David, but the Father saw him in his future as different.

TRAINEE: Does He see me different, too?

COACH: He sees you, through the power of His Son on the Cross, as transformed, healed and redeemed.

TRAINEE: So how do we train me to <u>be</u> different?

COACH: This is a tough course; listen first to the toughness of the Word.

WORD: **Thou shalt not commit adultery.** Exodus 20:14 (KJV)

Ye have heard that it was said by them of old time, Thou shalt not commit adultery: But I say unto you, That whosoever looketh on a woman to lust after her hath committed adultery with her already in his heart. Matthew 5:27-28 (KJV)

. . . on that day when, as my gospel proclaims, God will judge the secrets [all the hidden thoughts and concealed sins] of men through Christ Jesus Romans 2:16 (AMP)

Let there be no sex sin, impurity or greed among you. Let no one be able to accuse you of any such things. Ephesians 5:3 (TLB) [see, also, Pr. 6:25-26, Rom. 1:24, Jer. 2:19]

TRAINEE: This is too much! I am who I am! A leopard cannot change his spots.

COACH: That is not all of My Word. Listen to its continued toughness.

-continued-

AUGUST 10

WORD: **Listen to me, young men, and not only listen but obey; don't let your desires get out of hand; don't let yourself think about her. Don't go near her; stay away from where she walks, lest she tempt you and seduce you. For she has been the ruin of multitudes—a vast host of men have been her victims. If you want to find the road to hell, look for her house.** Proverbs 7:24-27 (TLB) [see, also, Pr. 7. 6-23; 9:13-18]

Therefore do not let sin reign in your mortal body so that you obey its lusts *and* passions. Do not go on offering members of your body to sin as instruments of wickedness. But offer yourselves to God . . . For sin will no longer be a master over you, since you are not under Law [as slaves], but under [unmerited] grace [as recipients of God's favor and mercy]. Romans 6:12-14 (AMP)

. . . The body is not intended for sexual immorality, but for the Lord, and the Lord is for the body [to save, sanctify, and raise it again because of the sacrifice of the cross] . . . Do you not know that your bodies are members of Christ? Am I therefore to take the members of Christ and make them part of a prostitute? Certainly not! Do you not know that the one who joins himself to a prostitute is one body *with her*? For He says, "The two shall be one flesh." But the one who is united *and* joined to the Lord is one spirit *with Him*. Run away from sexual immorality [in any form, whether thought or behavior, whether visual or written]. Every *other* sin that a man commits is outside the body, but the one who is sexually immoral sins against his own body. Do you not know that your body is a temple of the Holy Spirit who is within you, whom you have [received as a gift] from God, and that you are not your own [property]? You were bought with a price [you were actually purchased with the precious blood of Jesus and made His own]. So then, honor *and* glorify God with your body. 1 Cor. 6:13b, 15-20 (AMP. B.)

AUGUST 11

-continued-

TRAINEE: Heavy! Again, how do we train me to be different?

COACH: Your mind is like a computer; its contents can be both programmed or deleted. True wisdom [*fear: (great awe and respect) of the Lord*] begins in training your mind on the Father's Word. As you see, that Word will continue to discipline you to achieve change and growth [*repentance.*]

WORD: **In particular, I want to urge you in the name of the Lord, not to go on living the aimless kind of life that the pagans live. Intellectually they are in the dark, and they are estranged from the life of God, without knowledge because they have shut their hearts to it. Their sense of right and wrong dulled, they have abandoned themselves to sexuality and eagerly pursue a career of indecency of every kind. Now that is hardly the way you have learned from Christ, unless you failed to hear Him properly when you were taught what the truth is in Jesus. You must give up your old way of life; you must put aside your old self, which gets corrupted by illusory desires. Your mind must be renewed by a spiritual revolution so that you can put on the new self that has been created in God's way, in the goodness and holiness of the truth.** Ephesians 4:17-24 JB [see, also, Romans 12:2]

For as he thinketh in his heart, so is he: . . . Pr 23:7 KJV

My son, keep my words, And treasure my commands within you. Keep my commands and live, And my law as the apple of your eye. Bind them on your fingers; Write them on the tablet of your heart. Say to wisdom, "You *are* my sister," And call understanding *your* nearest kin, That they may keep you from the immoral woman, From the seductress *who* flatters with her words. Proverbs 7:1-5 (NKJV)

-continued-

AUGUST 12

COACH: So, what's on your <u>mind</u>? You are spirit, you have a mind, and you live in a body. In relating to other people, we need to train and renew your mind to love the <u>person</u> who lives in the house [*body*], not just the house. You do not have to be a prisoner to your thoughts—thoughts that mistakenly see the enemy's glitter unfolding from the macrocosmic universe of multiple relationships [*houses/bodies*] as more desirable than the microcosm of one mate [*person within the house*]. All that glitters is not gold.

TRAINEE: I know; it's like the old mountaineer's used to say: "You can't keep the birds from flying over your head, but you sure can keep them from building a nest in your hair."

COACH: Not a bad way to describe your new freedom of the mind. If that freedom wanes, look to Jesus to "make His strength perfect in (your) weakness." Thank Him, using your faith gift, in advance for what your mind does not yet see. The deceiver's suggestions of forbidden fruit are temporary pleasures and always rob joy. Sex is not a three-letter word for sin; it can be a beautiful celebration of the marriage—the Father's creative gift.

WORD: **Casting down imaginations, and every high thing that exalteth itself against the knowledge of God, and bringing into captivity every thought to the obedience of Christ;** 2 Corinthians 10:5 (KJV) [see, also, Pr. 4:23-27; Pr. 5:15-21]

So be careful how you act; these are difficult days. Don't be fools; be wise: make the most of every opportunity you have for doing good. [17] **Don't act thoughtlessly, but try to find out and do whatever the Lord wants you to.** Ephesians 5:15-18 (TLB)

"'Then it will be as though I had sprinkled clean water on you, for you will be clean—your filthiness will be washed away, your idol worship gone.

-continued-

AUGUST 13

And I will give you a new heart—I will give you new and right desires—and put a new spirit within you. I will take out your stony hearts of sin and give you new hearts of love. Ezekiel 36:25-26 Living Bible (TLB)

I advise you to obey only the Holy Spirit's instructions. He will tell you where to go and what to do, and then you won't always be doing the wrong things your evil nature wants you to. For we naturally love to do evil things that are just the opposite from the things that the Holy Spirit tells us to do; and the good things we want to do when the Spirit has his way with us are just the opposite of our natural desires. These two forces within us are constantly fighting each other to win control over us, and our wishes are never free from their pressures.

But when you follow your own wrong inclinations, your lives will produce these evil results: impure thoughts, eagerness for lustful pleasure, But when the Holy Spirit controls our lives he will produce this kind of fruit in us: love, joy, peace, patience, kindness, goodness, faithfulness, Galatians 5:16-17, 19, 22 (TLB)

TRAINEE: I'm deciding to trust You to work with my mind—helping me move my thoughts in this mental 'marathon'—just as You help me decide to move my legs in physical marathons, using the *"nevertheless of faith."*

COACH: Again, standing tall over all these Words confronting your sinfulness stands the Word secured by the Cross:

WORD: **If we say that we have no sin, we deceive ourselves, and the truth is not in us. If we confess our sins, he is faithful and just to forgive us our sins, and to cleanse us from all unrighteousness.** 1 John 1:8-9 (KJV)

AUGUST 14

COURSE: THE WISDOM OF OBEDIENCE

COACH: Obedience is the beginning of wisdom.

WORD: **Give instruction to a wise man, and he will be yet wiser: teach a just man, and he will increase in learning.**

The fear of the LORD is the beginning of wisdom: and the knowledge of the holy is understanding.

For by me thy days shall be multiplied, and the years of thy life shall be increased.

If thou be wise, thou shalt be wise for thyself: but if thou scornest, thou alone shalt bear it. Proverbs 9:9-12 (KJV)

The fear of the LORD *leads* to life, And *he who has it* will abide in satisfaction; He will not be visited with evil. Proverbs 19:23 (NKJV)

TRAINEE: How is being afraid of God a beginning of wisdom?

COACH: The original Word for fear, used in the Hebrew language, does not mean fear in sense of being afraid of a rattle-snake; it means to have a great awe and respect.

TRAINEE: As I consider respect for God, what do I see first?

COACH: Take the very Name of God; the Hebrew Old Testament Word for God is Yahweh and translates: "*I am Who I am.*" Recall, still again, when Moses went to Egypt to lead Israel out of bondage, he asked God who he should say sent him. God answered: "Tell them '*I am*' sent you." When speaking to His disciples of His identity, Jesus said: "*before Abraham was, I am.*" Also, think on this: God created out of nothing—"creatio- ex-nihilo." When Jesus was asked by those seeking to arrest Him, "Are You the Christ," He answered by saying: "*I am.*" When He spoke that answer, His opponents fell to the ground as though dead.

-continued-

AUGUST 15

TRAINEE: That's too deep for my mind. Why is wisdom so great?

COACH: Do you remember what Solomon chose when asked to choose one thing among anything he could have?

TRAINEE: Wisdom. But, why was the Father so pleased with that choice that He, also, gave Solomon a multitude of other riches?

COACH: To choose wisdom is to choose <u>love</u> of the Father's Word, which **is** His very Own Son, Jesus. Meditate deeply on the following Word!

WORD: **In the beginning was the Word, and the Word was with God, and the Word was God. The same was <u>in</u> the beginning with God. All things were made by him<u>; and</u> without him was not <u>any thing</u> made that was made. In him was life<u>; and</u> the life was the light of men . . . And the Word was made flesh, and dwelt among us, (and we beheld his glory, the glory as of the only begotten of the Father,) full of grace and truth.** John 1:1-4, 14 (KJV)

COACH: Read what Jesus said to the Father in His High Priestly prayer to the Father right before He was arrested in the Garden of Gethsemane.

WORD: **And now, O Father, glorify Me together with Yourself, with the glory which I had with You before the world was.**

"Father, I desire that they also whom You gave Me may be with Me where I am, that they may behold My glory which You have given Me; for You loved Me before the foundation of the world. John 17:5, 24 (NKJV)

TRAINEE: I'm beginning to see the connection between Word and Jesus; how does wisdom fit in?

-continued-

AUGUST 16

COACH: Wisdom, in the Old Testament, is a personification of Jesus, the Word. It is all in all. The following Words will deepen your understanding.

WORD: **Can't you hear the voice of wisdom? She is standing at the city gates and at every fork in the road, and at the door of every house. Listen to what she says: . . . Listen to me! For I have important information for you. Everything I say is right and true, . . . My words are plain and clear to anyone with half a mind—if it is only open! My instruction is far more valuable than silver or gold." . . . Those who love and follow me are indeed wealthy. I fill their treasuries. The Lord formed me in the beginning, before he created anything else. From ages past, I am. I existed before the earth began. I lived before the oceans were created, before the springs bubbled forth their waters onto the earth; before the mountains and the hills were made. Yes, I was born before God made the earth and fields and the first handfuls of soil.**

I was there when he established the heavens and formed the great springs in the depths of the oceans. I was there when he set the limits of the seas and gave them his instructions not to spread beyond their boundaries. I was there when he made the blueprint for the earth and oceans. I was the craftsman at his side. I was his constant delight, rejoicing always in his presence. And how happy I was with what he created—his wide world and all his family of mankind! And so, young men, listen to me, for how happy are all who follow my instructions. Proverbs 8:1-3, 6, 9-10, 21-32 Living Bible (TLB) [see, also, Pr. 3:13-19; 4:6-13; 9:1-3, 9-12]

TRAINEE: When God said: *"Let there be,"* wisdom was the *"craftsman at His side."*

AUGUST 17

COURSE: REACHING/FULFILLING HIGHEST NEEDS

TRAINEE: Again, to borrow a military phrase, I want to *"be all I can be!"*

COACH: Great minds in the field of psychology agree that people have a hierarchy of needs, ranging from: physical, safety, belonging, esteem, performance needs.

TRAINEE: I need for God to speak to these needs with His Word.

COACH: If the Father feeds the sparrows and clothes the lilies of the fields, will He not provide for your basic needs? Read all of the Word in Matthew 6:25-33, especially verse 33.

WORD: **But seek ye first the kingdom of God, and his righteousness; and all these things shall be added unto you.** Matthew 6:33 (KJV)

COACH: Solomon had a lot of 'other things' added to his life, didn't he? Trusting God, your identity, self-worth, is rooted not so much in "who" you are but in the realization of "Whose" you are!

TRAINEE: The Cross forms my new identity as I see me standing there.

COACH: Read John 17; let each Word of Jesus's High Priestly Prayer deeply soak into your mind and heart, especially the part where He asked the Father to secure your true identity in Him!

WORD: **. . . that they all may be one, as You, Father, *are* in Me, and I in You; that they also may be one in Us, that the world may believe that You sent Me. And the glory which You gave Me I have given them, that they may be one just as We are one: I in them, and You in Me; that they may be made perfect in one, and that the world may know that You have sent Me, and have loved them as You have loved Me.** John 17:21-23 (NKJV)

AUGUST 18

COURSE: DEVELOPING SPIRITUAL MUSCLES - STEPS OF FAITH

TRAINEE: I don't feel like practicing any of these runs: physical, mental, or spiritual.

COACH: These are the times you have to let go and say: '*I now run on faith, period.*' This faith must be a choice, a <u>decision</u> you make over against feelings.

TRAINEE: But I want to know how exactly God is going to help me with these runs. I want to see my future—the missing pieces of the puzzle.

COACH: That's for God to know and you to find out. Run the present mile; you do not need the weight of the remaining miles. Hindsight will allow you to see His intervening steps in your running.

TRAINEE: This is hard!

COACH:	I know, but it's God's way. Run by faith and not by sight. Your training in the Month of August will center your exercise on the hope that arises through such faith. The '*child within you*' must learn to use the '*faith-0-scope*' of a trusting relationship with the Father. You have yet to train on the courses laid out for the months of memory and praise.
TRAINEE:	Why so much?
COACH:	So the weight of your prayers can be matched by this spiritual muscle. "Now faith is the assurance (the confirmation, the title deed) of the things [we] hope for . . ." Hebrews 11:1 AMP.B.

AUGUST 19

COURSE:	RECONCILING GOD'S JUSTICE WITH HIS LOVE
TRAINEE:	I have trouble dealing with God as a loving Father, so severe with His children in the days of the Old Testament, allowing so many of them to be killed.
COACH:	Read the whole book of Hosea where God describes Himself as a husband and Israel as an unfaithful wife. Take note of how he constantly told the Israelites the consequences of their pursuit of '*other gods.*' God is a just God; this means wrongdoing requires punishment.
TRAINEE:	But why did the people of the '*Old Testament days*' have so much rougher punishment than we do?
COACH:	You, living the *New Testament days*, have been given a new agreement or covenant with God. It helps motivate you to obey Him more than the old one.
TRAINEE:	I don't understand.
COACH:	When the time was ripe [Mark 1:15], the Father poured out His love in an amazing way. Would you raise your hand and volunteer to take the punishment that your brothers and sisters, or even your enemies, deserved?
TRAINEE:	No way!

COACH: That's the arrangement Jesus and the Father worked out before the very foundation of the earth.

TRAINEE: He was thinking about me and my need for His forgiveness even before creation itself?

COACH: Let His Word describe for you His plans. Tomorrow's exercise will unfold the Old Testament, New Testament covenants, and how the New Testament fulfills the Old Testament.

AUGUST 20

-continued-

TRAINEE: I'm ready.

COACH: Read the prophetic Word given to the people of the Old Testament [old covenant] and an expressive Word about the people under the New Testament [new covenant].

WORD: **"Behold, the days are coming," says the LORD, "when I will make a new covenant with the house of Israel (the Northern Kingdom) and with the house of Judah (the Southern Kingdom), not like the covenant which I made with their fathers in the day when I took them by the hand to bring them out of the land of Egypt, My covenant which they broke, although I was a husband to them," says the LORD.**

              But this is the covenant which I will make with the house of Israel after those days," says the LORD, "I will put My law within them, and I will write it on their hearts; and I will be their God, and they will be My people. Jeremiah 31:31-33 (AMP)

              You show that you are a letter from Christ, delivered by us, written not with ink but with the Spirit of the living God, not on tablets of stone but on tablets of human hearts. 2 Corinthians 3:3 (AMP)

TRAINEE: How will what's *"written on my heart"* from the New Covenant hold the power to motivate or move me into obedience?

WORD:	**God showed how much he loved us by sending his only Son into this wicked world to bring to us eternal life through his death. In this act we see what real love is: it is not our love for God but his love for us when he sent his Son to satisfy God's anger against our sins.** 1 John 4:9-10 (TLB)
TRAINEE:	I'm loved that much?
COACH:	Yes, you are!

AUGUST 21

COURSE:	DOUBT, THIEF OF GOD'S BLESSINGS
WORD:	**For verily I say unto you, That whosoever shall say unto this mountain, Be thou removed, and be thou cast into the sea; and shall not doubt in his heart, but shall believe that those things which he saith shall come to pass; he shall have whatsoever he saith. Therefore I say unto you, What things so ever ye desire, when ye pray, believe that ye receive them, and ye shall have them.** Mark 11:23-24 (KJV)
COACH:	This Word will not work with doubt in your heart.
TRAINEE:	How do I tackle the doubt problem?
WORD:	**So then faith *comes* by hearing, and hearing by the word of God.** Romans 10:17 NKJV
COACH:	Why did Peter, one of Jesus's closest disciples, step out on the water but then start doubting? He took His eyes off Jesus and centered them on the water.
WORD:	**And immediately Jesus stretched out *His* hand and caught him, and said to him, "O you of little faith, why did you doubt?"** Matthew 14:31 (NKJV)
COACH:	Another faith event found Jesus pleased. Read about the centurion [Mathew 8:5-10, 13].
TRAINEE:	If I'm going to receive God's greater blessings, I need to keep my eyes off circumstances and feelings and keep them fixed on Jesus [The Word].

WORD: **So then faith *comes* by hearing, and hearing by the word of God.**
          Romans 10:17 NKJV

TRAINEE: I sense the Holy Spirit and the Word coaching me on the truth.

AUGUST 22

COURSE: HEAD FAITH OR HEART FAITH

COACH: You place natural faith in what your physical senses tell you: e.g., looking before starting across the street. Faith, a trusting relationship with God, comes from His Word. Read how Abraham exercised faith in God's promise to be a father of many nations when he didn't <u>see</u> any nations [Romans 4:17-21]

TRAINEE: But Abraham was a great patriarch of old and could have great faith.

COACH: You are telling me that, since you are not like Abraham, you can't have faith. Read and head:

WORD: **So understand that it is the people who live by faith [with confidence in the power and goodness of God] who are [the true] sons of Abraham. And if you belong to Christ [if you are in Him], then you are Abraham's descendants, and [spiritual] heirs according to [God's] promise.** Galatians 3:7, 29 (AMP)

          In hope against hope Abraham believed that he would become a father of many nations, as he had been promised [by God]: "So [numberless] shall your descendants be." Romans 4:18 (AMP)

COACH: Faith begins where the will of God is known. Find Scriptures that harmonize with your faith. Abraham did not go by what his physical senses told him; he simply believed what God had said.

TRAINEE: If I pray, for example, about my financial needs, will God hear and answer?

WORD: **But my God shall supply all your need according to his riches in glory by Christ Jesus.** Philippians 4:19 (KJV)

AUGUST 23

COURSE: FAITH OR HOPE

COACH: If you say, "I'll believe God if He answers my prayers, you are practicing hope. How big is the word "*all*" in the next verse?

WORD: **And we know [with great confidence] that God [who is deeply concerned about us] causes all things to work together [as a plan] for good for those who love God, to those who are called according to His plan *and* purpose.** Romans 8:28 (AMP)

TRAINEE: Can I see some evidence when I pray?

COACH: Practice trusting Him when you don't see anything. Recall: "*assurance of things hoped for; conviction of things not seen.*" God used Abraham as an example of this kind of faith.

WORD: **These men of faith I have mentioned died without ever receiving all that God had promised them; but they saw it all awaiting them on ahead and were glad, for they agreed that this earth was not their real home but that they were just strangers visiting down here.** Hebrews 11:13 (TLB)

TRAINEE: What will strengthen my faith to carry out such practice?

COACH: The practice of praise. Your training in October will show you the relationship between praising and trusting God.

TRAINEE: Can You give me a taste of that relationship?

COACH: The more you thank God, the more you trust Him; the more you trust Him, the more room He has to work for your good—answering your prayers as He says He can:

WORD: **Now to Him who is able to do exceedingly abundantly above all that we ask or think, according to the power that works in us,** Ephesians 3:20N (NKJV)

AUGUST 24

COURSE: THE HOPE OF IMMORTALITY

TRAINEE: Why do we believe there is life after death? Where did that feeling inside us come from?

COACH: God put it in you. He has *"set eternity in the hearts of men."* Ecclesiastes 3:11 [see, also, Romans 1:20; Hebrews 11:10; 2 Corinthians 5:1] The resurrection is proof of death's defeat.

WORD: **Jesus said to her, "I am the resurrection and the life. He who believes in Me, though he may die, he shall live. And whoever lives and believes in Me shall never die. Do you believe this?"** John 11:25-26 (NKJV)

  Let not your heart be troubled; you believe in God, believe also in Me. In My Father's house are many mansions; if *it were* not *so,* I would have told you. I go to prepare a place for you. John 14:1-2 NKJV

  Because I live, you will live also. John 14:19 NKJV

TRAINEE: How vast a place is Heaven?

COACH: The Kingdom of Heaven has no limit or end to It, all light and joy; joy in Heaven when man was created [Job 38:7]; joy when one sinner repents [Luke 15:7]; it is a place of reunion. Moses and Elijah had been dead to earthly life for hundreds of years before they appeared with Jesus on the Mount of Transfiguration.

WORD: **And I say unto you, That many shall come from the east and west, and shall sit down with Abraham, and Isaac, and Jacob, in the kingdom of heaven.** Matthew 8:11 (KJV)

  . . . for I know whom I have believed, and am persuaded that he is able to keep that which I have committed unto him against that day. 2 Timothy 1:12 KJV

AUGUST 25

COURSE: WHO IS JESUS?

WORD: **And there is salvation in no one else; for there is no other name under heaven that has been given among people by which we must be saved [for God has provided the world no alternative for salvation].**" Acts 4:12 (AMP)

COACH: In John 1:1-14, you see the answer to the question. Jesus is God. He lived and died and rose. Great historians such as Tacitus and Josephus wrote of these events, which are confirmed facts of history.

TRAINEE: Describe His nature to me.

COACH: Only in Jesus do you find the characteristics you would expect in God if He were to become a man. His intellect confounded the greatest minds of His day. His frankness confronted the religious "leaders" of that day of their hypocrisy. Read the account of the repentant prostitute and the prominent religious leader named Simon [Luke 7:39-49]. His forgiveness reached even His enemies; as they crucified Him, He asked the Father to forgive them. His moral authority caused even those who were plotting against Him to return to their superiors stating: "**Never did a man speak the way this man speaks.**" [John 7:46] "**The multitudes were amazed at His teaching; for He was teaching them as one having authority, and not as their scribes.**" [Matthew 7:28-29] Read what St. Paul wrote about Him:

WORD: **Let this mind be in you which was also in Christ Jesus, who, being in the form of God, did not consider it robbery to be equal with God, but made Himself of no reputation, taking the form of a bondservant,** *and* **coming in the likeness of men.** Philippians 2:5-7 NKJV

COACH: Jesus: omniscient; omnipresent; omnipotent; way, truth, life

WORD: "**I and the Father are one.**" [John 10:30]

AUGUST 26

COURSE: FAITH OR HOPE—ANOTHER LOOK

COACH: You can never place your hope too high because of the message of the *empty tomb*. Recall that the Apostle Paul stated the three greatest values in life are faith, hope, and love. He made it clear that, of those three, love is the greatest. What is different about faith and hope?

TRAINEE: Hope looks to the future.

COACH: And faith looks to the present. Think on the Word "Now" in the following Scripture; it is a word of time or tense. Next, center your mind on the Words "substance and evidence." Note that they are centered on a present reality. Faith is phrased in terms of the present and even the past. Faith allows you to be assured of your hope. After meditating on these verses, read and think on all of chapter 11; it is full of examples of the faith exercise.

WORD: **Now faith is the substance of things hoped for; the evidence of things not seen . . . By faith we understand that the worlds were framed by the word of God, so that the things which are seen were not made of things which are visible . . .** Hebrews 11:1-3 NKJV

TRAINEE: Are there other Words that address faith in this manner?

WORD: **Therefore I say unto you, what things so ever ye desire, when ye pray, believe that ye receive them, and ye shall have them.** Mark 11:24 NKJV

                Now this is the confidence that we have in Him, that if we ask anything according to His will, He hears us. And if we know He hears us, whatever we ask, we know that we have the petitions that we have asked of Him. 1 John 5:14-15 NKJV

TRAINEE: I need steps to take linking my prayers with this gift.

AUGUST 27

-continued-

COACH: The Gospel is very clear about the steps you are to take in using His gift of faith—the "*measure of faith*" He has given to each of His children.

Step one: see what His Word says concerning your prayer.

Second: place your belief/faith in that Word.

Third: let your feelings celebrate what the Word says and what your heart knows—keeping in mind that faith is not a feeling but a <u>decision</u> to trust Him at His Word, sometimes over against feelings.

TRAINEE: But it is so natural for me to begin with feelings.

COACH: When this is your response to Him, you are really saying that you trust your feelings and not His Word. God tells you to begin with His Word. The clash between feelings and the Word needs to be there. Recall Abraham's faith; now contrast it to "Thomas faith." When the disciples told Thomas about the resurrection of Jesus, he said he would not believe unless he touched Him. So, when Jesus came back, He had Thomas place his hand in His hands and His side. Crushed, Thomas fell and said, "My Lord and my God." Jesus said to him: "Thomas, do not be faithless but believing. You have believed because you have seen; blessed are those who have not seen and yet believe." [see John 20:24-29; Romans 4:17]

TRAINEE: How does this difference between "Abraham faith" and "Thomas faith" affect me?

COACH: Are you going to let circumstances and feelings be the boss of your decisions, words, and actions? You remember the account of Peter in the boat on the Sea of Galilee; he saw Jesus on the water and asked permission to come to Him. When Jesus said: "Yes, Peter, come forth," Peter began stepping out with Abraham faith, walking on the water. How? He was standing on the Word Jesus gave.

-continued-

AUGUST 28

Then Peter started looking at his circumstances and feelings, which were not firm enough to hold him up.

TRAINEE: I still need some encouragement that I can make a faith decision. How do I, by an act of my will, choose to stand on God's Word?

COACH: St. John presents "children of Abraham [John 8:37-40;" that is part of your inheritance because you who have been given "the measure of faith." God's Holy Spirit begins to speak to your human spirit—that part of you that can wrestle with feelings and doubt.

TRAINEE: I've got to be realistic and consider circumstances and feelings.

COACH: God's Word never puts down feelings; He created them, too, but they need to be placed in their proper relationship to faith. After describing His Word as working like the rain and snow in the production of crops, He says:

WORD: **So shall My word be that goes forth from My mouth; it shall not return to me void, but it shall accomplish what I please, and it shall prosper in the thing for which I sent it.** Isaiah 55:10-11 NKJV

TRAINEE: His Word then never comes back to Him empty handed.

COACH: In the beginning, God sent out His Word the first time to create the world; He can send it out again to re-create; this applies to your prayers. Use your imagination for a minute. Picture a big, complicated mass of puzzle pieces—huge, cumbersome; and you can't even begin to find a piece to match, not even the first one. God is the one capable of redeeming circumstances in the puzzles of our lives—back together in His hand. You may not recognize it at first, but He works a little bit up here, a little down here, and at some point, you begin to see "yes, He's put part of it—moved some of the pieces—together."

-continued-

AUGUST 29

Now, all is together, but there is one piece missing. You look everywhere and just can't find it. God knows where that missing piece is; with His redeeming will he knows when and how to put the missing pieces of your life back together. To best answer your question on how to trade Thomas faith for Abraham faith:

WORD: **So then faith cometh by hearing, and hearing by the word of God.** Romans 10:17 KJV

TRAINEE: In other words, God's Word is not only strong enough for me to stand on, It also builds up my faith.

COACH: Your thoughts, feelings, decisions can reach out and connect with your faith; faith that has been standing on His Word. Together, connected, they become the "evidence/conviction of things not seen, the assurance/substance of things hoped for"—no matter what circumstances or feelings are. This is the great *"nevertheless of faith"*!

TRAINEE: If I pray for God to build a hunger in me for His Word, I believe I can have confidence that I'm asking something that He wants and, therefore, will answer it.

COACH: Yes! Read what Peter wrote concerning a faith in God's Word that will guard your faith your hope.

WORD: **Blessed be the God and Father of our Lord Jesus Christ, who according to His abundant mercy has begotten us again to a living hope through the resurrection of Jesus Christ from the dead, to an inheritance incorruptible and undefiled and that does not fade away, reserved in heaven for you who are kept by the power of God through faith for salvation ready to be revealed in the last time.** 1 Peter 1:3-5 NKJV

AUGUST 30

COURSE: TRAINING DAILY ON THE WORD

COACH: The worn, torn, ragged Bible is usually owned by someone who isn't.

TRAINEE: But . . .

COACH: There are no 'buts' about it; train on the Word!

WORD: **For the Word that God speaks is alive and full of power—making it active, operative, energizing and effective; it is sharper than any two-edged sword, penetrating to the dividing line of the breath of life (soul) and [the immortal] spirit, and of joints and marrow [that is, of the deepest parts of our nature] exposing and sifting and analyzing and judging the very thoughts and purposes of the heart.** Hebrew 4:12 AMP. B.

COACH: Would you normally go a whole day without feeding your body or nurturing your mind?

TRAINEE: No

COACH: Well, your human spirit needs a daily diet, too.

WORD: **But He replied, It has been written, Man shall not live and be upheld and sustained by bread alone, but by every word that comes forth from the mouth of God.** Matthew 4:4 AMP. B. [see, also, Deuteronomy 8:3]

TRAINEE: How is a full year of 'taking in' God's Word going to train me?

WORD: **Spend your time and energy in the exercise of keeping spiritually fit. Bodily exercise is all right, but spiritual exercise is much more important and is a tonic for all you do. So exercise yourself spiritually and practice being a better Christian, because that will help you not only now in this life, but in the next life too. This is the truth and everyone should accept it.** 1 Timothy 4:7b-9 TLB

AUGUST 31

-continued-

TRAINEE: How exactly is this 'spiritual exercise' to take place?

COACH: Your part is to <u>meditatively read</u> the Word, letting the Word become the centering point [mantra] for your mind. Like a computer, your mind places into the memory banks what is programmed. The Holy Spirit can press the right 'keys'—bring up the 'Rhema-Word' [*see exercises for March 6 and July 27*] onto the screen of your mind—at the right time. Again, the following Word defines His work with the Word:

WORD: **As the rain and the snow come down from heaven, and do not return to it without watering the earth and making it bud and flourish, so that it yields seed for the sower and bread for the eater, so is my word that goes out from my mouth: It will not return to Me empty, but will accomplish what I desire and achieve the purpose for which I sent it.** Isaiah 55:10-11 NIV

    Every Scripture is God-breathed—given by His inspiration—and profitable for instruction, for reproof and conviction of sin, for correction of error and discipline in obedience, and for training in righteousness [that is, in holy living, in conformity to God's will in thought, purpose and action], so that the man of God may be complete and proficient, well-fitted and thoroughly equipped for every good work. 2 Timothy 3:16-17 AMP. B.

TRAINEE: His Word doesn't leave anything out; It lets me know that It knows me as I read and meditate on It.

COACH: A good understanding!

Month of Memories

COURSE:	THE MIND IN TRAINING AND IN HEALING
COACH:	Next time you try to resume piano playing or typing and your right hand nerve endings don't perform, give them verbal command to respond to your brain's signals.
TRAINEE:	Sounds weird, but here goes. [*After carried out*]: They're working; my fingers are rhythmically moving; my mental messages are connecting. Now, I remember the recent major medical university research which proved a connection between the central-autonomic nervous systems and the spoken word.
COACH:	God knows how He had made you. Before you can realize that your brain has sent a message to your foot to move, it is done.
TRAINEE:	What about my brain messages and my need to know Him?
COACH:	He knew the longing in you before you could acknowledge it yourself. Before you could realize that your brain had sent a message to your heart to move toward Him, He was already there—filling you to overflowing.
TRAINEE:	He knows me that well?
WORD:	**Then the word of the Lord came to me, saying: "Before I formed you in the womb I knew you;."** Jeremiah 1:4-5 NKJV [Read all of <u>Psalm 139</u>, slowly and thoughtfully!]
COACH:	You do not have to take steps to reach Him; you do not have to walk a fiery mile alone. You take His hand and He makes the steps for you. It is not a process of reaching a destination. Before you move your foot or your heart, He is there.
WORD:	**He will keep in perfect peace all those who trust in Him, whose thoughts turn often to the Lord.** Isaiah 26:3 TLB

SEPTEMBER 2

COURSE: REMEMBERING GOD'S BENEFITS

WORD: **Bless the Lord, O my soul, and forget not all His benefits**; . . . Psalm 103:2 NKJV

Blessed be the Lord, Who daily loads us with benefits, the God of our salvation! Psalm 68:19 NKJV

What shall I render to the Lord for all His benefits toward me? Psalm 116:12 NKJV

TRAINEE: I need to practice this memory.

COACH: It is a wise and helpful exercise, leading you deeper into your desire to be pleasing to Him with your obedience.

WORD: **Remember His marvelous works which He has done, His wonders, and the judgments of His mouth.** 1 Chronicles 16:12 NKJV

Remember now your Creator in the days of your youth, before the difficult days come, and the years draw near when you say, "I have no pleasure in them." Ecclesiastes 12:1 NKJV

Remember therefore from where you have fallen, repent . . . Revelation 2:5a NKJV

TRAINEE: Sometimes I think about the Kingdom of Heaven and imagine everyone there praising God for His Grace.

COACH: The glory of His Grace deserves praise coming from the very core of your being! The more you recall and celebrate His Grace to you while here on earth, the greater your desire to be in that Heavenly celebration. Recall, *"For as he thinks in his heart, so is he."* Proverbs 23:7a NKJV

SEPTEMBER 3

COURSE: THAT 'ALONE' TIME

TRAINEE: Every time I hit the pavement I run into that engulfing *'alone' time*, and sometimes I'm aware [sense] that I am not. Is there anyone watching?

COACH: The Father and the hosts of Heaven watch and applaud those times you put into practice the "nevertheless of faith." These times are *"moments of truth"* when His time merges with yours.

TRAINEE: Help me understand that last part about the two times merging.

COACH: There are two words in the original text of the Word for the word "time." One is "Chronos"—meaning measurable [*watch or calendar*] time; the other is "Kairos"—meaning unmeasurable, meaningful, filled-up, unending time: e.g., you say a minute seems like an hour, vice versa. Kairos is that Word from the Word that refers to the Kingdom. When you run the race by using the gift of faith in deciding your thoughts, your words, your actions—*forming moments of truth*—you step into the arena of His time, giving shape and direction for your time.

WORD: **"For He says, "At the acceptable time (the time of grace) I listened to you, And I helped you on the day of salvation." Behold, now is "the acceptable time," behold, now is "the day of salvation"**— 2 Corinthians 6:2 (AMP)

           "He made known to us the mystery of His will according to His good pleasure, which He purposed in Christ, with regard to the fulfillment of the times [that is, the end of history, the climax of the ages]—to bring all things together in Christ, [both] things in the heavens and things on the earth." Ephesians 1:9-10 (AMP)

SEPTEMBER 4

COURSE: TIME REDEEMED

COACH: God is in your future now. He is in your past now.

TRAINEE: How can this be?

COACH: Even His Name explains. As mentioned earlier, He told Moses that His Name is *"I Am."* The Hebrew word also means, "I will be Who I will be." As already noted, Jesus, when asked about His origin and identity, answered by saying, "<u>Before</u> Abraham was I <u>am</u>." God is not limited to space or time as we are.

TRAINEE: Can He work my past with my present and my future?

COACH: Pray for Him to heal your memories. September will train you long and well on this. He can use present relationships and events to exercise that healing—worked out in your future.

TRAINEE: Are you telling me that prayer about my past will make a difference in my present and future.

COACH: Yes, be expectant of God to act; there is nothing or no one He cannot redeem when He sees an open heart and mind.

TRAINEE: When I go to a redemption store, I often find something of value that others considered worthless. Is this along the lines of what He can do? I need a Word on this.

WORD: **"Now to Him who is able to [carry out His purpose and] do superabundantly more than all that we dare ask or think [infinitely beyond our greatest prayers, hopes, or dreams], according to His power that is at work within us,"** Ephesians 3:20 (AMP)

COACH: Pray for Him to help you see people and circumstances from the perspective of what He can do with them.

SEPTEMBER 5

COURSE: HEALING OF MARRIAGE AND FAMILY

TRAINEE: This looks absolutely impossible!

COACH: The Father does not recognize the word "impossible." He sees marriage and family as a permanent bond, capable of standing the tests of time, distance, and people.

WORD: **But Jesus looked at them and said, with men this in impossible, but all things are possible with God.** Matthew 19:26 AMP. B.

COACH: Remember that you and your wife are partners in receiving God's blessings. [see 1 Peter 3:7]

TRAINEE: I thought the wife is to submit to the husband as the head of the household in all things.

COACH: The Word directs the husband to see headship as love for the wife like Jesus [the Groom] has for the Church [the bride]. Again, it does not suggest that the husband can say "jump" expecting the wife to say "how high." The Father wants children from the union who belong to and follow Him. This gives them both roots and wings.

WORD: **For from the very first he made man and woman to be joined together permanently in marriage; therefore a man is to leave his father and mother, and he and his wife are united so that they are no longer two, but one.** Mark 10: 7-8 TLB

-continued-

SEPTEMBER 6

That is how husbands should treat their wives, loving them as parts of themselves. For since a man and his wife are now one, a man is really doing himself a favor and loving himself when he loves his wife! ... [That the husband and wife are one body is proved by the Scripture which says, "A man must leave his father and mother when he marries, so that he can be perfectly joined to his wife, and the two shall be one."] Ephesians 5:28, 31 TLB

TRAINEE: What if we see that bond as broken?

COACH: Re-read yesterday's training log. Simply ask that the Father build the desire of your heart for the marriage and family according to His perfect will. Your efforts to build that desire will cave in against the mountains ahead; but the Father's work will endure, leaving the mountains.

TRAINEE: What about the mountain 'unfaithfulness'?

COACH: Your arch enemy makes the macrocosmic universe of multiple relationships appear very attractive. The Father's truth is centered on the depth and fulfillment found in the microcosmic universe of faithful-honest marriage. Train well during the 'month of water'; those cleansing streams wash with forgiveness and renewal.

TRAINEE: What about divorce and remarriage; can a new marriage be of the Father's will?

COACH: Review the training exercise for January 5. Remarriage following divorce is not the Father's perfect will; it, however, can be His redeeming will.

SEPTEMBER 7

-continued-

His redeeming will is not a 'second class' will, either. Note the 'first class' forgiveness, redemption, salvation accomplished on the Cross.

TRAINEE: Now, consider this one! We all have free will to think, speak, act, feel, decide—using a diametrical 180 degrees from the Father's will.

COACH: Timely comment; rest well tonight. Tomorrow, re-connect with training days July 24-28 on freedom versus bondage of the will. Let the Cross event speak to your heart and spirit!

SEPTEMBER 8

COURSE: REMEMBER, REPENT AND RELATE TO GOD

TRAINEE: I need a summary of those repentance steps.

COACH: First step from the Word:

WORD: **Casting down imaginations, and every high thing that exalteth itself against the knowledge of God, and bringing into captivity every thought to the obedience of Christ; and having in a readiness to revenge all disobedience, when your obedience is fulfilled**. 2 Corinthians 10:5-6 KJV

COACH: NKJV reads *"readiness to revenge"* as *"ready to punish all disobedience."* This step stops sin in its tracks, freeing you to not make plans to sin—sparing you the evil consequences of it.

COACH: Second step from the Word:

WORD: **For if you live according to (the dictates of) the flesh you will surely die. But if through the power of the (Holy) Spirit you are habitually putting to death—making extinct, deadening—the (evil) deeds prompted by the body, you shall (really and genuinely) live forever.** (Rom. 8:13 AMP)

COACH: This step protects you from conditioning your mind by sinful activities—saves you from missing out on God's best.

COACH: The third step from the Word:

WORD: **I have been crucified with Christ; it is no longer I who live, but Christ lives in me; and the life which I now live in the flesh I live by faith in the Son of God, who loved me and gave Himself for me.** Galatians 2:20 NKJV

SEPTEMBER 9

-continued-

COACH: Most crucifixion deaths were caused by suffocation. Just like water replaces the air in the lungs when someone drowns, you need to replace wrong thinking with right thinking (see Phil. 4:8). Exercise—*"renewing of the mind"*—by replacing the junk in your mind with what the four gospel writers have to say about the passion of Christ. This is a vivid picture of how God wants you to *"crucify the self."*

You need to let the following Word be your training guide, especially the words italicized: "… **that I may know Him and the power of His resurrection, and the** *fellowship of His sufferings*, **being** *conformed to His death*, **if, by any means, I may attain to the resurrection from the dead**" (Phil. 3:10–11).

TRAINEE: I'm beginning to see that this means for me to be "found in Christ," to be a "new creation," and to "have the mind of Christ" (see 2 Cor. 5:17; Phil. 3:9; 1 Peter 4:1)?

COACH: Yes, you're progressing in your training on the Word. Do you remember how King David expressed such a need for transformation?

WORD: **Your word I have hidden in my heart, that I might not sin against You.** Psalm 119:11 NKJV

SEPTEMBER 10

COURSE: THE RENEWED MIND

WORD: **And be not conformed to this world: but be ye transformed by the renewing of your mind, that ye may prove what is that good, and acceptable, and perfect will of God.** (Rom. 12:2 KJV)

COACH: Take a Scriptural journey as you pray on the road to repentance.

Thank you, Father, that today I can stop having a "form of Godliness and denying the power thereof" (2 Tim. 3:5) and that I can be "transformed by the renewing of (my) mind" (Rom. 12:2) because I am going to "cast down the imaginations of (my) heart—making all of (my) thoughts captive to the obedience of Jesus" (2 Cor. 10:5); "deaden the deeds of (my) flesh" (Rom. 8:13); "crucify (my) self." (Gal. 2:20, 2 Cor. 5:15)

so that

"I can do all things through Christ who strengthens me" (Phil. 4:13); become **"more than a conqueror through Christ who loved me and gave himself up for me"** (Rom. 8:37); have **"God's strength made perfect in my weakness."** (2 Cor. 12:9)

so that

"It is no longer 'I' who live but Christ Who lives within me." (Gal. 2:20)

TRAINEE: Why?

SEPTEMBER 11

-continued-

COACH: Because He is the Word and the Word is Him. The Word now lives in you; therefore, so does He. And,

WORD: **"There hath no temptation taken but such as is common to man: but God is faithful, who will not suffer you to be tempted above that ye are able; but will with the temptation also make a way to escape, that ye may be able to bear it.** (1 Cor. 10:13 KJV)

COACH: Your personal "Declaration of Independence:"

WORD: **Bend down and hear my prayer, O Lord, and answer me, for I am deep in trouble…. Be merciful, O Lord, for I am looking up to you in constant hope…. O Lord, you are so good and kind, so ready to forgive; so full of mercy for all who ask your aid. Listen closely to my prayer, O God. Hear my urgent cry. I will call to you whenever trouble strikes, and you will help me…. May every fiber of my being unite in reverence to your name. With all my heart I will praise you. I will give glory to your name forever, for you love me so much! You are constantly so kind! You have rescued me from deepest hell.** (Ps. 86:1, 3, 5, 6–7, 11b–13 TLB)

COACH: As you *'deaden the deeds of the flesh'* (Rom. 8:13), *'crucify the self'* (Gal. 2:20), and *'cast down the imaginations of the heart'* (2 Cor. 10:5), the Holy Spirit can bring something beautiful out of you.

SEPTEMBER 12

COURSE: GROWTH, ADVANCEMENT, IMPROVEMENT

TRAINEE: I would like to see progress in what I know, do, and have.

COACH: God formed you and knows you better than you know yourself. He, therefore, is the best One to help you with that progress.

TRAINEE: I'm ready.

COACH: Matthew 25:14-28 is one of His major instructions; take some time and read the whole story. Then, ask yourself: "Can I see myself doing like the "faithful servant?"

WORD: The Parable of the Talents:

"For *the kingdom of heaven is* like a man traveling to a far country, *who* called his own servants and delivered his goods to them. And to one he gave five talents, to another two, and to another one, to each according to his own ability; and immediately he went on a journey. Then he who had received the five talents went and traded with them, and made another five talents. And likewise he who *had received* two gained two more also. But he who had received one went and dug in the ground, and hid his lord's money. After a long time the lord of those servants came and settled accounts with them.

"So he who had received five talents came and brought five other talents, saying, 'Lord, you delivered to me five talents;

-continued-

SEPTEMBER 13

look, I have gained five more talents besides them.' His lord said to him, 'Well *done,* good and faithful servant; you were faithful over a few things, I will make you ruler over many things. Enter into the joy of your lord.' He also who had received two talents came and said, 'Lord, you delivered to me two talents; look, I have gained two more talents besides them.' His lord said to him, 'Well *done,* good and faithful servant; you have been faithful over a few things, I will make you ruler over many things. Enter into the joy of your lord.'

"Then he who had received the one talent came and said, 'Lord, I knew you to be a hard man, reaping where you have not sown, and gathering where you have not scattered seed. And I was afraid, and went and hid your talent in the ground. Look, *there* you have *what is* yours.'

"But his lord answered and said to him, 'You wicked and lazy servant, you knew that I reap where I have not sown, and gather where I have not scattered seed. So you ought to have deposited my money with the bankers, and at my coming I would have received back my own with interest. So take the talent from him, and give *it* to him who has ten talents. Matthew 25:14-28 NKJV

TRAINEE:	I can reason from this parable that my efforts to do my best to use and apply what God has given me will be rewarded.
COACH:	Yes, when you pray for God's guidance and then step out with your best.
TRAINEE:	I will do my best and leave the rest to God.

SEPTEMBER 14

COURSE:	HIDING GOD'S WORD IN YOUR HEART
WORD:	**But his delight and desire are in the law of the Lord, and on His law—the precepts, the instructions, the teachings of God—he habitually meditates (ponders and studies) by day and by night.** (Ps. 1:2 AMP) **"For thou hast magnified thy word above all thy name."** Psalm 138:2 (KJV)
COACH:	Reading, meditating and memorizing God's Word are steps in hiding His Word in your heart. The rest of this "*month of memories*" will give you an opportunity to let His Word "*speak*" to your mind and heart concerning some crucial concerns in life. Memorize what you sense has been "*spoken*" to you.
WORD:	**My son, give attention to my words; incline your ear to my sayings. Do not let them depart from your eyes; keep them in the midst of your heart; for they are life to those who find them, and health to all their flesh. Keep your heart with all diligence, for out of it spring the issues of life.** Proverbs 4:20-23 NKJV
TRAINEE:	I will look for memories that linger in both mind and heart.
COACH:	That "looking" is a step of faith; God likes that.
WORD:	**But you be watchful in all things . . .** 2 Timothy 4:5 NKJV

SEPTEMBER 15

| COURSE: | GOD'S WORD ABOUT HIS WORD |
| WORD: | THE WORD about the WORD |

<u>1 Thessalonians 2:13</u> (New King James Version)

For this reason we also thank God without ceasing, because when you received the word of God which you heard from us, you welcomed *it* not *as* the word of men, but as it is in truth, the word of God, which also effectively works in you who believe.

<u>Hebrews 1:1-3</u> (New King James Version)

God, who at various times and in various ways spoke in time past to the fathers by the prophets, has in these last days spoken to us by *His* Son, whom He has appointed heir of all things, through whom also He made the worlds; who being the brightness of *His* glory and the express image of His person, and upholding all things by the word of His power, when He had by Himself purged our sins, sat down at the right hand of the Majesty on high,

<u>Hebrews 11:3</u> (New King James Version)

By faith we understand that the worlds were framed by the word of God, so that the things which are seen were not made of things which are visible.

<u>1 Peter 1:23-25</u> (New King James Version)

. . . having been born again, not of corruptible seed but incorruptible, through the word of God which lives and abides forever, because *"All flesh is as grass, And*

all the glory of man[as the flower of the grass. The grass withers, And its flower falls away, But the word of the LORD endures forever.

1 Peter 2:2

SEPTEMBER 16

-continued-

. . . as newborn babes, desire the pure milk of the word, that you may grow thereby,

<u>2 Peter 3:5-7</u> (New King James Version)

For this they willfully forget: that by the word of God the heavens were of old, and the earth standing out of water and in the water, by which the world *that* then existed perished, being flooded with water. But the heavens and the earth *which* are now preserved by the same word, are reserved for fire until the day of judgment and perdition of ungodly men.

1 John 1:1 (New King James Version)

What Was Heard, Seen, and Touched

That which was from the beginning, which we have heard, which we have seen with our eyes, which we have looked upon, and our hands have handled, concerning the Word of life—

1 John 5:7 (New King James Version)

For there are three that bear witness in heaven: the Father, the Word, and the Holy Spirit; and these three are one.

Revelation 19:11-13 (New King James Version)

Now I saw heaven opened, and behold, a white horse. And He who sat on him *was* called Faithful and True, and in [cont]

righteousness He judges and makes war. His eyes *were* like a flame of fire, and on His head *were* many crowns. He had[a] a name written that no one knew except Himself. He *was* clothed with a robe dipped in blood, and His name is called The Word of God.

SEPTEMBER 17

-continued-

John 1-4, 14 King James Version (KJV)

In the beginning was the Word, and the Word was with God, and the Word was God.

The same was in the beginning with God.

All things were made by him; and without him was not any thing made that was made.

In him was life; and the life was the light of men . . .

And the Word was made flesh, and dwelt among us, (and we beheld his glory, the glory as of the only begotten of the Father,) full of grace and truth.

Philemon 4-7 (NKJV)

Philemon's Love and Faith

I thank my God, making mention of you always in my prayers, hearing of your love and faith which you have toward the Lord Jesus and toward all the saints, that the sharing of your faith may become effective by the acknowledgment of every good thing which is in you[a] in Christ Jesus. For we have great joy and consolation in your love, because the hearts of the saints have been refreshed by you, brother.

SEPTEMBER 18

COURSE: MOVING CLOSER TO GOD'S HEART

COACH: God created you free to obey or disobey Him.

TRAINEE: Why?

COACH: He wanted to form you in His Own likeness and image. This means He had to make you free, as He is free. As stated, if He created robots that would always do what He wanted, they would not be created in His likeness and image.

TRAINEE: Didn't He know that Adam and Eve and the rest of humanity would continuously fail to obey?

COACH: That's the reason He and His Son, from the very beginning of time, made a plan to save and redeem His children from their sins. And, as you know, that plan involved Jesus and a Cross.

TRAINEE: But today's course looks at moving closer to His heart. How can I with my weak nature?

COACH: Read the following Word, centering your attention on three words: *confess, humbled, and accept.* The whole chapter is God's dealings with Israel over their perpetual history of sinning against Him.

WORD: **But if they <u>confess</u> their iniquity and the iniquity of their fathers, with their unfaithfulness in which they were unfaithful to Me, and that they also have walked contrary to Me, and that I also have walked contrary to them and have brought them into the land of their enemies; if their uncircumcised hearts are <u>humbled</u>, and they <u>accept</u> their guilt—then I will remember My covenant with Jacob, and My covenant with Isaac and My covenant with Abraham I will remember; I will remember their land.** Leviticus 26:40-42 NKJV [*Continue with the following supportive Word.*]

-continued-

SEPTEMBER 19

. . . but with the precious blood of Christ, as of a lamb without blemish and without spot. He indeed was foreordained before the foundation of the world, but was manifest in these last times for you. 1 Peter 1:19-20 NKJV [foreordained, planned before creation, to move hearts by the Cross—"the power of God" (1 Corinthians 1:18).]

Then shall ye call upon me, and ye shall go and pray unto me, and I will hearken unto you. And ye shall seek me, and find me, when ye shall search for me with all your heart. And I will be found of you, saith the Lord: . . . Jeremiah 29:12-14a KJV

Whoever has been born of God does not sin, for His seed remains in him; and he cannot sin, because he has been born of God. [Here, John is not speaking of our physical being, but of our spirit; our spirit is the person we are and who is saved by the "power of the Cross." It does not mean I have become sinless, but I am, nevertheless, training to sin less. **"Let your heart therefore be perfect with the Lord our God"** (1 Kings 8:61a KJV). The footnote in the Scofield Reference Bible (p. 399) states that the word *perfect* in that verse "implies whole-heartedness for God, single-mindedness, sincerity"—not sinless perfection.]

-continued-

SEPTEMBER 20

In this the children of God and the children of the devil are manifest: Whoever does not practice righteousness is not of God, nor *is* he who does not love his brother. 1 John 3:9-10 NKJV

. . . that I may know Him and the power of His resurrection, and the fellowship of His sufferings, being conformed to His death, if, by any means, I may attain to the resurrection from the dead. Philippians 3:10-11 NKJV [This is the righteousness of Jesus that the Father "imputes" to us as we accept and hold what Jesus accomplished for us on the Cross. **But for us also, to whom it shall be imputed, if we believe on him that raised up Jesus our Lord from the dead;** ... Romans 4:24 KJV]

And do not be conformed to this world, but be transformed by the renewing of your mind, that you may prove what *is* that good and acceptable and perfect will of God. Romans 12:2 NKJV

COACH: Look for a minute at St. Paul's journey through this. A sharp, honest, confessional and introspective look at himself surfaced this summary of his identity: *"I am chief of sinners;" "there's nothing good that dwells within me;" "I deserve only condemnation and death;" "the things I would (should be) do, I find myself not doing;" "the things I would not (should not) be doing, those things I find myself doing;" "wretched being that I am, who will deliver me from this body of death?"* (see: Rom. 5:16, 18; 7:13-25; Tim. 1:15)

Now, due to Paul becoming confessional, repentant and honest with God, look at what he discovered in his identity with Christ: *"I can do all things through Christ Who strengthens me;" "I am more than a conqueror through Christ Who loved me and gave Himself up for me;"*

SEPTEMBER 21

-continued-

"God's strength is made perfect in my weakness;" "It is no longer I who live but Christ within me;" "If we would judge ourselves, we would not be judged." (see Phil. 4:13; Rom. 8:37; 2 Cor. 12:9; Gal. 2:20; 1 Cor. 11:31]

WORD: **. . . and saying, "The time is fulfilled, and the kingdom of God is at hand. Repent, and believe in the gospel."** Mark 1:15 NKJV

So they went out and preached that *people* **should repent.**
Mark 6:12 NKJV

The LORD *is* **near to those who have a broken heart, and saves such as have a contrite spirit.** Psalm 34:18 NKJV

Repent ye therefore, and be converted, that your sins may be blotted out, when the times of refreshing shall come from the presence of the Lord. Acts 3:19 KJV

"But if a wicked man turns from all his sins which he has committed, keeps all My statutes, and does what is lawful and right, he shall surely live; he shall not die. 22 None of the transgressions which he has committed shall be remembered against him; because of the righteousness which he has done, he shall live. Ezekiel 18:21-22 NKJV

Therefore do not let sin reign in your mortal body, that you should obey it in its lusts. And do not present your members *as* **instruments of unrighteousness to sin, but present yourselves to God as being alive from the dead, and your members** *as* **instruments of righteousness to God . . . I speak in human** *terms* **because of the weakness of your flesh.**

SEPTEMBER 22

-continued-

For just as you presented your members *as* slaves of uncleanness, and of lawlessness *leading* to *more* lawlessness, so now present your members *as* slaves *of* righteousness for holiness. Romans 6:12-13, 19 NKJV [One tolerated sin often leads to others: e.g., Cain's envy to jealousy to murder; David's lust to adultery to murder . . .]

But go and learn what *this* means: 'I desire mercy and not sacrifice.' For I did not come to call the righteous, but sinners, to repentance." Matthew 9:13 NKJV

No temptation has overtaken you except such as is common to man; but God *is* faithful, who will not allow you to be tempted beyond what you are able, but with the temptation will also make the way of escape, that you may be able to bear *it*. 1 Corinthians 10:13 NKJV [Note here God's use of the word "able." When you and I say "we can't obey; we can't repent," God, *Who knows us better than we know ourselves*, says: "yes, you can!]

For godly sorrow worketh repentance to not to be repented of: but the sorrow of the world worketh death. 2 Corinthians 7:10 KJV

TRAINEE: There's no escaping God's serious eye on repentance.

COACH: The honesty and heart-felt sorrow of repentance, when we see the error of our ways, opens us to move closer to His heart.

WORD: **But God demonstrates His own love toward us, in that while we were still sinners, Christ died for us.** Romans 5:8 NKJV [see, also, Romans 5:10; 2 Corinthians 5:18-19]

TRAINEE: Yes.

SEPTEMBER 23

COURSE: A CHRISTIAN, YET SINFUL

WORD: **For what I am doing, I do not understand. For what I will to do, that I do not practice; but what I hate, that I do. If, then, I do what I will not to do, I agree with the law that it is good. But now, it is no longer I who do it, but sin that dwells in me. . . For the good that I will to do, I do not do; but the evil I will not to do, that I practice. Now if I do what I will not to do, it is no longer I who do it, but sin that dwells in me.**

I find then a law, that evil is present with me, the one who wills to do good. For I delight in the law of God according to the inward man. But I see another law in my members, waring against the law of my mind, and bringing me into captivity to the law of sin which is in my members. O wretched man that I am! Who will deliver me from this body of death? I thank God—through Jesus Christ our Lord! Romans 5:15-25 NKJV

TRAINEE: I can identify with every single Word!!!

COACH: Good! The next several training days will take you deeper into the freedom needed from such bondage of the will. For now, meditate on the following Word in preparation:

WORD: **The fear of the Lord is the beginning of wisdom**; [modern translation reads "fear" as *"fearfully shrink from anything that might offend God."* Ps. 111:10 NKJV

SEPTEMBER 24

-continued-

COACH: Review the January 2 training exercise on the three levels of the "fear of the Lord." The following Scriptures are center pieces for prayers addressing confession and repentance:

. . . for it is God who works in you both to will and to do for *His* good pleasure. Philippians 2:13 (NKJV)

Let no one say when he is tempted, "I am tempted by God"; for God cannot be tempted by evil, nor does He Himself tempt anyone. But each one is tempted when he is drawn away by his own desires and enticed. Then, when desire has conceived, it gives birth to sin; and sin, when it is full-grown, brings forth death. James 1:13-15 (NKJV)

So then, with the mind I myself serve the law of God, but with the flesh the law of sin. Romans 7:25 (NKJV)

For observe this very thing, that you sorrowed in a godly manner: What diligence it produced in you, *what clearing of yourselves, what* indignation, *what* fear, *what* vehement desire, *what* zeal, *what* vindication! In all *things* you proved yourselves to be clear in this matter. 2 Corinthians 7:11 (NKJV)

For the message of the cross is foolishness to those who are perishing, but to us who are being saved it is the power of God. 1 Corinthians 1:18 (NKJV)

TRAINEE: I'm looking forward to the message of freedom and redemption from my sin.

COACH: Rest up for tomorrow's training.

SEPTEMBER 25

COURSE: FREEDOM FROM SIN

COACH: Let God's Word coach you concerning the "freedom" that comes from His Grace to you.

Then I will sprinkle clean water on you, and you shall be clean; … I will take the heart of stone out of your flesh and give you a heart of flesh. I will put My Spirit within you and cause you to walk in My statutes, and you will keep My judgments and do *them*. Ezekiel 36:25-26 NKJV

Therefore, if anyone *is* in Christ, *he is* a new creation; old things have passed away; behold, all things have become new. 2 Corinthians 5:17 NKJV

This *is* a faithful saying and worthy of all acceptance, that Christ Jesus came into the world to save sinners, of whom I am chief. 1 Timothy 1:15 NKJV

COACH: There is no too great a sinner that Jesus cannot save through what He achieved on the Cross.

There is therefore now no condemnation to them which are in Christ Jesus, who walk not after the flesh, but after the Spirit. For the law of the Spirit of life in Christ Jesus hath made me free from the law of sin and death.

For what the law could not do, in that it was weak through the flesh, God sending his own Son in the likeness of sinful flesh, and for sin, condemned sin in the flesh: Romans 8:1-3 KJV

For thou, Lord, art good, and ready to forgive; and plenteous in mercy unto all them that call upon thee. Psalm 86:5 KJV

SEPTEMBER 26

COURSE: REDEMPTION FROM SIN

COACH: God is the one who can reach in with his redeeming will and bring something good out of it all, again, much in the same sense of going to a "redemption store." As you will see, God can take the garbage Satan brings in through the "back door" and "work it toward good" so that it glides gracefully through the "front door" of your life. [Ref. Romans 8:28]

WORD: **. . . who gave Himself for our sins, that He might deliver us from this present evil age, according to the will of our God and Father,** Galatians 1:4 NKJV

. . . who Himself bore our sins in His own body on the tree, that we, having died to sins, might live for righteousness—by whose stripes you were healed. 1 Peter 2:24 NKJV

For by one offering He has perfected forever those who are being sanctified. Hebrews 10:14 NKJV

But He *was* wounded for our transgressions,
He was bruised for our iniquities;
The chastisement for our peace *was* upon Him,
And by His stripes we are healed.
All we like sheep have gone astray;
We have turned, every one, to his own way;
And the LORD has laid on Him the iniquity of us all.
Isaiah 53:5-6 NKJV

In Him we have redemption through His blood, the forgiveness of sins, according to the riches of His grace Ephesians 1:7 NKJV [The problem, see: 1 Cor. 6:8-10; Heb. 10:26-30; 1 Tim. 1:9-11; Mark 7:20-23; Gal. 5:19-21; the Answer, see: 2 Cor. 7:10; Rom. 12:2; Phil. 2:13; James 1:12; 1 Cor. 10:13; 1 Jn. 1:8-9; Rom. 8:1-3]

SEPTEMBER 27

COURSE: OBEDIENCE

COACH: Let your obedience serve as a way you thank God for His Grace and all His provisions for you.

Therefore keep the words of this covenant, and do them, that you may prosper in all that you do. Deuteronomy 29:9 New King James Version NKJV

The things which you learned and received and heard and saw in me, these do, and the God of peace will be with you. Philippians 4:9 NKJV

Jesus answered and said to him, "If anyone loves Me, he will keep My word; and My Father will love him, and We will come to him and make Our home with him. John 14:23 NKJV [see in context verses 21-24]

If you know these things, blessed are you if you do them. John 13:17 NKJV

. . . (for not the hearers of the law *are* just in the sight of God, but the doers of the law will be justified; Romans 2:13 NKJV

COACH: Paul's statements of your no longer being *"under the law"* [Galatians 5:16-18] do not mean the law is no longer your standard; it means you, through Jesus, are no longer under the guilt, dominion, and penalty of the law. (see Rom. 6:14-15; Gal.3:23; 5:18]

WORD: **"Most assuredly, I say to you, he who hears My word and believes in Him who sent Me has everlasting life, and shall not come into judgment, but has passed from death into life."** John 5:24 NKJV [Life and Judgment are through the Son.

SEPTEMBER 28

-continued-

COACH: The word: *"hears"* is like the military expression: *"attention to orders."* It means with intention to follow through/obey. Again, for your earthly father to give a corrective word and then tilt his head to the side and look at you sharply saying, *"Do you hear me,"* he would be asking you if you were hearing him with the mind to obey. "Hear," is what Jesus said about the faith that obeys:

WORD: **"I tell you that He will avenge them speedily. Nevertheless when the Son of man cometh, shall He find faith on the earth?"** Luke 18:8 KJV

COACH: Like Joshua, you need to say in these deceitful and divergent times: **"but as for me and my house, we will serve the LORD."**]

WORD: **"Not everyone who says to Me, 'Lord, Lord,' shall enter the kingdom of heaven, but he who does the will of My Father in heaven.** Matthew 7:21 NKJV

And whatever we ask we receive from Him, because we keep His commandments and do those things that are pleasing in His sight. 1 John 3:22 NKJV

So Samuel said: "Has the LORD *as great* delight in burnt offerings and sacrifices,
As in obeying the voice of the LORD?
Behold, to obey is better than sacrifice,
***And* to heed than the fat of rams.** 1 Samuel 15:22 NKJV [see, also: Philippians 2:13, 2 Corinthians 7:10-11, 2 Corinthians 10:5, Galatians 2:20, 1 Corinthians 1:18, 2 Corinthians 12:9]

COACH: Tomorrow's course will make summary of these training days for obedience and repentance.

SEPTEMBER 29

OBEDIENCE: FIVE-FOLD SUMMARY

(1.) God is concerned not only about the *obedience of wisdom* but the *wisdom of obedience* (protecting me from the bad consequences of going against his will). "Casting down the imaginations of my heart" accomplishes this. Why? Because what gets my mind gets me! "***Casting down imaginations, and every high thing that exalts itself against the knowledge of God, and bringing into captivity every thought to the obedience of Christ; and having in a readiness to revenge all disobedience, when your obedience is fulfilled.***" 2 Cor. 10:5-6 KJV

(2.) He is concerned about the *obedience of faith* and also about the *faith of obedience* (protecting me from missing out on God's best) because I make a faith-decision over against feeling to: "*deaden deeds of my flesh*" (Rom. 8:13). His Word says, "***Be it done unto you according to your faith.***" MT. 9:29 KJV

(3.) He is interested in the *obedience of sacrifice,* but He also watches to see if I will make the cost or *sacrifice of obedience* in my giving up my sin desire as I "*crucify my flesh*" (Gal. 2:20; 2 Cor. 5:15) (protecting me from wounding his heart anymore with my sin). He told the people of Israel that he wanted their obedience more than their sacrifices: "***And Samuel said, Hath the LORD as great delight in burnt offerings and sacrifices, as in obeying the voice of the LORD? Behold, to obey is better than sacrifice, and to hearken than the fat of rams.***" 1 Sam. 15:22 KJV

(4.) He certainly desires my *obedience of praise* and equally looks for my *praise of obedience.* *"True worshipers will worship the Father in spirit and truth; for the Father is seeking such to worship Him."* Jn. 4:23-24 NKJV

(5.) He wants me to show him the *love of obedience.* *"If a man love me, he will keep my words..."* <u>Jn. 14:23</u> KJV

Get wisdom, get understanding: forget it not; neither decline from the words of my mouth. Forsake her not, and she shall preserve thee: love her, and she shall keep thee. Proverbs 4:5-6 KJV

SEPTEMBER 30

COURSE: PRAYER

COACH: Consider prayer as talking to God and that reading His Word is Him talking to you. He listens, also, to the "thoughts of your heart."

WORD: **. . . I lifted up my voice in prayer . . . If I had cherished evil thoughts, the Lord would not have heard me;** . . . Psalm 66:17-18 NEB [The NKJV reads *"If I regard iniquity in my heart, the Lord will not hear."*]

TRAINEE: Why does my sin block my prayers?

COACH: Your heart holds your deepest desires, therefore:

WORD: ". . . **For the righteous God tests the hearts and minds."** Psalm 7:9b NKJV

The heart is deceitful above all things; and desperately wicked; who can know it? I, the Lord, search the heart, I test the mind, even to give every man according to his ways, according to the fruit of his doings. Jeremiah 17:9-10 NKJV

For out of the heart proceed evil thoughts . . . These are the things which defile a man." Matthew 15:19-20a NKJV [see also Job 23:16; Psalm 139:23; Proverbs 23:7]

OCTOBER 1

Month of Praise

COURSE: BASIS FOR PRAISE TO GOD

COACH: God's Grace to you is the greatest reason for giving Him praise! This includes your answered prayers.

TRAINEE: His love reaches that far for me?

COACH: Jesus endured the cross for you, personally, in total empathy, not sympathy. It would be tantamount to blasphemy for you to give in to the suggestions of the enemy and, thereby, believe that God can't forgive someone so wretched as you or me.

TRAINEE: This understanding is what moves and motivates me, more than any other force, to want his will to be done in my life—for true repentance.

COACH: Herein lays the power of God from the cross.

WORD: **For the message of the Cross is foolishness to those who are perishing, but to us who are being saved it is the power of God.** 1 Cor. 1:18 (NKJV)

COACH: Praise for Grace and answered prayer in your past, in your present, and in your future!

TRAINEE: Thank You for coaching me on the Word of praise!

OCTOBER 2

COURSE: PRAISE FOR TRANSFORMATION

COACH: Do you recall the Apostle Paul confessing to being *"chief of sinners"*?

TRAINEE: Yes, he would find himself doing things against God's will that he really did not want to be doing.

COACH: Recall the effect the Cross, Passion of Christ, had on Paul, causing him to write that the Cross *"is the power of God."* Look, again, at yesterday's training Word:

WORD: **For the message of the cross is foolishness to those who are perishing, but to us who are being saved it is the power of God.** 1 Corinthians 1:18 NKJV

COACH: Read the changes Paul experienced:

WORD: **"I can do all things through Christ which strengtheneth me."** Phil. 4:13 (KJV)

     "God's strength is made perfect in my weakness." 2 Cor. 12:9 (KJV)

     "We are more than conquerors through him that loved us." Rom. 8:37 (KJV

     "It is no longer I who live but Jesus within me." Gal. 2:20 (NIV)

-continued'

OCTOBER 3

COACH: Pray yesterday's Word about the changes the Apostle Paul experienced—making them your prayer, a Scriptural journey on the road to repentance. Give Him <u>praise</u> for His answers, even before you see them! Pray:

     Thank you, Father, that today I can stop having a "**form of Godliness and denying the power thereof** (2 Tim. 3:5)" and that I can be "**transformed by the renewing of (my) mind** (Rom. 12:2)," because I am going to "**Cast down the imaginations of (my) heart—making all of my) thoughts captive to the obedience of Jesus** (2 Cor. 10:5);" "**deaden the deeds of (my) flesh** (Rom. 8:13);" "**Crucify (my) self** (Gal. 2:20, 2 Cor. 5:15)" so that "**I can do all things through Christ who strengthens me** (Phil. 4:13);" become "**more than a conqueror through Christ who loved me and gave himself up for me** (Rom. 8:37);" have "**God's strength made perfect in my weakness** (2 Cor. 12:9)" so that One day I can say, "**It is no longer 'I' who live but Christ Who lives within me** (Gal. 2:20)."

TRAINEE: How will praying these Words help me change?

COACH: Because Jesus is the Word and the Word is Jesus. The Word now lives in you; therefore, so does Jesus. Let that truth settle deep down inside you.

TRAINEE: I need to pray those Words again.

OCTOBER 4

COURSE: PRAISE FOR THE MODEL PRAYER

COACH: Again, one regimen of fitness to help produce a repentant mind centers in a profound manner on the prayer Jesus taught his disciples to pray as a model prayer. Repeat the training exercise from April 22. Again, ask yourself, "Can I pray—

Our—while I am self-centered;

Father—and not show that I daily look to him that way;

Who art in heaven—if I pursue only earthly things;

Hallowed be thy name—if I am not "set apart" for him;

Thy kingdom come—and not trade my control for his control;

Thy will be done—and continue to give in to my will, not his;

On earth as it is in heaven—and not be a willing instrument of his peace here and now;

Give us this day our daily bread—and not feed others in need;

Forgive us our trespasses as we forgive those who trespass against us—and continue to nurture bitterness and resentment;

Lead us not into temptation—if I seek out settings as open targets for temptation;

Deliver us from evil—while not using the sword of the Word;

Thine is the kingdom—and not continually be his servant;

Thine is the power—and fear people and circumstances more;

Thine is the glory—if I act primarily for self-recognition;

Forever and ever—and worry about the footsteps ahead;

Amen—and not really mean it."

OCTOBER 5

COURSE: PRAISE FOR GOD'S HELP

TRAINEE: How does God work his Word for my good?

COACH: Look, again, at the following Words with an expectant eye:

WORD: **"And we know that all things work together for good to them that love God, to them who are the called according to his purpose."** (Rom. 8:28 KJV)

[Not in your own strength] for it is God Who is all the while effectually at work in you—energizing and creating in you the power and desire— both to will and to work for His good pleasure and satisfaction and delight. Philippians 2:13 AMP. B.

TRAINEE: "How does God actually *do* this?"

COACH: We have already seen how God can take "all things"—even the works of the enemy—and work them, redeem them for His good purpose and for your fulfillment and blessing.

TRAINEE: Yes, I need to "forget not all His benefits" (Ps. 103:2) to me and to remain faithful and have an expectant trust about Him working in my future.

COACH: What you just said is one example of how He is "at work in you" so that you have "the power and desire— both to will and to work for His good pleasure and satisfaction and delight."

OCTOBER 6

-continued-

WORD: **"Jesus answered, If a person (really) loves Me, he will keep My word— obey My teaching" (John 14:23a AMP). And "For it is not merely hearing the Law (read) that makes one righteous before God, but it is the doers of the Law who will be held guiltless and acquitted and justified."** Rom. 2:13 (AMP)

COACH: Again, God's two greatest commandments not only summarize all the other commandments, they hold the power to move your heart toward faith and obedience; look on and into them again:

WORD: **'Hear, O Israel, the Lord our God is one. Thou shalt love the Lord thy God with all thy heart, all thy mind, all thy soul and with all thy strength. And thou shalt love thy neighbor as thyself** [Matthew 22:36-40].'

TRAINEE: I'm beginning to have not just knowledge itself about his Word but an understanding in my heart of the boundaries of God's thoughts—thinking His thoughts after Him.

COACH: Just like reading a good conversational book can make you feel like you know the author, reading God's book (the Holy Scriptures) brings you closer to Him.

OCTOBER 7

COURSE: PRAISE FOR THE WORD & ANSWERED PRAYER

TRAINEE: So, how can I <u>*know*</u> whether or not my prayer (*talking/listening relationship with God*) on a given concern is in God's will, that I've heard God's "*rhema*?" I need a <u>review</u>.

First "Know"

COACH: If conviction is there, it is "the assurance of things hoped for, the conviction of things not seen" (Heb. 11:1). (The KJV reads, "*substance of things hoped for, the evidence of things not seen.*" Something substantial gives great assurance; evidence goes with conviction.)

TRAINEE: I need something to back up my conviction, to know God is really talking to me when I pray.

Second "Know"

COACH: Second, does God's Word confirm and address your conviction? Does the Word echo your prayer? If so, you have the strongest confirmation possible. When you pray God's own Word right back to Him, then you *know* you are praying in his will! The Word assures and gives substance to the prayer. That Word feeds your spirit. Inspired by the Word, your spirit will launch and renew the activity of your body and mind, including feelings.

Third "Know"

COACH: Do you have godly, wise counsel of others who are steeped in the faith? **"For by wise counsel you can wage your war, and in an abundance of counselors there is victory and safety"** (Prov. 24:6 AMP). Do they witness to your convictions and confirmation from the Scriptures? If so, you have still further confirmation.

OCTOBER 8

-continued-

Fourth "Know"

COACH: Do you have an inner peace, much like that *"eye of the hurricane"*—calm, balanced, and stable while everything around you is chaotic? Can you turn over and go to sleep? If so, that's another confirmation.

Fifth "Know"

COACH: Is there circumstantial evidence? Do thoughts, conversations, actions, feelings, decisions, plans, and so on point toward what you believe is "meant to be"? This may occur following some prayers; with others, it may not exist. Should it not, rest firmly on the confirmation of God's Word. That Word will lift up faith. God's Words are events! A "tug-of-war" may ensue where faith in the Word overrules whatever feelings and circumstances may be trying to dictate—"(walking) by faith and not by sight." When you let feelings or circumstances win, you lose; when you let faith win, you win! Recall, again, Peter trying to walk on the water (Matt. 14:22–32), standing at first on the *rhema* (personal) Word of Jesus when He said to Peter "come forth;" but, then, trying to stand on his feelings as they dwelt on the wind and the waves, he began to sink.

-continued-

OCTOBER 9

TRAINEE: I like the story of Gideon as he questioned God about His promise to deliver Israel from the Medians with a small clan under Gideon's leadership:

WORD: **"Then Gideon said to God, 'If you are really going to use me to save Israel as you promised, prove it to me in this way: I'll put some wool on the threshing floor tonight, and if, in the morning, the fleece is wet and the ground is dry, I will know you are going to help me!'**

And it happened just that way! When he got up the next morning he pressed the fleece together and wrung out a whole bowlful of water!

Then Gideon said to the Lord, 'Please don't be angry with me, but let me make one more test: this time let the fleece remain dry while the ground around is wet!

So the Lord did as he asked; that night the fleece stayed dry, but the ground was covered with dew!" Judges 6:36–40 (TLB)

TRAINEE: As you say, God might not show me an outward sign of his will; however, I am learning that he often honors an "emotional fleece." For me, this centers on Psalm 37:4 in that I sometimes say to God, "Dear Father, if this really is what you are going to work out in my life, then build the desire of my heart for it; if not, then let that desire die out."

OCTOBER 10

-continued-

COACH: To nervously put out that fleece can sometimes amount to nothing more than a lack of faith on your part.

Sixth "Know"

Sixth, is there unconfessed sin? This blocks God's hearing (1 John 5:13–15; Is. 59:1–3, 12–15) of your prayers. Confession and God's forgiveness clear the way. **"He that covereth his sins shall not prosper: but whoso confesseth and forsaketh them shall have mercy"** Proverbs 28:13 (KJV).

TRAINEE: "Dear Father, I have sinned against you; I confess *all* my sins (thoughts, words, deeds), including the secret thoughts and desires that I cannot fully understand but that are all known unto you. I do earnestly repent and am heartily sorry for these, my many offenses. Now, in the name of Jesus, I ask you to forgive (*cover, erase, forget, heal*) me and have mercy on me, to cleanse, strengthen, heal, guide, bless, and protect me. And deliver me from the consequences of not having the "*fear of the Lord*" on all three levels. By the power of your Spirit living in me, I place the name of Jesus above every thought in my mind. I ask that the Holy Spirit pray for me those prayers needed but not formed in my mind. And, like the disciples who, when they saw the intensity of His prayers, asked Jesus to teach them to pray, I ask that you teach me to pray more and more in your will, to become a true, tried, and tested prayer warrior, one from whom you want to hear. Amen."

-continued-

OCTOBER 11

Seventh "Know"

COACH: Look for the final/actual provision, the ultimate confirmation of God's will. In the military, you do not go anywhere until you have orders in hand. Your number one "*Commander-in-Chief*" does deliver those orders from his Word as a final provision.

Pray "*without ceasing.*" Seven days without prayer will make "one weak." Be like the woman who knocked on the door for a loaf of bread until, said Jesus, the householder, opened up to her. Jesus said to pray like that. Do not regard God as hard of hearing, but be persistent. "*Pray-through;*" "*go the distance.*"

WORD: **"For whoever would come near to God must (necessarily) believe that God exists and that He is the Rewarder of those who earnestly and diligently seek Him (out)."** Heb. 11:6b (AMP)

"You will seek me and find me when you seek me with all your heart. I will be found by you, declares the Lord." (Jer. 29:13–14a NIV; see Deut. 4:29; Prov. 8:17)

COACH: Following the above steps, be persistent in giving God thanks for his answer, even before your eyes see it. "*See it*" with the "*eyes of faith*." Read and meditate on Mark 11:23-24 and Romans 10:9–10; let them challenge and encourage your vision. What you say with your mouth, following a prayer-faith connection, adds strength to your conviction. Remind yourself of how well the Father can answer your prayer (Eph. 3:20).

OCTOBER 12

COURSE: THE PRACTICE OF PRAISE

COACH: The January 31 exercise introduced the following "praise prescription:"

WORD: **In everything give thanks: for this is the will of God in Christ Jesus concerning you.** 1 Thessalonians 5:18 KJV

Giving thanks always for all things unto God and the Father in the name of our Lord Jesus Christ; . . . Ephesians 5:20 KJV

By him therefore let us offer the sacrifice of praise to God continually, that is, the fruit of our lips giving thanks to his name. Hebrews 13:15 KJV

Be careful for nothing; but in every thing by prayer and supplication with thanksgiving let your requests be made known unto God.

TRAINEE: In January's training, you said I will see that day when "*gritted-teeth thanks*" and "*tearful thanks*" becomes "*joyful thanks*;" and that I should look to October's training.

COACH: A "*sacrifice of praise*" is not a feeling; it is a decision. Why did God allow Satan to do so much to Job? Regarding the practice of praise, do you recall the words of Job after he had lost and suffered so much that not even his friends could console him and his wife had finally told him to just curse God and die? He said, **"Though He slay me, yet will I wait for (trust, hope) in Him"** (see Job 13:15). **"The Lord gave, and the Lord hath taken away; blessed be the name of the Lord"** (Job 1:21 KJV).

OCTOBER 13

-continued-

God honored that posture of praise and trust with His peace and the seven-fold restoration of everything Job had lost.

TRAINEE: Yes, as you said, it is a decision.

COACH: Practicing such praise builds trust and faith, giving God room to act. There is, therefore, a vital link between giving God thanks in *all* things, the exercise of faith, and God's activity. The "*sacrifice of praise*" is neither a psychological gimmick nor the "*power of positive thinking,*" neither is it a leverage pole to somehow pry God's hand into action. It is a *trusting relationship.*

TRAINEE: How does the practice of praise affect the enemy?

COACH: Satan flees the praises offered to the Father. In charge of praise when he was still in the kingdom, he cannot stand it; it is his sore spot. Therefore, when you offer up praises to the Father—especially when those praises are for the garbage Satan has been "allowed" to deliver into your life, which God can wonderfully redeem into the stem of the rose—Satan is compelled to retreat. James 4:7 Scripture does tell you that God "inhabits" or lives in the praises of his people, so you have Satan running away and God moving in. The practice of praise is like the "Truman Decision" to use the bomb; it not only wins the battle, it ends the war. It is a spiritual "weapon—*good battle strategy.*"

OCTOBER 14

COURSE: PRAISE AND JUDGING

TRAINEE: I thought God said not to judge or we would be judged.

COACH: Yes, the Word says:

WORD: **Judge not, that ye be not judged. For with the judgment ye judge, ye shall be judged**: . . . Matthew 7:1 KJV

COACH: However, look at the following Word about judging:

WORD: **For if we would judge ourselves, we should not be judged. But when we are judged, we are chastened of the Lord, that we should not be condemned with the world.** 1 Cor. 11:31–32 KJV

Therefore let us not judge one another anymore, but rather resolve this, not to put a stumbling block or a cause to fall in our brother's way. Romans 14:13 NKJV (see, also, Prov. 3:11, 22:15; Heb. 12:5–6)

COACH: God will not only judge what you do, He will judge the hidden motivations of the heart; praise Him for that.

WORD: **They will give an account to Him who is ready to judge the living and the dead.** 1 Peter 4:5 NKJV [see, also, 2 Timothy 4:8]

A man's conscience is the Lord's searchlight exposing his hidden motives" Prov. 20:27 (TLB)

OCTOBER 15

COURSE: PRAISE AND HEALTH

COACH: In addition to the fact that God deserves your praise as creator and redeemer, He has also placed a powerful reciprocal blessing on you as you give Him praise! The wisdom of making the *"sacrifice of praise"* is like the *"treasure hidden in the field"* (Matt. 13:44)—so great, said Jesus, that the one who stumbled over it went out and sold everything he had and bought that field. Can praise become a spiritual treasure? Yes! In the midst of your stress and concerns, giving God that gritted-teeth and/or tearful thanks, your trust level is raised, giving God room to go to work. The rest becomes good history.

WORD: **My son, give attention to my words; . . . Keep them in the midst of your heart; for they are life to those who find them, and health to all their flesh.** Proverbs 4:20-22 NKJV

COACH: The sacrifice-of-praise is healthy for your whole being. Through *expression*, it keeps the evolving cycle of *sup*pression, *re*pression, and *de*pression from attacking your emotional system, not to mention the body's natural immune system for good physiological health, as well. To Israel, God said he would "appoint unto them ... the garment of praise for the spirit of heaviness (depression, worry . . .)" [Is. 61:3].

TRAINEE: I need to see praise as good medicine and a builder of my faith.

COACH: Carry on.

OCTOBER 16

COURSE: PRAISE FOR HIS GRACE

COACH: Grace, His *"unmerited favor,"* is what He sends forth to bring beauty even out of loss and defeat. All of nature, during this month, joins in with praise, as only God can bring forth beauty out of death. <u>Psalm 103</u> forms a diadem of praise for all He performs and forms in His people and in the created order.

TRAINEE: I'm glad He works in me to conform me more into the likeness of Christ. I also like it when I see how He *"works all things toward good."*

COACH: You are not to thank God in and for bad things as though He had somehow made them happen but to give Him thanks with the understanding that he had *allowed* them for a reason and is the One who can bring something good out of it all. As you will see, God can take the garbage Satan brings in through the "back door" and "work it toward good" so that it glides <u>grace</u>fully through the "front door" of your life.

Again, you will see God's twofold response to the *"sacrifice of praise"*: 1) "The peace of God that passes all understanding"—like the eye of a hurricane. The Hebrew word for *peace* does not refer to peace in the absence of war or stress but peace in the *midst* of it. "**And the peace of God, which passeth all understanding, shall keep your hearts and minds through Christ Jesus**" (Phil. 4:7 KJV). 2) Miracle, working good with those things you cannot do anything about.

OCTOBER 17

COURSE: PRAISE FOR GOD'S WORD IN THE FACE OF SIN AND OPEN REBELLION

COACH: In your day and time, you see historical duplication of the Days of Noah and of Sodom and Gomorrah: e.g., AIDS, Ebola… (*not in Noah's or Sodom and Gomorrah's time but unique latter day pestilence, biological warfare, plague*), homosexuality, self-gratification, occultism [see: <u>Genesis 19:1-28</u>; <u>Leviticus 18:22</u>; <u>20:13</u>; <u>Romans 1:18-32</u>; <u>1 Corinthians 6:9-11</u>; <u>Galatians 5:19-21</u>; <u>1 Timothy 1:8-11</u>; <u>2 Timothy 3:1-6</u>], and reprobate mind [see: <u>2 Timothy 3:7-9</u>; <u>Matthew 24:9-13</u>; <u>Mark 7:20-23</u>]. A quick glance at today's media underscores the intense level of immorality, random violence and rebellion as in those days [see: <u>Luke 17:26-29</u>]. Governmental persecution of Church-State issues and the de-humanization or de-valuations of life punctuate this prophetic word. Edward Gibbon's <u>History of the Decline and Fall of the Roman Empire</u> and William Shirer's epic history of <u>The Rise and Fall of the Third Reich</u> describe America today [see: John 15:18-25].

TRAINEE: History is repeating itself and taking steps for the worse.

COACH: Look at Edward Gibbon's notes in <u>History of the Decline and Fall of the Roman Empire</u> for a picture of that repetition:

(1.) "The rapid increase of divorce; the undermining of the dignity and sanctity of the home, which is the basis of human society.

(2.) Higher and higher taxes and the spending of public monies for free bread and circuses for the populace.

-continued-

OCTOBER 18

(3.) The mad craze for pleasure; sports becoming every year more exciting and more brutal.

(4.) The building of gigantic armaments when the real enemy was within the decadence of the people.

(5.) The decay of religion: i.e., faith fading into mere form, losing touch with life and becoming impotent to warn and guide the people."

(Quoted in the book: Pearls from the Prophets, Greg S. Pettys, Roger Alan Dennis. P. 184)

TRAINEE: Sounds pretty rough for Christian values.

COACH: Those who confess Jesus as God, the Bible as His Word, and the crucial role of obedience to God will face a growing persecution in the midst of a democracy of compromise, destined to pave the way for the anti-Christ. **Yes, and all who desire to live godly in Christ Jesus will suffer persecution** (2 Timothy 3:12 NKJV; however, see also: Psalm 125:1-2). Will democracy actually pave the way for the ultimate end of freedom as the world looks for unity one day under the authority of the Antichrist? Such a shift will not take place by force; the world will be hungry, ready for that leader.

WORD: **Now we beseech you, brethren, by the coming of our Lord Jesus Christ, and by our gathering together unto him, that ye be not soon shaken in mind, or be troubled, neither by spirit, nor by word, nor by letter as from us, as that the day of Christ is at hand. Let no man deceive you by any means: for that day shall not come, except there come a falling away first, and that man of sin be revealed, the son of perdition; who opposeth and exalteth himself above all that is called God, or that is worshipped; so that he as God sitteth in the temple of God, shewing himself that he is God.** 2 Thessalonians 2:1-4 KJV (see, also, Romans 1:18-24; Rev. 13)

"A wise man's heart is at his right hand; but a fool's heart at his left."
Ecclesiastes 10: 2 KJV

OCTOBER 19

-continued-

TRAINEE: We are becoming numb to our sin and the conditions it causes.

COACH: Gibbon's description fits not only America but also the entire world. The above prophecy concerning the "days of Noah" addresses how normal wickedness seemed to those living in the midst of that wickedness (see: Ez. 16:49). The people of Noah's time and residents of Sodom and Gomorrah lived what they considered "normal" lives (see: Ez. 16:49). They traded Godly lives for wickedness that they considered the norm. This applies to you today. The following constitute three big strike-outs for the U. S. A. as far as God is concerned:

Endorsement of killing the unborn (*56 million abortions since the 1973 Supreme Court Roe vs. Wade ruling,* Randy O'Bannon, *Live News.com, Jan. 12 2014*). The loud cry goes forth for animal rights and not to kill; yet, modern medicine gets paid to kill (abort) human babies! To the question as <u>when</u> life begins, read what God said to the prophet Jeremiah:

WORD: **Before I formed thee in the belly I knew thee; and before thou camest forth out of the womb I sanctified thee, and I ordained thee a prophet unto the nations . . .** Jeremiah 1:5 KJV.

Homosexual marriage. This is an affront to God's created order. "Dr. Francis Collins, who received the Presidential Medal of Freedom for his work sequencing the human genetic code, has in fact proven that homosexuality is not genetically 'hardwired' (<u>Midnight Call Magazine</u>, April 2013, p. 28)." Despite this evidence and high rates of sexually transmitted diseases, psychiatric illness, drug abuse, suicide, etc., schools now teach children that it is normal. Some U.S. City officials have informed pastors that if they refuse to marry homosexuals, they will face jail time and fines. Concerning this subject, the FCC has opened the door with some proceedings regarding "Open Internet" that have surfaced, for this author, some questions to free speech: e.g., Internet tech companies can now censor what they deem to be 'politically incorrect speech.'

OCTOBER 20

-continued-

Some early results: Facebook suspended postings of former governor Mike Huckabee because he supported traditional marriage; road signs on the Internet highway saying: "Conservatives stay out," "No preaching by Bible-believing Christians allowed," "This is not a pro-Israel town …" (*Israel My Glory*, September/October, p. 19) Not modern marriage but modern abuse of marriage is what you now face as legal steps are taken to require pastors to give the government evidence of what they preach. Paul describes such human deceitfulness as the "natural man" who has no spiritual discernment in (1 Cor. 2:14 *See in context: vs. 6-16*) [See also 1 Cor. 6:8-10; 1 Tim. 1:9-11; Gal. 5:19-21]

Freedom of religion is now replaced with freedom from religion: e.g., the Ten Commandments were removed from schools, partly, with the rationale that repeated, daily attention given to them would cause students to begin doing them. Further, while the Bible is being ousted, schools are now told to study the Quran. Prayer is not to be conducted at the White House, but the Day of Prayer for Muslims is to be acknowledged.

TRAINEE: There is something intrinsically wrong with this picture!

Billy Graham stated several decades ago: "If God does not judge America, He will have to apologize to Sodom and Gomorrah." Romans 1:29-32 and 2 Thessalonians 2:10-12 outline the rule of the day. However, as these pages are written to you, I want to lift up something for you to consider. God did judge Israel harshly for their stubborn rebellion against Him. Nevertheless, time and time again, God found a way to heal and redeem His people, making it clear that He was going to hold fast, be faithful, to the covenant He had made with His people through Abraham, Isaac, and Jacob. He was determined to do this "*for His Name's sake*" and for the everlasting purity and value of His covenant.

OCTOBER 21

-continued-

Now, let's consider what the Puritans held on to and valued at the formation of America. They and the Founding Fathers pursued a covenant relationship with God as they continually sought out His Word to guide the founding documents for our country; the Geneva Bible was the scholarly tool in their hands, minds, and hearts for this task! So, think how great God's Name is and that He has raised up His Word even above His Name (Psalm 138:2). Why? I believe it is because the Word is Jesus.

I will worship toward Your holy temple,
And praise Your name
For Your lovingkindness and Your truth;
For You have magnified Your word above all Your name. Psalm 138:2 NKJV

America as a nation, however, is not in a covenant relationship as Israel is with God. Not only is Israel chosen, but the land also was chosen. Jared Diamond, anthropologist and Pulitzer-prize-winning author documents how the geography of the Middle East was the early center for human development, having plants and animals easily domesticated and being the location man was first placed. (Diamond, Jared. *Guns, Germs, and Steel: The Fate of Human Societies.* 1999, New York, p. 162)

America has the most arable land, major ports, navigable internal waterways, two coasts serving as natural barriers to enemies… (Stratford. *The Geopolitics of the United States, The Inevitable Empire.* August 14, 2011). To Israel, as to America, certain physical and geographical formations were, from the foundation of the earth, assigned. Why did God call Israel His habitation (Ezra 7:15; 1Chronicles 23:25) and make Jerusalem, according to formative studies, the most central to all of the world's land masses? *https://www.jewishvirtuallibrary.org/jsource/loc/Center.html*).

OCTOBER 22

-continued-

It is safe to believe America has significance, as well, in the prophetic timeline; however, you do have free choice as to obey or disobey our Creator. God used the Roman Empire to change timing and events for the First Coming of Christ. Will America be part of timing and events for the Second Coming? It does seem like the more America learns about the creation, the less they want to know about the Creator!

Peter Marshall, in his book, <u>The Light and the Glory</u>, describes how Christopher Columbus had a calling in the discovery of America, as deeper search was made into the cellars of the files of Harvard, Yale, Princeton and the Library of Congress; the search unfolded that Columbus was convinced God was calling him to reach the ends of the world with the Gospel. The name Columbus means "Christ-bearer." A Scripture that spoke to him was Isaiah 49:1-6 (Dr. Dave Arnold, <u>Why a Good God Allows Bad Things to Happen</u>, p.48). Will God, despite rebellion in so many categories of life, hold fast to that covenant He cut for Americans? In November of 2013, Billy Graham delivered what he called his last message to America; just prior to the telecast he wrote:

"I believe God has given me a message for people in our nation today. On a television talk show the other night, I heard a commentator say, 'This country is headed straight to Hell.' When you listen to the news day after day or simply pay attention to what goes on around you, it's not hard to understand why someone might say that. Ungodliness floods our land. Moral decline has become normal. We see killing, theft, dishonesty, greed, and open immorality everywhere. Many flaunt what they do and even demand public approval.

The Bible says, '**They proclaim their sin ...; they do not hide it**' (Isaiah 3:9).

-continued-

OCTOBER 23

In an interview with Trinity Broadcasting Network, Graham's son, Franklin, expressed what is beginning to prevail the minds of many:

"I believe there'll be some persecution in this country... We see it now in some sense. Hollywood has demonized people of faith—pastors and Christians—and for 50 years [they've] been poisoning the minds of people against the church of Jesus Christ... You can't even pray now at football games. You can't have the Lord's Prayer read. I prayed at President [George W.] Bush's inauguration [in 2001], and he was sued because of my prayer because I prayed in Jesus's name; we're living now in a time where we see the spirit of Antichrist is at the governmental level." (Elwood McQuaid, "Is America a Christian Nation?" ISRAEL MY GLORY, March/April 2015, p. 6.)

TRAINEE: How can I wage war against such subtle and persistent forces?

COACH: For you to fight against that picture painted by the Grahams will only entangle you in the issues of the world, thereby draining your strength. Jesus and the leaders of the New Testament Church never fought against the political and military clout of Rome. We are to have "the mind of Christ" (1 Cor. 2:16.). Jeremiah spoke an assuring word to Israel:

WORD: **Nevertheless in those days," says the Lord, "I will not make a complete end of you."** Jeremiah 5:18 NKJV

In the same tone, Zechariah relayed to them:

"Therefore say to them, 'Thus says the Lord of hosts: "Return to Me," says the Lord of hosts, "and I will return to you," says the Lord of hosts. Zechariah 1:3 NKJV

-continued-

OCTOBER 24

A Scripture that speaks directly to you from Graham's message is: "**If my people, which are called by my name, shall humble themselves, and pray, and seek my face, and turn from their wicked ways; then will I hear from heaven, and will forgive their sin, and will heal their land.**" 2 Chronicles 7:14 KJV

COACH: To close our discussion, let the words of one of your great leaders speak. Give God praise for faithful servants and rulers who knew the wisdom of His Word to lead and provide midst challenging times!

Words of Abraham Lincoln

"At what point shall we expect the approach of danger? Shall we expect some transatlantic military giant to step the Ocean and crush us at a blow? Never! All the armies of Europe, Asia, and Africa combined . . . could not by force take a drink from the Ohio or make a track on the Blue Ridge in a trial of a thousand years. At what point, then, is the approach of danger to be expected? I answer, if it ever reach us it must spring up amongst us; it cannot come from abroad. If destruction be our lot, we must ourselves be its author and finisher. As a nation of freemen, we must live through all time, or die by suicide." (*Israel My Glory*, Sept./Oct., 2014, p. 39)

OCTOBER 25

COURSE: THE CROSS AS CENTER OF CREATION AND REDEMPTION

TRAINEE: Help me get a picture of the Cross and creation.

COACH: Beyond the research centered on the "God-Particle," another recent scientific discovery shows that "the Laminin molecule—*which holds the cells and tissue of our bodies together, and without which our bodies would literally fall apart*—has the form of a **cross** [Dec. 2012 Midnight Call p. 22]." Has God placed into the very fabric of creation a picture of what it would take to bring our hearts back to His heart?

WORD: For by Him all things were created that are in heaven and that are on earth, visible and invisible, whether thrones or dominions or principalities or powers. All things were created through Him and for Him. And He is before all things, and in Him all things consist. Colossians 1:16-17 NKJV

He has made the earth by His power, He has established the world by His wisdom, and has stretched out the heavens at His discretion. When He utters His voice, there is a multitude of waters in the heavens: "And He causes the vapors to ascend from the ends of the earth. He makes lightning for the rain, He brings the wind out of His treasuries." Jeremiah 10:12-13 NKJV

-continued-

OCTOBER 26

It was through what his Son did that God cleared a path for everything to come to him—all things in heaven and on earth—for Christ's death on the cross has made peace with God for all by his blood. This includes you who were once so far away from God. You were his enemies and hated him and were separated from him by your evil thoughts and actions, yet now he has brought you back as his friends. He has done this through the death on the cross of his own human body, and now as a result Christ has brought you into the very presence of God, and you are standing there before him with nothing left against you—nothing left that he could even chide you for; the only condition is that you fully believe the Truth, standing in it steadfast and firm, strong in the Lord, convinced of the Good News that Jesus died for you, and never shifting from trusting him to save you. Col. 1:20–23a (TLB)

COACH: The writer of Hebrews tells us the greatness of the New Covenant is the perfect fulfillment of the Old Covenant, the new Passover. Jesus surely recited and sang Psalms 113-118 as part of the Passover Meal (*Haggadah*) before his arrest in the Garden of Gethsemane. These psalms are a poetic summary of God's deliverance described in the Exodus out of Egypt. Was Jesus thinking, during this Last Supper, about what He was about to do that would pave the way for the new "exodus" out of bondage to sin? Let the two Covenants speak to you about the Word of prophecy and fulfillment in Jesus!

-continued-

OCTOBER 27

WORD: **For if the blood of bulls and of goats, and the ashes of an heifer sprinkling the unclean, sanctifieth to the purifying of the flesh: How much more shall the blood of Christ, who through the eternal Spirit offered himself without spot to God, purge your conscience from dead works to serve the living God?** Hebrews 9:13-14 KJV

COACH: Let, now, the Word from both the Old and New Testaments, covenants, speak to your heart, showing you the power of the "Cross!"

Old Covenant:

WORD: **Even my own familiar friend in whom I trusted,**
Who ate my bread, Has lifted up *his* **heel against me.**
Psalm 41:9 NKJV

New Covenant:

Then Judas Iscariot, one of the twelve, went to the chief priests to betray Him to them. Mark 14:10 NKJV

Old Covenant:

He was oppressed and He was afflicted,
Yet He opened not His mouth;
He was led as a lamb to the slaughter,
And as a sheep before its shearers is silent,
So He opened not His mouth. Isaiah 53:7 NKJV

New Covenant:

And the high priest arose and said to Him, "Do You answer nothing? What *is it* these men testify against You?" ⁶³ But Jesus kept silent. And the high priest answered and said to Him, "I put You under oath by the living God: Tell us if You are the Christ, the Son of God!" Matthew 26:62-63 NKJV

-continued-

OCTOBER 28

Old Covenant:

**I gave My back to those who struck *Me*,
And My cheeks to those who plucked out the beard;
I did not hide My face from shame and spitting.** Isaiah 50:6 NKJV

New Covenant:

Then some began to spit on Him, and to blindfold Him, and to beat Him, and to say to Him, "Prophesy!" And the others struck Him with the palms of their hands. Mark 14:65 NKJV

Old Covenant:

**So His visage was marred more than any man,
And His form more than the sons of men;** Isaiah 52:13-15 NKJV

New Covenant:

So then Pilate took Jesus and scourged *Him*. John 19:1 NKJV

Old Covenant:

"And I will pour on the house of David and on the inhabitants of Jerusalem the Spirit of grace and supplication; then they will look on Me whom they pierced. Yes, they will mourn for Him as one mourns for *his* only *son*, and grieve for Him as one grieves for a firstborn. Zechariah 12:10 NKJV

New Covenant:

And again another Scripture says, *"They shall look on Him whom they pierced."* John 19:37 NKJV [Joseph's brothers, seeing him in Egypt after rejecting him and the passage of time, did not recognize him at first, perhaps because of his Egyptian attire. In like manner, Jesus (Yeshua) will reveal Himself as the Promised Messiah of Israel. They will come to see the parallels of Israel 40-yrs. in the wilderness and Jesus 40-days in the wilderness; the Torah, great teaching, received by Moses on Mount Sinai and Jesus's teaching, Sermon on the Mount, on the Mount of Olives; Moses face shining after receiving the Torah and Jesus on the Mount of Transfiguration: **And was transfigured before them: and his face did shine as the sun, and his raiment was white as the light.** Matthew. 17:2 KJV]

OCTOBER 29

-continued-

Old Covenant:

Be not far from Me, for trouble *is* **near; for** *there is* **none to help.** Psalm 22:11 NKJV

New Covenant:

Then Jesus said to them, "All of you will be made to stumble because of me this night, for it is written:

'I will strike the Shepherd, And the sheep of the flock will be scattered' Matthew 26:31 NKJV

Old Covenant:

Surely He has borne our griefs   And carried our sorrows;
Yet we esteemed Him stricken,
Smitten by God, and afflicted.
But He *was* **wounded for our transgressions,**
He was **bruised for our iniquities;**
The chastisement for our peace *was* **upon Him,**
And by His stripes we are healed. Isaiah 53:4-5 NKJV

New Covenant:

. . . that it might be fulfilled which was spoken by Isaiah the prophet, saying: " *He Himself took our infirmities And bore our sicknesses.*" Matthew 8:17 NKJV

OCTOBER 30

-continued-

Old Covenant:

They divide My garments among them, and for My clothing they cast lots. Psalm 22:18 NKJV

New Covenant:

Then they crucified Him, and divided His garments, casting lots, that it might be fulfilled which was spoken by the prophet:

"They divided My garments among them,
And for My clothing they cast lots. Matthew 27:35 NKJV

Old Covenant:

My God, My God, why have You forsaken Me?
Why are You so **far from helping Me,**
And from **the words of My groaning?** Psalm 22:1 NKJV

New Covenant:

And at the ninth hour Jesus cried out with a loud voice, saying, "Eloi, Eloi, lama sabachthani?" which is translated, *"My God, My God, why have You forsaken Me?"* Mark 15:34 NKJV

Old Covenant:

They also gave me gall for my food, and for my thirst they gave me vinegar to drink. Psalm 69:21 NKJV

New Covenant:

. . . they gave Him sour[a] wine mingled with gall to drink. But when He had tasted *it,* **He would not drink.** Matthew 27:34 NKJV

Old Covenant:

He guards all his bones; not one of them is broken.
Psalm 34:20 NKJV

New Covenant:

But when they came to Jesus and saw that He was already

dead, they did not break His legs John 19:33 NKJV

But one of the soldiers pierced His side with a spear, and immediately blood and water came out. John 19:34 NKJV

OCTOBER 31

-continued-

Old Covenant:

He was taken from prison and from judgment,
And who will declare His generation?
For He was cut off from the land of the living;
For the transgressions of My people He was stricken.
And they made His grave with the wicked—
But with the rich at His death,
Because He had done no violence,
Nor *was any* deceit in His mouth. Isaiah 53:8-9 NKJV

New Covenant:

With Him they also crucified two robbers, one on His right and the other on His left. ²⁸ So the Scripture was fulfilled which says, *"And He was numbered with the transgressors."* Mark 15:27 NKJV

COACH:	Did the Old Testament Word of prophecy about Jesus and its New Testament fulfillment speak to you?
TRAINEE:	It more than "spoke" to me; I sense those Words were and are alive, knowing and speaking to my heart! I saw myself standing there, watching as His Passion unfolded.
COACH:	I'm pleased to see a heart connection with His Word!

TRAINEE: I can truly give thanks and praise for the Cross being the center piece for both creation and redemption!

COACH: You, therefore, are ready for the month of November—to train on God's peace.

TRAINEE: Looking forward to it!

NOVEMBER 1

Month of Peace

COURSE: PERFECT PEACE

COACH: As you have seen through this year of training, God's Word speaks to all needs and concerns in life. Therefore:

WORD: **Thou wilt keep him in perfect peace, whose mind is stayed on thee: because he trusteth in thee.** Isaiah 26:3 KJV

COACH: God is telling you that He will keep you in this "perfect peace" as you trust Him. Look at the middle part of that verse: "mind stayed on thee." To have your mind "*stayed*" on God's Word is the same as having it "*stayed*" on Him (see again John 1:1–14). Your trust, your faith comes from the Word:

WORD: **So then faith *comes* by hearing, and hearing by the word of God.** Romans 10:17 NKJV

TRAINEE: And the most effective Word now, for me, is the Word from the Cross.

COACH: "Mind stayed," also calls for meditation and memorization; like exercise, you need repetition with the Word. Look again into the Word of the Passion of Christ, especially the seven last Words Jesus spoke from the Cross.

SEVEN LASTING WORDS FROM THE CROSS

1. *"Father, forgive them, for they do not know what they do."* Luke 23:34 NKJV [Can you look at the Cross with everything happening there to Jesus, and then hear Him say these words and still find it hard to forgive others?]

-continued-

NOVEMBER 2

2. *"And Jesus said to him, "Assuredly, I say to you, today you will be with Me in Paradise."* [Can you take assurance of your salvation as you hear Jesus say this to a hardened criminal who asked to be saved as he, too, was dying? Jonathan Edwards remarked: "The only thing I can contribute toward my salvation is the sin which made it necessary." (*Midnight Call Magazine*, Int'l, June 2014, page 24)]

3. *"When Jesus therefore saw His mother, and the disciple whom He loved standing by, He said to His mother, "Woman, behold your son!" Then He said to the disciple, "Behold your mother!"* John 19:26-27 NKJV [In the midst of agony, He was thinking ahead for those He loved. Does He do the same for you?]

4. *"And about the ninth hour Jesus cried out with a loud voice, saying, "Eli, Eli, lama sabachthani?" that is, "My God, My God, why have You forsaken Me?"* Matthew 27:46 NKJV [Again, did He sense His identity being torn in two, separated from the Father Who will not look upon sin?]

5. *"After this, Jesus, knowing that all things were now accomplished, that the Scripture might be fulfilled, said, "I thirst!"* John 19:28 NKJV [Martin Luther used to say: "The Holy Scriptures are the 'crib' in which the baby Jesus lies… .(*Midnight Call Magazine*, Int'l April 2013, p. 7)" For Jewish people, as well as non-Jewish, to read Isaiah 53, Psalm 22, Jeremiah 31, Micah 5:2-5, Daniel 9:24-27, Isaiah 7:14, Zechariah 12:10, Matthew's gospel (focused on Jewish values), and a host of other passages is to see the direct connection with Messianic prophecy and the life of Jesus on this earth, especially what He experienced on the Cross!

6. *"So when Jesus had received the sour wine, He said, "It is finished!" And bowing His head, He gave up His spirit.* John 19:30 NKJV [Notice, He "gave up" His spirit; no one took His life from Him. His Cross was His gift to you!]

7. **And when Jesus had cried out with a loud voice, He said, "Father, 'into Your hands I commit My spirit.'" Having said this, He breathed His last.** Luke 23:46 NKJV [He reached the point where all had been paid; now He could be, again, one with the Father.]

NOVEMBER 3

COURSE: A SUMMARY

COACH: In the face of every temptation, can you turn and take that long, cold stare at the cross and see that it was personal and for you, glance back at the temptation, and then look still deeper at what he suffered for you? Here, again, is where the power for true repentance comes. [*Again, I mention for the reader the power of the "Cross-look!"*]

TRAINEE: I need to sharpen my Cross vision by looking at the Word.

COACH: The Old Testament is the New Testament concealed; the New Testament is the Old Testament revealed. The following parallels will make a good Bible study for the reader:

Psalm 41:9 – Mark 14:10
Isaiah 53:7 – Matthew 26:62-63
Isaiah 50:6 – Mark 14:65
Isaiah 52:13-15 – John 19:1
Zechariah 12:10 – John 19:37
Psalm 22:11 – John 20:25
Isaiah 53:4-5 – Matthew 8:17
Psalm 22:18 – Matthew 27:35
Psalm 22:1 – Mark 15:34
Psalm 69:21 – Matthew 27:34
Psalm 34:20 – John 19:33
Zechariah 12:10 – John 19:34
Isaiah 53:8-9 – Mark 15:27

TRAINEE: The cross becomes the platform for me to be "born again, God's Word conceived in my heart."

COACH: The Word clearly tells that it is the Spirit Who "baptizes" with the Word and Who, in turn, becomes born in you—a giant step up from the "churchianity" or "religiosity" of today!

NOVEMBER 4

-continued-

WORD: Jesus replied, "With all the earnestness I possess I tell you this: Unless you are born again, you can never get into the Kingdom of God.... Men can only reproduce human life, but the Holy Spirit gives new life from heaven; so don't be surprised at my statement that you must be born again! Just as you can hear the wind but can't tell where it comes from or where it will go next, so it is with the Spirit. We do not know on whom he will next bestow this life from heaven." John 3:3, 6–8 (TLB)

The Spirit gives life; the flesh counts for nothing. The words I have spoken to you are spirit and they are life... He went on to say, "This is why I told you that no one can come to me unless the Father has enabled him." John 6:63, 65 (NIV)

For you have been born again, not of perishable seed, but of imperishable, through the living and enduring word of God. 1 Peter 1:23 (NIV)

COACH: God is *always* as good as his Word, and he watches over his Word to see what it will perform in your heart. He is watching you to see if you trust Him to remove your sins "as far as the east is from the west" and impute to you the righteousness of Christ!

TRAINEE: Can I see the "righteousness of Christ" <u>imputed</u> to me?

NOVEMBER 5

-continued-

As <u>placed</u> in my account, thereby making it truly mine?

Can I see the "righteousness of Christ" <u>imputed</u> to me the same as being <u>placed</u> in my account as though someone "imputed" $10,000 to my bank account, thereby making it truly mine?

COACH: *Abraham's faith was counted as being the same as righteousness.*

WORD: **And being fully persuaded that, what he had promised, he was able also to perform. And therefore it was imputed to him for righteousness.** Romans 4:21-22

And because of what Christ did, all you others too who heard the Good News about how to be saved, and trusted Christ, were marked as belonging to Christ by the Holy Spirit, who long ago had been promised to all of us Christians. His presence within us is God's guarantee that he really will give us all that he promised; and the Spirit's seal upon us means that God has already purchased us and that he guarantees to bring us to himself. This is just one more reason for us to praise our glorious God. Eph. 1:13–14 (TLB)

These things have I written unto you that believe on the name of the Son of God; that ye may know that ye have eternal life, and that ye may believe on the name of the Son of God. 1 John 5:13 NKJV

NOVEMBER 6

COURSE: THE JUDGMENT: AT THE FEET OF JESUS

TRAINEE: When I stand at the Judgment Seat and Jesus shows me what my life should have been and how I chose my own path instead, will I see tears in His eyes?

COACH: He is the same there as He was here—honest with His feelings centered on His love for you. His grief will merge with His love.

TRAINEE: I will stand there with memories speeding through space and time. I could have been this, but… I see myself void of all but His Grace.

COACH: Let your vision give shape to your heart's desire to obey, serve and move closer to His heart.

TRAINEE: My wicked heart will come to the breaking point; tears will not amount to enough. I cannot expect to have my head crowned.

COACH: In light of what you now see, what will you do with the years that are left for you?

TRAINEE:	I will give them to Him. I will let Him mold me and give shape to the plans He has for me.
COACH:	He has a Word for you:
WORD:	**"For I know the plans I have for you," declares the Lord, "plans to prosper you and not to harm you, plans to give you hope and a future."** Jeremiah 29:11 New International Version
TRAINEE:	*"Nothing in my hands I bring; simply to the Cross I cling."*

NOVEMBER 7

COURSE:	PEACE IN THE MIDST OF STRESS
TRAINEE:	As Tevye says, "Life is a little like walking a tightrope, or like being a fiddler on the roof."
COACH:	The word *"peace"* comes from the Hebrew word *"shalom." Shalom* does not necessarily refer to peace in the absence of war or peace in the absence of stress; it most often means peace in the midst of war or in the midst of stress. Imagine your tightrope walker, walking along a very high wire, carefully placing one foot in front of the other. What is the most important instrument this person has in his or her hands? The *balance* pole. The English word *"balance"* is the best translation of the word *shalom.* God does not always remove the stressful conditions in your life, but he does provide the balance to move through them. *Shalom* does not refer to a spiritual endorphin; it refers to the balance that it takes to weather a storm and come out a winner.
WORD:	**Be anxious for nothing, but in everything by prayer and supplication, *with thanksgiving* (emphasis mine,) let your requests be made known to God;** [7] **and the peace of God, which surpasses all understanding, will guard your hearts and minds through Christ Jesus.** Phil. 4:6–7 (NKJV)
TRAINEE:	So, Paul wrote: **"For I have learned, in whatsoever state I am, therewith to be content"** (Phil. 4:11b KJV)

-continued-

NOVEMBER 8

COACH: It is significant that Paul, in the midst of his own on-going stressful conditions, was the author of those Scriptures coaching you to give thanks. God's response of peace to the practice or exercise of sacrificial praise creates this learning process of contentment in all circumstances.

The following centers more on what it takes to journey out of the pit of anxiety into trust in the Father's care:

Do not fret or have any anxiety about anything, but in every circumstance and in everything by prayer and petition (definite requests) with thanksgiving continue to make your wants known to God.

And God's peace (be yours, that tranquil state of a soul assured of its salvation through Christ, and so fearing nothing from God and content with its earthly lot of whatever sort that is, that peace) which transcends all understanding, shall garrison and mount guard over your hearts and minds in Christ Jesus. Phil. 4:6–7 (AMP)

TRAINEE: The words "all" and everything" are standing over me in an ominous manner.

COACH: God says for you to live "**by <u>every</u> word that comes forth from the mouth of God**" Matt. 4:4

The mind of sinful man is death, but the mind controlled by the Spirit is life and peace. (Rom. 8:6)

NOVEMBER 9

COURSE: CONTENTMENT

TRAINEE: I need to have anchors, reminders of God's love and care.

COACH: He has given you the most powerful anchor, His written Word. It is tangible; you can read it and touch it. Signed documents are binding in the truest sense of the word. Believers can, therefore, rely on what The Book says about being saved from the perils of the end times. Why? Because their names are written in God's Book of life.

WORD:	**In the beginning was the Word, and the Word was with God, and the Word was God.** John 1:1 NIV
	See, I have engraved you on the palms of my hands. Isaiah 49:16 NIV
	Deep within them I will plant my Law, writing it on their hearts. Then I will be their God and they shall be my people. Jeremiah 31:33 TJB
	. . . for I have learned, in whatsoever state I am, therewith to be content. Phil. 4:11b. KJV
TRAINEE:	How did Paul learn that?
COACH:	Review this "Month of Praise." Paul found peace in praise.

NOVEMBER 10

COURSE:	SCARS THAT HEAL
WORD:	**Unless I see in His hands the print of the nails, and put my finger into the print of the nails, and put my hand into His side, I will not believe.** John 20:25 NKJV
TRAINEE:	Why did Jesus keep those scars and wounds?
COACH:	The Apostle Thomas needed to see them to believe. This is a dramatic picture of how He understands your wounds. God wants to use your wounds, forming you into a *"wounded healer."*
TRAINEE:	How can my wounds be a healing factor for others?
COACH:	When they see your wounds and how God has been your strength, they are comforted and more willing to listen and consider the path you have modeled in seeking God's healing presence. Who is the best person to help an alcoholic?
TRAINEE:	Another recovering alcoholic.
COACH:	Recall that a wounded healer is someone who has been there, who has gone through the pain, problem, crisis, sin condition, weakness, habit, addiction, and so on. So, like an Army scout, he is the best person to come back and take the rest of the troops through the same territory.

-continued-

NOVEMBER 11

WORD: **For even to this you were called—it is inseparable from your vocation. For Christ also suffered for you, leaving you [His personal] example, so that you should follow on in His footsteps . . . He personally bore our sins in His [own] body to the tree [as to an altar and offered Himself on it], that we might die (cease to exist) to sin and live to righteousness. By His wounds you have been healed.** 1 Peter 2:21; 24 AMP. B.

But he was wounded for our transgressions, he was bruised for our iniquities: the chastisement of our peace was upon him; and with his stripes we are healed. Is. 53:5 KJV.

He delivers the afflicted by their affliction, and opens their ears [to His voice] by adversity. Job 36:15 AMP.B.

COACH: God can deliver you from suffering, and also deliver you <u>through</u> your suffering. Scars that remain train you into greater wisdom.

WORD: **But let patience have her perfect work, that ye may be perfect and entire, wanting nothing. If any of you lack wisdom, let him ask of God, that giveth to all men liberally, and upbraideth not; and it shall be given him.** James 1:4-5 KJV

TRAINEE: When I see Jesus face to face, will He be looking for my scars?

COACH: He will trade your crown of thorns for a crown of victory.

NOVEMBER 12

COURSE: PEACE OF GOD/PEACE WITH GOD

WORD: **He has not observed iniquity in Jacob, nor has He seen wickedness is Israel.** Numbers 23:21 KJV

TRAINEE: Surely God had seen the offenses and wrongs found in Israel.

WORD: **[God] has not beheld iniquity in Jacob [for he is forgiven], neither has He seen mischief or perversion in Israel [for the same reason]. The Lord his God is with Israel, and the shout of praise to their King is among the people.** Numbers 23:21 AMP. B.

COACH: The four words used in the Greek New Testament for *forgiveness* give the words *amnesia*, *erase*, *therapy*, and *cover*.

TRAINEE: He has forgotten, erased, healed, and covered my sin.

WORD: **For I will forgive their iniquity, and their sin I will remember no more** Jer. 31:34b (KJV).

He takes our sins farther away than the east is from the west Ps. 103:12 (Jerusalem Bible, or JB).

Blessed and happy and to be envied are those whose iniquities are forgiven and whose sins are covered up and completely buried. Rom. 4:7 (AMP).

NOVEMBER 13

COURSE: PEACE FROM THE POWER AND PRACTICE PRAISE

TRAINEE: Does giving God praise make for peace?

WORD: **Be happy (in your faith) and rejoice and be glad-hearted continually—always. Be unceasing in prayer—praying perseveringly; Thank (God) in *every*thing (*emphasis mine*)—no matter what the circumstances may be, be thankful and give thanks; for this is the will of God for you (who are) in Christ Jesus (the Revealer and Mediator of that will).** 1 Thess. 5:16–18 (AMP)

At all times and for everything giving thanks in the name of our Lord Jesus Christ, to God the Father. Eph. 5:20 (AMP)

Through Him therefore let us constantly and at all times offer up to God a sacrifice of praise, which is the fruit of lips that thankfully acknowledge and confess and glorify His name." Heb. 13:15 (AMP)

I will bless the LORD at all times: his praise shall continually be in my mouth. Psalm 34:1 (KJV)

COACH: Giving God thanks in *all* things builds trust, thereby freeing God's hand to work in *all* things. The above three Scriptures, therefore, "marry up" with the following two Scriptures.

-continued-

NOVEMBER 14

WORD: **(Not in your own strength) for it is God Who is all the while effectually at work in you—energizing and creating in you the power and desire—both to will and to work for His good pleasure and satisfaction and delight.** Phil. 2:13 (AMP)

And we know that in all things God works for the good of those who love him, who have been called according to his purpose. Rom. 8:28 (NIV)

COACH: Recall that God's twofold response to the sacrifice of praise is as follows:

Peace: "And the peace of God, which passeth all understanding, shall keep your hearts and minds through Christ Jesus" (Phil. 4:7 KJV).

Miracle—where he works with those things you and I cannot do anything about.

WORD: **For though we live in the world, we do not wage war as the world does. The weapons we fight with are not the weapons of the world. On the contrary, they have divine power to demolish strongholds.** 2 Cor. 10:3–4 (NIV)

TRAINEE: So, <u>from</u> praise <u>to</u> trust <u>to</u> His answers for my prayers and needs.

COACH: Carry on.

NOVEMBER 15

COURSE: DRAWING CLOSER TO GOD/ CLIMBING HIGHER

TRAINEE: Just how do I move into that third dimension of "the fear of the Lord"?

COACH: Review the exercise from May 2; the Word tells you how:

WORD: **Seek first his kingdom and his righteousness, and all these things will be given to you as well.** Matt. 6:33 (NIV)

Delight yourself in the Lord and he will give you the desires of your heart. Ps. 37:4 (NIV)

TRAINEE: How do I delight in and seek Him first?

COACH: By loving Him for just *who* He is. He is your heavenly Father. Think for a moment: do parents want their children to love them just because of what they can give them, or do they want their children to love them simply because of *who* they are?

TRAINEE: How does that happen?

COACH: It happens as you take in his Word. Recall the first chapter of John's gospel. He states that the Word, Jesus [see Rev. 19:13], was, in the beginning, sent out [see Gen. 1 and Is. 55:10–11].

NOVEMBER 16

-continued-

Then he says that the Word *was* God. You could stop right there and know that to delight in God's Word is to receive Him into your heart and mind. But John continues, saying, "And the Word was *with* God." This, in the ancient world, implies a face-to-face relationship. "Jesus, the Word, is an active Person Who is with the Father. The Word was of the very quality of God, while still retaining His personal distinction from the Father.

. . . God the Father created the world (Gen. 1:1) through the Son (Col. 1:16; Heb. 1:2) . . . Note that life is not said to have been created; life existed in Christ (John 5:26; 7:57; 10:10; 11:25; 14:6; 17:3; 20:31)." (Thomas Nelson New King James Study Bible Note, p 1756)

TRAINEE: What does that mean?

COACH: The creation narrative tells that God said, "Let there be …" and there was. He also said, "Let <u>Us</u> make man in our own image."

TRAINEE: To whom was he talking?

COACH: The answer to this comes in John, chapter one, where he states that "the Word became flesh and dwelt among us." You know this to be Jesus, born in Bethlehem, dying on a cross, and rising from the dead.

-continued-

NOVEMBER 17

WORD: **He is the image of the invisible God, the firstborn over all creation. For by Him all things were created that are in heaven and that are on earth, visible and invisible, whether thrones or dominions or principalities or powers. All things were created through Him and for Him. And He is before all things, and in Him all things consist.** Col. 1:15–17 (NKJV)

But in these last days he has spoken to us by his Son, whom he appointed heir of all things, and through whom he made the universe. The Son is the radiance of God's glory and the exact representation of his being, sustaining all things by his powerful word. Heb. 1:2–3a (NIV)

By the word of the Lord the heavens were made, and all the host of them by the breath of his mouth. Ps. 33:6 (KJV)

TRAINEE: Putting all the above together, what do we have?

COACH: You have a consistent and persistent message that God's Word *is* God and that Jesus was pre-existent at the very point of creation in the form of the Word (see John 17:5). That Word is still with you in written form. To take it in, read and meditate God's Word is to receive him (Jesus).

-continued-

NOVEMBER 18

WORD: **You are already clean because of the word I have spoken to you. Remain in me, and I will remain in you.** John 15:3–4a (NIV)

COACH: God wants you to desire and delight in his Word because to do so is to desire and to delight in Him! His own words say this:

WORD: **"My son, keep my words and store up my commands within you. Keep my commands and you will live; guard my teachings as the apple of your eye."** Prov. 7:1–2 (NIV)

O taste and see that the Lord is good: blessed is the man that trusteth in him. Ps. 34:8 (KJV)

When your words came, I ate them; they were my joy and my heart's delight. Jer. 15:16a (NIV)

How sweet are your words to my taste, sweeter than honey to my mouth! Ps. 119:113 (NIV)

COACH: When you eat something wholesome, it benefits your whole system.

-continued-

NOVEMBER 19

WORD: **But his delight and desire are in the law of the Lord, and on His law—the precepts, the instructions, the teachings of God—he habitually meditates (ponders and studies) by day and by night.** Ps. 1:2 (AMP)

TRAINEE: Is this the reason God was so pleased with Solomon's choice of wisdom for God's gift to him, out of all the things he could have selected; so pleased that He gave him everything else?

COACH: Remember, to choose wisdom is to choose God's Word, and to choose His Word is to choose Jesus.

WORD: **He was clothed with garments dipped in blood, and his title was 'The Word of God.'** Rev. 19:13 (TLB)

So we have these three witnesses: the voice of the Holy Spirit in our hearts, the voice from heaven at Christ's baptism, and the voice before he died. And they all say the same thing: that Jesus Christ is the Son of God. 1 John 5:7–8 (TLB)

TRAINEE: God promises to be close to me with His Word?

COACH: Read and head.

-continued-

NOVEMBER 20

WORD: **Let the word of Christ dwell in you richly in all wisdom, teaching and admonishing one another in psalms and hymns and spiritual songs, singing with grace in your hearts to the Lord.** Colossians 3:16 NKJV

And I heard a loud voice from heaven saying, 'Behold, the tabernacle of God is with men, and He will dwell with them, and they shall be his people. God Himself will be with them and be their God.' Revelation 21:3 NKJV

COACH: No wonder Paul told the early Church:

WORD: **I can do all things through Christ who strengthens me.**

Phil. 4:13(KJV)

God's strength is made perfect in my weakness. 2 Cor. 12:9 (KJV)

It is no longer I who live but Jesus within me. Gal. 2:20 (NIV)

COACH: The Father knows the Word you need; the Son is the strength and life of that Word in you; and the Spirit will deliver that Word to you in a most timely way—five words that describe the Names of the Holy Spirit and how He works among us "to help, teach, comfort, counsel and convict of truth."

NOVEMBER 21

COURSE: PEACE THROUGH REPENTANCE AND COVERED SINS

COACH: As stated, in a marathon, somewhere around mile twenty or twenty-one, the runner hits "the wall." This is where mind and body shake hands in agreement and say, "We wanna quit." And that's where most runners will do just that—quit.

TRAINEE: At that point, "mind over matter" no longer works. The walls and struggles I encounter in my mental and spiritual "marathons" cause my mind and body to say, "We wanna quit!"

COACH: The burning question is: "How does the Holy Spirit apply the Father's healing Word through the stripes of his Son, Jesus, to your wounded body, mind, spirit, and relationships? How does God heal lives broken from sin, and how could you train to run on the road to repentance? I repeat, what can you learn from the physical marathon that would apply to the mental and spiritual marathons, and vice versa?

WORD: **But he was wounded for our transgressions, he was bruised for our iniquities: the chastisement of our peace was upon him; and with his stripes we are healed** Is. 53:5 (NKJV).

TRAINEE: Therefore, to break through the "wall" in a marathon, I need to understand the hierarchy of Word over spirit over mind over body.

COACH: Well recalled!

NOVEMBER 22

COURSE: PEACE THROUGH ENDURANCE

TRAINEE: I'm still trying to break through those "marathon walls."

WORD: **But they that wait upon the LORD shall renew their strength; they shall mount up with wings as eagles; they shall run, and not be weary; and they shall walk, and not faint.** Is. 40:31 KJV.

COACH: Breaking through calls for endurance.

WORD: **Therefore then, since we are surrounded by so great a cloud of witnesses (who have borne testimony of the Truth), let us strip off and throw aside every encumbrance—unnecessary weight—and that sin which so readily (deftly and cleverly) clings to and entangles us, and let us run with patient endurance and steady and active persistence the appointed course of the race that is set before us.** Heb. 12:1 (AMP).

TRAINEE: I remember the exercise on the road to repentance—to "cast down, deaden, crucify."

COACH: But do you recall the "Cross look"?

TRAINEE: Yes. I need to stay close to those Gospel accounts.

-continued-

NOVEMBER 23

WORD: **I have been crucified with Christ: and I myself no longer live, but Christ lives in me. And the real life I now have within this body is a result of my trusting in the Son of God, who loved me and gave himself for me.** Gal 2:20 (TLB)

For if you live according to (the dictates of) the flesh you will surely die. But if through the power of the (Holy) Spirit you are habitually putting to death—making extinct, deadening—the (evil) deeds prompted by the body, you shall live forever. Rom. 8:13 (AMP)

And he said to them all, "If anyone desires to come after Me, let him deny himself, and take up his cross daily, and follow Me. For whoever desires to save his life will lose it, but whoever loses his life for My sake will save it." Luke 9:23–24 (NKJV)

Moreover—let us also be full of joy now! Let us exult and triumph in our troubles and rejoice in our sufferings, knowing that pressure and affliction and hardship produce patient and unswerving endurance. And endurance (fortitude) develops maturity of character—that is, approved faith and tried integrity. And character (of this sort) produces (the habit of) joyful and confident hope of eternal salvation. Such hope never disappoints or deludes or shames us. Rom. 5:3–5a (AMP)

NOVEMBER 24

COURSE: PEACE THROUGH OVERCOMING

TRAINEE: My feelings lead me into sin.

COACH: Feelings are thought choices; calling, as you said, for an intense conditioning and training program for the mind.

WORD: **Those who live according to the sinful nature have their minds set on what that nature desires; but those who live in accordance with the Spirit have their minds set on what the Spirit desires. The mind of sinful man is death, but the mind controlled by the Spirit is life and peace.** Rom. 8:5–6 (NIV)

TRAINEE: I need a picture of what this exercise would look like for me?

COACH: The scene unfolds showing you working on the beds in a greenhouse. As you turn the dirt for planting, your hand picks up a clump of fresh cow manure; instantly, you throw it down, quickly brushing your hands together as to remove any remains, not wanting to see it in your hand another second. In this vision, you are coached to *"cast down the imaginations of the heart"*—improper thoughts/feelings—with the same disgust and zeal, recalling what it could cause you. Next, see someone on a life-support system in a hospital; the decision is made to remove the supports and let the person die. You're further coached to understand this picture to mean that when you stop entertaining daydreams of acted out sins, you are *"deadening the deeds of the flesh."* Tomorrow, one more picture comes.

NOVEMBER 25

-continued-

Begin to see the connection with *"crucify the self."* Most crucifixion deaths were caused by suffocation. Just like water replaces the air in the lungs when someone drowns, you need to replace your wrong thinking with right thinking (see Phil. 4:8). So, I give you the exercise of replacing the junk in your mind with what the four gospel writers have to say about the passion of Christ. This is a <u>vivid picture</u> of how God wants you to *"crucify the self,"* a *"renewing of the mind."*

TRAINEE: As I have said, I need to let the Word be my training guide.

WORD: **… that I may know Him and the power of His resurrection, and the *fellowship of His sufferings*, being *conformed to His death*, if, by any means, I may attain to the resurrection from the dead"** Phil. 3:10–11.

TRAINEE: I see that this is part of what it means for me to be *"found in Christ,"* to be a *"new creation,"* or to *"have the mind of Christ"* (2 Cor. 5:17; Phil. 3:9; 1 Peter 4:1)?

-continued-

COACH:	You're still making progress in your training on the Word. When you see the obedience Jesus achieved on the Cross and the Grace showered on you, His righteousness imputed to you, your own obedience will become a natural response or fruit.
TRAINEE:	This broadens my vision and challenges my understanding.

NOVEMBER 26

COURSE:	FREEDOM TO OVERCOME
WORD:	**"Turn away my eyes from looking at worthless things, and revive me in Your way"** [Ps. 119:37 KJV; see in context of verses 33–40]
COACH:	Again, what captures your mind captures you. Recall that your thoughts, as Martin Luther wrote in his treatise, *On Bondage of the Will*, can place you in a state of bondage to sin, or you can place them in bondage to Jesus by *"bringing into captivity every thought to the obedience of Christ"* (2 Cor. 10:5 KJV). Luther, you recall, also wrote: *"You can't stop the birds from flying over your head, but you sure can keep 'em from building a nest in your hair."*
TRAINEE:	Without this exchange, I remain in bondage to sin and death and cannot free myself. I've allowed too much *"nest building."*
COACH:	You are free to choose which bondage you want.
WORD:	**Happy is the man who doesn't give in and do wrong when he is tempted, for afterwards he will get as his reward the crown of life that God has promised those who love him. And remember, when someone wants to do wrong it is never God who is tempting him, for God never wants to do wrong and never tempts anyone else to do it. Temptation is the pull of man's own evil thoughts and wishes. These evil thoughts lead to evil actions and afterwards to the death penalty from God. (James 1:12–15 TLB)**

NOVEMBER 27

COURSE: MOVING FROM WORRY TO TRUST

WORD: **Casting the whole of your care—all your anxieties, all your worries, all your concerns, once and for all—on Him; for He cares for you affectionately, and cares about you watchfully.** 1 Peter 5:7 (AMP)

TRAINEE: I need to understand all that is hitting my mind.

COACH: There is a form of pride in worrying or fretting. They expose your thoughts as saying that things are, or have to be, in your control. Matthew 6:25–34 focuses your mind on the stupidity of not trusting the God who looks after the smallest of creatures. The following Word tells you what it takes to journey out of the pit of anxiety into trust in the Father's care:

WORD: **Do not fret or have any anxiety about anything, but in every circumstance and in everything by prayer and petition (definite requests) with thanksgiving continue to make your wants known to God.**

            And God's peace (be yours, that tranquil state of a soul assured of its salvation through Christ, and so fearing nothing from God and content with its earthly lot of whatever sort that is, that peace) which transcends all understanding, shall garrison and mount guard over your hearts and minds in Christ Jesus. Phil. 4:6–7 (AMP)

NOVEMBER 28

COURSE: WOUNDS CAUSED BY SIN

TRAINEE: Like the walls and struggles encountered in my physical marathon, the simultaneous mental and spiritual "marathons" begin to, like chronic depression, cause my mind and body to say, "We wanna quit!"

COACH: The burning question is how does the Holy Spirit apply the Father's healing Word through the stripes of his Son, Jesus, to wounded bodies, minds, spirits, and relationships? How does God heal lives broken from sin, and how can you train to run on the road to repentance? In short, what can you learn from the physical marathon that would apply to the mental and spiritual marathons, and vice versa? Let this burning question that sears your soul find roots in the following Word:

WORD: **But he was wounded for our transgressions, he was bruised for our iniquities: the chastisement of our peace was upon him; and with his stripes we are healed** Is. 53:5 (NKJV).

TRAINEE: This Word, and the many others from this year's training, tells me that when I am sorry for my sin and confess it, I can count on Him to forgive me. I further understand this to mean He will erase, heal, cover and not remember my sins anymore.

COACH: Yes, He will remove them as far "as the east is from the west." Psalm 103:12

NOVEMBER 29

COURSE: STEPS ON THE ROAD TO REPENTANCE - A REVIEW:

1. Recognize your Condition and admit you are lost in sin. Romans 3:23 KJV says, **"For all have sinned and come short of the glory of God."** Sin has a penalty: **"For the wages of sin is death, but the gift of God is eternal life in Christ Jesus our Lord.** Romans 6:23 KJV

2. Religion and Good Works are not the Answer. **"There is a way that seemeth right unto a man, but the end thereof are the ways of death."** Proverbs 14:12 KJV Ephesians 2:8-9 KJV says: **"For by grace are ye saved through faith; and that not of yourselves: it is a gift of God: Not of works, lest any man should boast."** If you could work your way to heaven, then why did Jesus have to die?

3. <u>The Good News---Jesus Christ Provides the Way!</u> **"For God so loved the world that He gave His only begotten Son, that whosoever believeth in Him should not perish, but have everlasting life**." John 3:16 KJV He became the payment for our sin. In Romans 5:8 KJV, the Bible says, **"But God commendeth [meaning proved or demonstrated] His love toward us, in that, while we were yet sinners, Christ died for us."** Christ died for us so that we can go to Heaven with Him!

4. <u>Believe and Receive Christ.</u> **"For whosoever shall call upon the name of the Lord shall be saved."** Romans 10:13 KJV That promise, directly from God, tells us that if we pray to Him and ask Him to forgive our sin and turn to Him alone to be our Savior, He will save and give us the free gift of eternal life. You can make that decision today by sincerely praying something like this:

Dear God, I know that I am separated from you because of sin. I confess that in my sin, I cannot save myself.
Right now, I turn to You alone to be my Savior. I ask You to forgive and to save me from the penalty of my sin and I trust You to provide eternal life to me. Amen.

-continued-

NOVEMBER 30

COACH: I look forward to seeing your response announcing your decision for Christ as your Lord and Savior—that it has become settled in your heart and mind. This is a decision you will never regret!

WORD: **"For God so loved the world that He gave His only begotten Son, that whoever believes in Him should not perish but have everlasting life."** John 3:16 NKJV

". . . that if you confess with your mouth the Lord Jesus and believe in your heart that God has raised Him from the dead, you will be saved. For with the heart one believes unto righteousness, and with the mouth confession is made unto salvation." Romans 10:9-10 NKJV

TRAINEE: "Dear Father, in the Name of Jesus, I ask You to help me take the same faith journey as King David, moving from his sins of adultery, murder, and deceit to what he wrote in Psalm 51 where he found that Godly sorrow and later found You to say: *"David has a heart after my Own heart* 1 Samuel 13:14." Amen.

WORD: Psalm 34:18 NKJV **"The Lord is near to those who have a broken heart, And saves such as have a contrite spirit."**

Psalm 51:17 NKJV **"The sacrifices of God are a broken spirit, A broken and a contrite heart— These, O God, You will not despise."**

COACH: That person's sorrowful heart moves them to make changes!

Month of Victory

COURSE: SALVATION [Part one]

TRAINEE: As we journey through our lives toward the Day of Judgment (see Olivet Discourse in Matt. 24-25; Is. 13:9-11; Zeph. 1:14-17; Amos 5:18-20), what does it take in preparation so that we march toward it with a chord of victory about our salvation? In other words, what is our Creator's plan to bring us into His Kingdom?

COACH: Many times, you hear on television and radio the message that says all you have to do is accept Christ as your "personal Savior" or to just "believe" in order to be saved. Favorite Scriptures often quoted:

"For God so loved the world, that He gave His only begotten Son, that whosoever believeth in Him shall not perish, but have everlasting life." John 3:16 KJV

"But what does it say? 'The Word is near you; it is in your mouth and in your heart,' that is, the word of faith we are proclaiming: That if you confess with your mouth, 'Jesus is Lord,' and believe in you heart that God raised Him from the dead, you will be saved." Romans 10:8-9 KJV
But, let's look at another Scripture. Speaking about the last judgment, Jesus said:

WORD: **"Not all who sound religious are really godly people. They may refer to me as 'Lord,' but still won't get to heaven. At the Judgment many will tell me, 'Lord, Lord, we told others about you and used your name to cast out demons and to do many other great miracles.' But I will reply, 'You have never been mine. Go away, for your deeds are evil."** Matthew 7:21-23TLB

-continued-

DECEMBER 2

COACH: Did they believe? Yes, they called Him "Lord." But were they saved? No. Why? Like us, they have a sin problem. Jesus put it plainly when speaking to his own people in Galilee: "**I tell you, Nay: but, except ye repent, ye shall all likewise perish**." <u>Luke 13:3</u> KJV John 3:16 by itself is not enough; see the following verse:

WORD: **Thou believest that there is one God; thou doest well: the devils also believe, and tremble**. James 2:19 KJV [see: 1 John 5:3; 2 John 6; 14:21]

TRAINEE: Refresh me on how I can change and repent.

WORD: **Jesus answered and said unto him, Verily, verily, I say unto thee, Except a man be born again, he cannot see the kingdom of God. Nicodemus saith unto him, How can a man be born when he is old? Can he enter the second time into his mother's womb, and be born? Jesus answered, Verily, verily, I say unto thee, Except a man be born of water and of the Spirit, he cannot enter into the kingdom of God. That which is born of the flesh is flesh; and that which is born of the Spirit is spirit. Marvel not that I said unto thee, Ye must be born again.** John 3:3-7 KJV

COACH: Again, this is the Word of God living in your heart. Not emotional experiences but the Word, hidden and rising in the heart, creating an ever present hunger to read and meditate upon It, to pray It, (*all leading to a genuine repentance to overcome temptations*), constitutes what "*born again*" is all about, when it comes to "*working out your salvation with fear and trembling* [Philippians 2:12]." This person longingly and expectantly looks for the return of Jesus! What begins internal becomes external and then eternal; this is <u>victory</u>!

DECEMBER 3

-continued-

WORD: **Jesus said to him, "I am the way, the truth, and the life. No one comes to the Father except through Me . . . Jesus answered, "My kingdom is not of this world. If My kingdom were of this world, My servants would fight, so that I should not be delivered to the Jews; but now My kingdom is not from here."** John 14:6, 18:36 NKJV

And so we have the prophetic word confirmed, which you do well to heed as a light that shines in a dark place, until the day dawns and the morning star rises in your hearts; 2 Peter 1:19 NKJV

COACH: Read again the High Priestly prayer Jesus prayed for all who would turn to and accept Him, those whom God "foreknew":

WORD: **Father, I desire that they also whom You gave Me may be with Me where I am, that they may behold My glory which You have given Me; for You loved Me before the foundation of the world.** John 17:22-24 NKJV [see vs.1-26]

COACH: Again, Jesus's High Priestly prayer for us opens the way for Him to become our closest person. This will take place fully at the Rapture. Like Mary, visiting the tomb to find Jesus and thinking Him to be the gardener will we know Him by hearing Him call our Name? At the very least, this will be a most intimate time of meeting and knowing! **"Precious in the sight of the Lord is the death of his saints" (Ps. 116:15 KJV).** Why? Because he wants us to come home; the death of a believer is a homecoming!

DECEMBER 4

COURSE: SALVATION [*A Scriptural Look,* part two]

WORD: **Jesus answered and said unto him, Verily, verily, I say unto thee, Except a man be born again, he cannot see the kingdom of God.** John 3:3 . . . 7 KJV

COACH: Again, this is the Word of God living in your heart.

WORD: **It is the spirit that quickeneth; the flesh profiteth nothing: the words that I speak unto you, they are spirit, and they are life..... And he said, Therefore said I unto you, that no man can come unto me, except it were given unto him of my Father.** John 6:63, 65 KJV

COACH: Recall that God told Jeremiah that He "*knew him before he was conceived in his mother's Womb* (Jeremiah 1:5)." Who did He "know"? He knew the spirit (*life force*), the person who would have a mind and live in a body. God knows ahead of time each "spirit" who will choose Him and who will not. You are known before You arrive!

WORD: **And you *He made alive,* who were dead in trespasses and sins,** Ephesians 2:1 NKJV

TRAINEE: By Grace through Faith.

WORD: **For this *is* good and acceptable in the sight of God our Savior, Who desires all men to be saved and to come to the knowledge of the truth.** 1 Timothy 2:3-4 NKJV

And you, being dead in your trespasses and the uncircumcision of your flesh, He has made alive together with Him, having forgiven you all trespasses, Colossians 2:13 NKJV

But the free gift *is* not like the offense. For if by the one man's offense many died, much more the grace of God and the gift by the grace of the one Man, Jesus Christ, abounded to many. Romans 5:15 NKJV

-continued-

DECEMBER 5

COACH Grace is what allows you to whisper in your prayers as God hears you when you are empty, needy and humble. Again, **Thou knowest my downsitting and mine uprising, thou understandest my thought afar off.** Psalm 139:2 KJV (see also: 1Chronicles 28:9; Psalm 139:23; Hebrews 4:12)

WORD: **But after that the kindness and love of God our Saviour toward man appeared, Not by works of righteousness which we have done, but according to his mercy he saved us, by the washing of regeneration, and renewing of the Holy Ghost; Which he shed on us abundantly through Jesus Christ our Saviour.** Titus 3:4-6 KJV

But as many as received Him, to them He gave the right to become children of God, to those who believe in His name: who were born, not of blood, nor of the will of the flesh, nor of the will of man, but of God. John 1:12-13 NKJV

All that the Father gives Me will come to Me, and the one who comes to Me I will by no means cast out. John 6:37 NKJV

And this is eternal life, that they may know You, the only true God, and Jesus Christ whom You have sent. John 17:3 NKJV

These things I have written to you who believe in the name of the Son of God, that you may know that you have eternal life, and that you may *continue to* believe in the name of the Son of God. 1 John 5:13 NKJV

TRAINEE: These Words make a mark on my heart!

DECEMBER 6

COURSE: RETURNING AND REST

WORD: **For thus says the Lord God, the Holy One of Israel:**

In returning and rest you shall be saved;

In quietness and confidence shall be your strength."

But you would not, . . . Isaiah 30:15 NKJV

COACH: "Returning" is the action of being repentant. "Quietness and confidence" can be expressed as "utter trust." [Nelson Study Bible NKJV 1997 p. 1158]

TRAINEE: I need to remember that God is watching me to see if I can exercise the faith of obedience.

COACH: Well put!

TRAINEE: I understand that the only way I can be pleasing to Him is to exercise that faith. But I will need to have my faith strengthened.

COACH: Take His Word deeper into your heart.

WORD: **Thy word have I hid in mine heart, that I might not sin against thee** (Ps. 119:11 KJV). **So then faith cometh by hearing, and hearing by the word of God.** Romans 10:17 KJV

COACH: Keep the Word about the Cross at the center of your heart.

DECEMBER 7

COURSE: CROSS TRAINING

TRAINEE: Your name for this course throws me; I don't understand what constitutes "Cross Training."

COACH: 18-days 'til Christmas!

TRAINEE: What does Christmas have to do with "Cross Training"?

COACH: In a day and age when you see growing evidence of a world wanting a global government, global economy and even a global religion, the name 'Christian' is becoming more segregated or isolated. The Bible, in a most comprehensive way, tells you that that Name is sentinel to world history and to eternity. The word Christmas was taken from two words: Christ [*the anointed one who is sent*] and Mass [*to celebrate*]; so, the true meaning of Christmas [*shortened name*] means we are to "celebrate Christ." That makes every day Christmas! Picture this: during the Christmas season, a manger with a Cross in the center of the cradle with straw around it to see "how silently the wondrous gift is given!"

Carrying this vision can help you pray in your heart. *"Be born in us today!"* Again, you find your identity secure and safe as you see that it is not so much *"who"* you are but *"whose"* you are!

DECEMBER 8

COURSE:	OVERCOMERS
TRAINEE:	How does being an "overcomer" relate to salvation?
WORD:	**He who has an ear, let him hear what the Spirit says to the churches. To him who overcomes I will give to eat from the tree of life, which is in the midst of the Paradise of God.** Revelation 2:7 NKJV
COACH:	The Nelson NKJV Study Bible, p. 2167, explains three views of the overcomers: 1. They are all believers, and failure to overcome means they were not really believers; 2. They are believers, and failure to be obedient or overcome means they have lost their salvation; 3. They are believers, and failure to be obedient means a loss of rewards. Based on all seven "overcomer" passages, the third view best holds the content and context of those seven passages.
TRAINEE:	When in grade school I, read John Milton's "Paradise Lost and Paradise Regained." The scene in those books that most impressed me, staying with me over the years, is the one depicting the difference between those in Hell and those in Heaven. Milton gave us a picture of people in both dimensions, all of whom had locks on their elbows, preventing them from being able to bend their arms and feed them. The folks in Hell were starving; those in Heaven were well fed and happy. The difference? People in Heaven knew they could reach out with their hands to pick up the food on the table, but then, to reach across the table and place the food in the mouth of the one sitting opposite from them. Those in Hell could not conceive of doing that.
WORD:	**He who has an ear, let him hear what the Spirit says to the churches. He who overcomes shall not be hurt by the second death.** Revelation 2:11 NKJV

-continued-

DECEMBER 9

COACH: The second death is eternal torment; believers who use their faith to be obedient/overcome will not experience this second death nor loss of rewards.

WORD: **He that overcometh shall inherit all things; and I will be his God, and he shall be my son.** Revelation 21:7 KJV

COACH: Great reward will come to those who practice overcoming. See some of those promises in the following: Matthew 5:12; 16; Mark 9:41; Luke 6:35; Ephesians 6:8; Colossians 3:24; Revelations 22:12

WORD: **He who has an ear, let him hear what the Spirit says to the churches. To him who overcomes I will give some of the hidden manna to eat. And I will give him a white stone, and on the stone a new name written which no one knows except him who receives *it*.** Revelation 2:17 NKJV

COACH: Hidden manna, white stone, new name all point to intimacy as co-rulers with Christ.

WORD: **And he who overcomes, and keeps My works until the end, to him I will give power over the nations** . . . Revelation 2:26 NKJV

COACH: Again, believers who persevere in obedience are promised to rule and reign with Jesus in the millennium—1000yr reign on the earth—and in the Kingdom of Heaven, sharing in His splendor and glory. In the millennium, Jerusalem will be the majestic city of honor and victory as nations flow to her, and she will constitute the ethical-moral and religious center of the earth (Micah 4:2). No more anti-Semitism. To a certain extent, the millennium will be a part of eternity; as the Garden of Eden, before the fall. **Blessed be the Lord out of Zion, which dwelleth at Jerusalem. Praise ye the Lord.** Psalm 135:21 KJV

-continued-

DECEMBER 10

WORD: **He who overcomes shall be clothed in white garments, and I will not blot out his name from the Book of Life; but I will confess his name before My Father and before His angels.** Revelation 3:5 NKJV

COACH: Jesus will make sure that faithful service and obedience, motivated by love (see 1 Corinthians 13), will not be erased. For Him to publicly confess your name will give you His nod of approval.

WORD: **He who overcomes, I will make him a pillar in the temple of My God, and he shall go out no more. I will write on him the name of My God and the name of the city of My God, the New Jerusalem, which comes down out of heaven from My God. And *I will write on him* My new name.** Revelation 3:12 NKJV

Behold, I stand at the door and knock. If anyone hears My voice and opens the door, I will come in to him and dine with him, and he with Me. To him who overcomes I will grant to sit with Me on My throne, as I also overcame and sat down with My Father on His throne. He who has an ear, let him hear what the Spirit says to the churches. Revelation 3:20-22 NKJV

COACH: Co-rulers are those whose humble, faithful obedience stood up even in the midst of suffering (*see first three chapters of Revelation for the full context of the above passages*).

TRAINEE: These Words about the Kingdom broaden my vision of eternity. It places a different view of the temporary present.

COACH: The Apostle Paul well expressed this difference.

WORD: **For I consider that the sufferings of this present time are not worthy to be compared with the glory which shall be revealed in us.** Romans 8:18 NKJV

DECEMBER 11

COURSE:

[*At the Graveside*]

TRAINEE: What can be said of us when our last breath is drawn; when we've said our final good-bye with heaved exit sigh? What will they say, those we've left behind . . . were we cruel or were we kind?

Did we leave tears on faces to mark our trail, or smooth out wrinkled foreheads to ease their sail? Whatever we do, life is soon spent, and our tales are told however life went. Did we win or did we lose, who is to say, except Christ our Lord on the final day?

Did our words hurt those who even now gather? Do they remember anger spit out as fire? Or do they recall calmness and quiet, a word wisely spoken?

Was our love deep or only a token?

Oh, friends, hear me, a spirit now gone; love well while you may for it won't be long; your children are grown, your grandchildren you see ... reflections of lives that used to be.

10-16-03   Connie Snider Coffey

COACH: Well said!

DECEMBER 12

COURSE: <u>VICTORY</u>

WORD: **And I beheld, and I heard the voice of many angels round about the throne and the beasts and the elders: and the number of them was ten thousand times ten thousand, and thousands of thousands; Saying with a loud voice, Worthy is the Lamb that was slain to receive power, and riches, and wisdom, and strength, and honour, and glory, and blessing.**

And every creature which is in heaven, and on the earth, and under the earth, and such as are in the sea, and all that are in them, heard I saying, Blessing, and honour, and glory, and power, be unto him that sitteth upon the throne, and unto the Lamb for ever and ever.

And the four beasts said, Amen. And the four and twenty elders fell down and worshipped him that liveth for ever and ever. Revelation 5:11-14 KJV

But every man in his own order: Christ the firstfruits; afterward they that are Christ's at his coming. Then cometh the end, when he shall have delivered up the kingdom to God, even the Father; when he shall have put down all rule and all authority and power. For he must reign, till he hath put all enemies under his feet. The last enemy that shall be destroyed is death. 1 Corinthians 15:23-26 KJV

And the glory which You gave Me I have given them, that they may be one just as We are one: I in them, and You in Me; that they may be made perfect in one, and that the world may know that You have sent Me, and have loved them as You have loved Me.

"Father, I desire that they also whom You gave Me may be with Me where I am, that they may behold My glory which You have given Me; for You loved Me before the foundation of the world. John 17:22-24 NKJV

DECEMBER 13

-continued-

And so we have the prophetic word confirmed, which you do well to heed as a light that shines in a dark place, until the day dawns and the morning star rises in your hearts; 2 Peter 1:19 NKJV

COACH: The written Word in the days of the Old Covenant was even more trustworthy than the personal experience of Peter and the other apostles. Again, not emotional experiences, but the Word, hidden and rising in the heart, creating an ever-present hunger to read and meditate upon It, to pray It—all leading to a genuine repentance to overcome — constitutes what "born again" is all about, when it comes to "working out our salvation with fear and trembling (Philippians 2:12)." This person longingly and expectantly looks for the return of Jesus! The Word, *"hidden in our hearts,"* always points to Jesus and His return. What begins internal becomes external and then eternal; this is <u>victory</u>!]

WORD: **Jesus said to him, "I am the way, the truth, and the life. No one comes to the Father except through Me . . . Jesus answered, "My kingdom is not of this world. If My kingdom were of this world, My servants would fight, so that I should not be delivered to the Jews; but now My kingdom is not from here." John 14:6, 18:36 NKJV**

COACH: Any form of religion that strives to erect a "kingdom" on earth is diametrically opposed to God's will and plan!

WORD: **He who believes in the Son has everlasting life; and he who does not believe the Son shall not see life, but the wrath of God abides on him." John 3:36 KJV**

TRAINEE: Victory now takes on new meaning for me!

COACH: Carry on!

DECEMBER 14

COURSE: RUNNING IN HIS GRACE

WORD: **Moreover the law entered that the offense might abound. But where sin abounded, grace abounded much more, so that as sin reigned in death, even so grace might reign through righteousness to eternal life through Jesus Christ our Lord.**

What shall we say then? Shall we continue in sin that grace might abound? Certainly not! How shall we who died to sin live any longer in it? Or do you not know that as many of us as were baptized into Christ Jesus were baptized into His death? Therefore we were buried with him through baptism into death, that just as Christ was raised from the dead by the glory of the Father, even so we also should walk newness of life.

For if we have been united together in the likeness of His death, certainly we also shall be in the likeness of His resurrection, knowing this, that our old man was crucified with Him, that the body of sin might be done away with, that we should no longer be slaves to sin. For he who has died has been freed from sin. Now if we died with Christ, we believe that we shall also live with Him, knowing that Christ, having been raised from the dead, dies no more. Death no longer has dominion over Him. For the death that He died, He died to sin once for all; but the life that He lives, He lives to God. Likewise you also, reckon yourselves to be dead indeed to sin, but alive to God in Christ Jesus our Lord.** Romans 5:20-6:11 NKJV

TRAINEE: I find no questions that I need to ask. Why?

COACH: Those Words speak of an accomplished work that has no need of further work.

WORD: **I have finished the work which You have given me to do . . .** John 17:4b; **He said, "It is finished!" And He gave up His spirit.** John 19:30 NKJV

DECEMBER 15

COURSE: READING THE BIBLE

TRAINEE: I need some clear and reasonable steps in reading It.

COACH: Listen to how this one couple has approached reading it: *"My wife and I, for most of our 30 years of marriage, have been reading one chapter in the morning and one in the evening; this "sandwiches" the day in a good way. We have worked our way through the Bible [Genesis – Revelation] many times with this approach. Each time through brings countless insights and understandings!"*

TRAINEE: As I read, what will happen?

COACH: God's Word can become, as he describes it, "sent out" (Is. 55:10–11); "active and alive" (Heb. 4:12); "watched over and performed" (Jer. 1:12). The central task and goal for you is to take the opportunity to see how God's Word can speak to and change real-life concerns, leaving a sense of wonder and comfort about His Word. Theologically, it would mean that encounter of Scripture—not just as logos (*an idea or concept*), but as rhema (*word spoken directly, meant to be personal*). Again, how could the Scriptures become more than words on a page? The Bible is the revelation of His nature and desire for all people.

TRAINEE: Why should I read the Bible?

COACH: The Bible is God's Word to you. It's His message of love and forgiveness, and it shows you how you can have eternal life. It can also answer questions you have as you try to live a life that pleases Him. That's why Christians should try to read the Bible daily.

TRAINEE: Tomorrow, I need some "*how to*" suggestions.

DECEMBER 16

-continued-

COACH: First, read one chapter from the Gospel of John each day. John is the fourth book in the New Testament. It will help you understand what Jesus did and why we should believe in Him.

Second, read Acts, the exciting story of how Jesus Christ's first disciples told others about how He died and rose again.

Third, read the letters that Christ's apostles wrote to His first followers— all who were new in their faith. These letters are the book of Romans through the book of 3 John.

Fourth, go back and read the other three gospels: Matthew, Mark, and Luke. [*A good commentary at the back of a Bible would be helpful as well. The New King James Study Bible has proven to be good for many. You will find the Old Testament to be prophetic of the New Testament and the New Testament as fulfillment of the Old Testament.*]

WORD:	**Be diligent to present yourself approved to God, a worker who does not need to be ashamed, rightly dividing the word of truth.** 2 Timothy 2:15 NKJV
TRAINEE:	I may need motivation to get started.
COACH:	God says He will answer prayers that are in His will.
WORD:	**Now this is the confidence that we have in Him, that if we ask anything according to His will, He hears us. And if we know that He hears us, whatever we ask, we know that we have the petitions that we have asked of Him.** 1 John 5:14-15 NKJV

DECEMBER 17

COURSE:	GOD CELEBRATES YOUR EXISTENCE
COACH:	Did you know that God rejoices over you with singing! Zephaniah 3:17 says, "**The Lord your God is in the midst of you, a Mighty One, a Savior [Who saves]! He will rejoice over you with joy. He will rest [in silent satisfaction] and in His love He will be silent and make no mention [of past sins, or even recall them]: He will exult over you with singing** (AMP)."
TRAINEE:	So, recalling my training exercises on faith, I need to make a faith-decision that as I start off each morning, I can enter into His presence knowing that He rejoices over me. My confessed sins are in the past and His mercies are new every morning. Whatever struggles or stresses I might face today, I can know for sure that God is with me and that He delights in me.
COACH:	Well said! The love poured out on the Cross imputes the righteousness of Christ to you. Can you make a faith-decision to let _____ love _____, based on how much you are loved by our Creator and Savior!
TRAINEE:	Dear Father, in the Name of Jesus, I ask that Your Holy Spirit would coach me through the Scriptures as my teacher, counselor, comforter, helper, and One Who convicts me of what is true. I've made my decision for Jesus as my personal Lord and Savior. Help me through Your Word to move closer to Him. Amen

WORD: **"For by Him all things were created that are in heaven and that are on earth, visible and invisible, whether thrones or dominions or principalities or powers. All things were created through Him and for Him. And He is before all things, and in Him all things consist."** Colossians 1:16-17 NKJV

DECEMBER 18

COURSE: MOVING CLOSER TO GOD BY MOVING CLOSER TO HIS WORD

COACH: What if God were only all-powerful or only all judging?"

TRAINEE: I would be in a "pickle!"

COACH: As you know, He found a way to show you that He is also all loving and that He brought that picture to us in His Son, Jesus.

WORD: **"Jesus said to him, "Have I been with you so long, and yet you have not known Me, Philip? He who has seen Me has seen the Father; so how can you say, 'Show us the Father'?"** John 14:9 NKJV

WORD: **"I and My Father are one."** John 10:30 NKJV

            ". . . that is, that God was in Christ reconciling the world to Himself, not imputing their trespasses to them, and has committed to us the word of reconciliation." 2 Corinthians 5:19 NKJV

COACH: I want to salute your prayer about moving closer to God by moving closer to His Word. His answer to that prayer will make the rest good history, even in the midst of stress or turmoil. The Apostle Paul put it this way:

WORD: **Not that I speak in regard to need, for I have learned in whatever state I am, to be content**: Philippians 4:11 NKJV

TRAINEE: How did he "learn" that?

COACH: God says: "We'll talk about that tomorrow."

DECEMBER 19

-continued-

WORD: **Thou wilt keep him in perfect peace, whose mind is stayed on thee: because he trusteth in thee.**" Isaiah 26:3 KJV

TRAINEE: To have my mind stayed on His Word is the same as having it stayed on Him. Why?

COACH: Again, He is the Word and the Word is Him. See John 1:1-14. The following speak to your need for peace and hope:

Psalm 4:8

Psalm 85:8

Matthew 11:28-30

Romans 5:1-5

John 14:27

Isaiah 53:5

Isaiah 26:3-4

Philippians 4:6-7

Isaiah 57:2; 14-19

Luke 2:1-20

TRAINEE: You want me to just read these?

COACH: Read them as a historical message personally written to you about Jesus—the prophecy of His coming, the reality of His being here and His future return—and the fact that all this is for you!

TRAINEE: I want and need to continue training on the Word!

COACH: Glad to hear that! As we march closer to the celebration of His birth in Bethlehem, let the Word paint a picture for you of the events and people surrounding that birth.

DECEMBER 20

COURSE: THE END

TRAINEE: Dear Jesus, I know I am a sinner, and I ask for your forgiveness. I believe you died for my sins and rose from the dead. I trust and follow you as my Lord and Savior. Guide my life and help me to do your will. Lead me into Your Kingdom!

WORD: **For this is good and acceptable in the sight of God our Savior, who desires all men to be saved and to come to the knowledge of the truth. For there is one God and one Mediator between God and men, the Man Christ Jesus,"** 1 Timothy 2:3-5 New King James Version (NKJV)

COACH: Be trained by saving Grace

WORD: **For the grace of God that brings salvation has appeared to all men, teaching us that, denying ungodliness and worldly lusts, we should live soberly, righteously, and godly in the present age, looking for the blessed hope and glorious appearing of our great God and Savior Jesus Christ, who gave Himself for us, that He might redeem us from every lawless deed and purify for Himself *His* own special people, zealous for good works."** Titus 2:11-14 (NKJV)

COACH: God's Grace is something no human being can achieve or deserve. God's Grace is His freely given unmerited favor when we place our believe in Him—more directly, it is when we believe and accept what His Son, Jesus, accomplished for us on the Cross. "**For by grace are ye saved through faith; and that not of yourselves: it is the gift of God: Not of works, lest any man should boast.**" Ephesians 2:8-9 KJV Train today on: John 6:37; John 14:6; John 17:3; 1 John 5:13; Galatians 2:16; Titus 3:5.

DECEMBER 21

COURSE: LOVE

TRAINEE: Love hurts and it doesn't last.

COACH: Erotic love [Eros], friendship love [Philia] and sexual love [Libido] are limited. Too often "self" is at center stage. The Father's "Agape" love is unlimited, unconditional, and unending.

TRAINEE: How can I get some of this kind of love?

COACH: Mr. James Stewart once wrote a book entitled <u>Fire</u>. He describes a deep, silent and very dark forest. Suddenly, a bolt of lightning from a storm slashes into one of the large trees there. One single spark jumps out the end of the tap root into a little clump of leaves where the sparks begin to smolder and grow, but a puff of wind would come and almost blow it all out. Then, slowly but surely, it would begin to grow again, moving to a larger group of leaves, then some bushes . . . trees . . . and finally, you read of the worst forest fire California ever had.

    Sometimes people's lives are like that fire—sometimes up, sometimes down, sometimes almost on fire, sometimes almost burned out. God's Agape love is the fire.

TRAINEE: I see that last point, but there are certain things that tear this love down. I don't have the power to love on my own; I can't get this FIRE off the ground.

COACH: You've noticed a baby crying; the mother or father take this little person up in their arms and the pain is forgotten. This is the way it is with the Father and His children. The simple answer to your question about the need for love is: The Father loves you! His indwelling Spirit empowers you to know/show such love.

DECEMBER 22

-continued-

COACH: But this love does not grow unless it is shared; this FIRE needs the wind of communication to heat it up. You need love; you also need <u>to</u> love.

TRAINEE: Rummaging around in Mama's attic, I found an old dusty book. As I turned the pages, a piece of paper dropped to the floor. I picked it up and read: *"Whoever finds this note and reads it, I love you."*

COACH: Empty yourself in service to others—even to those who fret you—and you create a web of personal relationships, like dropping a pebble into a still pool of water, the effect reaches all sections.

WORD: **I have loved you even as the Father has loved me. Live within my love . . . I have told you this so that you will be filled with my joy . . . I demand that you love each other as much as I love you.** John 15:9' 11-12 TLB

TRAINEE: Times come when I count my problems and sins; I begin to feel they will never run out.

COACH: Counting the grains of sand at the beach or the stars in the universe, pretty soon you get the idea that they're never going to run out. Neither does the Father's love! Learn to live in and by the greatest commandment.

TRAINEE: What is that one?

COACH: The Hebrew nation gathered over 600 commandments; out of that context, a lawyer tried to test Jesus by asking which was the greatest. See, tomorrow, how He addressed the question.

DECEMBER 23

-continued-

Jesus reversed the pitch by asking him the same.

He answered correctly by stating: *'the Shema.'*

TRAINEE: Tell me again what the Shema is.

COACH: The Hebrew word, Shema, means 'hear thou.' It is the first word of what became the primary creed for God's people. '**Hear, O Israel, the Lord our God is one. Thou shalt love the Lord thy God with all thy heart, all thy mind, all thy soul and with all thy strength. And thou shalt love thy neighbor as thyself** [Matthew 22:36-40].' Jesus said there is no other greater commandment than these and that they summarize all of the commandments. The crowning summary of these two great commandments is the new one He gave.

TRAINEE: Which was?

WORD: **And so I am giving a new commandment to you now—love each other just as much as I love you. Your strong love for each other will prove to the world that you are my disciples.** John 13:34-35 TLB

Pay all your debts except the debt of love for others. For if you love them, you will be obeying all of God's laws . . . If you love your neighbor as much as you love yourself you will not want to harm or cheat him, or kill him or steal from him And you won't sin with his wife or want what is his, or do anything else the Ten Commandments say is wrong. All ten are wrapped up in this one, to love your neighbor as you love yourself. Love does no wrong to anyone. That's why it fully satisfies all of God's requirements. It is the only law you need. Romans 13:8-10 TLB

DECEMBER 24

COURSE:	MOVING DEEPER IN GOD'S LOVE
COACH:	Begin today's warm-up exercise with I John 4:7-19. Let each and every Word sink deep into the crevice of your inner thoughts and feelings!.
TRAINEE:	Talk to me about this, coach.
COACH:	You do not please the Father by your education, position or any other factor; the only way to His heart is through faith in what His Son accomplished when He said: "It is finished!" It can be said that the heart of the Father is lonely for His children, yet there is nothing He needs from them. Nevertheless, He chooses to know you intimately.
WORD:	**You did not choose me, no, I chose you** . . . John 15:16-17 J. B
COACH:	The Father, Himself, chose relationship over position. Jesus stepped down from His position of power and glory to be born as one of you. You cannot comprehend love that is this broad and this deep!
TRAINEE:	Then, how do I put this love I'm receiving from the Father into motion in my everyday life?
COACH:	I like the hunger pangs I'm hearing from you. Imagine if Adam and Eve had responded to Satan by saying: *"We need to talk these matters over with the Father first."* Intimacy would have been an invincible weapon.
WORD:	**So you can find out how much you love God's children—your brothers and sisters in the Lord—by how much you love and obey God** . . . 1 John 5:2-4 TLB

DECEMBER 25

COURSE: CELEBRATE CHRIST

WORD: **Behold, the virgin shall be with child, and bear a Son, and they shall call His name Immanuel,' which is translated, 'God with us.'** Matthew1:23 KJV

COACH: Go back and study the December 7th devotional. Let the cradle and contents speak to your heart. Recall that *"Christmas"* literally means to *"celebrate Christ."*

TRAINEE: How do I best do that celebration?

COACH: Consider that the Price He paid for your forgiveness, healing, and salvation is so priceless that the only way you can respond is to obey Him. And, as you know, this means to obey His Word. He is the Word! Celebrate the announcement of His birth:

WORD: **Then the angel said to them, "Do not be afraid, for behold, I bring you good tidings of great joy which will be to all people. For there is born to you this day in the city of David a Savior, who is Christ the Lord. And this will be a sign to you; You will find a Babe wrapped in swaddling clothes, lying in a manger.** Luke 2:10-12 NKJV

COACH: Your life needs to become a "Bethlehem" for the new birth!

DECEMBER 26

COURSE: -CHRISTMAS-

COACH: The Bible, in a most comprehensive way, tells that the Name "Christ" is sentinel to world history and to eternity. Picture, during the Christmas season, a manger with a Cross in the center of the cradle to see how *"wondrously the gift is given!"* This gives a picture of what was actually born in a stable in Bethlehem 2000 years ago. One of the verses of the hymn, Oh Little Town of Bethlehem, states: *"How silently, how silently, the wondrous gift is given..."*

Carrying this vision can help a person pray in their heart what another line from the above hymn says: *"Be born in us today!"* Again, you find your identity secure and safe as you see that it is not so much *"who"* you are but *"whose"* you are! Because of the Cross, a line from another famous hymn forms good posture at the judgment before Christ: *"Nothing in my hands I bring; simply to the Cross, I cling!"*

Christmas is not just a birth but a "coming" that was planned from the foundation of the earth [see: John 17:24; Ephesians 1:4; Revelation 13:8]. These writings in the Bible about Christmas are factual accounts of what actually happened in history. God forgives and saves because of what His Son accomplished on the Cross—the only answer to humanities sin condition. His death was not martyrdom; it was a divine, eternal decree!

DECEMBER 27

COURSE: GOD: A SUMMARY [A Review]

On the one hand He:

Is a just God demanding punishment of evil. [Deut. 32:4; Is. 45:21; Acts 3:14]

Grants no remission without repentance. [Mt. 3:7-9; Lu. 3:3, 8; 24:47; Acts 2:38; 26:18-20; 2 Cor. 7:9-10; Heb. 6:1, 6]

Will not hear prayer when iniquity is regarded in the heart. [Ps. 66:18]

Says to love Him is to obey Him. [Jn. 14:15, 21 23]

On the other hand He:

Has paid for it all. [1 Cor. 6:20; 7:23]

Makes His strength perfect in weakness. [2 Cor. 12:9]

Says that faith is a decision not a feeling. [Lu. 22:42]

Is a rewarder of faith. [Col. 3:24; Heb. 11:6; 2 Jn. 1:8; Rev. 22:12]

Says that if you judge yourself you will not be judged [1 Cor. 11:31-32]

Helps you do what He wants [Phil. 2:13; 4:13, 1 Cor. 1:18, Rom. 12:2]

Says sorrow for what is done against Him leads to repentance [2 Cor. 7:10]

Coaches to:

Make the *sacrifice-of-obedience*

Exercise the *faith-of-obedience*

Have the *wisdom-of-obedience*.

Offer Him the *praise-of-obedience*.

Show Him the *love-of-obedience*.

DECEMBER 28

POWER	1. Honest Confession
OF	**If we confess our sins, he is faithful and just to forgive us our sins, and to cleanse us from all unrighteousness.** 1 John 1:19
HIS	2 Corinthians 7:10
WORD	*Godly sorrow brings repentance that leads to salvation and leaves no regret, but worldly sorrow brings death.*

{PRAY THE WORD}

That if you confess with your mouth the Lord Jesus and believe in your heart that God has raised him from the dead, you will be saved. Rom. 10:9

THOUGHTS   CAPTIVE TO JESUS

2 Corinthians 10:5
We demolish arguments and every pretension that sets itself up against the knowledge of God and we take captive every thought to make it obedient to Christ.

Galatians 2:20
I have been crucified with Christ and I no longer live, but Christ lives in me. The life I live in the body, I live by faith in the Son of God, who loved me and gave himself for me.

1 Corinthians 1:18
For the message of the cross is foolishness to those who are perishing, but to us who are being saved it is the power of God.

Romans 8:13
For if you live according to the flesh you will die; but if by the Spirit you put to death the deeds of the body, you will live.

-continued-

DECEMBER 29

2 Corinthians 12:9
But he said to me, "My grace is sufficient for you, for my power is made perfect in weaknesses." Therefore I will boast all the more gladly about my weakness, so that Christ's power may rest on me.

PLACE THE NAME   OF JESUS OVER YOUR MIND

Philippians 2:9
*Therefore God exalted Him to
highest place and gave Him the
Name that is above every name.*

Philippians 4:13
*I can do everything God
asks me to with the help
of Christ who gives me
strength and power.*

Romans 8:37
*In all these things we are more
than conquerors through Him
Who love us.*

Romans 12:2
*. . . Be ye transformed by the
renewing of your mind . . .*

BUILDING TRUST

PRAISE

1 Thessalonians 5:16-18
*Be joyful always; pray
continually; give thanks
in all circumstances, for
this is God's will for you in Christ Jesus*

Ephesians 5:20
*Always giving thanks to God
the Father for everything in
the Name of our Lord Jesus
Christ.*

-continued-

DECEMBER 30

Hebrews 13:15
*Through Jesus, therefore,
let us continually offer to
God a sacrifice of praise—
the fruit of the lips that
confess His Name.*

*If you remain in me and my
Words remain in you, ask
whatever you wish and it
will be given.* John 15:7

RESULTS OF PRAISE AND TRUST
AROUND US IN AND THROUGH US

Romans 8:28
*And we know that in all things
God works for the good of
those who love Him, who have
been called according to His purpose.*

Philippians 2:13
*For it is God at work
within you, helping you
want to obey Him, and
then helping you do what He wants.*

Jesus answered and said unto him, If a man love me, he will keep my words: and my Father will love him, and we will come unto him, and make our abode with him. JOHN 14:23 KJV

DECEMBER 31

COURSE: KEEPING RESOLUTIONS

WORD: **In a race, everyone runs but only one person gets first prize. So run your race to win. To win the contest you must deny yourselves many things that would keep you from doing your best. An athlete goes to all this trouble just to win a blue ribbon or a silver cup, but we do it for a heavenly reward that never disappears.** 1 Corinthians 9:24-25 NKJV

TRAINEE: Could you give me a thought for the day?

COACH: Walk the talk then talk the walk.

TRAINEE: What does this mean?

COACH: These are times of beginning, times to be aware of God's presence—to practice His presence. Take a message from the story about the vine and the branches [John 15:1-8]. Your guidance and growth come from this relationship with the Father through His Son and by His Spirit.

TRAINEE: This relationship will help me keep my resolutions.

WORD: **How blest are those who know their need of God; the kingdom of Heaven is theirs.** Matthew 5:3 NEB

TRAINEE: Yes, I see my need of God for all resolutions as I stand on the brink of a new year of training.

WORD: **Show me Your ways, O Lord; teach me Your paths. Lead me in Your truth and teach me, for You are the God of my salvation; on You I wait all the day.** Psalms 25:4-5 NKJV

POSTSCRIPT

COURSE: PRACTICING THE PRESENCE

COACH: God says we are "blessed" when hungry for His Word [Matthew 5:6]; and that His Word "endures forever [Isaiah 40:8]." When you and I read His Word, what are we taking in? In the 55th chapter of Isaiah, God talks in "living-room" conversation style about His Word. He says that It is like the rain and snow that comes down and waters the earth, causing the seeds to germinate and bear forth fruit/grow. Then He says that It "always accomplishes that which It is sent out to do, never returns to Him void or empty." The Apostle Paul speaks about the Word as "active and alive, sharper than a two-edge sword, able to divide between bone and marrow, soul [personality] and spirit [that part which is eternal] and to discern and know the deepest thoughts and motivations of the heart [Hebrews 4:12]." And God says that He "watches over His Word to perform It [Jeremiah 1:12]." The wisdom writer tells us that God's Word is "medicine to all (our) flesh [Proverbs 4:22]." St. John wrote that the "Word became flesh and dwelt among us [John 1:14]."

To meditate and memorize His Word [God's M & M's] is to receive into the hierarchy of our being [spirit-mind-body] the same force sent out at the beginning of creation when God spoke His Word and said: "Let there be . . . and there was." Recall that He says His Word shall "accomplish and prosper" in what It is "sent out to do" and "shall not return to [Him] void." [Isaiah 55:11]

Right prayers bring right results! Again, like wartime infra-red computerized weapons, the most on-target form of praying is to pray God's Own Word right back to Him. He says that prayers prayed in His will are "heard and answered [1 John 5:14-15]." His Word is His will! Let's increasingly engage spiritual "readiness training" by exercising daily on His Word.

-continued-

Paul wrote to Timothy: "**For bodily exercise profiteth little; but godliness is profitable unto all things, having promise of the life that now is, and of that which is to come** [1 Timothy 4:8]."

One reminder from the heart of this book in your hands: Through the finished work of Jesus on the Cross, His Grace delivers us from being sin-conscious to being "righteousness-conscious," and from being "judgment-consciousness" to being "forgiveness conscious." Our obedience then becomes a natural or spontaneous response to the massive love showered upon us!

Because of the "imputed" [Rom. 4:11; 23] righteousness of Jesus, the Heavenly Father looks at each of us as His Beloved child in whom He is well pleased! [Mt. 3:17; Rom. 11:28; Eph. 1:6]

SHALOM

[The <u>peace of God</u> that passes all understanding keep your hearts and minds through Christ Jesus]

-continued-

ADDENDUM

THE REAL VALUE IN

READING GOD'S WORD

IS NOT JUST THE KNOWLEDGE ITSELF,

BUT

THE HEART UNDERSTANDING IT SETS

TO

THE BOUNDARIES OF GOD'S THOUGHT

THINKING GOD'S THOUGHTS AFTER HIM

FRAMES HIS PURPOSE AND COUNSEL

IN A

BELIEVER'S HEART.

AND,

IT SETS THE BOUNDARIES FOR

FERVENT & EFFECTUAL PRAYERS

-continued-

AUTHOR BIO

Arthur Coffey has served as a parish pastor for fifteen years, an Army chaplain for twenty-three years, and a Veterans Affairs Medical Center chaplain for twelve years. He was mobilized for Operation Desert Shield, Operation Desert Storm, Operation Joint Endeavor, and the Humanitarian Aid tour to Guatemala.

Coffey is the recipient of the **Witherspoon Award** for *"most creative use of Scripture,"* presented by the National Bible Association and the Armed Forces Chief of Chaplains.

He is also the recipient of a Veterans Affairs National Chaplain of the Month award for *"outstanding service in the promotion of the Bible in ministry, healing and research."*

In addition, Coffey presented his Alzheimer's research, centered on Scripture, at the Mayo Clinic, where it was voted the most outstanding of those presented and declared to be *"pioneer research"* because no other known research had ever used Scripture as the independent variable.

Coffey earned a doctorate in "[w]holistic" health care; the exam committee proclaimed his research to be the best they had seen in the field.

CPSIA information can be obtained
at www.ICGtesting.com
Printed in the USA
BVHW010502180119
538098BV00014B/66/P